Spinners

Tony Sheppard

Splinters

*For Mij, with best
wishes,
Tony Sheppard.*

Matador
9 De Montfort Mews
Leicester LE1 7FW, UK
Tel: (+44) 116 255 9311 / 9312
Email: books@troubador.co.uk
Web: www.troubador.co.uk/matador

ISBN 10: 1 905886 09 8
ISBN 13: 978 1 905886 09 8

Cover design: Graham Higgins

Typeset in 11pt Stempel Garamond by Troubador Publishing Ltd, Leicester, UK
Printed in the UK by The Cromwell Press Ltd, Trowbridge, Wilts, UK

Matador is an imprint of Troubador Publishing Ltd

For myself, and Alison

Whatever man has wrought or made,
In time will surely crumble and fade;
But youth and beauty come again,
Conceived in love, and born in pain.

Profits from the sale of this book will be invested in the future of mankind, via *JMA*, a children's charity.

Writing a novel is relatively easy. Producing it to the required standard takes meticulous scrutiny. I am therefore grateful to author and tutor Chris Morgan, copy editors Sue Browning BA, Joel Lane, and author Shirley Thompson for their expertise in this area.

Also, my thanks to proofreaders Margaret Hayward, Annie Clarke and Chris Sawyer of Authors' Aid, Cheshire, for their valuable contributions and kind comments.

Special thanks to Enid, Happy and Eyvonne, who always believed.

Haslemere 2050 October 1950 to August 1999

Prologue
Haslemere – 2050

An empty house on a plateau appeared, dark and brooding, through early morning mist, its vacancy expressed through grime-covered windows. Everyone had gone, each in their way. Died, lapsed, or just couldn't stay.

"Who owned this place, then?" said Barry.

Ron ignored him and carefully negotiated his new, blue and white Hovawagun through a pair of lodge gates, and set off up an incline leading to where the house stood.

"Ron."

"What?"

"I said, who owned this place?"

"Bloke called Bates. Moved abroad. Used to be a stud farm, but after hunting with hounds got banned, thoroughbred horses weren't needed anymore. I got the place at the auction at Guildford."

"What you gonna do with it?" said Barry.

"Dunno, yet. Might knock it down, and build a Chinese Cemetery. It'd look alright with oval-shaped graves dug into the hillside. Bet you didn't know that's why Chinese graves are shaped like that. Like a womb. It's symbolic of returning to their ancestors."

"No. I always wondered."

Ron smirked. "First thing we're gonna do is see if they left anything of value. It cost me a grand, just to have 'Ron Millward – Demolition & Renovation' painted on the side of the van."

* * *

Ron squeezed the brass doorknob with both hands, and drew in a deep breath. Then he yanked, as hard as he could. "I can't budge it. You have a go," he said.

Barry looked at Ron's dust-covered scalp, glistening two inches from his nose. *I'm not surprised. You're so fat, your sweat stinks worse than this hallway*, he thought.

Barry let Ron slide the short distance from cellar door to wall behind them. "Move," he said. Gauging the angle between his foot and a spot just above the doorknob, Barry pressed his back against plasterboard, restricting his backward movement. *I'm sick of this*, he thought. *Every time there's humping or chopping to do when we knock these places down, I'm the one who has to do it. You don't pay me enough, mister.*

Harnessing his pent-up anger in his right thigh, Barry imagined the brass plate to be Ron's head and unleashed his steel-toecapped boot against it. Then he leapt forward, grabbed the doorknob, and pulled.

The door cracked, then creaked open slightly as the mould- and dust-sealed oak gave up. Old, musty air sighed out thankfully into the cramped confines of the passage.

"Yuk," said Barry.

With a further three, easier pulls, the door opened. Ron squeezed past, and flicked the light switch. Nothing. He took the Ever Ready sticking out of his pocket, and pressed the button. Fragile-looking nine-by-two-inch steps, held together by a handrail, disappeared into the gloom below.

"Er, you go first," said Ron, handing the torch to Barry. "I'll fetch the tools."

Tell me something new, fatso, screamed Barry, wordlessly.

The pencil beam swept over a brick floor, then broke into shafts of light as it pierced cord-like cobwebs. Barry surveyed the empty cellar. *They must've cleared it out before they left. Kuh. Nobody could've been down here for years*, he thought. *Time for an early tea-break, I reckon.*

He ducked to avoid a light bulb hanging in front of him, then gasped, and shook his head as it revealed itself to be, instead, an enormous spider, dangling from the ceiling. *This place is spooky*, he thought.

Barry paused, letting his eyes adjust to give a better perspective of the layout. A carpenter by trade, he knew all about angles and shapes. *This room isn't right*, he thought.

He ran his fingers over a brick wall flaking on his left, and shone the torch into that corner of the room. He stopped and looked at the wall to his half-right, angling away – not at ninety degrees, but slightly off true. He tapped it. The vibration, echoing inside paint-covered plasterboard, told him there was a void behind.

Barry jumped, as Ron came, unnoticed, from behind. "What you trynna do? Scare me to death?"

"Sorry. Just being careful."

"Hand me that claw hammer."

Ron wiped dust-caked sweat off his face with a filthy handkerchief. "Found something?" he said.

Barry took the hammer by its head, avoiding the part the cotton touched. *Bet your missus loves you,* he thought. He wiped the handle on his jeans, then flipped it over and crooked its head over the top corner of the plasterboard. "Dunno. Might've," he said. He gently eased the handle up, pulling at the same time. The whole thing came away in a crumbling sheet. "Get a generator, will you? There's another room behind here."

"Will do. What's in there?" said Ron, straining to see more than the beam allowed.

"Why d'you think I need a generator?"

"Oh. Yeah, OK."

Brilliant white light gave the cellar an atmosphere of being, at least, not the morgue-like place it had seemed before. Still, both men had the definite feeling of having been transported back in time as the recess revealed its secrets.

The sound of Barry's footsteps was muffled as they transferred from brick to a musty carpet. Dust billowed up into Ron's face, prompting him to whip out the handkerchief again. Small nasal deposits remained on his face when he put it back in his pocket.

Barry's gaze traversed from left to right. A wheelchair came first into view. Then a pair of crutches, propped against a writing desk. Barry's arms spontaneously jerked up to protect his face as what seemed to be a bird of prey, perched on top of the desk, prepared to leap at him. A stuffed owl fell forward and over the edge. As if completing a successful moon landing, it plopped onto the carpet and rolled towards the men, leaving a crazy line in the dust.

"Bring up that rig," said Barry.

Ron pushed the trolley of lights (pinched off the side of the M3 one night) nearer to where Barry stood.

"What you got?" he said. "Looks like junk to me. Might be money in them drawers. You have a look. I'll put the kettle on."

Barry sighed. *Are money and your gut the only things you ever think about?* he thought.

Barry took off his jacket and wiped the surface of the desk. Bad idea, he thought, as a cloud of dead matter exploded into life.

A faint glint, coming from a small statue, lying in an empty shoebox, caught Barry's eye. He picked up the statue, pulling a drawer open with his other hand at the same time. Several photographs, the top one of which appeared to be a family portrait, clung together inside. He picked them up too.

"Tea up," said Ron.

"Hmmm. Coming," said Barry, looking again at the statue. Stuffing the photographs in a back pocket, he turned it over and looked at its base. "Blimey," he said.

"What's happened?"

Barry smeared grease and dust off the figure. "It's an Oscar. An old one, as well. The date on it's 1991."

"Oscar who?"

God, you're thick, thought Barry, sitting on an edge of the trolley. "No, an Oscar. One of those things you got – if you were lucky – after sitting in a room that smells like a brothel, surrounded by clicking people, for five hours."

"Clicking?"

"Clicking. You know, top and bottom sets. In your north and south."

"North?"

"Oh, for God's sake, Ron. Top and bottom sets – of teeth."

"Oh. I get you. False teeth. It is old, then."

Somewhere between receiving the sounds of Barry's words and "Oh. I get you" coming out of Ron's mouth, the signifi-cance of Barry's explanations went AWOL, resulting in him contradicting his own last statement, when he next said, "Where would that be, then?"

Barry gave up. "Hollywood," he said.

"Yeah, but, so what?"

Ohhh, What a gob I've got. Story of my life. Should've stuck it in me pocket, thought Barry.

"So what? If it's a real one, it's solid gold, that's what."

Half a soggy biscuit spewed back into Ron's mug. "Give it here," he spluttered.

Barry gave it to him, and bent down to pick up his tea. As he did so, extra pressure in his back pocket reminded him of the photographs. He took them out, downing a slurp of warm Typhoo at the same time. "Huh," he said.

"What?" said Ron, squinting at the statue, trying to find the best place to scratch it.

"This photograph was taken outside, by the side of this house. You can see the top paddock. And the Devil's Punchbowl over the trees in the background. There's an old bloke. Those crutches are propping him up. He's only got one leg. I think he's only got one arm, too. And there's an old woman, sitting in the wheelchair."

Ron laughed. "Got his hand caught in a safe, and fell under a bus running away."

Barry, deciding to keep his mouth shut, let weary thoughts limp into his brain. *God, you're as useful as an exhaled breath of air. I'm packing it in after this job.* He moistened his fingers, wiped the picture, and looked again. His low whistle broke the silence.

"What now?" said Ron.

Barry was too entranced to reply straight away. Standing between the crippled man and the old lady was the most beautiful woman he'd ever seen. She was taller than the old man. Her right arm lay, snakelike, across his back. Her long, well-manicured fingers seemed to point to something offstage. Her left hand rested comfortably on the old woman's right shoulder.

Wiping the picture again brought a smile to Barry's face, as a pair of blue eyes – a blue seemed to surround the woman's body – seduced him. Perfect teeth, accentuated by full lips – the colour of a guardsman's tunic and the curve of her bosom just visible by the side of the old woman's head, triggered a rush of testosterone to his brain. "Don't bother scratching it, Ron. It's real."

"How d'you know?"

"There's another woman in this picture. I didn't notice her, what with her blonde hair and the white, summer dress. She's the one who won that Oscar."

"An old woman?"

Barry sighed a martyr's sigh, then said, "I'll bet you this picture was taken in the 1990s. Before you could grow your own body parts. That's why he's on crutches. Come on. Drink up. We'll be here all day at this rate."

* * *

As Ron's Hovawagun rose and carried them away from the house, Barry allowed himself to fantasize a little. Looking out past the top paddock to his left, the woman – projected from his mind in one glance, like a hologram on the horizon - accepted her Oscar to thunderous applause. *She was some beautiful woman*, he thought. *Wow! I wish I'd looked through the lens that took that picture.*

The name of the woman Barry was so taken with was Esther. The man on crutches her father, Terry Clayton. The lady sitting in the wheelchair was Esther's mother, Joan. Her once jet-black hair, white-flecked in the photograph, gave her the appearance of being older than her forty-nine years.

Ron hadn't been far from the truth. Shortly after Terry started work in 1970, he reached out his left arm to pick up something he shouldn't. That greed-prompted decision changed his life. Had he not lost his forearm, he might never have met Joan.

The person who took the photograph was Esther's husband, Ricky. His finger trembled slightly as he looked through the view-finder that day. Looking at the faces of the people he loved in the compacted environment of the camera was causing a flashback. A thin film of sweat began to form on his forehead as he prepared to press the button. He knew that if he hadn't been there to take the photograph, the world would have been dominated by a force of almost unimaginable evil. Millennium parties throughout the world would not have taken place. Nor would the popping of champagne corks have been heard. That joyful sound would have been replaced by something far more sinister.

An epic story of true love, greed, selfishness, murder and political intrigue as mankind descended into a secular way of life began with a storm, many years before Ricky took the picture and later sealed away the wheelchair, the crutches and other things he saw as symbols of a victory for mankind, in the cellar. Many years before any of the people who lived in the house were born, in fact.

Chapter 1

The Great Oak Tree
Solihull, England – 1950

The phone rang in Tim Howell's workshop. He wasn't surprised. The storm last night had been a lulu. He put down the chisel he was using, and picked up the receiver. "Hello," he said.

"Hi, Tim. It's John Barratt at the council offices."

"John, I was expecting a call from you."

"Yeah, sure was a bad one. I need you to have a look at the woods behind St Mary's Church. The big oak tree came down, at least. We need it shifting, as soon as possible really."

"OK, mate. I'll get on it straight away."

The Great Oak tree had stood for a thousand years, becoming the tallest tree around. Its presence dominated the scene, before the storm.

The oak had braced itself against autumn gales that fateful night. Thin branches at its crown flailed the air, like a drowning man's arms looking for a purchase. They found none, and every leaf fell. When it was over, the Great Oak stood like a crucified martyr against a dark, brooding sky.

Then the storms began. Thunder and lightning raged through the upper atmosphere. Positive and negative atoms smashed into each other with increasing ferocity, violating the air around.

Memories that had once lived in the minds of men and women—now a part of the universe—were stirred in this hotch-potch of chaos. From prehistoric man, who discovered how to make fire, down through the age of Greek philosophers and scholars; the mathematical genius of the Chinese, and heroic conquerors of lands such as Ghengis Khan and

Alexander the Great. Down through the age of the Roman Empire, the Renaissance, and the greatest empire the world has ever seen—the British Empire—*all* memory was disturbed in its rest. For hour after hour, opposing forces of nature battled against each other. At last, and with no other option, a massive bolt of lightning *exploded* from the sky. But the lightning didn't take electricity alone with it. Memories of the dead also found themselves drawn in.

The Great Oak had no defence as the lightning raced from the heavens in an instant, looking for its nearest escape route. With an ear-splitting crackle which reverberated throughout the woods, it struck the uppermost branches of the tree, and surged through every branch and fibre until it burst through its roots and into the ground. Finally, the Great Oak lay in smouldering pieces.

What remained cooled. The swollen, bubbling, sap-filled veins contracted, but whereas the electricity had dissipated, the memories had been mixed up in the coagulating mess. And there they stayed, as everything around them hardened.

Tim was astonished as he surveyed the scene. The Great Oak was part of local folklore. Generations of children had swung on ropes tied to its branches, carved their initials into its bark, and daydreamed of tomorrows while under its protective canopy. Now the oak tree was lying in pieces, Tim realised how much ground it had stood over. He began to retrieve what he could. All that remained after he'd finished was a stump, surrounded by blackened earth. He trimmed and tidied the corpse before cutting it into manageable pieces. Tim smiled as spiders and woodlice scuttled away from his saw. Even when cut, the tree provided dozens of planks, each more than twenty feet in length. They'd a rich, dark colour, and a strongly defined grain. He knew they'd make strong, sturdy furniture and the like, which would last many years.

Tim worked the timber with a trained, loving eye. His father before him had been a Master Carpenter, highly respected by his peers. He was a good teacher too, and proud of his sons, who had followed him into the trade. Tim's grandfather had done privileged work on Westminster Cathedral, and his great-grandfather had been in charge of the workmen who built Birmingham Cathedral. *I'm the man to breathe life back into this timber,* he thought.

As he sawed and planed Tim imagined what he'd do with all this fine oak. *A new Magistrate's Court's planned for the city centre. They'll need the best wood for that. I'll even make a special gavel, and present it to the Lord Chief Justice on opening day.*

The Botanical Gardens. They've ordered six new benches, for putting amongst the flowers and hedgerows, he mused. *The buying of benches by the loved ones of the departed has become popular recently. A good, solid bench will outlast us all,* he thought.

Cemeteries. That's another outlet, too.

When he'd finished, Tim found he had one hundred planks of the finest oak timber in the world. Each over twenty feet long, eighteen inches wide, and two inches thick. All were as straight as a gun barrel. There was even enough to make fifty benches, half of which he wholesaled to cover his costs. He sold what was left to a man who made furniture for children's nurseries. His favourite things to make were rocking horses and doll's houses, but he also fashioned toys.

Tim sold the shavings to the local huntsmen, and the sawdust to the licensee of a pub near his workshop. Nothing went to waste.

Tim had no idea what he was sealing in with every coat of varnish, after the wood had seasoned six months later. All over the world, those who came into contact with remnants of trees similarly affected, be it bench, plank, dust or splinter, would be influenced in their decision-making by memories of the dead.

Some memories were those of people who'd led good lives. Some were erotic, and used the opportunity to relive pleasures of the flesh. Some were wicked, and had murderous and malevolent intent. Some used their energy to prey on weak and vulnerable people, creating havoc in their minds.

The population of the British Isles was particularly susceptible to temptations of greed and avarice. The years between 1950 and 1990, commonly referred to as "boom and bust" years because of recurring periods of high inflation and interest rates, but fuelled by, amongst other things, rapid rises in the price of property, led to consumerism on a scale never previously known. More people owned their homes. Each family came to own cars and electrical goods of every kind; and went on holidays abroad, often buying a holiday-home, or getting involved in "Time-Share" organisations while there. In short, the people were ripe for exploitation, and not only by corporations or bankers, who encouraged them to live for the moment with advertisements such as "Buy Now—Pay Later." and made finance available. The memories took over. *Yes, that's a good offer. I can have it now, and not worry about having to pay for it*, were easy thoughts to give in to.

* * *

Inside the stump, the awesome memories of the brilliant sixth-century philosopher, mathematician and mystic, Pythagoras, and his servant, Audeus, also waited. It was said that Pythagoras used to write on a looking glass in blood and place it opposite the moon, when the inscription would appear reflected on the moon's disc; and that he tamed a savage Daunian bear by "stroking it gently with his hand", and held absolute dominion over beasts and birds by "the power of his voice" or "the influence of his touch".

Born on the island of Samos in about 529 BC, Pythagoras was noted for his manly beauty and long, fair hair. He grew up showing extraordinary mental power and foresight. A forward-thinking man, who employed the Samian Letter (Y) and the Harmony of the Spheres in his philosophy, he travelled widely, witnessing many unusual happenings in the known world.

On his return to Italy Pythagoras taught that the human soul is immortal. That all things in the universe belong to the macrosystem and are assigned and recognised within the matrix of perfected numbers. He sought to devise principles by which many questions the world struggled with in his time and in all time since could be understood and answered. All of life, the whole heaven, he said, was designed for harmony and ordered to function as a number, the universe, the body and the soul, together, and in natural potential to the divine. It's said

Pythagoras was the first to call the world "kosmos".

Pythagoras, like Socrates, and later Jesus, left no written accounts of his work. Instead his knowledge and speculations were delivered by disciples and biographers by word of mouth legends, and later in letters by people who called themselves, aptly, Pythagoreans.

But, as with Jesus, people were suspicious of Pythagoras and the brotherhood. They killed most of the members in a political uprising, after which Pythagoras was never seen again.

Unknown to his contemporaries, Pythagoras was on the verge of a great discovery when he disappeared. Only his faithful servant Audeus suspected that his master had broken into the world of the Harmony of the Spheres. Audeus carefully broke the seal on his master's great ledger and read Pythagoras' words:

"Through my experiments using the first book of Euclid as a guide, I believe that man's soul has three vehicles. (1) the ethereal, which is luminous and celestial, in which the soul resides in a state of bliss among the stars; (2) the luminous, which suffers the punishment of sin after death; and (3) the terrestrial, which is the vehicle it occupies on Earth. I believe that man's soul transmigrates into other things at the point of death."

This was, to Audeus, a true revelation but when he read the accompanying notes, which expanded the tenets of Euclid's geometry, and ended with the sentence "All of life—the whole of heaven—is designed for harmony and ordered, to function as a number," he was enthused to carry on his master's work.

Audeus concentrated on the third of the harmonies, the *terrestrial*. But he didn't know he was following the path his master took, and when the critical point came he too was taken.

On that day, Audeus set out his master's books and charts on the ground outside. He took pots containing all the elements of the Earth, and placed them round a fire. Finally, he mixed the elements and poured them on the ground in the shape of the letter Y. Massive electrical activity built up in the atmosphere, and swirled above Audeus as he raised his arms to the heavens and spoke: "Divine Master, most revered Seer. I make the sign of the letter Y on the ground, with the elements of the earth. This is the sign; the emblem of the straight and narrow, which is one, but if deviated from, becomes wider, and the breach extends. Master—show your humble servant the way."

At this point Audeus threw a mixture of graphite, sulphur and iron filings into the fire. When he then raised his arms to continue, lightning, attracted by the exploding metallic elements, and bringing with it the Harmony of The Spheres, burst from the sky, striking him down.

When Audeus' body was discovered, it was found that his skull was empty. Both his memories and those of his master remained in the universe—until they were returned to Earth via the bolt of lightning.

Chapter 2
St Mary's Church

St Mary's Church was built just before war broke out in 1939. Behind the church is an incline, leading to a flat, wooded area of about three acres. On this plateau, a Celtic homestead once bustled with life. No buildings remain to give an idea of what the homestead looked like, but a dried-out moat surrounds the inside perimeter. This is where the Great Oak stood, some seventy-five metres from the edge of the wood. Its long roots still stretch down the incline, and underneath the north end of the church.

Standing on top of logs which look like buffalo horns, lying upright on the ground, you'd notice the whole area was virtually symmetrical, even after a thousand years.

In autumn, as in the year of 1950, the scene is ablaze with rustic colouring. If you jumped from the log, a crunch of dead and dying leaves would breathe their last beneath your feet. Crisp, brown beech leaves, rolling around like locks of human hair, would, perhaps, inspire imaginings of the people who once lived there. A musty smell, rising unseen from decomposing vegetation and bonemeal, would bring visions of long-dead people to your mind. Foraging birds and squirrels would dart away, their cries of protest at the disturbance of your presence echoing in your ears.

Dead ash trees, stripped of bark, lie upturned like naked thighs, embarrassed by their unflattering position. Sounds of woodpeckers, drilling for any remaining insects under bark, would remind you of the chattering of human teeth soon to come.

A harsh breeze worries the last few expiring leaves from their anchorages. Soon, all above ground will be frozen. But underneath the topsoil, many different insects and animals sleep, waiting for warmer days.

Above ground the only movement would be ropes children had tied to branches so they could swing out over the moat. The ropes sway gently, like halters waiting for the next hangman's victim. All would be silent, like glass.

The scene is remarkably different in summer, when Nature's pageant is re-enacted. Trees unfurl fresh growth, which spreads like a peacock's boasting fan. Wild brambles throw out runners that twist and turn along the ground, before being swept into the air by limbless shoots, straining to outdo each other. They seem to dance in a warm breeze, like serpents writhing in courtship. Their efforts are applauded by many different mating calls, and the flutter of nest-building by those similarly affected. An orgasmic burst of new life rises all around.

In May, fairy-capped bluebells appear, seemingly overnight, as if bringing the message that it's safe to come out and play. Days get longer, and warmer.

In the summer of 1951 the only remaining signs that the Great Oak ever lived were the stump and two roots, rising from the ground like the Loch Ness monster. Children came back to explore in Nature's busy fairground. For some it would be the summer of the loss of their innocence, hiding in the undergrowth which envelops such roots, giving perfect cover for young boys and girls to conduct their society in.

After Tim Howell, fifteen-year-old Michael Jobson was the next to come into contact with the Great Oak tree. While hurtling up and down the dried-out moat on his bike, Michael fell, scratching his knee on the stump in the process. Inside an oak splinter, left sitting under the first few layers of his skin, were the memories of Pythagoras and Audeus.

Michael dusted himself off, and looked for a cool place to eat his apple. Spotting a den of vegetation covering the roots of the Great Oak tree, he crawled inside, and ate. Afterwards, he laid his head on a moss-covered root, and looked at the sky through tiny holes between leaves, twitching in the breeze.

He soon became drowsy, as the dry, balmy atmosphere and the humming of insects lulled him to sleep. As he dreamt he saw himself in his favourite place, St Mary's Church.

Michael's whole existence outside school revolved round the church. Apart from being a member of the Youth Club and

Bible reading class, he was a patrol leader in the Scout group, revelling in the close relationship with nature that being a Scout brought. And it suited his extrovert character, being as he was a natural leader. Apart from these interests, Michael was head choirboy.

Some of the sung parts of services in the Book of Common Prayer could have struck sinners with fearful dread, if spoken. Michael's perfect soprano voice smoothed these supplications and other reverences to God performed by the congregation. All felt that no god would deny prayers offered in such a beautiful way.

Each Sunday morning the bell tolled, calling the faithful to go to church. The sound of Michael's voice not only stood out from Nature's sounds as it lifted melodiously upwards to the heavens, but echoed in the routes underneath the church, now empty of flesh and resembling an underground railway system. His clear, penetrating tone soothed even the memories of the dead.

Michael left school determined to join the army, thereby giving satisfaction to those who'd nourished the leadership qualities he'd shown within the Scout group. That would be in a year's time, when he was seventeen so he sought, in the meantime, temporary employment by attending the recruitment drive organised by a team of American salesmen.

The product Michael would try to sell was *The Children's Encyclopaedia*, published by Field Enterprises. Michael felt sure that many parents would want to invest in their children's education by buying the books.

The atmosphere at the meeting, encouraged by American football-style cheerleaders, was charged with emotion by the time the head-man took the stage. Dressed in a white suit, he strode to the footlights with an air of confidence designed to inspire his young audience.

Wow! thought Michael. *I want to be just like him.*

The first question the head-man asked was, "You have one person on your team who's not doing as well as the rest. What d'you do about it?"

Michael's answer, "Give them my full support and encouragement," wasn't what the man wanted to hear.

"No." he said. "You dump him, and concentrate on the ones who can make you money."

This was Michael's introduction to the American business philosophy, "The world's a shop, and all the people in it customers."

Five years later, having worn out his shoes trying to sell encyclopaedias that nobody wanted, and completed his three-year National Service stint in the army, during which time he had the opportunity to see more of how Americans thought and behaved abroad, Michael returned to his roots thoroughly discouraged by what he saw as extreme capitalism and complacency, but convinced that he could serve his local community.

Michael remained a part of the church and eventually became vicar at St Mary's.

In the meantime, Tim's benches had proved to be popular buys, especially with the clergy.

Chapter 3

Louisa Rhodes

The solemn-faced director of a cemetery in Birmingham, England, purchased an oak bench from carpenter Tim Howell to set in the children's garden amongst sycamore, oak and maple trees.

"To give clients the opportunity to reflect," he said.

The funeral of Louisa Rhodes took place in the summer of 1965. Her parents, Peter and Anne, had battled for her life since she had been born, eleven months before. It became clear soon after her birth that Louisa was struggling to survive. Born severely disabled, she was also in considerable pain, and thought to be blind. Doctors controlled her pain with drugs, but reluctantly came to the conclusion that her prognosis was very poor indeed. They recommended that no attempt be made to keep Louisa alive if she became critically ill. She had died two weeks before the funeral.

The funeral cortège made its slow, winding way through the cemetery and into the children's garden. Peter and Anne and the rest of her family accompanied the tiny coffin to its final resting place. Even the doctors, who hadn't been attempting to help a child live for the first time, were present.

Later that evening, after the cemetery was shut, a bright moon shone its white, Tiffany-veiled light over the countryside. Foxes barked while skipping through parks, and pigeons cooed, perched, hidden away as they were amongst the evergreens. In the cemetery, an owl blinked and swivelled its head round three hundred and sixty degrees, looking for any small, unwary animal that would make a tasty meal.

A human being would not have noticed anything out of the ordinary going on, but the memories of the dead were conversing in their special way. All the graves had no souls in, of course. They'd left their bodies, and were waiting for loved ones who had predeceased them to come and fetch them. Memories, feeling the grief of mourners, knew another child had passed away.

"Why don't we go and see who it is?" said one old man's memories to his brother's—his brother had been shot down in the Battle of Britain, and waited for him.

When they got to Louisa's grave they found her apparition sitting on top of it.

"Hello, who are you?" she said.

"I'm George, and this is my younger brother William. You can call him Bill. I'm seventy-six—sorry, *was* seventy-six. Haven't quite got used to it, yet. Bill was shot down by the Luftwaffe in 41..."

Louisa cut him short. "Forty-one what?"

"Sorry again, I forgot. You're too young to remember. I meant 1941. That was a long time ago. You've got a lot of history to catch up on. You come from the finest stock. This country's provided some of the best soldiers and sailors the world's ever seen. Take my brother here. He shot down twelve Fokker-Wulfs before he bought it. Bomber's Moon. That was his problem. If the moon hadn't..."

"Come on, George. She doesn't want to hear about all that," said Bill. "I bet your mom was upset, Louisa."

"Yes, and I'm worried about them. Great-Nanny and Grandad have been to tell me I'm going with them, but I hadn't learnt to talk before I died, and couldn't tell my mom and dad I'd be OK."

"Well, you don't have to worry about that now. We use telepathy, so just think. I don't know what to do, but the bench will."

The oak bench had settled in well. The timber kept its shape throughout winter, spring and summer. But natural gaps between its tenon joints left enough space for sound to get in. The memories heard every sound and conversation that came their way.

"We can do something to help this girl, can't we?" said Bill's memories. "She only wants to get a message to her parents."

"I'll go," said a soft, friendly voice.

"Who's that?" said another.

"My name's Paul. I haven't been here long, but I used to live in the same road as Louisa's parents. Besides, I want to have a word with my missus. She's been spending my insurance money like there's no tomorrow."

The Same Day

Peter and Anne were exhausted. The adrenaline that had kept them going had disappeared now they'd laid Louisa to rest, and they just flopped when they got home. When tiredness overcame them, they linked arms and walked upstairs to bed.

"You go the bathroom first. I'm going to shut the windows in the nursery," said Anne.

"OK. But don't be too long. I know you're grieving, but we both have to try to get some sleep."

Anne decided it was probably displacement of air as she opened the door to the nursery that caused the cot to rock. But the window was open. Cartoon faces on pink and blue wallpaper stared back at her as she looked around. She and Peter hadn't known the sex of the baby when they had decorated. The cot, bought when she had first realised she was pregnant, swayed emptily.

There, on a small chest of drawers, lay a white bone teething ring Anne's mother had bought when they told her she was going to be a grandmother again.

Louisa won't need it, now, she thought. She sighed, and walked over to close the window. As she reached up, she could have sworn she felt *something* warm caress her cheek. Closing the window, she sat on a tiny stool by the cot for a moment. Tears began to flow, as she thought of the precious part of her she'd been forced to give up in such sad circumstances.

She wouldn't have had much of a life, even if she'd survived, she thought.

As she turned to look at the room one last time, Anne fancied that one of the cartoon faces reminded her of Louisa.

A serenity that Anne could only give herself to suddenly

overwhelmed her, as Paul's telepathic message flooded into her mind. "Hello, Mummy. Don't worry. I'm alright. I know you and Daddy didn't think I had much of a life, but I felt loved."

The face. It *was* Louisa.

"What?" said Anne.

The face continued, "I wanted to tell you both, whatever decision you made would be OK. I already knew what my future would be. Perhaps you thought I was alone? I wasn't. Great-Nanny and Grandad were watching over me all the time. They told me they'd be waiting, if I was eventually drawn to the light."

Anne shook her head in disbelief. But the face kept on speaking.

"I didn't mind when they came to fetch me. My thoughts were concentrated through a sort of window. All I could feel was love and understanding. After my body died, my memories—that's what you called my soul, by the way—left my body, and now I'm here with all the rest. I met a lovely old man called George. He's going to tell me all about my ancestors. Thanks to the Great Oak tree, and Paul who brought you this message, I can stop worrying about you now. Thank you for giving me life. This life."

It took Anne a while to realise the room was quiet again. Then she regained her senses.

"What? ... How? ... I don't understand. Great Oak tree? Old man called George? Great-Nanny and Grandad? They've been dead for years. Oh. Peter... Must tell Peter."

Anne jumped off the stool and, running from the nursery, met Peter coming from the bathroom. His face was ashen. He pointed. "I've just seen... it was... in the mirror..."

"I know. It was Louisa," Anne said. "Come on, let's go and tuck the girls in. Then I'll put the kettle on, and you can tell me all about it."

Peter and Anne sat drinking coffee in the kitchen, each going over the experience they'd been through in silence. Peter spoke first. "It's logical when you think about it."

"What is?" said Anne.

"Well, Louisa just spoke to us, right?"

"Yes."

"How?"

"I don't know. I just know that she did."

"I'll tell you how. But you've got to look at it differently. Not as a living person."

"I haven't a clue what you're talking about."

"Look. We thought Louisa had no life, right? That's because we relate everything to what we know about living. We don't know what it's like to be dead until we're dead, do we?"

"Suppose so," said Anne.

"Right. And when you're born, you have to go to school to learn about everything. If you want to know about life after death, you go to church. You need language to do that. When you're dead, you don't need language, because communication between souls, or memories, or whatever you want to call it, is telepathic. Everything Louisa needs to know is in the minds of the people who died before her. All she has to do is think."

"My God. She knows more than we do now, then," said Anne.

"Suppose she does," said Peter, taking Anne's hand.

"Well, I believe what I saw," said Anne.

"I do too."

In the cemetery, memories in the bench congratulated themselves on the success of their mission, and sent a message to Pythagoras and Audeus. It may have been coincidence that brought the memories of these good and great men back to Earth. But as a pattern of selfishness and greed emerged all over the western world, their positive energies were needed to redress the balance.

Having gained an enormous amount of knowledge in a short time, and relieved of the daily struggle merely to survive, rich societies indulged themselves, neglecting and using those less well off. Tremendous innovations in technology led to the mass production of cheap consumer goods in the 1960s. Capitalism of the worst kind perverted science, and market forces dominated lifestyles, resulting in a clash of cultures which brought Armageddon ever closer. And nowhere more so than in the district where the Great Oak had once stood.

Chapter 4

Roy and Eve

A thunderstorm was raging. Rain poured down for hours, filling drains and culverts. Under St Mary's Church the roots of the Great Oak tree were filling to bursting point. Michael Jobson completed his tour outside St Mary's. Invariably there'd be one or two youngsters messing about round the back. Occasionally he'd find condoms and discarded syringes lying around.

He looked at the sky and watched the sleeting rain for a moment before going inside. *This is a bad one*, he thought. *Hope the gutters stand it. Better check the windows.*

Once everything was secure Michael knelt and prayed to his God, as usual. He'd seen his congregation diminish rapidly since the advent of Rock and Roll and television. Privately, he also felt the changeover from the Book of Common Prayer to a more modern service hadn't helped. *I'm used to the old service,* he thought. *It's what I was brought up on. Besides, the people who devised these new services took out the poetry as sure as if they were atheists.*

Michael crossed himself, and got up. The sound of rain beating against the windows and the gale blowing outside became, in a way, comforting to Michael; as if Heaven was maintaining contact with him through the elements and his church. He closed his eyes to meditate. For a moment he saw a vision of a woman on a journey. He felt somehow that her path was entwined with his. Words within the rhythm of wheels, rumbling on a track, seemed to be spoken but he couldn't quite make them out, or her face. Then a brief lull in the storm enabled him to hear, "...So that he set the royal crown upon her head, and made her queen instead of Vashti." Michael recognised this as a passage from the Bible.

Wind and rain, renewed in its ferocity, blocked out all chance for him to think further, but Michael had no doubt this was a sign. *Is this the second coming, Lord? Thy will be done. All I have to do now is wait*, he thought, crossing himself again.

Memories spilled out everywhere from the drains under St Mary's Church. One murderous set disappeared in a rage, and seeing a light in a house in Castle Lane, which ran behind the woods, made straight for an upstairs window. Inside the bedroom Eve Marshall was in the throes of a difficult labour. Roy and Eve Marshall were twenty and twenty-two respectively, when they married in 1966. They had met on a coach trip to Blackpool three years before. The trip was organised by somebody at the hotel where Roy was apprenticed to be a chef. Eve worked in a bank, and only went along because a friend who worked in the offices invited her.

The party spent the first few hours wandering around Blackpool, then chilled out on the beach, sunbathing. Somehow the teenagers paired up during the afternoon and Roy and Eve ended up snogging on the back seat of the coach on the return journey.

Roy and Eve were from entirely different backgrounds, but fell in love almost at once. He, tall and handsome, oozed the confidence of a young man who'd left home to live in a hotel. Roy's mother had worked as a decoder in the Second World War and married a Post Office messenger boy, who weaved in and out of the bombs on his bike to deliver messages, or so he said. After the war ended, and she'd given birth to Roy, she went to work at a teleprinter's in a factory in Small Heath, while Roy's father got promoted to a management position at a Post Office depot not far away.

In the early fifties they joined a Post Office self-build group, along with two hundred other couples who wanted to build their own houses. At that time the site they chose was far enough away from the city for families to fragment, even though it was only seven miles south of Birmingham.

Eve's family lived in a two up, two down terraced house in Aston, where as well as Eve, her parents and brother, her maternal grandparents also lived. A large sheet nailed to the ceiling, dividing the largest bedroom, was the only thing to protect Eve's modesty, and that of her grandmother who slept in the same bed. Eve's brother and grandfather shared the bed on the other side of the sheet.

Roy fell in love with this close-knit family. Although he wasn't sure about Eve's mother, whose first words on meeting him were "We speak our minds in this house."

Roy wasn't sure if this was an invitation to speak his mind, or a warning to be prepared to receive the sharp end of her tongue.

He was invited to sit in the parlour, which was the room the family lived in, mostly. It had a huge fireplace with a hob in the grate that Grandad used to keep a jug on. When she was young, Eve was sent several times a week to an Out-Door from which alcohol was dispensed, returning with a jug of ale. Then she'd stand mesmerised as Grandad stuck a hot poker in it.

A tiny kitchen opened out onto what was really just a chicken run. There was a coal bunker too, in which the coal was painted white so they'd know if anybody pinched any. The kitchen was the only other room Roy saw for the first six months of his relationship with Eve. The front room, which contained a piano, a settee, a dining table and chairs, and an aspidistra plant in a pot, was used only on special occasions, such as for laying out the dead.

When Roy was allowed into the front room it was to sleep on the settee, after a Christmas party. In the middle of the night Roy woke, suddenly. "What's the matter?" he said. The only sound was that of a Westminster chiming clock on the mantelpiece. Then a horrible feeling he was going to be sick came over him.

He looked frantically round the room. "The aspidistra pot. No—better not," he decided. Stark naked, he jumped off the settee, flung the door open and ran up the stairs. Actually, he only made it to the fourth step before the thick-cream-topped sherry trifle, plus copious draughts of beer he had consumed earlier, attained a frightening velocity on their way back up.

Roy, to his eternal shame, spent his first overnight stay sitting naked, halfway up the stairs, trying to clean up the mess with a bucket of cold water. Next morning, Eve's mother let him know she'd heard every sound he'd made, of course.

Fortunately for Roy his faux pas was overshadowed by Grandfather George's. George, a tall, silver-haired, retired policeman, was trusted with plucking the turkey that Christmas Eve while the family went to the pub. George had drunk a skinful and retired to bed when they returned. In the middle of the floor (covered with feathers) in the parlour, they found the naked turkey, plucked and drawn. Its legs were splayed open with a note saying, "Why don't you come up and see me some time?" attached to its chest by a cocktail stick.

Roy loved Eve completely. He thought her dark, curly hair, her blooming complexion, and her round, dark brown eyes entrancing, making her the most beautiful girl he'd ever seen. Her love for him shone through her personality, so that a heady mix of young love and laughter filled their lives. It wasn't long before they announced their plans to wed.

They consummated their commitment to one another on Eve's huge bed one afternoon in a giggling fumbling of passion and inexperience. No couple were more in love than they.

After the wedding Roy and Eve settled into a council house and set about starting a family. Eve proved to be fertile, and gave birth to her first child, Stephen, the same year.

She was overjoyed to find herself pregnant again so soon after giving birth to Stephen. But things were not going well.

Roy, now at the Chamber of Commerce, was working when the call telling him Eve had gone into labour came. He jumped onto his battered old scooter and made his way home. It was just after 8 p.m. November 23rd 1967.

Rain began to fall as Roy made his way back, making it difficult to see. But he didn't care. He was going to be a father again. The howling gale accompanying him could have been the congratulations of the family, and the arrow-like darts of water, slaps on the back, as he walked up the path leading to his front door.

A midwife, Nurse Galloway, was already at the house when he arrived. She seemed, to Roy, to be flustered as she greeted him. "Watch that kettle. When it's boiled, bring it to me," she said. Then she shot off upstairs.

Roy kept one eye on the kettle while struggling to get out of his rain-sodden clothing and was still towelling off when the nurse shouted down, "Hasn't that kettle boiled yet?"

Roy rushed upstairs and into the bedroom with the kettle just in time to see Eve writhing around on the bed. "What's happening?" he said.

"She's having a baby, that's what. Haven't you ever seen a baby being born?"

"No, I..."

At this moment, unnoticed by those present, the murderous apparition appeared at the open window. Its eyes sparkled as it surveyed the scene. Eve was having problems. Roy didn't realise it, but the baby's head was too big to pass through Eve's vagina. After struggling for several hours she was weak. Something had to be done, quickly.

"Hold her legs open," said Nurse Galloway. Roy held Eve's legs open, while trying to comfort her. He blinked in disbelief as the midwife then plunged a syringe into Eve's thigh. She screamed.

Then, as if from nowhere, the midwife produced a pair of surgical scissors. As she reached down to cut the skin holding the baby's head back, a scalpel appeared in the apparition's hand. In a millisecond, the scalpel overtook the midwife's hand and slashed at Eve.

Then the apparition disappeared.

Roy, eyes bulging, stood transfixed as the midwife sprang into action. "Phone for an ambulance," she said.

Eve fainted as the baby's head popped out. It was struggling to avoid choking.

Roy jumped as the midwife again said, louder this time, "*Phone for an ambulance, will you.*" Roy fled downstairs while the midwife tried to staunch the flow of blood and secure the umbilical cord at the same time.

The response from the emergency services was immediate. Eve was made comfortable and sedated, and the baby, a girl, whom they named Annette, seemed none the worse for her traumatic entrance into the world. Soon, the memories of their painful experiences left Eve and Annette and life returned to normal, apparently.

The family would all pay a heavy emotional price later though, as Roy became tormented by memories of the appalling mutilation of his beloved wife.

Annette was a beautiful baby and thrived in the months that followed. Unlike Stephen, who'd conned both Roy and Eve all night, every night, Annette slept through from the start and was no trouble whatsoever.

None knew that the glint in her eye was a reflection of the evil she'd sucked in as she took her first breath of life. Even now it was invading her mind, implanting evil thoughts.

Roy struggled to come to terms with what he'd seen. He loved his family, but things seemed different now. He couldn't bring himself to make love to Eve any more. It was all his fault, he felt. He'd caused her pain and suffering by making her pregnant. But it was the scissors, and the blood, he couldn't forget.

A friend of Roy's suggested he take the vacant job at a local nightclub. It wasn't far away, and was well paid, so he accepted.

Roy found working in a nightclub a novel experience. His hours of work were different, of course, but it wasn't that which caused the breach between him and his family to expand. Massive indoor arenas and football stadia would soon generate much more income for cabaret performers, but for the time being Roy was in charge of a part of the glamorous world of entertainment. Pop stars, such as Lulu and Cliff Richard, and a host of bands and comedians, such as Bob Monkhouse and Bruce Forsyth, filled the place night after night.

Eve let herself go after the birth of Annette. Bringing up two children and running a household at the same time left her little opportunity to make herself attractive for Roy, whose eyes beheld stunningly pretty, and hot, young women nightly.

When Sue, a waitress, made a pass at Roy he embarked on a passionate affair with her. Roy was in the habit of dropping staff off after the club wound down, and one night found himself alone with Sue, the last to be dropped off. As he leaned across to open the door she turned to say goodnight. Their eyes met, and she brought one hand up to the side of his head. "Thank you," she said, kissing him lightly on the cheek. Roy automatically responded, but as he let go of the door handle and withdrew his arm he brushed a nipple. She gasped, and said, "Come on."

Sue grabbed Roy's hand and led him up the path to her

parents' house. What began as a goodnight kiss ended up as a moment of lustful madness.

Roy was lost after that. Confused and tormented beyond help, he used his relationship with Sue to block out the terrible scene of Annette's birth from his mind.

Living with Eve inevitably became a strain for Roy, and his dealings with the children conflicted with his daytime arrangements with Sue. On one of the few occasions he did take them out he noticed Annette fidgeting about under her seatbelt. "You haven't wet your knickers have you?" he said. He felt her crotch. It was wet. "Oh, hell. That's all I need," he said.

After months of mentally divorcing himself from his family Roy declared his love to Sue, who said she loved him too, but didn't want children. He left Eve and the children, convincing himself they'd be better off without him. This decision had far-reaching consequences for both Roy and his family.

The years which followed saw the memories take hold of Annette's character, causing Eve to worry for her sanity.

Chapter 5
Terry and Joan

Terry (Hammer) Clayton peered through blood, trickling down from cuts above his eyes. Fortunately, the bell sounded to end round two, saving him from further punishment. He turned away from his tormentor, a boy half as big as him again but the same age—fifteen—and staggered back to his corner. The year was 1968. The place—Nuneaton, Warwickshire.

He flopped onto his stool, exhausted, while his trainer worked feverishly to staunch the flow of blood. "Terry," he said, "This is madness. He's got you beat. I'm going to throw the towel in."

"If you do, I'll knock *you* out." Terry said. "Give me this one last round."

His trainer shrugged his shoulders. "Be it on your own head. I give up."

The bell rang to start the final round. Terry put both gloved fists on his knees, hauled himself wearily to his feet, and ambled to the centre of the ring.

Terry lost yet another fight, and the trainer had difficulty finding enough fresh skin to stitch around Terry's bloody eyes in the dressing room afterwards. "That's your last fight for me. If you want to carry on, you'll have to find another trainer," he said. "You've got a terrific right, and you're as game as they come, but you can't keep on giving height and reach away to opponents."

Terry sighed. He knew the trainer was right. He was just too small, and didn't have the scope to grow enough to catch up with taller, heavier opponents.

"OK, I'll pack it in," he said. Terry never fought again.

When he left school the following year, Terry went to work in a local factory, his dreams of becoming a professional boxer put firmly behind him.

He was fit and healthy, and had no trouble reaching the piecework targets set him to produce coil tops. It was hot work. He stood, stripped to the waist, in front of a massive press, doing four eight-hour shifts, days and nights, a fortnight about. At least he was *supposed* to do four eight-hour shifts. Terry had a strategy which enabled him to finish long before his fellow workers.

When production workers filled a box with 100 units, they put it onto a shelved trolley. The target for each man was ten boxes per shift. When the trolley was full with ten boxes, the worker pushed it to a checking-in point. There, each box was weighed. If found to be correct, a tag with the worker's number on it was tied to it. Then the worker pushed the trolley to a place of storage.

This was an easy fiddle for Terry. At the end of his shift, he'd stack only nine boxes at the storage area, rip the tag off the remaining one, cover it up with an apron, and wheel the trolley back to his place of work. Then, making sure no one was watching, he'd lift up the floorboards beneath the press, and stash the box in the hole. That way he would have an easy night once a week.

Terry began work when the press reached its required temperature. First he would place two brass terminals into each of twelve impressions in a mould, then put a pellet of powdered plastic into each. Pull down the safety guard, and press a button. Wait for the press to come down and do its work, while having a quick look round to see if anyone was watching. Lift the safety guard when the press finished its cycle, and take out the cooked tops. Clean out each impression with a brush dipped in wax, and start over again. Easy money.

This wasn't good enough for Terry, though. Pulling down the safety guard and raising it again took time, and time was money.

His foreman was in the habit of retiring to his office for a kip shortly after midnight. This was the signal for Terry to switch off the safety guard, and work like a maniac. He could then finish early, and get his own head down at about 3 a.m.

Terry got careless one night, however. He'd worked even more frantically than usual, and was shattered by the time he started the last of his ten boxes. He almost threw the plastic pellets in, one of which flopped into the impression of its neighbour. Terry noticed this as he pressed the button to bring the press down. He reached in to right it, but the pellet had started to melt, and slipped from his gloved fingers. He tried again, but it was too late.

Terry screamed, and passed out, as the twenty-tonne press squashed his entire forearm between its plates.

Terry's mate heard the scream. Knowing of Terry's habit, he switched the safety guard back on when he rushed over to help. Terry got £30,000 for his arm, and became eligible to receive incapacity and other related benefits, because he was too stressed to work again. His useful working life had lasted a mere eighteen months.

Terry met a pretty young thing named Joan at the local Social Security Office, and married her. She liked to sleep on the left hand side of the bed, conveniently.

Joan was even more skinny than Terry. Her daily intake of fluid was a large glass of hot water, into which she squeezed the juice of one lemon. Her favourite and main meal of the day was a burger and fries. This she topped up with vitamin and other pills. A multi-vitamin tablet was followed by a Glucosamine with Chondroitin capsule, and a garlic tablet.

Joan wore long, black, sleeveless dresses, which she bargained for at any of several charity shops lining the local high street. And she wore open-toed sling-back shoes, whatever the weather. She went to bingo three nights a week, which suited her dreamy character. Her hair was black and shoulder length, worn swept back behind her head, secured by a rubber band.

In the summer of 1970, Terry and Joan moved to Margate, as her sister, Elizabeth, had done when marrying a local man, Alan Bennet, two years before. This was in order to enjoy their lifelong holiday at the expense of the taxpayer in more clement surroundings.

It would be hard to find sisters more opposite in character. Unlike Joan, whose formative years were spent during the relaxation of social and eating habits in the Sixties, during which period the emancipation of women was completed when female contraception via the Pill became freely available, and take-away restaurants suddenly took the place of Lyons' Cafes, Elizabeth, five years older, retained the air of quiet competence her mother had instilled in her. A pre-war period of high unemployment among men and post-war austerity produced a generation of women who fed and clothed their families on very little, and seemed able to cope with almost anything.

Although absent in Joan, this indomitable spirit resurfaced in her firstborn. Quickly becoming pregnant, she gave birth to a beautiful, blonde-haired girl, whom they named Esther.

One evening, late that summer, Terry and Joan ambled along the seafront. Joan, pushing the pram, was window shopping and eyeing brightly-coloured fashion, wondering, *will I ever get into them again?*

Terry's thoughts meandered along the same lines, but on a different subject. *It's been three months. Wonder if she's ready for a bit of hanky-panky, yet?*

Deep in thought, Terry swerved to avoid his foot descending on something a local dog had left on the pavement, causing him to lose his balance. Terry lurched into the arms of a man, standing in a shop doorway. "Buy a paper, mate? Read about the big issues in the world today," the man said.

Terry looked into soft brown eyes, and instantly felt as if he'd known this man all his life. "Sure. How much?" he said.

Although his reply was delivered in little more than a whisper, Terry heard each word as clearly as if the man were a sailor ringing eight bells. "This is the only one left. Take it."

"Thanks. Nice one, mate," said Terry.

Terry looked at the magazine as he and Joan walked off. He looked back, sure the man pictured on its cover was the same man he'd just spoken to. Terry felt he was still there, but... *Must've stepped back into the doorway*, he thought.

"You alright?" said Joan.

"Yeah, I'm fine."

Joan hoicked the pushchair round a corner. Terry, still scanning the cover and noting that the man pictured appeared to be standing outside a cathedral this time, looked up. He stopped, as if petrified. A tile-covered church steeple pointed, like a ladder, to the sky on the other side of the road. The words, "We ought to have Esther baptized," came in a spontaneous rush.

"Of course, we will," said Joan. "Shall we organise it, now. While we're here?"

Three weeks later, Terry, Joan, Elizabeth and Alan sat in Margate Methodist Church—each absolutely convinced the minister was thinking, *I only ever see any of this lot at Christmas, weddings, baptisms, and funerals.*

Alan, glad they were in a crowd, kept his head down.

Sure the minister would be impressed if he looked heavenwards, Terry raised his eyes when the minister looked in his direction during the singing of a hymn. Terry squawked as two red eyes, below a crown of thorns, bored into him. An effigy of Christ Crucified loomed over him, like a giant condor hanging in the sky. Terry felt as if it would pounce down, and admonish them for their sins, at any second.

Terry eased his way past Joan. "Got to go to the toilet," he said.

"What?" said Joan, to an empty space.

Terry returned in time to reply to the minister's question: "Will you love your children, committing yourselves to care for them in body, mind, and spirit?"

"Yes," said Terry and Joan, in unison. Then it was the godparents' turn.

"Will you help these parents to nurture their children?"

By the time Terry left the church, he felt different. It was obvious to him that there was real meaning to the service. After the baptism, each child was taken amongst the congregation. *Sort of introduced*, Terry thought.

Later, Terry confided to Alan, "I thought it was great. Did you see that little boy? He shook my hand."

Alan, a more sombre man, gave it some thought, then said, "Y'know, there's a lot to be said for it. I got the impression those children will remember that experience. I noticed Esther took it all in. I bet if you ask her in thirty years' time if she remembers being baptized, she'll say 'yes'. Fancy a pint?"

"Joan. We're going for a pint."

"Well make sure it's one. Not a skinful. And bring me and Elizabeth back a Snowball."

"OK."

* * *

"Watch out." Alan grabbed Terry's arm. The driver of the bus Terry was about to walk under blared his horn.

"Thanks. I was just thinking."

"Well, if I was you, I'd try looking at the same time."

Terry opened the door to the Railway pub. "Yeah, thanks. What d'you want? Bitter?"

"Bitter-shandy, please. The bitter will need livening up at this time of day. By the way, what got to you in the church?"

"I dunno. I just felt uneasy. I mean, it was my idea as well as Joan's to have Esther christened. But why do we feel we have to? We only ever go to church for christenings, weddings and funerals."

Terry gave Alan his pint. "There's two seats over there, by the window."

"Thanks. Why do we go to church? That's a difficult question. I think about things like that. I felt the same as you, you know."

"Oh."

"Yes. I've got a theory. What d'you think a caveman would do if you showed him how to cook with one of those new-fangled microwave ovens?"

Oh, God. He's on his favourite subject, now. I suppose, if I were the caveman, I'd wonder where he got the electricity from, thought Terry. "Dunno. Think I was an alien?"

"Why d'you think he'd think that? And why does it always have to be something from up there?" said Alan, pointing to the heavens.

Terry sipped his pint, and looked out the window. *God. I don't know. Hope they don't eat all that sherry trifle. Mustn't forget her Snowball,* he thought. "Because even though he's only a caveman, he knows there's something else up there? Another force he doesn't understand," he offered.

"Exactly. Now, d'you believe in telepathy?"

I know if I stay in this pub too long she'll send me a message, and it won't be by hand, thought Terry. "Erm. Sometimes I get the feeling someone's watching me," he said.

"Right. And that's how we all felt, inside that church. And that's empathy. What did you have for dinner on August 31st 1970?"

"How the hell should I know? I bet you do, though. What sort of a question's that?"

"Well, can you remember the Lord's Prayer?"

"Of course," said Terry.

"I bet everybody else does, too. It's not just something you learned when you were a kid. You could've forgotten it, like you forgot maths. You want to believe there's a force up there. I think there is. It's mental energy. And it's powerful. Like what you feel when you look into a woman's eyes. A meeting of minds."

Oh God. Where's he going, now? There'll be more than a meeting of minds if we don't get back soon. Her fist'll meet my stump. "Yeah. I get the message. Come on. We've got to get back."

Alan wasn't going to let him get away with the last word. "Course, the issue about christenings and things is that we do them because we feel uncomfortable if we don't. We *know* there's something else out there. We just don't know what, yet. At the moment, mankind communicates either by speaking face to face, or on the phone. He's bound to discover how to transmit thoughts sometime and do away with wires. Same with electricity pylons. Case proved, m'lud?"

Alan's words came back to Terry as they walked home. *"The issue,"* he said. *The big issue.* Terry looked for the man who gave him the copy. *Funny. I only ever saw him that once.*

*   *   *

After Esther was weaned she refused to be spoon-fed, giving the world a preview of her single-minded nature. Terry watched with amusement as every time Joan attempted to prise Esther's lips apart with a spoonful of food, Esther turned her head away, lips clamped shut. Finally, Joan exploded, "Oh, I can't be bothered with this. Here, you try."

Terry took the spoon and swirled it round in the bowl of Heinz creamed chicken Joan had prepared. Then he offered it to Esther. She looked at Terry, clamped her teeth shut even more tightly, and shook her head. Then she held out her hand for the spoon.

At first the puree went everywhere, except in Esther's mouth. But she quickly got the hang of it, and took only a few seconds to advance to a fork when later sharing the same diet as Joan. A diet of burger and fries meant that her early growth was a little stunted, however.

The years passed quickly by. Four years later Esther's sibling twins, Margaret and Andrew, were born and she started school, quickly becoming best friends with Sheila Watson, who lived in the same street. Before long she began to stay over, and take her evening meals at Sheila's house—which was a blessing, and evened out the poor diet she was more used to. Joan didn't mind, now she'd twins to worry about.

Late one afternoon that summer Esther was enthusiastically riding Billy—a rocking horse—in Sheila's bedroom. Over the years it had become smooth and polished after providing hours of fun for children. Its dark colour and strongly defined oak grain gleamed as the afternoon sun touched it.

Then came a shout from downstairs. "Dinner's ready."

Esther swung a leg over the horse and jumped off. As she did so, she caught the inside of a thigh on one of its ears, causing a tiny splinter to lodge just under the skin. And there it stayed, causing her no discomfort whatsoever. In Esther's teens, the erotic memories of Erato, seventh daughter of Zeus and Mnemosyne, would take advantage of Esther's sexual awakening. But it was the buying of a book which had more significant consequences for her future.

In an attempt to keep up with Esther's voracious appetite for learning, Terry and Joan scoured the local car boot sale that summer. As they walked down the aisle, looking from side to side to see what was on offer, Terry came across a table covered with videotapes, cassettes and books. The man standing behind was the same man who had given him the magazine when he stumbled on the pavement on Margate seafront when Esther was a baby. "Haven't seen you for ages, mate," said Terry.

The words came as softly as before. "I get around."

"What d'you do, anyway?"

"I'm looking."

"What for?"

The man didn't reply, but kneeling down, took a book

from a box lying on the grass beside him. He gave it to Terry. "*Snow White*, sir. Perfect for any child. An introduction to the world of politics and the complexity of relationships for a young mind, in a fairy story. Ingenious, don't you think?"

Terry looked into those soft brown eyes, thinking, *What on earth are you talking about?* Still, he took the book.

* * *

No one knew the name of the man who gave Terry the book. He never offered it. Nor could they have discerned his origin by his accent. Indeed, any accent this nomadic character (who was in fact American by birth) might once have had was now a blend of verbal sounds so neutral, accommodating, and disarming as to be immediately understood by all who heard it. There was a reason for this.

* * *

On July 16th 1969 a rocket named Apollo 11 took off from Kennedy Space Center. The mission of the crew was to attempt a landing on the moon and, if successful, the exploration of it.

Each man had a job to do, which took their minds off the enormity of what they were attempting. Still, the nervous shifting of their eyes from dial to computer monitor while cramped together in the juddering confines of a tiny module, bolted onto the nose of the rocket straining against the force of gravity, was evidence enough of the way they were feeling.

As the rocket left the Earth's atmosphere the crew began to experience emotions far different from those of passengers in aeroplanes, who would have clouds and the ground beneath them to keep the scene in perspective. Witnessing the Earth slowly shrinking in size was an awesome sight. And a fearsome sight, with only a small, man-made machine propelling them further and further away into space.

The crew completed their mission, and returned safely to Earth. But they weren't the same. Only they, out of the five billion people living on Earth, had reached out into the Universe. Had felt the mighty power in the void; that embracing stem-cell from which all things emanate, and one day return to. Only they had been held in the womb of creation. And they were profoundly moved by the experience.

* * *

The power and presence of that environment, so pure as to be closer to that which mankind thinks of as God than any other, was now present on Earth. Carried by the brown-eyed, softly-spoken man, in a splinter nestling in the palm of his right hand.

Terry never saw the man again. But others would meet him as he travelled the continents. They too would become changed people.

And the king loved Esther above all the women and she obtained grace and favour in his sight more than all the virgins; so that he set the royal crown upon her head, and made her queen instead of Vashti.

Esther 2:17

Chapter 6

Esther

Hilda Watson, now becoming more of a mother to Esther than Joan, took both girls to school, and brought them back each day.

It became routine for Esther and Sheila to improve their reading skills by reading from a book of their choice after tea. On one occasion, Esther read from *Snow White and the Seven Dwarves*. She sat next to Hilda while Sheila watched. Sheila's father, Norman, videoed the process.

Esther spoke slowly and deliberately. "Snow White put the tablecloth on the table." Esther paused and looked at Hilda, as if needing confirmation she'd got it right. Getting a nod of approval, she glanced at the camera before continuing. "Can you see me, Mister Watson?"

"Yes, I can see you, Esther. Tell the story."

"Yes, and perhaps I can see me," she piped. She went on. "Then Snow White put seven plates, seven cups, seven knives, seven forks, and seven saucers on the table." Esther paused again. "And there were seven beds against the wall. And Snow White lay upon one of the beds and went to sleep." Esther sniffed, before carrying on.

"It happened," she paused, and looked at Hilda. Getting a smile in return, she continued, "that seven dwarves lived in the cottage. When the dwarves returned to the cottage, Snow

White was still..." Esther turned to Hilda again, and grinned. Hilda winked back at her, and Esther finished the sentence with a flourish: "asleep."

The next sentence was difficult for her, and she struggled with the syllables. "They—grunted."

"No," said Hilda, gently. "Well, they probably did, but you're wrong."

Esther flung her arms round Hilda's neck, and shouted "Granted" in her ear.

"No," said Hilda, more firmly this time. Esther turned back to the book, taking a peep at the camera to see if her admonition had been recorded. Hilda pointed at the first syllable. "What does that say?"

Esther looked. "Ga," she said. Then, getting it in a rush, flung her arms round Hilda's neck, and shouted "Gather." Then she carried on. "They gathered round the bed to look at her. Snow White was *so* surprised when she woke up. She told them all about her wicked stepmother, and the..."

At this point, Esther scrunched herself up a little, and put her hands round her throat, before saying, "...*hunter,* and how she ran..." Esther turned to Hilda, hands still round her throat, and finished the sentence, "...through the forest to their cottage."

Esther began again. "'May I stay with you?' Snow White asked." Esther slowed up now, as if trying to take in the meaning of the word before she said it. As a result, the narration stuttered.

"'Shee, cud, keep, the house clean,' the first dwarf said. 'She, cud, cook,' said the second dwarf. 'She, cud...'" a pause, and a sniff this time, before exclaiming, "'Sew,' said the third dwarf. 'She could.'" Esther sighed a big sigh. Another sniff followed, before a rise in the pitch of her voice. "'Knit,' said the fourth dwarf. 'She could make the birds...'"

"No, Esther."

She jumped as Hilda brought her back to reality. "Bees."

"No."

"Beds. 'She could make the beds,' said the fiveth..."

"The what?" said Hilda. "Well, you are right, but it's..."

"Thyfth," Esther shouted.

They all fell about laughing at this, while Esther blushed. She turned to Hilda and said, quietly, "Thyfth."

"Yes, you are right, Esther. But it starts with a f, not a th."

"OK, fifth. Every day, the dwarves would go out to dig for..." another pause, before "Cuppa."

"No, look, what's the word?" said Hilda, pointing at the page. Esther put her nose onto the page, sniffed, then looked at Sheila in desperation. Sheila shrugged.

Esther raised her head from the book, and prepared to continue, unaware that as she put her nose on the book, and sniffed, a minute flake of paper was dislodged, and disappeared up her nose. Inside this flake of paper , which lodged in Esther's lungs, this tiny wisp containing wood from a tree struck in the same way as the Great Oak tree, a protective force settled and became part of her being. If Sheila had been reading the book and bent her head down and sniffed, she would have been its host. Fate alone decreed that Esther should be chosen.

"Cuppa," Esther repeated.

"No, where's the uh?"

Esther looked, and slowly got it. "O—Op—Cop."

"Yes. And what does that say?"

"Air. Coppair."

"Yes. But it's copper."

"OK. Copper. They looked for copper."

Esther continued. "When they came home at night, Snow White cooked them supper, and the wicked Queen thought Snow White was dead." This stopped Esther in her tracks. Her eyes widened as she looked at everyone in the room in turn. "Did you hear that, everybody? *Dead.*"

Then she turned back to the book, picked up the pace and read to the finish. "But one day, the wicked Queen looked at the mirror on the wall and asked, 'Who is the fairest of them all?' And the mirror answered, 'Snow White is more fair than thee, and she's living with the dwarves.'"

Norman broke in at this point. "Right, Esther, it's time for you to go home, now."

With that they all spontaneously broke into a rendition of "Hi ho, Hi ho, it's off to work we go."

That night, Esther dreamed the dreams of a little girl with the whole of her life before her. Shortly, however, Fate would see her cross paths with a solitary local man, who lived in a shack in the woods behind Esther's school playing fields.

Chapter 7

Jim Pascoe

Jim Pascoe was full of bitterness and hate. The world owed him. But he'd have revenge when he let loose his pent-up vat of hate. He was born on April 30th 1942, the date on which Hitler would later commit suicide. He admired Hitler and his maniacal ideas of genocide. Those gas chambers. The smell of burning flesh. Fantastic. Jim wouldn't commit suicide after, like Hitler, though. He had plans; but it was late now, and he needed to get back.

The man, deep in thought, didn't notice a dog, lying just off the path. As he stepped on its tail, the dog jumped up and bit him with a snarl. A blade appeared instantly in his hand and with one mighty thrust, he severed the dog's spine.

"That'll teach him," he muttered as he went on his way.

Jim Pascoe was tall and slim. He didn't eat much—his hate kept him going. His bald, blackhead-covered forehead glistened with sweat as he shuffled along in a gait resembling something like a cross between Charlie Chaplin and a crab.

"That dog made me jump," he muttered. "Well, he won't do it again."

* * *

If Jim Pascoe's childhood days had been different he might have grown up mentally stable. As it was, the treatment he received from a resentful stepfather ensured that he was a very disturbed man indeed.

Jim's mother took a chance with a married sergeant behind the NAAFI one night in 1941, and Jim was born as a result of that one-night stand. Two years later she took up with Jim's stepfather, to whom the boy's development was of no interest whatsoever.

Jim then contracted rickets, due to a lack of sunlight and calcium. Left untreated, the condition caused his legs to become as bent as a chicken's wishbone as he grew.

Jim's half-sister was born four years later. That was when Jim Pascoe began to think of himself as worthless. Enough food was put on the table for Jim, and he never went without shoes on his feet, or clothes on his back, but that was as far as it went. His stepfather, reminded every time he saw Jim that he was another man's child, never mentioned the fact, but the look on his face couldn't conceal his loathing for the boy. Jim's sister's welfare, emotionally and practically, came first.

Meals were eaten in silence, except for a growl if his stepfather felt he'd put too much food on his fork. Jim craved a loving relationship with him, but there was very little other communication from the man who had adopted him. Jim very soon realised he could get attention by misbehaving, though.

Violence was the form of contact his stepfather reserved for him, so a blow on the head, as he struggled to comprehend basic maths, followed by bleatings of "Don't hit him so hard, Rod," from his mother was a form of consolation. Jim never cried.

In the evenings Jim usually sat on the kitchen floor with the light switched off. The rest of the family would be in the lounge. Hidden in the dark, he'd stare into the warm red light of a coke-burning stove, and imagine heroic scenes in the flickering flames. At times he was a Crusader, fighting the cause of freedom. Or a Knight of King Arthur's Court, battling with a dragon to save a maiden in distress.

While Jim's mind was far away in flights of fancy, he'd breathe in the masculine aroma of his stepfather's jacket, draped round a farmhouse chair by the stove, and feel its herringbone cloth. Occasionally, Jim would be attracted to coins jingling in its pockets, and take a penny or two. When discovered, he was branded a thief, and beaten again.

Always in trouble at school, Jim's mother would send him to bed until she could relate his latest misdemeanours. Jim would hear murmurs coming from the kitchen. Then there would be silence, prompting him to huddle further down under the blankets of his bed. He knew what was coming.

The sound of the kitchen door being opened was the sign his stepfather was on his way. Footsteps, gathering pace on a tiled, carpetless floor, echoed down the hall. Jim's bedroom door would be flung open, and his stepfather would strike the nearest bump he could see. Not a word would be spoken during this drama, or as the door slammed shut behind him on his way out. Then, with all quiet again, Jim would read his comics by torchlight.

Stories of Batman and Robin, Flash Gordon, Superman, and the like, fired his imagination. But it was always the baddies who were his favourites. As a boy, Jim grew up in a world of his own, and of superheroes. He suppressed his caring and loving nature, the legacy of his blood father. But the hurt, bottled-up and festering, gradually turned to hate.

Jim simply scavenged his way through life after he left school, quietly taking advantage of the system of benefits the Welfare State provided to support those who wouldn't work.

* * *

Now a man, and unable to respond to anyone who might care for him, Jim Pascoe was ready to wreak havoc on society as a whole. His first target would be Esther.

After more than thirty years of his feet hitting the ground at a forty-five degree angle, Jim's knees and hips were riddled with arthritis. The pain made him even more angry, but he didn't care. Reading about the slaughter of the children of Israel by King Herod in the Bible interested Jim. Then he read about the debauchery the Marquis de Sade enjoyed in his castle, in the eighteenth century. That was a good one.

Lately, though, he'd been reading accounts of the behaviour of Japanese soldiers in the Second World War. They used Samurai swords to behead prisoners, and bayoneted Malayan women. Just to see what sex the unborn child would have been. They'd taken bets on it.

That made Jim laugh. A laugh that would have made the hairs on a sane person's head stand up, if they had heard it.

When he got back to his miserable shack, he ate slowly, devouring his food with slavering jowls. He imagined how he'd eat the flesh of human beings. He wanted young flesh, though. "Soon. Very soon," he growled. Later that night Jim Pascoe tossed and turned in his bed, demons tormenting his addled brain.

* * *

Esther was in fine form one morning, shortly afterwards. She'd packed her top and trainers herself before going to bed the previous night, and was looking forward to running about with the rest of class at exercise. They were doing "jumping and stuff", as she called it.

The children looked like a flock of new-born lambs as they leapt about in the playing fields. When lunch-time came, they all showered, and changed back into their uniforms. All except Esther, that is. She'd fallen asleep, exhausted, under a hedge at the far end of the playing field.

Jim Pascoe woke early that day. He had pains in his stomach to go with the pain in his knees, now. His mood darkened as the morning wore on. Unable to stand it any longer, he grabbed his blade, and stomped out of the shack. He ran into the woods behind the school, slashing and hacking as he went. This calmed him a little, and he'd slowed to his more crab-like gait by the time he reached the spot where Esther lay. As he stepped through a gap in the hedge, it was her he trod on this time.

Esther woke with a start.

Jim froze—the reaction costing the dog its life absent, as pain numbed his senses. He just stood there, mouth open.

"Hello, who are you?" said Esther. "Are you the hunter in the forest?"

"Er, no. I'm the Beast. You know, Beauty and the Beast." He looked round. *Perhaps this is my chance. There's no one about. I could just take her.* he thought.

"Oh, I know you. You're not really a beast, are you? You love the princess, even if you do look sad," said Esther.

"Yes, but I can't find her. Can you help me look for her?"

"I know exactly where to look," said Esther.

This is my chance, Jim thought. *This is the opportunity I've*

40

been waiting for. They won't like it when they find her in the morning, all slashed, and half eaten.

Rage boiled up inside him. He gripped Esther's hand, and took her into the woods.

* * *

Teacher Pat Clark missed Esther immediately she saw Sheila wander into the dining hall alone. Her heart missed a beat. She knew the pair were inseparable.

"Sheila. Where's Esther?" she said.

"Please, Miss. I don't know, Miss."

"Go and sit down, please."

"Yes, Miss."

Pat looked at her watch. Looking down the corridor, she spotted the school secretary and waved her over. "Jenny, where's the Head?"

Inwardly, Jenny smirked. *The last time I saw him he was trying to explain to his wife where he was last night, so don't think you'll get a quickie in his office today, Miss Toffee-nose. One of these days I'm gonna blow the whistle on you two.* "In his office, talking to his wife on the phone," she said.

"Take over here for a minute, will you?"

Pat didn't wait for a reply, but went quickly to the door. Running down the hall she caught sight of Esther's teacher. "Rose. Have you seen Esther? She hasn't come in for lunch yet."

"No. I haven't seen Esther since the children were in the playing field. She must be in the changing rooms," said Rose.

"Well, go and see if she's there, then report back to me, please."

* * *

Pascoe punched himself in the stomach to try and dull the pain as Esther led the way. Presently, he saw the shack through the trees. *There it is. She's leading me right to it.* he thought.

"Oh, I'm tired," he said. "Can we sit on this bench for a minute? Look, there's a shack. Shall we see who lives there?

41

They might give us a drink of water."

While they sat on the oak bench a faint blue glow appeared on Esther's breath. Swirling out from her nose and mouth, the force from the flake of paper wrapped itself around her body, and went with her as Jim Pascoe led her towards the shack. "The door's open. Let's go inside," he said.

Once inside, Jim motioned Esther to a grubby stool by a window. "You sit there, while I go and see if anyone's here. Would you like a glass of lemonade?"

"Yes please."

Esther hummed to herself, and looked through the window. *Wonder where the princess could be?* she thought.

Back at the school, Pat burst into the headmaster's office. Geoffrey Wilkinson put his hand over the phone. "Pat. What the..."

"Esther Clayton's missing. We can't find her anywhere."

"I'll call you back, Mary," said Wilkinson, putting down the phone. "Well, where have you looked?"

"Everywhere. She's just disappeared."

"Well, look again. Get some help. But keep this quiet. And don't run."

Jim Pascoe put his hands over his face as excruciating pain threatened to blow his brain apart. Esther was still looking out the window with her back towards the kitchen, as he lurched in. The blade was in his hand.

Esther, noticing Hilda's car go by in the distance, jumped up. "Sorry. Got to go. Byee."

As Esther opened the door, the blue light put itself between her and Pascoe. The blade came slashing down, but didn't find its mark. The swirling spectre of light deflected the point of the blade, which, carrying on its new trajectory, thudded into Jim Pascoe's thigh, severing an artery.

Jim Pascoe's face turned purple with rage. His eyes bulged. He screamed, then choked, as black bile and spew bubbled from his every orifice. The spectre's eyes glowed, and grew wide. As if drawn from a reservoir containing all the power of the universe, twin bolts of cold, blue fire were hurled at Pascoe.

Jim Pascoe, petrified in the light, froze, then collapsed to the floor. Slowly, his evil body dissolved and seeped through the floorboards. The spectre then dispersed, becoming a mist which drifted under the door and into the air outside.

* * *

Hilda, looking in her rear view mirror as she pulled up outside the school gates, saw Esther walking the last few yards across the playing field alone. Leaning across to open the car door for her, Hilda missed seeing the blue mist, highlighted by sunshine like a warm breath in winter's air, disappear back up Esther's nose.

Pat Clark, having caught sight of Esther while on her way out with Sheila, arrived at the school gates in the hope Hilda hadn't noticed. But after the girls were ushered into the car, Hilda turned on her. "Why didn't they come out together?" she said.

"Their last period was PT. Esther probably showered and changed, then made her own way to you."

This was just plausible to Hilda, who didn't want to believe Esther had been in danger. "Well, I'd prefer it if Esther came out with Sheila and the other children in future, please."

"Certainly, Mrs Watson. I'll make a note of it, and make sure it doesn't happen again. I'm sure she didn't leave school premises."

Hilda wasn't entirely satisfied. Pat Clark seemed to be nervous, and was perspiring. On the drive home, she decided to tell Norman about it. In the meantime she wanted a word with Esther. But Esther got the first word in when she got into the car. "Hello, Hilda. Have you had a nice day?" she said.

Hilda looked directly at her. "Yes, thank you. Did you?"

"Yes, thank you. D'you know what happened to the princess in *Beauty and The Beast*?"

Hilda waited until she was alone with Norman before she told him about the incident.

"Something happened today," she said.

"Oh. What's that, dear? Have you won the pools?"

"Don't be frivolous. I'm serious. Esther wandered off on her own. It really worried me."

Norman knew a lot more than Hilda thought. "You've grown attached to Esther, haven't you?"

That was enough to bring a flood of tears from Hilda, who turned away, sobbing. "I was so worried. She came from across the playing fields. For a minute I panicked, then she asked me if I knew what happened to the princess in *Beauty and The Beast*."

"Look, I love Esther, too. It's like having another daughter. But she isn't our child. As parents we can only do our best. We can't know where they are all the time. You shouldn't be taking all this on. I'm going to have a word with Terry."

"But she's too young, and Joan isn't all that bothered."

"I know, but what can you do? Esther already knows there's something other than her family at the end of her nose. She spends half her time here. She knows who she is now."

"Yes, but don't stop her coming."

"Course I won't. You know, it's nothing but a steady release of a child from the day it's born. I'll tell you something else. It'll get worse. You've seen the youngsters on the front. Wait till Sheila starts to bring boys home."

"Oh, God."

"All I'm saying is, we've got to get used to it. Even with Esther. I'll talk to Terry."

Hilda stopped shaking, dried her tears, and smiled. "You're not as green as you're cabbage-looking, are you?"

"Well, you didn't marry me for my good looks, did you?"

Chapter 8

The Exorcism

In the woods behind St Mary's Church, nine-year-old Annette and her brother, Stephen, were huddled in the den camouflaging the roots of the Great Oak tree. Annette was about to give up her most precious secret.

"I saw a ghost," she said.

Stephen stopped carving his initials into one of the roots, and looked at her. "Don't believe you," he said.

"Did too."

"Where?"

"In church. The other day."

"What happened?"

"When the vicar was singing. I saw a ghost come out of his mouth. It floated in the air."

"Rubbish," said Stephen. "There's no such thing. I'm telling Mom on you."

"I don't care. I saw it, you didn't. It's my secret, and you can't tell."

The years following Roy Marshall's desertion of his family were difficult for them. Annette and Stephen formed an even closer bond than sisters and brothers normally do. Much of their time was spent playing in the woods behind St Mary's. Occasionally they picked up splinters, each containing more memories of the dead.

Inside Annette, a ferocious battle for control of her soul ensued. Her behaviour was a constant source of worry for Eve. Having not spoken a word until she was three years old, Annette now came out with a vocabulary that would make a footballer blush. And yet on other occasions she could be so angelic, Eve thought perhaps she wasn't too bad, after all.

Then she noticed cuts on the insides of Annette's arms. At

first she thought nothing of it. *Just kids, playing.* Then she realised they were more frequent than they should be, and always the same. Parallel lines, as if drawn by a blade. Eve was frantic, and took her to their doctor. He didn't know what to do, except refer her to a child psychiatrist, and suggest Annette start nursery school, "to stimulate her mind," he said.

Eve also enrolled Annette at a kindergarten which took pre-school aged children, and even tried to get her into the Brownies at St Mary's. This made things worse. One minute she'd be the caring and motherly one in whichever group she was in. The next, she'd be rolling around the floor, spitting fire and trying to scratch somebody's eyes out.

Finally, Eve began to hope. Annette joined the choir, and seemed to calm down a little.

At the Sunday Family Service, all the children knelt down in front of Michael Jobson to be blessed, while the adults received bread and wine. He always felt a reaction when he put the palm of his hand on the top of Annette's head.

In the months and years that followed, Annette fought him as he tried to instruct her, but she kept going to choir practice, and never missed a Sunday service. Somehow he felt for her, and was aware of the mental struggle she was involved in.

Eve was lonely, despite having the children to look after. It took a long time for her to accept that the man she loved, and had thought loved her and his children, wasn't coming back. She coped, with the help of her parents and friends. After a while she even got a part-time job at the Law Courts in Birmingham. But she was a young woman, and had needs. Family get-togethers provided the only social life she had for a while. She rejected the offers of men callers who asked, "Fancy a drink down the pub?"

Finally she gave in. Flattered when a friend of a friend's son made a pass at her, Eve let him seduce her, but soon finished the affair when he declared his undying love for her. He was seventeen.

Three years after Roy left, and responding to urgings from Hilary, a friend and neighbour, she went out for a drink. Meeting Harry Campbell that night produced another twist in her life, and uncovered emotions she didn't know she had.

Harry swaggered into the pub, and made straight for the bar. This was his patch, and if anyone wanted to make anything of it, they could see him outside, or inside. Harry raised his pint to his lips, swivelled and had a look round, leaning back against the bar. He spotted Hilary and Eve, getting up to leave. He locked eyes with Eve for a second, and nodded as the girls passed him on the way out, before carrying on his surveillance.

The girl making conversation with friends next to Harry threw back her head and laughed, bumping against him. Harry put down his pint and embraced her, putting a hand over a breast at the same time. "Hi, chick," he said softly.

Petrified by what she saw in Harry's eyes, the girl froze. Not so her boyfriend, who took a swing at him. This was what Harry wanted. Needed, in order to satisfy his lust for violence. This was the moment Harry would savour, later on. After the adrenaline rush he knew was coming had gone. He stood perfectly still for a second, then threw the girl aside, picked up his glass, and, like a rattlesnake striking, drove it into the man's face in one swift movement.

"You all saw it," Harry shouted. "He threw the first punch."

Silence.

Harry looked slowly round the room, then at the barman. "Did you see it?"

The barman knew Harry. "I didn't see anything, sir. I was ringing up on the till." If he wanted to live he wouldn't be in a hurry to phone the police, either.

Harry looked down at the unfortunate man at his feet and sneered. "Good. Now get this piece of junk a towel."

Eve and Hilary had crossed the road, and were waiting by a bus stop, when Harry pulled up and opened the door of his Mercedes. "Give you a lift, girls?"

"No thanks. We only live down the road," said Hilary.

Harry directed his next comment at Eve. "Suit yourself, catch you later."

Eve had noticed Harry when he'd walked into the pub. His confident nature reminded her of Roy, when she'd first met him.

Harry pursued her with a vengeance. She knew nothing

about his nature, or his reputation, and he, as charming in female company as he was violent, made sure she took the bait. Vulnerable, and needing the companionship only a man can bring, Eve gave in eventually, thinking perhaps this man would share her life in the way she so desperately needed.

Harry soon showed the brutal and domineering side of his nature, however.

Two months after their relationship was consummated, Harry disappeared. A fortnight later, he reappeared, demanding to know where his dinner was. He stayed the night, and for several weeks, beginning what was to become a routine. Harry's routine.

Harry Campbell thought himself a clever chap. He had several women on the go. Even had children with a couple of them, although Eve didn't know. He knew he could keep control of his little brood by returning to them, each at their time of the month, like a stallion in the wild. He'd satisfy one, then go to the next. Before they knew where they were, they were enjoying the freedom his lapses afforded them.

Eve was in a rut. Harry dominated her. She was frightened of him, but he satisfied her sexual needs. He was all right with the children, too, letting them watch him tinker with old cars and help him do odd jobs. Annette in particular seemed to get on well with him. So Eve let him back into her bed. For the children's sake, she told herself. Eve told herself many lies, just to get through each day.

* * *

Annette and Stephen came back from the woods. Stephen didn't mention Annette's story about the ghost—just in case the ghost was watching. They were about to eat when Harry came in, through the back door. "Where's me dinner?" he said.

Eve said nothing. She didn't want a scene with the children about. She set about dividing what she had between the four of them, and gave him his share. Harry took one look at it and threw it up the wall. "What the bloody hell's this?"

"Go to bed," Eve said to the children, quietly. "Take your dinner with you. I'll be up in a minute."

Annette and Stephen took their dinners upstairs to their bedroom, and ate in silence. Then Annette said, "I like him."

"I hate him. I'm gonna kill him," said Stephen.

"I—*LIKE HIM*," Annette spat out. "I like him. And I hate Daddy."

Stephen felt himself being thrown across the room as Annette's words came as a burst of vile energy from her mouth, in a deep, male voice. As he hit the bedroom wall, a picture of Christ, hanging above his head, was seemingly ripped away and hurled to the floor. Stephen cowered in the corner as Eve came into the bedroom, her eyes stained with tears. The look Annette gave Stephen left him in no doubt what would happen if he told on her.

Eve cuddled the children, and put them to bed. "I love you very much," she said. "Don't worry, Mommy will be OK." Then she left them.

Harry had never done this before. Eve was shocked, but told herself this sort of contact was better than none at all. Besides, maybe it was her fault.

Harry knew exactly what he was doing. After Eve came down, he apologised profusely. "Sorry, chick. You know I love you." He took her in his arms and kissed her, hard. "I'm mad for you," he said. Eve gave in, she couldn't combat his strength.

He knew the passion of anger he'd aroused in Eve would make her senses alive to his touch. Tomorrow's guilt was far away. She dug her nails into Harry's shoulders, in a half-hearted effort to push him away. She looked into his eyes. "You sod," she said. Then she gave herself to the moment. The certainty of a cold place by her side in the morning if she made him go away, accompanied by the knowledge that she'd jump out of bed quickly, before rose-coloured thoughts of happier days crept into her brain, was enough for her to abandon herself to the ground rush of the most explosive orgasms she'd ever had.

The next day, Harry did some DIY for her, gave her money, and left.

* * *

Annette and the rest of the congregation were in full flow at

49

St Mary's the following Sunday morning. She loved singing and was taking her cue from Michael, not the choirmaster, as usual.

Singing was the one time Annette felt safe. During one particularly beautiful sung part of the communion service she became distracted by a shaft of brilliant sunlight, shining down through a window. It lit up Michael Jobson as if a staircase to heaven had been revealed to him. She wouldn't have been surprised if he'd just walked straight up it. She couldn't take her eyes from it.

Then she stopped singing as what looked to her like snowflakes twinkled down the beam, and took form. Annette saw her ghost.

She nudged the boy next to her. "He's back," she said.

"Who?"

"The ghost."

The boy nudged her back, hard. "Leave me alone," he said.

They both shut up as Michael Jobson turned and looked at them. Annette almost shouted "Watch out!" to him as the ghost appeared to hit him on the head. Pythagoras and Audeus were returning to their sanctuary.

Pythagoras was aware of the emotions coming from Annette. As he completed his transmigration into Michael, he caused him to look in her direction. Their eyes met. Annette held her breath under Michael's gaze. Pythagoras was searching her mind. Then she heard a voice in her head say, "Who are you?"

Annette was terrified. She heard the question, and the answer that came. A cold, spiteful answer, "None that you would know."

This time, Pythagoras and Audeus, together, searched deep into her mind. Then they knew. They saw Eve's labour, and the scalpel. They saw the blood, and Annette suck in the apparition as she took her first breath of life. Annette cringed as an immense power filled the church.

Members of the choir around Annette stopped singing. Michael approached, an aura of heavenly blue light surrounding him. The organist stopped playing when Annette fell to the floor.

There was utter silence as the drama unfolded in front of a stunned congregation. Pythagoras' memories, enraged by what they'd seen inside the girl, called on Audeus. Michael Jobson stopped in front of Annette, now curled up in a ball on the floor, frothing at the mouth. Still she couldn't avert her gaze from those eyes, from which two brilliant, blue shafts of light reached out and formed a perfect emblem of the letter Y over her.

Annette heard the words in her head, but all she could see was the blue of the Universe. To all in the congregation, there seemed to have been an explosion, as Pythagoras and Audeus as one hurled a telepathic exorcism at the thing inside Annette;

"LUCIFERA. Miserable chief of the seven sins. We see you in your carriage of splendour. And SATAN, who is your coachman. You cannot ascend to the heavens and make yourself higher than the Harmony of the Spheres. We call upon all the forces of nature to PUT YOU OUT. By all that is known, and yet to be known. With all the power of the Universe, and the memories of the dead. We command you, GO—BACK TO THE PLACE FROM WHENCE YOU CAME."

The foundations of the church shuddered as these words burned into Annette's psyche. Then a noise began to rumble inside Annette. She convulsed, and opened her mouth. The sound rose in volume as if coming from the Pit itself. Finally, it *burst* from her in a dark, screaming mass. A sound, like a gunshot, reverberated around the Church, and it was all over.

Reverend Michael Jobson looked down at Annette, still curled up in a ball. He saw a small cut on her forehead, in the perfect shape of the letter Y. He watched the letter fade away, leaving her sleeping peacefully, then smiled, nodded, and turned to the congregation, saying, "Let us pray."

Eve didn't know what to make of what happened at church that Sunday. Annette was brought home by parishioners, who said some sort of miracle had happened. Eve was glad when Michael Jobson called round to explain; not that he was sure himself.

"I know you've been worried about Annette for some time, Mrs Marshall. We've had many a conversation about her in the past. You know I've always felt that her father leaving had a lot to do with it. Last Sunday, I knew there was more to it, though." Michael paused, not quite sure of how to tell Eve what had happened without alarming her. He'd long since realised he was host to a force for good. A force his faith allowed him to suppose was related to his Christian beliefs. Still, he knew that telling Eve about what he suspected could bring all sorts of baggage. He decided there was only one kind way. "What happened is something I've read a lot about, but only seen once before. I performed—it seems—an exorcism. It happened on the spur of the moment. What I can tell you is whatever has been tormenting Annette has gone forever. Of that I'm certain."

For a moment Michael thought Eve was about to faint. He offered a comforting squeeze of the hand. Recovering her composure, Eve said, "She doesn't remember a thing. All I know is, after she was brought home she was more content."

"Well, it's probably a good thing she doesn't remember. If there's anything else I can do, don't hesitate to call me."

"Thanks for all you've done, Father. I will."

When Harry didn't return, Eve put it down to the fact he'd got fed up. Then Hilary asked, "Shame about Harry. Will he get better?"

"Haven't seen him. What's happened?"

"He had a stroke, didn't he?"

Eve found she didn't care. "Oh, well, I expect he'll get over it."

*　*　*

The reality was that when Pythagoras called on all the powers of the Universe to banish the evil thing inside Annette, Harry collapsed and began to see things. One by one, his sins were made clear to him, in visions of telepathic clarity. He heard the exorcism in his brain. When he woke, he found his co-ordination had gone. Harry Campbell would suffer mental torment, and physical deformity, until he died at a great age. No longer was Harry Campbell attractive to women. He scratched around on crutches, and spent the rest of his life alone with only the light from long-dead stars to keep him company at night.

When remembering Annette and her family in his prayers, later, Michael realised how difficult it had been for Eve to cope with the situation. *Eve's a good woman,* he thought. *But like most people, she's finding it difficult to keep her religious balance in today's society. Her soul's under siege from the sins of the world. Her husband, whom she loved, abandoned her to bring the children up on her own, but the spirit of Jesus Christ still lives in her. She brought Annette to the church, for baptism, where I spoke his words. 'Suffer little children to come to me, and forbid them not; for of such is the kingdom of God.'*

"Thank you, Lord, for fulfilling your promise, by evicting, through me, the evil spirit from Annette. And if it be thy will, make the sun to shine on her, now and forever. And give me the strength to carry on your work. The reconciliation of the minds and spirits of your people. Amen."

Chapter 9

Roy and Eve's Reconciliation

Yellow street lights seemed to Roy Marshall like flying saucers hovering in the sky, showing him the way. It was 4 a.m. on July 8th 1979. *I could just keep driving*, he thought. *There's nothing and no one behind me to go back to.* He flicked a cigarette butt out the car window, and wound it up. It was cold. Air still whistled through a crack in the rubber lining of the battered old Maestro. That, and engine noise, was the only sound keeping him company. Mind you, he didn't feel half as lonely as in the daytime, when the world he hated bustled around him. He remembered another occasion when he'd driven all night.

At one minute past midnight on Christmas Eve 1974, the phone rang in the kitchen at the nightclub. The place was humming. Roy put one finger in his ear, and picked up the phone.

"Hello," he shouted.

"You are coming home tonight, aren't you, Roy?" said Eve.

"Of course I am. I'll see you later," he said. He heard Eve sob as he replaced the receiver.

Roy didn't go back that night, and had not seen his wife, or children, since.

As the last few punters left, and the club wound down, Roy's lover, Sue, came into the kitchen. She knocked his chef's hat off, and threw her arms around his neck. "Happy Christmas," she said, and kissed him. "Phew. Must've made a hundred quid in tips tonight." Roy looked at the floor. Her nervous smile punctured the atmosphere. "Are you sure you want to do this?"

Roy looked at her. She was so different. Unlike Eve, she was tall and blonde, and her make-up perfectly complemented her fair complexion. To Roy she was as attractive as any of the glamorous female stars who came to perform at the club. She'd been a willing outlet for his pent-up sexual frustrations, too. And a way for him to forget the blood. Except he could only forget while in the throes of passion. For that reason, Roy frequently made love to Sue.

"Of course I do. I love you," he said. Sue looked at him for a moment, then, satisfied, took his hand and said, "Come on, then."

Roy had no doubts as he drove to Sue's house to pick up their suitcases. He'd convinced himself Eve and the children would be better off without him. Roy set off for Weymouth at 2.40 a.m. on Christmas Day. He thought about his plans. *I'll get a job, easy enough. Sue can get a job waitressing, if she wants.* That was as far ahead as he'd looked. They had one apple each. Still, he was determined. He reached across and kissed her on the cheek. "Whoa, mister, keep your eyes on the road." She squeezed his knee to let him know it was alright, really. "Later," she said.

Snow began to fall, lightly at first, but it wasn't long before a build-up on the windscreen made it awkward for Roy to see. By the time they got to Salisbury, the wipers were only moving a couple of inches in the middle of the windscreen, and he had to stop and clear it away.

Such a long time ago now, it seemed.

The sound of a horn behind Roy brought him back to reality. He put his hand up to apologise to the driver behind, and pulled away from the traffic lights. He turned left, retracing his route. He had to go back.

Next day Roy made his way to swear an affidavit at the Law Courts. His life had been a mess since he'd left Eve and the children. Sue had run off with a waiter, after Roy stopped making love to her so often. He reckoned she was a nymphomaniac on the side. She'd done nothing but moan about how Roy compared her to Eve all the time they were together.

He returned to the place he knew best and decided to make a change from the unsocial hours being a chef entailed. He set up a business, selling bankrupt stock with a man he knew. Roy raised the finance, with his partner providing a van.

Six months later his partner disappeared with his van, and half the stock. Roy was faced with a decision. *What is it they say? When the going gets tough, the tough get going*, he thought.

Roy tried. He borrowed money to re-stock, and with the help of a neighbour threw himself into turning things around. He kept the warehouse open later, and when it was closed on Sundays, got up at 4 a.m. and did the markets. It couldn't last.

Roy was fit, but the combination of overwork and a poor diet led to physical exhaustion. Rest might have cured him, but when his friend died suddenly, he realised he couldn't carry on. He was bankrupt, financially and emotionally. But he kept his sense of humour, and saw the irony of it. "At least I know people who'll give me the best price on my stock," he said.

Nowadays, Roy walked with the aid of a stick, the result of breaking his leg falling down concrete stairs at the warehouse. Its oak handle was carved in the shape of a kestrel's head. He stopped, and looked around. *The city has changed so much*, he thought. *New buildings, and pedestrian areas. Wide open spaces.*

He noticed two boys chatting to a girl. "This is their time. I hope they don't waste their lives, like me," he said, as if anyone would gain any benefit from hearing him say it.

Looking down from the top of Corporation Street, he saw the site of the coffee bar he'd spent so many happy hours in with Eve. It was an office for the Citizens Advice Bureau now. The date on the clock in Priory Circus showed 11 a.m. July 9th. His resolve wavered a little, but he kept on.

Tall, camouflage-grey buildings loomed in front of him. Then he spotted the Law Courts. After being given the once-over by security, he walked to reception. He stopped, and looked at noticeboards covering the wall. His eyes lit on the department he wanted. It was on the second floor. *At least there'll be a lift*, he thought.

Roy was struck by the aura of the place. It seemed to give off a feeling of solemn purpose. He got out of the lift and looked around. More notices, and pictures of old Birmingham. Signs pointed the way. "Chancellery", "Magistrate's Court", "Chambers", "Family Division". Then finally, "Bankruptcy —

This Way". Roy sensed power. More than that, he felt safe. *This is where laws are proclaimed*, he thought. *The place where people come for guidance, under the law of the land. The law. The only means society has to live in harmony. This place will never change, no matter what the fashion of the day is.*

A woman brushed past him as he went into the Family Division. She approached a young man standing behind a counter, and said loudly, "Is this the one for Divorce, or Bankruptcy?" Roy cringed, and looked around. Seeing a sign for affidavits he made his way to it. *Thank God there isn't a queue*, he thought.

While Roy was sorting himself out, Eve was seeing the last of her appointments before the end of her shift in the Family Division next door. The lady she was going through the procedure for divorce with was close to tears, and clearly finding it difficult to cope with the emotional strain of what she was doing. Eve shuffled the papers together and put her pen down on top of them.

"Let's have a break, shall we, Rita? Bet you could do with a cup of tea, yeah?"

Rita, who had been close to hyperventilating, let it all go with a rush. "I don't know what's happening. When I got married I thought that was it, we loved each other completely, I was never so sure. Then the children came along and everything..."

Eve went round to Rita's side of the desk, knelt down and put an arm on her shoulder. "Whoa," she said softly. "Take a breath and settle down. I'm not going anywhere. You've got plenty of time. I'll fetch us a cuppa and you can talk all you want. I'm here for you."

Rita had no qualms about telling a stranger about what had happened. It was as if she had no feelings or personality any more. She sipped her coffee and looked across at Eve.

"Are you married?" she said.

"Sort of. My husband left me a long time ago, but for some reason I never wanted to divorce him."

"I know what you mean, but I just don't know what else to do. Have you got children?"

"Two. A boy ten, and a girl nine. I know you've children

but they're grown up now, aren't they?"

A sob caught in Rita's throat at the mention of her children. She sighed. "What's happening, Eve? My son divorces and comes back home to live. Then I find him injecting drugs in his bedroom. My daughter hates me because I won't put up with his lies and stealing from all and sundry. I think she's doing drugs and supporting his habit at the same time. I'm sure she's having affairs with women as well as men. I just can't get through to them. I've had to cope with it all by myself, and now I find my husband's been having it off with a barmaid. And just look at me. I'm a mess. What's happening to everyone? Everybody I know has problems like ours. I sometimes wonder if it's something in the air."

"Oh, I dunno. All I know is that I have to carry on. And so do you. I'll give you my number. You can call me any time, OK?"

*　*　*

Roy pressed a button marked "Press For Service", and waited. Presently, a young man came out. "Can I help you?" he said.

Roy gave him the paperwork. The young man looked it over, then scribbled something on the bottom. Then he went into overdrive. "Are you Roy Douglas Marshall, herewith named in this affidavit?"

"Yes," Roy whispered.

"Have you read the affidavit, and found everything to be correct?"

"Yes."

"Initial where I've initialled," said the young man. The stick seemed to grow warm in Roy's hand as he rummaged around for a pen. "It's hot in here," he said. "Hang on a minute."

He found a pen, and signed the document at the spot the clerk was pointing to. He was putting the pen back into his pocket, expecting that to be the end of it, when the young man started again. "Have you any objection to swearing on the Bible?"

Roy wasn't expecting that. "No," he said.

The young man produced a copy of the Bible, and held it up in the air. Then he picked up a card with his other hand. "Hold up your hand, and repeat the words on the card," he said.

At this moment Eve was putting her coat on next door, preparing to go home.

Roy looked at the card, and began to speak. "I, Roy Douglas Marshall, swear that..." Words flooded Roy's brain, confusing him. The stick was red hot in his hand. He found himself saying the betrothal speech he had said to Eve, at his wedding. "...I take thee, Eve, to have and to hold..." Tears welled up in his eyes. Why was her face all he could see? "No, that's not right, it's too hot in here. I'll have to go outside for a minute," he said.

Roy burst into the corridor as Eve turned the corner and spotted him. "Roy. What are...? Why?" Her heart went out to him. She'd never really stopped loving him. Now, seeing him like this, all her old feelings for him came back. "You look as if you could do with a cup of tea. There's a canteen downstairs. Come on, I'll buy you one."

She grabbed an arm and supported a wobbling Roy while they walked to the canteen. Roy told her about his life since he'd left her, but more importantly about the guilt he'd felt after her traumatic labour, and the nightmares. Neither mentioned anyone else during their conversation, but as they prepared to leave, Eve asked Roy, "Has there been anyone else?"

He thought for a moment, then said, "Not really."

"Why don't you come home with me?" she said. "Annette and Stephen need you. *I* need you."

Roy remembered his walking stick when they were on the way out. It wasn't there when he went back to look for it. Somebody probably found it where he dropped it, and took it. He didn't mind. He didn't seem to need it any more.

It was as if Roy had never been away. There were old wounds to be healed, but they all tried, with the help of the memories. They walked as a family in the woods behind St Mary's Church, acknowledging people they passed. Occasionally, Roy and Eve got a warm feeling, and a smile, when they looked into people's eyes.

Chapter 10

Esther Grows Up

Blissfully unaware of her fortuitous escape from the clutches of Jim Pascoe, Esther thrived. She hardly missed a day at school, and was industrious while there. A lovely-natured girl, her generous attitude to her fellow human beings endeared her to students and teachers alike.

The four-year age gap between Esther and the twins gave her an advantage, in that, apart from Sheila, adults were the people she interacted with mostly. The Watsons became loved as second parents, with Elizabeth and Alan a close third.

Joan wasn't too bothered about anything other than mooching about in charity shops and playing bingo, but Terry adored his firstborn. And Esther idolised him. They could be seen walking along the seafront holding hands at any time.

Terry would sit Esther down on a bench facing the sea and tell her about his exploits in the boxing ring (with the only deviation from the truth being that Terry always won). Dancing around, chin on chest, he'd feint with his one arm. "He thought he'd got me," Terry would say. "But I'd lulled him into a false sense of security. The bell went for the last round. He came at me, smirking all over his face, then wham. I got him with me right hook. I tell you, if I hadn't lost me other wing, I'd've been World Champion."

Esther would wave her legs under the bench, giggle, and clap as Terry went through his routine. Then he would buy her an ice cream before taking her home.

One afternoon Esther surprised Terry with a question that would change fundamentally his attitude to people and life. "Dad," she said.

"Yes, darling."

"Will you teach me to box the bloody hermans?"

"The what?"

"Well, I heard Mr Bowen talking to the headmaster yesterday and he said they'd given the bloody hermans a right punch on the nose in the last war."

Terry's first reaction was to burst into laughter, but, seeing that Esther thought he was laughing at her, dropped to one knee and took her hand. Two half-closed blue eyes atop a smile so fresh and warm it would melt an iceberg, never mind his heart, twinkled back at him. Terry paused, seeing his first-born in a totally different light for the first time. He knew then that he had the power to mould his children; that it was his duty to do so, in fact, and in the right way.

"Darling, I'm going to teach you everything you need to know. It's for all the mommies and daddies to teach their children what they need to know so that when they grow up they can be happy. I'll never tell you a lie, and nothing will ever happen to you that you can't overcome. Do you believe me?"

"Yes, Dad. But will you teach me about the bloody hermans?"

It was after the twins had begun to walk around, and take an interest in their surroundings, that differences in the children's characters became apparent. A typical occasion was when Esther had been given a doctor's outfit on her eighth birthday. She dressed up, and sat the twins down. "Now then, Mrs Watson. What seems to be the problem today?" she said. When Margaret picked her nose and looked away. Esther went into schoolteacher mode. "Don't do that, Margaret," she said. Then she turned her attention to Andrew, who was staring at her with adoring eyes as usual, and said, "I'll have to examine you, Mister Watson. Take your clothes off, and lie on the couch, please."

Andrew lay down on the settee, and put his arms above his head. Esther put on a stethoscope, and made as if to listen to his heartbeat. Margaret smirked, and put out her tongue at Andrew, who puffed up his chest.

Esther gasped, and showed the first signs of the talent that would have Hollywood at her feet just twelve years later, saying, "Oh, this is terrible. I'll have to operate immediately. Quickly, nurse. Help. This is a matter of life or death."

Margaret ignored her and wandered off, returning later carrying a potty full of water, which she threw all over them, leaving Esther to do the operation by herself. Margaret always spoiled play between the children and it was only the fact that she could boss Andrew herself, when Esther was at Sheila's house, that prevented a major rift between them as they grew up.

* * *

Esther had less to do with Andrew and Margaret after she passed her tenth birthday, feeling she was somehow more grown-up than they. Inside the splinter, the erotic force sensed her impending transformation from girl to young woman. At the same time, a period of teenage angst came in a rush for Esther, beginning after her twelfth birthday, as Sheila found out when she called round one Saturday morning. Terry answered the door to her.

"Hi, Mr Clayton. Is Esther about?"

"Hi, Sheila. She's up in her room. You know what she's like on a Saturday morning. Go on up."

Joan came into the lounge as Terry was saying this. "If you're going up to Esther, take her these aspirin," she said.

Sheila looked at Joan, then the aspirin, then Terry. He shrugged. She took the aspirin and a glass of water from Joan, saying, "Has she got a headache?"

"Just take her the aspirin. She'll tell you all about it."

Sheila tapped Esther's bedroom door. Getting no reply, she put the glass down, and turned the handle. "Hi," she said, picking the glass up, and pushing the door open with her foot. Esther lifted her head from under the duvet. Her eyes were red, and tear-stained. She burst into tears when she saw Sheila, and buried her head again.

Sheila put down the glass and aspirin and ran to her friend. "What's happened?"

Distraught snufflings filtered through the duvet. "I'm bleeding. Down there, and I've got spots on my face."

Sheila gently pulled the duvet back, and pushed her fingers through Esther's hair. "Move over, silly. I'm coming in," she said.

Sheila slid under the duvet, and cuddled up. "Hey," she said.

Esther sniffed, and looked at Sheila, who smiled, and said, "That's so weird. I did, too. Last night. That's what I was coming to tell you about. Your mom gave me some aspirin for you. D'you want them?"

"Will you just lie with me for a bit? I'm frightened." She burst into tears again when Sheila laughed.

Sheila put her arms around her. "I'm sorry. I'm not laughing at you. I love you so much. It's nothing, believe me. Hasn't your mom told you about it?"

"No. I couldn't talk to her. You know what she's like. She just said, 'Now don't get experimenting. Familiarity breeds contempt.' What does she mean?"

"Boys."

"Yes. But how experimenting?"

"You know exactly what she means. Sex."

"No. I don't. Nobody's ever told me anything. You and I have never had anything to do with boys. It's not like saying, 'Here, try this. It's ice cream—you'll like it.'"

"So that's what you're crying about. Well, Mister Lister covered it in class."

"You know Mom wouldn't let me go to that class. She said it was disgusting they were teaching kids some of those things."

"Well, what about your dad?"

"No, I couldn't."

"OK. I'll tell you, then. Come on. We'll go to mine. I've got some books."

During the next couple of years, Esther became even closer to Sheila, as they shared flirting experiences. She enjoyed kissing boys, but was horrified at their loutish behaviour. And the language they used on Margate sea-front. She knew some of them were sniffing glue, even during the day, and trying other drugs. She had seen girls older than her doing things in the back row of Margate cinema, and heard them bragging about it afterwards. When one of them became pregnant, Esther decided that if that was what experimenting got you, she wouldn't bother.

Something constantly nagged at Esther from then on. A mental battle ensued, in which lewd imaginings flooded her mind. This just made Esther more frightened, and she'd never date without Sheila being present.

Even at this tender age, she noticed the difference between the relationship Sheila's parents had and the one between her own mother and father. She even felt she was closer to Terry than her mother was. It was as if she already knew she was different.

Margaret and Andrew felt no such allegiance, and by 1986 were making plans.

Chapter 11
Esther's Awakening

Esther's brother and sister were growing up to be almost moronic. Andrew, aged ten, had finally learnt to speak, reciting the six times table. Not the mathematical version, though. These were the six different numbers of Social Security forms he'd to memorise before he left school in five years' time, or sooner if he could swing it.

Andrew reckoned that if he bunked off a bit more each month, in a couple of years' time nobody would miss him, and he could stay at home playing games on his computer. Occasionally, Andrew stopped, after failing to reach level two for the umpteenth time, and sat, staring accusingly at the screen.

A pet owl, which sat perched in a huge, golden cage in the corner, blinked, as if wondering if the boy had become petrified. The owl was fed one mouse or day-old chick each day. Sometimes it ignored the offering, but pounced and gulped it down on other occasions. If the meal was a mouse, it paused and tilted its head back. The tail would slither down its gullet, like a strand of spaghetti. Then it would jump back on its perch, and spend the next twenty-three hours and fifty-eight minutes excreting the remains of its meal.

Margaret became plump, and took no interest in her appearance whatsoever. Her long hair (blonde again) was matted and unkempt. And she smelled. But she didn't care. She knew exactly what she was going to do when she left school. Have babies. Lots of them, and it didn't matter to her how many different fathers they had. The only important thing as far as Margaret was concerned, was that she would be able to give birth six times. This was the optimum number of children she'd need to produce in order to be given a large council house and about £800 a month, which she thought would be enough to feed them on, and provide her with a social life.

Margaret practised, charging local boys 50p for a look, and £1 for a feel. "Downstairs" had been off limits, but her hormones were raging, and she was already wondering which of the spotty-faced, testosterone-flooded youths would be the father of her first offspring.

Margaret reasoned if she gave birth next year, the father would be too young to have a maintenance order taken against him. That way, he'd ignore the child, hopefully, and she wouldn't have to worry about him. Also, she'd qualify for the top range of benefits straight away. The bonus was, if she started now, she'd be able to get it all over and done with before she was twenty. Then she could relax and enjoy herself.

Esther was different. At around 5'6", blonde and slim, her demure and respectful behaviour meant she was attractive to boys. But she wasn't interested, even after she started to menstruate. Hormones flooding her bloodstream brought spots, and painful losses each month. Her doctor brought the erratic nature of her cycle under control by putting her on the Pill, and things settled down enough for her to concentrate on schoolwork.

When Esther was almost fifteen years old, and with her body well into the process that differentiates girls from boys, the bumps erupting on her chest sprouted into perfectly rounded breasts. Her pert nipples thrust out and upwards, looking like a pair of ripening lemons. Her pelvis widened to produce a birth canal, and her fat turned to firm flesh. Soon, the spots disappeared and she began to give the appearance of being exactly what she was, a beautiful, blonde-haired young woman. Esther still experienced a little pain each month but found that a warm shower every day, before going to school, eased her aching muscles.

One morning she dropped the soap, and in bending down to pick it up, touched the spot on her inner thigh where the oak splinter lay. The erotic force inside the splinter immediately took over. A warm, tingly sensation spread through the area, and up through Esther's entire stomach. *Ooh, that feels good,* she thought. Warm water ran down her neck, over her breasts and torso, before caressing her special place with rippling rivulets.

She tilted her head back to let the water stream over her, frothing up the soap as she did so. This movement of hands over her body caused her to catch her breath, and suddenly the spot on her inner thigh *demanded* she touch it.

As Esther moved her hand downwards, she brushed against herself. The reaction was electrifying. She almost fainted with the intensity of orgasmic waves sweeping over her. Prompted by the erotic force inside the splinter, orgiastic scenes involving Esther and members of her family and Sheila—the people Esther were most emotionally involved with at the time— flooded her brain. She instinctively knew these were forbidden sexual pleasures, and quickly banished the thoughts. But she gave in to her body, which reacted helplessly to the stimulation.

Then it was all over.

Esther's outlook changed forever from that day. She noticed boys, and they certainly noticed her. The camera-mad anorak in her class at school asked if he could take photographs of her, which she agreed to, so long as Sheila could be there.

Esther bashfully declined his offer to take one or two more revealing shots. He did a fair job of lighting her, but it wouldn't have mattered if he hadn't. The camera loved her. Esther was stunning, and there wasn't a blemish on her body, except the tiny dark spot on her inner thigh, where the oak splinter lay.

It was Sheila's reaction to the photographs that made her think of modelling after leaving school. "You're absolutely beautiful," she said. "You should enter a competition or something."

Esther didn't let this, albeit flattering, praise from her friend, or the new-found sexual sensation, interfere with her schoolwork. It was only after passing her exams comfortably, and everyone was thinking about what to do, that her thoughts returned to the photographs.

"Go on. Send them off," said Sheila.

Esther looked at the prints, then Sheila. "I don't know if I wouldn't rather go to college with you, after the summer holidays."

"Look. You might only get one chance. You've got to do it while you're young. It's not as if you've got to go to the other end of the country. There's loads of studios in Margate. I'll come with you, and if it doesn't work, then you've lost nothing. But if you don't try, you'll never know."

Esther knew Sheila was right. "OK. I'll do it, so long as you come too. You know what Mom will say, though."

"Well, ask your dad, then."

Esther chose her moment carefully. Assuming Terry would ask what she wanted to do now she was leaving school, she waited until they were alone on Margate front. Then, when he did ask, she showed him the photographs. "I want to be a model," she said. Then, as a second thought, "and I'd like to get a job on the front, this summer. Earn my own money."

Terry looked at the photographs. *God. All of a sudden she's a woman*, he thought. Memories of her sitting on the same bench they were sitting on now, while he danced about and told his stories, came. He looked at her, wanting to hold her close, and tell her not to grow up yet. *It'll kill me to let her go. Perhaps she won't leave if she gets a summer job. She might meet a nice lad, and settle down in Margate. It'll be a long summer*. He smiled at her, and kissed her on the cheek.

"I think that's a great idea," he said.

Esther flung her arms around him. "You're great, Dad. Would you do one other thing for me?"

"Of course."

"Tell Mom for me."

"Humph. Thinks a lot of herself, that one," said Joan.

"You've only got yourself to blame. You've ignored her since she was born," said Terry. "If she wants to do it, she can. She's got guts."

The summer didn't drag for Esther. And, like many before her in the same situation, the opportunity to fulfil her dream came unexpectedly.

By mid-August, the cafe Esther worked at was packed every day. After a few dropped plates and rows with the cook, she got into the routine and learned to take care of herself. Her attitude to boys softened too, as youths on holiday and local lads vied for her attention by dropping things on the floor in the hope they'd get a look down her cleavage when she picked them up.

Esther knew exactly what was going on. She enjoyed the attention, and flirted a little, but wouldn't get involved with any of them. Her break came when she met Motti Freedman. On that day Esther was flustered. The cafe was busy. She licked the tip of her pencil, fixed the youth nearest to her with a steely look, and said, "Right. What would you like?"

The youth stood up and adopted an Elvis Presley pose, toes pointed inwards, and mouth open. Then, strumming an imaginary guitar, he burst into song. "One nighyite with youoo."

Smiling through her eyes, Esther put him down. "I'd rather stab myself in the eye with a piece of dried dog pooh. Now, are you lot going to order, or sit twiddling your cheese-sticks all day?"

The lads hooted, and banged the table in unison. "Nice one, gorgeous."

Unable to keep a straight face, Esther glanced away. As she did so the man sitting on the next table raised his arm, catching her attention. "Could I have the bill, please?" he said.

"Certainly, sir," she said, putting away her pad and pencil. Then, turning her attention back to the lads, "And hurry up, you lot. I'll be back in a minute."

Esther walked towards the counter accompanied by a chorus of "Hurry up. Hurry up," from the lads.

The cafe owner, Joe Harper, winked at her, then looked over her shoulder. "Won't be a minute," he said.

Esther turned to find the man who'd asked for his bill had followed her. He ignored Joe, and addressed Esther. "Motti Freedman. Here's my card. I'm staying at the Grosvenor Hotel until Saturday. I'd like to talk to you before I go back to London."

Esther looked at the card, then back at the man who'd offered it. "I don't understand. It says you're a literary agent," she said.

"Let's say I've other interests, too."

"Such as?"

"I've been watching you. You're obviously beautiful, but I like the way you handled those boys. You seem to work twice as hard as the other waitress, too. There are opportunities in fashion and photography, if the camera likes you. What d'you say?"

Esther caught sight of Motti's shoes as she looked back at the card, and was impressed. She took the bill from Joe, and gave it to Motti. "Thanks. I'll think about it. Excuse me. Before I make my fortune I've got some waitressing to do."

Esther could hardly contain herself when she later told Sheila about her meeting with Motti. "I can't believe how cool I was," she said. "I just said, I'll think about it, and went back to work."

"Are you going to phone him?"

"No. I'm going to see him. At the Grosvenor, if you'll come as well."

Sheila drew in a deep breath. "Wow! D'you think he'll buy us dinner?"

Esther was lucky, in that Motti Freedman was a businessman. He introduced her to a friend who owned an agency in London. A photo-shoot was organised and the agency not only offered her a contract after seeing the proofs, but taught her how to apply make-up and dress her hair to show it off to its best advantage. By the time she was eighteen, Esther was number one on the lists of advertising executives who wanted a sexy young girl to adorn their products. She was on her way.

Esther's private life was virtually non-existent as she travelled to and from London. She soon found that being whisked from one venue to another was hard work, and a lot less glamorous than she had imagined. She had to grow up quickly. Seeing less of Sheila was a wrench, but both she and Terry encouraged her, giving her confidence.

Then there were offers of pick-me-ups, in the form of the white powder other girls sniffed up their noses when they were all tired. Esther refused them, while all the time keeping an eye open for the main chance. She got to recognise certain looks that men gave her. Looks that triggered a reaction inside her, tempting her to give in to her sexuality. The barriers finally came down when she met wealthy socialite Graham de Courcey. Their eyes met briefly from across the room at a party one night. In that instant more information than can be stored on a computer was exchanged. She danced with him later, and accepted his invitation to dinner the following evening.

Graham behaved like the perfect gentleman he was throughout, and followed up an exquisite evening's entertainment with flowers the next day. Their paths crossed several times after that, and when Graham invited her to join other friends for a party at his apartment, hinting that she could stay overnight if she wished, she accepted.

Esther decided it was time to make her move. She almost always pleasured herself whilst taking a shower. The warm water running over her body invariably triggered the same reaction, sending her into raptures of ecstasy. But the urges inside Esther were impatient. They encouraged her to want to feel like a *real* woman, and the decision to offer herself to Graham came when she was on her way to his apartment in Connaught Square, W1.

During the evening, Esther drank only two glasses of champagne, and was in a perfect mood as guests began to drift away. Finally, the moment came. She was alone with him at last.

Graham was much older than her. Twenty years, at least, she reckoned. She didn't mind. She knew his experience would allow her to give herself completely to the moment.

Not a word was spoken as he took her in his arms. Esther could feel his muscular frame as she put her arms around him and looked into his eyes. She was drawn into their deepness, and hoped he couldn't hear her heart beating faster and louder. He couldn't, but he could feel it.

He kissed her gently. They didn't close their eyes. Hers, deep ocean blue, answered his unspoken question. He took her hand, and led her to his bedroom.

She was a picture of elegance in a long, white, off-the-shoulder evening dress. The neckline showed merely a little of what lay beneath, by only slightly revealing her cleavage. Two threadlike straps on the dress disappeared over her shoulders, before crossing in the middle of her back. They weren't needed to hold the dress up. Her breasts would have done that on their own. The whole thing clung to her, like an aura round a full moon.

As they stood by the bed, Esther slipped the straps off her shoulders, and let the dress fall to the floor.

The sight of her naked took Graham's breath away. "You're the most beautiful creature I've ever seen," he said, gazing at her, as if to implant a picture of her in his brain forever.

Her short, curly hair seemed to be petals adorning a white rose. Wide, confident eyes returned his gaze. Her pink, healthy complexion reddened a little, as he too took his clothes off.

They were so close that Esther could feel his breath on her body. She didn't dare look down. She realised she was breathing more heavily herself now, as feelings she'd never experienced before came over her. She *wanted* him.

Graham kissed her again, more urgently this time. Then he broke off, saying, "I haven't got any..."

Esther put a finger to his lips. "Don't worry. That's all taken care of," she whispered.

He laid Esther gently on the bed, and kissed her. She spread her arms, causing her breasts to rise. He took a nipple in his mouth and rolled his tongue round it. Esther took Graham's head in her hands, and ran her fingers through his hair. She shuddered as waves of pleasure coursed through her body. *This isn't lust*, she thought. *This is heaven.*

Graham transferred his attentions to Esther's neck and ears. When his hand descended smoothly to her special place, she turned her head to one side. *Yes*, she heard in her mind. When Graham touched her the response was immediate. She stiffened, and her arms shot upwards, grabbing the brass headboard. Esther abandoned herself. She seemed to be in a dream as the erotic force inside spoke through her, *I want you, now*.

She held her breath as Graham entered her. *What would happen? Would it hurt?* she wondered. These and all other apprehensions were melted away by the incredible sensation of that first gentle coupling.

They lay motionless for a moment, then Graham began to gyrate against her, sending tremors of pleasure through her body. Esther found herself moving against him, as he guided her through the stages approaching her first orgasm while making love. When she was almost there, she felt him rising to passion. The warmth of his seed surging inside her brought an emotion that lit her like a firework, and spread as if it would break out through every pore in her body.

Afterwards, Esther relaxed onto the bed with Graham following her down, as if consolidating the union. Esther felt ever-decreasing climaxes dissipate from her body as they lay entwined. The last thing she remembered before she drifted into sleep was a twitch in her inner thigh. Erato was also satisfied—for the time being.

In the morning Esther looked at herself in a full-length mirror in Graham's bathroom. *I don't look different*, she thought. Then she threw her arms in the air, and shouted, "But I feel different. Oh, how I love life."

She no longer felt the need to pleasure herself in the shower. There would be plenty of men who would want to do that for her, from now on.

A casting director Esther was introduced to at one of the many parties she attended asked her to do a screen test. Again the camera loved her, and she was offered a contract to make two films with a Hollywood production company. Six weeks later Esther said goodbye to Sheila and the family, and flew to Hollywood with her agent. The fluttering of apprehension and excitement in her stomach was not entirely due to the plane driving down into take-off mode, or the unknown.

Chapter 12
The President

The studio gave Esther acting lessons, but her natural talent soon showed through. She was easy to work with, which made her popular, and a quick mind meant learning lines was straightforward.

Esther became a star almost overnight, captivating all who saw her grace and beauty.

A hectic schedule left her exhausted most of the time, giving her little chance of accepting offers of this and that, made by drooling, middle-aged, married men. She politely fended off their attentions with a fib when cornered, explaining that she was engaged to be married. Esther was in love, and hoped to carry on with Graham where she had left off.

Transatlantic affairs usually fizzle out, especially when one party lives in Hollywood. Nightly rounds of socialising, the need to advertise herself and the time difference back home, left her with virtually no opportunity to phone even her family.

"Huh," said Joan, while reading the papers in Margate. "After all I've done for her."

Twelve months later, Esther was nominated for and won "Best Supporting Actress" at the 1991 Oscar ceremonies. Her face was now all over the world's press. This brought her to the attention of people in high places. People who liked to bathe in the reflected glory of relationships with movie stars.

Esther was introduced to President Jefferey at his inaugural celebration party, and accepted his offer to spend a weekend at Camp David, thinking that other people would be there, too.

She was impressed with the limousine sent to pick her up, and the accompanying escort. It made her feel important. The limousine had been refurbished to bring it up to the standard required to protect a President of the United States. Part of this was replacing the dashboard fascia with the finest oak veneer, imported from England.

Esther took in the incredible views at Camp David, Maryland, as the limousine purred its way through the 200 acres of the presidential retreat. Established by Franklin Roosevelt in 1942, this "Shangri-La" of places, with its beaches and spectacular mountain views, was seen by successive presidents as an ideal place in which to conduct high-level conferences with foreign heads of state.

But this president had other plans for Esther. It mattered nothing that he could take his pick of older women. He got his kicks by using his power to impress and subdue impressionable young women. If Esther had been more worldly she'd have noticed a distinct lack of security, but as it was thought nothing of it, as she was shown into a huge lounge and given a cocktail on arrival. Hors d'oeuvres were also served. After chatting for a while she took her drink and snacks outside. She sat, admiring stunning views from a veranda. *There's definitely nothing like this back home*, she thought. When the time to retire came Esther felt quite light-headed.

Her eyes shot open. Someone was in the room. And that spot on her thigh was itching. Pain raked her temple as she tried to raise her head. Then she felt movement. She tried to get up, but was only able to lift her head and arms a little.

Again movement. Through a bleary haze Esther realised someone was on the bed, and they were trying to touch her, down there. She tried to protest, but the President pinned her down. He forced her legs open.

NO, she thought, but couldn't say.

As he reached for her, his hand touched the spot where the oak splinter lay. Her body reacted as before. Her arms shot up, and grabbed the headboard. Her legs opened, and she arched her back.

The President saw this as complicity, and fell on her. He took her, not gently as Graham had before, but roughly, rudely, *violently*.

Esther couldn't help herself. Her body responded with animal-like passion, as erotic imaginings swirled in the air around her.

The President suddenly realised he wasn't in control. Esther's muscles closed round his member, and drew him in. She smiled a sadistic smile.

They thrashed and writhed on the bed for what seemed, to him, an eternity. He lost his stimulus, but she wouldn't let him withdraw, or lose his erection. On and on it went. He tried to push her away, but she just drew him back in, more securely each time. It only served to spur on the madness.

In a frenzy of thrusting, the zip on his trousers rubbed the spot where the oak splinter lay. As one last gigantic heave sated her voracious appetite and brought her to a screaming orgasm, the zip ripped open the flesh on her thigh. Released from Esther, the splinter was now transferred to the President, who flopped onto the floor on his bottom as he parted from Esther in an orgy of blood and violence.

Esther collapsed unconscious onto the bed.

Three days later, and unable to remember anything, Esther woke in a private room in hospital. She seemed to remember she'd been admiring the view at Camp David, but after that there was just a haze. An aide brought an enormous bunch of flowers, plus a note from the President, which read:

Dear Esther,
You had me worried for a moment. Thank goodness my aide was there to help you, when you collapsed on the patio. Doctors have completed their tests, and found you had a severe allergic reaction to fish in the hors d'oeuvres.

Matters of State have taken me back to Washington, but I hope to see you when you're better. Don't worry about a thing. My secretary will take care of the bill,
Yours sincerely,
William Jefferey

Esther read the note, and looked at the aide. "Did I collapse on the patio?" she said.

"Sure did, honey. Thought you were having a fit.

Squirming around on the floor like a fish on a hook, you were. Whoosh. I thought you were a goner, for sure."

"Oh—well, thanks for helping me," said Esther dolefully.

"Why, you're very welcome, Miss. That's mah job. You take care, now."

Esther recovered quickly enough, but was weak, and decided to fly back to the UK for a break. She still didn't remember a thing when she left hospital. Nor was there any sign of a wound on her thigh where the oak splinter once lay. Bemused and bewildered, Esther booked a flight, unaware that fate was about to deal her an ace in the hole.

Chapter 13

Ricky's Adventure — March 1991

"I'll be OK when my ship comes in," meaning that one's fortune would be assured when the fishing boats returned, was a popular saying at one time. As far as Ricky Bates, taxi driver and part-time poker player, was concerned, *his* ship had gone down somewhere in the Bermuda Triangle. Whichever way he looked at it, his ship definitely hadn't come in.

Ricky usually turned his For Hire sign off as he approached the city boundary, but the next person to flag him down seemed sober enough. Ricky pulled his battered old cab over, and the man jumped in.

"Where to, Guv?" he said.

"Tamworth, please."

Blimey. This is my night, thought Ricky. *Birmingham to Tamworth. Easy money at this time of night.* He turned to the punter and said, "It's about thirty quid, mate. Sure you've got enough?"

"You'll get paid."

Ricky swung Old Faithful round, and put his foot to the floor. He looked at his watch, and decided this job would see him nicely up to Rainbow time. Rainbow Casino, that was. Ricky wasn't a gambling man, really. He liked the odd flutter, but carried his money in a purse. He and his mates were in the habit of forming an unofficial rank outside the casino. It suited the owner, because it meant he'd a ready source of transport available when his punters needed to fetch more money. The cab drivers could avail themselves of the free buffet (provided for gamblers) in the quiet time between pub turn-out time and the rush when nightclubs emptied, just after 2 a.m.

Ricky turned onto the Aston Expressway, and looked at the man in his rear-view mirror. *A bit rough*, he thought. But he never knew. The ones he expected to do a runner usually paid up sweet as a nut. It was, more often than not, the posh ones who disappeared over the nearest garden wall after the child locks came off.

The man directed Ricky to a scruffy block of flats in the suburb of Glascote as they reached the outskirts of Tamworth. Ricky pulled up, and turned to ask for the fare.

"I'll have to go and get the money," the man said.

Here we go, thought Ricky. He reached for a nightstick he kept in the compartment divider, and closed his fingers round its smooth oak handle. He'd never had cause to use it since his beloved whippet, Jenny, had brought it as a lump of wood while he was walking in the woods behind St Mary's Church. He hoped he wouldn't have to now.

"No problem, mister. I'll come with you," he said, turning the ignition off. "It's thirty-two quid." He added a bit for the inconvenience.

"Have you got a screwdriver?" the man asked.

Ricky looked at him for a moment, then said, "Yes, why?"

"Bring it with you, then."

Ricky shrugged, sorted a screwdriver out, and followed him into the flats. When they got to the second floor, the man stopped outside number six, and turned to Ricky. "Got the screwdriver?"

Ricky nodded, and gave it to him, keeping the nightstick gripped firmly in the other hand.

Once inside, the man opened a cubby hole and used the screwdriver to rip open the gas meter. Ricky got paid his fare— in fifty pence pieces.

"Sorry, I can't give you a tip, mate. I'm skint," he said.

Ricky reflected on some of the weird situations he'd been in as he limped back to his cab. *That was just about the queerest*, he thought. *He's definitely one for my memoirs.*

It was almost ten years since his wife Rosie had left him. They'd met at college, and fallen in love. When they finished their courses, Rosie told Ricky she'd big ideas. She was a clever fashion designer, whose talent had already caught the eye of at least one scout. She encouraged Rosie to set up business straight away, dangling as an incentive the offer of a contract to supply Marks & Spencers if she came up to scratch. Trouble was, neither Ricky nor Rosie had any capital. After talking to Ricky's father it was agreed that he would lend them the capital, and Ricky would give up his opportunity to go to university in order to support Rosie and himself until the business got off the ground.

"I can earn a good living, Dad. I'll learn 'the Knowledge', pass the test, and rent a cab. I know blokes who pay £100 rent, spend about £60 on diesel, and still clear £300, all cash."

"D'you know what a worker at the Rover factory earns? And they're the best paid workers in the country," said Ricky's father. "Sixty quid a week, that's what. You've been listening to too many stories. Go for a job at the factory."

Still, Ricky passed 'the Knowledge' and rented a cab. Within five years he'd bought and paid for a large house in a salubrious area of Solihull. He then saved for and bought his own cab, and a small cruiser, which he kept moored at Lapworth. She provided them with many a pleasant summer's evening, boating on local canal routes.

Then Rosie fell out of love with him, and in love with her production manager. That was when Ricky realised there were only two sorts of people alive. Those who dumped on people, and those who got dumped on. Rosie was doing well, but still took him to the cleaners in court. He hadn't bothered to find another woman since. Sometimes, he'd take a girl up on her offer to pay the fare 'in kind', if she was pretty enough. But mostly he just went to 'Grab a Granny' night at the Reservoir Dance Hall, downed several barley wines, followed by pints of *Ansells*, and had a fling with the first willing partner. But he hadn't had the urge for a long time.

Ricky pulled onto the car park at the Rainbow Casino just after 1 a.m. Nicely in time to have a bite to eat, and see who was playing poker. Poker was one area where his frugal nature deserted him. After the cards were dealt, a rush of adrenaline surged through his blood, caution went, and a basic animal instinct took over. He felt alive.

A crowd was beginning to gather round one of the tables in the Rainbow. Ricky joined them, quickly followed by a man cascading chips from one hand to the other. "What's going on?" he said.

"Poker. 'Texas Hold 'Em,'" said Ricky.

"Why Texas Hold 'Em? What's the difference?"

"'Texas Hold 'Em' is a form of poker where each player is dealt two cards, which they keep face down in front of them. A round of betting takes place, based on each player's view of the value of those two cards. Those who don't like the look of their cards throw them away, losing an ante in the process." Ricky looked at him to see if he was following.

"What then?" he said.

"Then three community cards, they're called the 'flop', are dealt face up in the middle of the table. They're cards each player uses to make the best five-card hand they can at the end. Another round of betting takes place. Then the 'turn card', so called because it can turn a previously losing hand into a potentially winning one, is dealt. Another round of betting takes place. Are you sure I'm not boring you?"

The man shrugged.

Ricky carried on. "The 'River' card, so called because many a player who had the best hand before this card was dealt, lost (drowned at the river) when it gave another player a better hand, is the last card to be dealt. A final round of betting takes place, then the cards are revealed to show who has the best hand. That's it. It's easy to learn, but takes a lifetime to master. Why don't you have a go?"

"Nah. Thanks. I'll stick to something I know."

Ricky wasn't playing tonight. He'd won free entry to the world's biggest poker competition, due to take place in Las Vegas in a fortnight's time, by winning a knockout version at the Rainbow Casino a month before. He just wanted to watch. The entrance fee for the competition in Las Vegas was $20,000, so winning at The Rainbow had been a tremendous stroke of luck. Professionals preferred to pay the entry fee up front, but amateurs could qualify cheaply by winning one of hundreds of games, either in casinos around the world or on the Internet.

Nothing much happened at the table Ricky was standing behind for a while. Then a big pot built up, leaving two players by the time the River card was dealt. After the last card was dealt, one of the players pushed his money to the centre of the table. "All in," he said.

This is the strongest move a player can make in poker. It means he, or she, is willing to bet all their money on this one hand. If they lose, they're out.

Fool. He hasn't got a chance, thought Ricky.

The other player was the chip leader (the one with most chips in front of him). He looked at his opponent for a while.

Beads of sweat began to form on the first player's face. The chip leader folded his arms and looked at the ceiling, replaying the hand in his mind. Then he looked back at his opponent. A look as cool as an ex-lover's stare.

The oak nightstick grew warm in Ricky's pocket. The first player squirmed in his seat, and felt his collar. The chip leader looked at him again, holding his gaze. Finally he made his decision. "Call," he said, turning over his two cards, one of which was the ace of diamonds, matching four other diamonds amongst the community cards.

"Nice hand," the first player said. Then he got up and walked away from the table. "That's me finished."

Ricky congratulated himself as he went back to his cab. For some reason, he always knew when a player was bluffing. He'd been only an average player until the night he noticed that other players brought a good luck charm, or mascot, to the table. Ricky slipped his nightstick into his pocket the next time he went, and his luck changed. He took it with him everywhere now.

Chapter 14
The Poker Championship

Ricky boarded a jumbo jet bound for Las Vegas at Birmingham Airport and settled himself in his seat. First stop was Manchester, to pick up several more passengers, one of whom was the legendary poker player 'Piranha Fish' Johnson. Once a dealer in gold, he had long since left the running of that business to a son. A fearless gambler, with a reputation for ruthlessness, Johnson now indulged his passion, but only played big cash stakes games, or major tournaments. Ricky had no idea who was sat across the aisle from him on that flight.

Some eight hours later the jumbo swooped into McCarran Airport, Las Vegas, where courtesy buses waited to ferry passengers to their hotels. Ricky got on the one marked Stratosphere Hotel, along with Johnson, and several others.

There isn't a word in the English language to describe the Stratosphere Hotel. It stands over 1,000 feet high, and has a roller coaster on top of its roof. Each of the 2,444 bedrooms has every conceivable facility, from bottled water through Game Boy consoles to a Xerox machine.

Ricky was shown to his room by a bellboy who Ricky thought was a bit old for the job. He also had the feeling he knew him, but put the thought from his mind. He couldn't do, this was his first visit to the States. Ricky went to bed as soon as he'd unpacked, leaving the nightstick in a suitcase.

The competition was due to begin the following day. Six hundred players from all over the world would compete in a knockout competition, until there were only nine left. These nine would all receive prize money, ranging from $100,000 for ninth place to $2,000,000 for the winner.

First, Ricky had to book in and find his table. Fresh enough at breakfast, it was perhaps jet lag which caused him to forget the nightstick when he went downstairs for the start of play.

He only needed to identify himself as the winner at the Rainbow Casino to be given a table, a seat number, and the $20,000 in chips each player started with. Then he looked for the table with his number on it. *This place reminds me of a Mecca bingo hall,* he thought.

Hundreds of people were in the process of doing exactly the same as him, but he felt terribly alone. He located the kidney-shaped table with his seat number on, and sat down. The recess was for a dealer of the cards to sit in. The organisers of the tournament also employed waitresses to tend to players' refreshment needs, free of charge. All the players had to do was play.

Ricky's table filled up as the time for play to start neared. But there was still one empty seat as the bell went to start the action. Someone would come to sit there, though. Twenty thousand dollars worth of chips were stacked on the table in front of it.

Turning up late was a favourite ploy of 'Piranha Fish' Johnson. Each player had to put an ante in the pot before each hand was played. If a player wasn't there, the dealer took it anyway. By showing up late, Johnson was showing disdain for his opponents. Poker is very much a mind game.

Ricky started nervously. He played a few hands he shouldn't have, and passed a few that maybe he ought to have played. He won enough to keep his stack of chips at about the level he'd started with, however, and grew a little in confidence after the first players were knocked out. He took liberal advantage of the free soft drinks offered him, which meant after a while he needed to go to the bathroom.

The only empty seat when he returned was his. 'Piranha Fish' Johnson had arrived.

Ricky was lucky and ended the first day's play with more chips than he'd started with. He was exhausted, and crashed after a steak dinner. Even so, he only just made it back to his table as the bell sounded to start play the following morning.

Lady Luck had been at her most fickle, knocking out a quarter of the field, including previous winners. *That's some-*

thing, thought Ricky. *I'll have to pull my socks up today, though*.

Johnson spent the first session weighing up the opposition, while making sure he took advantage of any easy pickings that came his way. A natural bully, he enjoyed making people squirm, and occasionally threw his hand face upwards into the middle of the table just to show he'd bluffed them all. Ricky didn't like that. He'd have to watch him. But he still couldn't 'read' him.

Ricky studied the dour, expressionless man, taunting his opposition without speaking, except to say "Call", "Raise", or "Check". Ricky imagined him to be about forty-five years of age. His full head of ginger hair looked like a carrot top, as it tapered to a pointed chin. He was smartly dressed, if casual. This allowed freedom of movement in a warm, crowded environment. Another good strategy in competitions. Each of Johnson's fingers had a gold ring on it, and on his left wrist he wore the diamond-encrusted bracelet which denoted a previous winner of the tournament. As far as Ricky was concerned, it was all a bit over the top. *Still, he must be good*, he thought.

Johnson stopped revolving six chips round the fingers of one hand, and peered at Ricky over the top of solid gold-rimmed spectacles. Ricky quickly averted his eyes. *Don't think he saw me looking at him*, he thought.

Ricky made a little progress that day, but still slumped wearily into bed after a good meal.

Feeling fresher next morning Ricky showered, and ate a good breakfast, before going downstairs. All the same, he decided to pack, just in case he was eliminated and had to take an early flight home.

The oak nightstick gleamed at him when he opened his case. *Perhaps that's it*, he thought. *I'll take it with me today*. He took it out, and placed it on a coffee table. It rolled behind a vase of flowers as he turned to answer a knock at the door. It was a waiter, come to clear the breakfast things away. Ricky left him to it, and went to get the lift, leaving the nightstick behind.

Ricky's pile of chips got lower as play continued. *I'll have to make a stand soon*, he thought.

The first two cards he'd been dealt this time looked prom-ising. Ace of Spades and Queen of Hearts. It was his turn to start the betting, too. He bet the minimum amount, and sat back in his chair, trying to appear confident. The players next to him folded, but the cowboy opposite called the bet. The next two folded, and it was up to Johnson. "Raise," he said.

Johnson looked at the dealer, then said, "Fifty thousand."

Ricky wondered what the cowboy would do if he matched this bet. It would take almost half his chips. The players to the right of Ricky threw their hands in, and it was up to him. While he was deciding what to do, a tap on his shoulder diverted his attention from the play. It was the bellboy. "Excuse me, sir. The waiter asked me to give you this."

Ricky absent-mindedly took the nightstick, and slipped it into one of the pockets of his flannel trousers. "Thanks," he said, then returned to his thoughts. He wondered if his oppo-nent was bluffing. Looking at the diminishing pile of chips in front of him, Ricky decided he was committed. "Call," he said.

The cowboy also called, and the first three community cards were dealt. Two Kings — and a Jack. One of the Kings and the Jack were spades.

Ricky only needed a ten to make a run. But a lot of hands beat a run. He could represent a flush in spades, if he bet strongly enough. But Johnson was first to bet.

"Check," said Johnson.

What shall I do now? thought Ricky. *If I bet, he might come back over the top, and bet much more. I need to see the next card.* "Check," he said.

The cowboy checked as well. Ricky sat back in his seat, and put his hand in his pocket as the dealer turned over the Ace of Diamonds, matching Ricky's Ace of Spades. The dealer then turned over the Two of Spades. Disaster for Ricky. His hand hadn't improved at all, but he could still represent a flush. His fingers closed round the handle of the nightstick, which imme-diately warmed to his touch.

"Check," said Johnson. Ricky looked at him. Johnson was like a statue.

Suddenly, the background noise seemed to Ricky to fade

away. He toyed with the handle of the nightstick, and looked at the cards in front of Johnson.

Ricky played the hand over in his mind. *He raised before the flop, so he could have a big hand. He's a bully, though. Could be bluffing.*

Then, Ricky slowly became convinced that Johnson was bluffing. *He's got nothing. Absolutely nothing. He's got even less than me.*

Ricky let go of the nightstick, and confidently pushed his chips into the middle of the table. "All in," he said.

Johnson was stunned by such a bold move. He glanced at Ricky, and decided he'd wait for a better opportunity. "Fold," he said.

Johnson didn't have enough chips in front of him. All the chips in the room wouldn't have been enough. Ricky wiped the floor with him, and became winner of the *World Poker Tour Championship 1991* and the two million dollars that went with it.

Chapter 15

Adam Gibson

Ricky decided to treat himself on the flight back to the UK. By the time he boarded the plane the magnitude of his achievement had set in, and he was in celebratory mood.

Spotting a lone woman reading a book, feeling pretty full of himself, and not a little gallant, he approached her. "Hi. My name's Ricky. Hope you don't mind, but I'm sort of celebrating and wondered if you'd like to join me in a glass of champagne."

That's the last thing I need, thought Esther, but, on looking up and seeing Ricky grinning all over his face, wasn't offended. About thirty, and sixish feet tall, with eyes that, like hers, were blue. The hint of crow's feet in their corners showed a sense of humour. He didn't have as much hair on his head as he once must have, but he had a kind face.

"Why not?" she said, holding out her hand. "The name's Esther, how d'you do?"

Pleased at his success, Ricky shook Esther's hand, and poured her a glass of champagne.

"What are we drinking to?" she asked.

Ricky raised his own glass. "To the two luckiest days of my life."

"Why two?"

"Because yesterday I won two million dollars, and today I met you."

Esther blushed, and looked down at her glass. "Thank you for that," she said.

"Right, have you eaten?"

"I'll be honest, the food on planes doesn't inspire me. I'm not hungry anyway, thanks."

"Right. I'm now going to show you what a difference having money makes. We'll go upstairs and eat in club class."

Esther lightened up. "OK. But I'll pay for the champagne." The cabin crew rose to the occasion by finding a couple of fillet steaks and some paté, which they turned into Tournedos Rossini with the help of a rich Burgundy sauce. First, Ricky and Esther enjoyed hot asparagus tips, smothered in salty butter and dipped in Hollandaise sauce, accompanied by a chilled bottle of Chablis.

Esther loved the attention Ricky paid her, but was still troubled by her inability to remember what had happened at Camp David.

The effects of champagne and wine loosened her inhibitions after a while, but after the alcohol rush subsided, tears came.

"What on earth's the matter?" said Ricky. "I thought you were enjoying yourself."

Esther, recovering her composure a little, said, "It's not you. And the meal was lovely. It's just that I'm having such a good time. On top of what's happened lately it's all a bit too much."

"Well fancy bursting into tears because you're having a good time. I don't mean to intrude, but you can tell me tell me about it, if you want to."

Esther didn't tell him where she'd been, just that she'd collapsed with food poisoning, and been in hospital for a few days.

"Well you're OK now. That's the main thing," he said. "Why don't you have a nap? You must be exhausted. I'll get the stewardess to call you when we get close to Heathrow."

"OK. Thanks for the meal. It was lovely. I'm sorry to have spoiled it for you."

Ricky tut-tutted, and fussed her a little. "Nonsense. It's been a real pleasure. I wouldn't have much of a good time on my own, would I? And don't think you're going to slip away from me now we've met. Is anyone meeting you at Heathrow?"

"No. I hadn't thought about it really. It was a spur of the moment thing, coming home."

"That's it, then. I'm seeing you home. Where d'you live?"

"With my mom and dad in Margate, I suppose. I haven't got a place of my own yet."

"Margate it is. I could do with some sea air."

"No, really. I couldn't impose."

"I won't hear another word on it," said Ricky, pressing a button to summon a stewardess.

After she'd gone, he settled down to think. *Wonder what upset her. God, she's a looker. But different. It's as if I've known her all my life. She can't tell a lie, either. She wears her emotions on her face. No wedding ring, either.*

Ricky realised he knew absolutely nothing about her. Not even her second name. But for the first time since Rosie left him he was interested enough to find out more about another woman.

The contented effects that a good meal brings caused Ricky's eyes to grow heavy. As he dozed, the nightstick grew warm in his pocket.

As they slept, Esther and Ricky dreamed the same dream. Of being part of a gathering in a cemetery. Their spirits seemed to lift from their bodies, and be given an insight into the life and memories of Adam Gibson, one of a special breed of men who was approaching his death.

Adam was seventy-three years old, and deep in reflection. He'd grown up in a small village called Coesau Bach, some ten miles from Oswestry. When he was nineteen he fell in love and married his sweetheart, Olwyn. Their son, David, was two years old when World War II broke out and Adam joined up.

"Keep your chin up," he said to Olwyn at Swansea station. Tears were streaming down her face. She was immensely proud of Adam, but frightened too, and couldn't control her emotions.

"Look after yourself, Adam. Please come back to me," she sobbed.

"Don't worry. Mom will look after you and the boy. I'll write often, and I'll come back. You can depend on it."

Olwyn wasn't so sure as she waved him goodbye. Shivers ran down her spine as the train pulled slowly away to the strains of *Land Of My Fathers*, sung by a local male voice choir.

Adam distinguished himself many times in war and was soon given a commission. He had no fear, convinced as he was that the cause was just. His men loved him, and followed his lead without question.

When it was his side's turn to endure the barrage he let his mind go. Amidst the madness of war, and with heightened senses, Adam began to see a depth to his surroundings unnoticed in peacetime. Small things took on greater significance, which was plain to see in his letters, sent home each day.

Adam wrote in poetic verse—the tradition of his forefathers. Bombs became rain, pattering around him like tiny feet. The sodden earth beneath his feet was, to him, Heaven's clouds to walk upon, and the screams of dying men, the songs of angels.

Adam led a charmed life while his comrades fell, one by one. By the time hostilities ended he'd come through it unscathed. That was when his *real* problems started.

While he was away Adam was reported missing on several occasions, only to return later carrying a wounded comrade, or leading his patrol to safety. The news of Adam being missing filtered through to Olwyn, but after she was bombed out she was more difficult to get hold of, and didn't know Adam was safe. All she knew was that the letters stopped.

When David was five years old, Olwyn, convinced Adam was dead, took up with another man.

Adam returned as promised, but there was no place for him with his family. He took this badly but felt, for the boy's sake, who'd begun to call the man who replaced him "Daddy," he shouldn't stand in their way. Adam left Coesau Bach forever.

There was plenty of work about. The country needed rebuilding. And the general feeling was that things could only get better. New houses were being built, along with shops and factories. Adam, swept up by this mood of optimism, drifted from job to job taking solace in drink as he needed to. But he didn't settle. He'd spent almost a quarter of his life outdoors, after all.

In spring and summer Adam spent his time travelling from one racecourse to another. His job, along with others, was to walk the course after each race, replacing any divots kicked up by horses' hooves.

Esther and Ricky saw all this in their dream and followed

Adam when he found warmth and employment in hotels during winter. An upsurge in technology brought by war led to hotels being packed out with businessmen from all round the world.

After many years of this alternating lifestyle Adam decided to stay at the Grand Hotel, Manchester, instead of joining his mates when spring came. He stayed there for fifteen years.

The Grand Hotel lived up to its name, having an impressive facade. Inside, the foyer and bedrooms were appointed to the highest standards, matched only by the huge number of staff employed to cater for customers' needs. In the 1960s, and for the time being, this was still the age of gracious living, exemplified by bishops and cardinals who ate well in sumptuous surroundings in à la carte restaurants. The kitchen at the Grand was a noisy, French-speaking hive of activity, as legions of workers seduced the palates of the middle and upper classes.

Adam worked as a washer-upper in the main kitchen. The aluminium sink that was his workplace ran across the entire width of the space at one end. A beautiful Victorian hotplate with sliding doors, decorated with scrollwork along its backplate, ran across the other end. Down the middle and in groups of two were eight massive gas-fired stoves. In the middle of each was a set of rings. Starting with the smallest, chefs could expose more and more of the pan they were using to the flame by taking off another, larger ring.

Four main 'corners', the Roast, the Veg, the Sauce, and the Fish corners, surrounded these stoves. A chef was in charge of each corner, with a commis chef (a chef just out of his apprenticeship) as his assistant. A couple of apprentices did the peeling and running about.

Fresh ingredients, needed to make any dish a customer ordered, were delivered daily in a stream of butcher's vans, drays, and greengrocer's vans, before being sorted through and dispensed as ordered from an adjoining larder room.

The air in the main kitchen was full of the sounds of guttural, male voices, shouting orders or cursing, staccato-like, and the squeaky, shrill sounds of nervous apprentices, rushing to obey.

Steam rose everywhere from boiling pots on stoves, or huge

vats of consommé leaching out the contents of cracked beef bones, minced beef, vegetables, egg shells and parsley stalks for days on end, until all that remained was a crystal clear, tasty soup.

Adam stood washing the same silver and lead-lined copper sauté pans over and over again. Cruel apprentices who called him 'le plongeur' made his life a misery. They were supposed to take hot pans to him for washing but when the kitchen was at its highest rate of production were allowed to slide them along the floor, so long as they shouted "Hot pan coming" before they did so. They forgot on many occasions.

Washing the same pots continually creates a rhythm. Adam would be standing there, going through the motions when a sizzling pan not long out of the oven would come hurtling down. He'd stretch out a hand, and...

The palms of Adam's hands were covered with scars which sometimes took a long time to heal. His hands were under water for much of the time with the result that damp got into the joints of his fingers, which then became permanently white and wrinkly.

One apprentice, named Richard, saw more in Adam than the others. To him, Adam was a quiet, proud man who took all that came his way without complaining. He also saw a man who didn't break, only bend. Richard respected him.

With Christmas approaching Richard went to Adam. "Taff, I was wondering if you'd like to come to my girlfriend's for Christmas lunch. I could take you and bring you back."

"Well, that's nice of you, Dai Bach. Why would you want an old man like me to do that?"

"I just thought—well, it's a family time of year and you don't seem to have one."

Adam studied the fresh-faced youth standing in front of him. He felt pain as his family was mentioned, but the boy seemed genuine enough. *My son could be the father of a lad like you*, he thought. A warmth spread from inside Adam and smiled through his face.

"That's very kind of you, Dai. I'd be happy to come."

In fifty years this was the only time Adam experienced the community of family life.

Adam's routine at the Grand Hotel was much of a muchness. He'd wake and the same sequence of events would thieve another day of his life.

In their dream Esther and Ricky went with Adam as he climbed narrow, winding stairs leading to staff quarters situated on the top floor after he finished his shift. They smelled each smell he did. Baking pastry on one floor; roasting coffee beans on another.

Adam was in the habit of availing himself of a freshly baked loaf of bread on his way up. In his tiny room he'd slice it down the middle and smother it with butter and jam. He'd poke bits of bread through a mesh-covered, bottom-hinged window, for pigeons to peck at.

Sometimes the salty butter mingled with tears as he thought of his son, then dribbled down his cheeks, before falling onto a cold, hard floor.

Adam's room was situated halfway down a dimly-lit corridor, which ran the whole length of the top floor of the hotel. The floors were covered with tiles, as were the walls. The only difference was the walls were of a glazed, flowery pattern, while the floors were matt in colour, with a pattern at the edges only. Much easier to keep clean in the sanitized setting of Victorian Britain, which was when the hotel was built.

The corridor was typical of those inside asylums, which is where many of Adam's comrades were put after being demobbed. So many soldiers presented symptoms of shellshock and other related mental conditions, after the war ended, that the authorities couldn't cope. Doctors didn't understand the symptoms at the time, so they simply committed them to asylums. Some of the soldiers were only in their twenties when they went in.

Adam considered himself lucky. He'd kept his head above water, just. Outside he looked a wreck but inside he remained straight and true. He'd done his duty and never counted the cost. He possessed an inner warmth and tranquility which cushioned him against emotional blows.

To supplement his meagre wage Adam sold newspapers during the afternoon break. This he did from an oak hut, shaped like a sentry box. Inside the wood, memories of the compassionate dead sensed his unhappiness and comforted him. It was Adam's sanctuary. He felt safe and could vent some of his pent-up frustration by shouting "Spatch a Mail" as people passed by.

One afternoon Adam was found slumped inside his box.

The Social Services, which the conscience of society set up to cater for the casualties of its now profligate and more liberal-minded society, nursed him back to health, then abandoned him to live in a block of flats. Enough money to enable him to live was paid into a bank account each week. But the phone never rang, and no one knocked on his door. He spent most of his time watching the world go by through the bay window in his second storey flat.

The flats lay behind a tall hedge of yew and holly, bordering a main road. Traffic noise kept him awake but the location allowed him to see people, especially children. Buses passing by caused maple and sycamore trees to shiver and sway. Birds swooped down to pluck berries from hedges, or rummage around in food packaging that people threw on the pavement.

Adam was content to sit and watch and think of old times. He hadn't eaten for a while, but didn't mind. He didn't hunger for anything and there was no bitterness in his heart. Besides, that inner warmth was wrapping itself round his outside now.

In their dream, Esther and Ricky returned to the cemetery. Once again they were aware of a conversation.

One of Adam's comrades' memories had arrived. They were glad to find they weren't alone, and were joining in, telling stories about what happened in the war. And about the fearless officer who led them into battle.

"What was his name?" asked one set of memories.

"Captain Gibson. Why? Did you know him?"

The bench broke in. "Did he have a wife and son, who he was forced to leave behind after the war? And did he work in a hotel for many years?"

"Why, yes. That's him."

"The memories are with him now. He'll be joining us soon."

Adam was sitting, as usual, remembering the places he'd

been to and the people he'd met; the situations he'd been in, good or bad; the emotions they'd inspired at the time, happy or sad.

He looked through the window and into a garden far away. He could see a little boy sitting there, and recalled being in a garden like it when he was a boy.

It was summer and he was in his godmother's garden in Coesau Bach. His seat was a patch of buttercups and mayweed. Warm, safe air supported thistle seeds, which, teased aloft by goldfinch beaks, floated by nymph-like in the breeze. Reverberating sounds of dragonflies and bumblebees gave orchestrated music to the business in the sky.

Lost amid the lavender, the blackcurrant and raspberry bushes, entrancing scents of honeysuckle, buddleia, and rose moistened dry air with a heady perfume.

His fingers became magic wands, as an orange-tipped butterfly found a warm, salty resting place on his outstretched hand. Time was irrelevant.

Suddenly a voice said, "Come, it's time for tea." Adam thought it was his godmother calling, but, as he turned, it was an old man's face he saw, high up in the sky. *He* was smiling at himself.

His name was called—he had to go—drawn back to a place where the old are put in tall flats and desolation becomes a view. And stifling space colours thoughts.

Adam was drawn back as rain, trickling down the window pane, misted his view. He liked rain but was tired now. As he laid his head back to rest on his chair a feeling of peace and understanding came to him. His senses isolated themselves in readiness, much as they had in war; became poised to leave his body and fulfil Nature's promise to every man and woman; which is that even as the body prepares to give up the spirit, the brilliance of everlasting creation is revealed to them.

As the moment of his death approached, Adam looked at his poem hanging on the wall. Written as a soldier, hoping to survive and return to his wife and child, with all the fear of failure that being able to choose one's own destiny brings, the words "When will the warming mist arise, lifting all back to the skies? Will this day my soul return to the place for which I yearn?" took on new meaning.

The gentle drone of the Jumbo 36,000 feet above the Earth gave a sense of reality to Ricky and Esther's dream. A swirling mist surrounded Adam and became a spectre, whispering, "Yes, old man. This is that day. Come."

Adam's face took on a look of serenity as his spirit rejoined his comrades.

He now waits for his son, David, in that place of overwhelming love and understanding. A part of all there is.

*　*　*

This soon to be forgotten telepathic experience created in Ricky and Esther a closeness that would help them in difficult times ahead, for by the time they met, society had descended into godlessness and secularity.

In this her twentieth year, Esther, in her naivety, and having had such a fortuitous start to life with virtually no effort, knew nothing of the choices adults were confronted with. Choices no previous generation had to make.

Her science master hadn't told her that rapid advances in medical technology, and a greater demand on resources, had presented doctors with moral issues. Who to treat? and who not to? Like most people, Esther wasn't aware of how much worse things had become since Louisa had been left to die, forty years before. Nor had he explained fully the possible consequences of the unravelling of the DNA mystery, which, to some experts, was like opening Pandora's box.

Politics was something Esther didn't yet know she ought to think about. Abortion—now made legal and available on demand—presided over, and actively condoned by weak and indulgent politicians, gave rise to sexual promiscuity. Banks, dispensing with restraints on borrowing, released enormous amounts of money into the economy with the result that a fundamental change in the way people viewed themselves had occurred. Now able to fund almost hedonistic lifestyles, people had become slaves to their egos. Relationships, like jobs, were easy to change, so that being young, free and single took precedence over family values.

Confused, but not knowing why, because of her amnesia,

Esther would soon learn that using one's position for selfish gain, as Jefferey had done, was merely symptomatic of attitudes held by countless people the world over. That some men and women saw the world as a trough from which to gorge themselves, and their community's coffers, their own personal bank accounts to draw on at will.

The plane carrying Esther and her new friend was nearing Heathrow. Ricky was street-wise, but nothing he'd experienced in life so far had prepared him for the furore their arrival was about to cause.

Chapter 16
Esther and Ricky Arrive at Heathrow

The first rays of sunshine peeped over the horizon as the Jumbo bringing Esther and Ricky back from America made its approach to Heathrow. "Look. The dawn," said Ricky.

A suffusion of colour lifted over the skyline, and with all the magnificence and power its heat promises, the sun burst through the porthole, illuminating Esther's face. Once again Ricky was awestruck by the aura this beautiful but seemingly vulnerable woman gave off. "God, you're lovely," he blurted out.

Ricky's heart leapt when Esther's eyes found his. An emotion, so powerful that it threatened to burst from him and embrace her, welled up from inside him. His legs seemed paralysed, and, for a sublime moment, he was overwhelmed. He blushed, and said, "Sorry, I wasn't thinking. I didn't mean to embarrass you. It's just that—when the sunlight caught you—I thought..."

Esther smiled. "That's OK. What a nice welcome to a new day." She kissed him lightly on the cheek. "You're one of the nicest people I've met. I'll never forget your kindness."

A feeling of panic swept over Ricky, as he realised she wasn't expecting to follow up their meeting by getting to know each other. He decided there and then he'd make it his business to find out if she was free. He very soon had a shock.

They collected their luggage at Heathrow and were making their way through Arrivals when all hell let loose. Camera flashes blinded them, and a cacophony of shouting voices stopped Ricky in his tracks. Esther pulled him back into Arrivals.

"Was that for us?" he said.

"Well, you're a famous poker player now. Come on, we'll have to order a car to get us out of here."

Ricky was bemused, and a little lost, as they made their way into the VIP Lounge. Esther knew her way around, and took charge. "You sit there while I organise some coffee. D'you want breakfast?" she said.

"No, thanks. My stomach is churning. Can we just get a car and get gone?"

"OK. You see the manager about a car. I need coffee."

A pin-stripe burst from an office as Ricky was getting up. The man inside it ignored Ricky and ran straight to Esther. "Miss Clayton. Please accept my apology. I'd no idea you were coming through today. Someone should've told me. Can I get you anything? Anything at all?"

Ricky wondered what was going on. *Clayton. He called her Miss Clayton.*

"Thank you. Yes, well, we didn't want any fuss. Could we have some coffee? and maybe some toast? And we need a car, if you can arrange one," said Esther.

"Of course. Straight away," said the pin-stripe. "Please make yourself comfortable. I'll tend to everything myself."

"What was that all about? Who are you?" said Ricky.

"Oh, nobody really. I made a film last year which was well received. I didn't star in it, though."

"That's it. You're Esther Clayton, the actress. Didn't you get an Oscar for it?"

"Yes. I was very lucky. But I haven't been back since. I wasn't expecting this. It was only one film."

Ricky laughed. "Only one film? They'll be all over you from now on."

Esther's face suddenly went pale. "Oh, no," she said.

"What's up?" said Ricky.

Esther showed him the front page of the daily she was reading. The headlines seemed to leap off the page. March 28th 1991.

"FILM STAR MISSING
STAY IN HOSPITAL FOR STARLET BRINGS FEARS OF
DRUG ABUSE"

Ricky wished he hadn't said "Is it true?", but the words

sprang from his lips before he could stop them. "No. Of course not. You know what reporters are like. I had an allergic reaction to fish, that's all. I had blood poisoning, or something, and spent a fortnight in hospital. All of a sudden I'm a junkie."

"Well, first thing is to get you down to Margate so you can regroup. I'll go and find out what's keeping that car," said Ricky.

* * *

Meanwhile, 150 miles away, Tim Howell, now in his fifty-sixth year, was about to receive devastating news.

Chapter 17

Tim Howell

In the cemetery, the recently departed memories of Tim Howell's mother, Jean, were communicating with the bench. No longer shackled by confusion and coaching by her daughter, Jean realised she'd disinherited Tim shortly before her death. She regretted this now. Tim was due in court within the hour. "What can I do?" she said.

"Don't worry," they said. "We'll send a message to Audeus."

Tim's problems began when he answered the phone one morning. The news his sister had for him was shocking in two ways. "Hi, Doreen, how you doin'?" he said.

"Mom died," she said.

Tim was stunned. He didn't even know she was ill. "What d'you mean? How? I don't understand."

"She died in hospital, three days ago. She was living in a home and had a fall. She broke her hip. After an operation to set the hip complications set in and she died, suddenly."

"Why was she in a home?"

Doreen wasn't very forthcoming with her answers so Tim asked her what they did now.

"What d'you mean?"

"Well, we're joint executors of Mom's Will, aren't we?"

"Not now we're not," said Doreen.

"I don't understand. Mom told me we were joint executors and beneficiaries."

"If you want to know any more, contact the solicitors disposing of the estate," said Doreen, testily.

Dismayed, Tim put down the phone. He hadn't seen much of his mother lately, but that was because of circumstances. *What's the matter with Doreen? We've always been so close.*

Why is she being so nasty now? he wondered.

Tim had breathed in a lot of dust as he worked to retrieve what he could from the Great Oak. As he sawed and planed dozens of planks of timber the air became thick with dust containing memories of the dead. Politicians, doctors, sailors, scientists; all sorts of memories were mixed up in this permeating cloud of dust. They got in his hair and clothes. They even got into his food and drink. By the time he'd finished he was riddled with them. As Tim struggled to make sense of it all, the memories prompted him to do just what Doreen had said. Consult a solicitor.

* * *

The solicitor had another shock for Tim. "The solicitors representing your mother's estate say they themselves executed the Will. Your mother was clear that she was disinheriting you because, and I quote, 'He's not a very nice man, and I never see him.' You have no case."

"But my mother gave me to understand that my sister and I would be treated the same."

The solicitor sighed. "I'm afraid cases of contentious probate have grown out of all proportion in recent years."

"What are you saying?"

"Well, we've become an affluent society. People have a lot more to leave these days. Estates of a quarter of a million are not uncommon anymore. And that means people are tempted to undermine other members of the family while the testator is alive, in the hope they'll take them out."

"You're joking."

"Wish I were, Mister Howell. But many people in your predicament come to me. Mom has told them what they can expect, but when it comes down to it, they find that their brother, or sister, or even an aunt or uncle, has persuaded their mother, or father, to disinherit them in their favour. Proving it to a judge is the problem."

"Judge? Surely a jury would believe me."

"No. Only judges are allowed to hear these cases. You see, the court isn't interested in what is fair, or what you may see as

103

an injustice. Was the testator sound in mind and body? That's the only thing the judge has to establish. I'm sorry."

* * *

Stunned for the second time, Tim felt he'd no choice but to accept what the solicitor said. But something niggled him. He suspected something was wrong.

The memories Tim had breathed in all those years ago now came to the fore. He'd many talents at his disposal. The detective in him drew him to conclude that he'd better make his own enquiries.

Tim put a caveat against the Will, so that Doreen couldn't rush her application for probate through. Sure enough, Tim found that Doreen had applied for probate within two days of his mother dying. Convinced that Doreen had something to do with the Will change, he began to dig a little.

The only clue Tim had was that his mom had died in Stoke Hospital. He phoned, and was put through to a girl in charge of patient support. "Mrs Howell was brought in by ambulance after having had a fall," she said.

Tim phoned the ambulance service and was given the address of the home Jean had been living in at the time. Tim made an appointment to see the proprietor.

Mixed thoughts harried Tim as he drove to Stoke Hospital. His mother's estate, which must amount to over £500,000, he reckoned, was the issue, but it was the possibility that she'd rejected him, and his not having been there to say goodbye, that distressed him most. And his sister's attitude.

Tim wasn't that bothered about the Will. If she'd disinherited him there wasn't anything he could do about it. He'd always told her she could leave her money to a lamp post if she wanted to. This was a shock, though.

He remembered the conversations he'd had with her. She told him several times what she'd done, and seemed to need to confirm to him that everything was OK. He'd always said the same thing. "Well, it's nice to know you've put everything in order, Mom. But you've got to look after yourself first."

He remembered calling round one day and finding toast on

fire under the grill. But she said there was nothing wrong with her. *Perhaps the owner of the home will tell me more*, he thought.

Matron Boyle managed the nursing home as well as being the proprietor. She had plenty to say in answer to Tim's questions.

"D'you know why Mom came to you?" he asked.

"It was decided that Jean needed stimulation," she said. "She was living with your sister, in her boyfriend's house. They left Jean with sandwiches and a flask when they went to work each day. But Jean refused to eat, and stayed in bed all day till they came home."

"What? They left her on her own all day with just sandwiches and a flask?"

"Your sister had tremendous influence over your mother, you know."

"What d'you mean?"

"At first I thought it was just a case of a loving daughter taking a healthy interest in her mother's affairs. She came in every day and laid out your mother's clothes. Each set of clothes had a label with the day written on it. She even put toothpaste on your mom's toothbrush."

Tim was beginning to smell a rat. He knew his mother bowed to whatever his sister said. As Matron Boyle paused to take a sip of water, the memories inside Tim prompted him to believe his fears about Doreen. *My God. Doreen got Mom to leave me out,* he thought. More words came. *"Absolute power corrupts absolutely."* What Matron Boyle said next confirmed his fears.

"Then I noticed there'd be a terrible row if your mother wasn't wearing what your sister had labelled for her. One day an infection broke out in a burn on your mother's arm. I thought it odd because the nurse had dressed it the day before. It turned out your sister hadn't liked the way the nurse had bandaged the wound, took the dressing off, and re-dressed it herself. That was when the infection set in."

Matron Boyle had even more to say.

"Things came to a head after that. I asked Doreen and her boyfriend to come in for a meeting. I asked her if she was happy with the care we were providing. Some of the staff felt intimidated by her. She said she was perfectly happy with Jean's care and admitted to being a bit of a 'control freak'—her words—where your mother's concerned. I suppose you know there were concerns about Jean's mental health?"

Tim went cold at this. Doreen had dismissed *his* concerns years ago and told him to stay out of it.

"No, I didn't. Please continue," he said.

"Well, I felt I had to make a stand, for your mother's sake. When the hospital rang to ask if Jean could come back here after recovering from her fall I said she could, on the condition your sister didn't interfere with her care and welfare. I didn't hear any more."

"What? You didn't even know she'd died?"

"No. I only knew when another resident told me. Doreen came into the home early the day after Jean died and cleared her room out. I didn't even know she'd been here until staff checked."

Tim thanked Matron Boyle, gave her the flowers he'd taken with him, and took his leave. He was furious. But he knew Doreen had been found out. *Undue influence, that's what it is. After they persuaded her to leave me out, they kept her locked in a home, and fobbed me off every time I asked about her*, he thought.

Tim wrote to the solicitors executing the Will, expressing his concerns. Also, he applied for his mother's medical records to be released. He didn't have long to wait for a reply from Doreen's solicitors, who reacted angrily.

"We give you notice that if you continue to hold probate up unnecessarily, an action will be sought stating that you personally be held responsible for the extra costs of defending this Will."

They also issued an "Appearance To Warning". This meant Tim had to give his reasons for holding up probate in court. Undaunted, he decided to represent himself.

A court date was set, but when the day came the medical records hadn't arrived. He'd have to start without them. He wasn't too worried. He felt it was obvious that Doreen had controlled their mother.

Chapter 18

The Court Case

Tim began to construct his case, while inside him memories stirred. The rhetorical skills of legendary barrister Sir Montague-Peregrine-Murray Hill (whose character wouldn't have been out of place in a Victorian farce), sharpened themselves.

Tim was too preoccupied to notice that the Family Division at the Magistrates Court had been furnished using the fine oak timber he himself had supplied. He just knew he didn't feel out of place there.

The case began with the judge asking if the Will had been properly executed. Counsel for the estate stood up. "Your Honour, this case is straightforward. Solicitors acting for the executor received a letter from the deceased, in her own handwriting, asking them to go to her house and execute a Will. When they arrived the lady was able to let them in herself. She made them comfortable, and gave them tea."

At this point, the barrister raised his hand to swat away the wasp which only he could see, buzzing under his nose. Mischievous memories in the oak bench were making things as uncomfortable as possible for him.

"Are you alright?" the judge asked.

The barrister nodded, and continued. "The solicitors asked the testator if she was aware of what she was about to do. She replied that she was, and reiterated her intention to disinherit her son because, and I quote, 'He is not a nice man, and I never see him'."

It was now Tim's turn to present his case. He stood up. "Your Honour, I have a previous Will executed by my mother, in which she clearly states that my sister and I should inherit jointly should she predecease us..."

The barrister, still bothered by the wasp and trying to scratch the back of his neck, raised his hand, but the judge interjected. "There's no need for Counsel to interrupt. I'm quite capable of seeing points of law myself, thank you. Is there a revocation clause in the Will?"

"Sorry, Your Honour. There is indeed, Your Honour. All is in order," said the barrister.

"Thank you. Are you allergic to something?"

"No, Your Honour. I've an itch."

"Well try to control yourself. You look like a constable on traffic duty."

The judge addressed Tim. "The Will you speak of cannot be accepted in court. Do you have anything else?"

Tim looked at his papers. "Your Honour, I have a statement from Matron Boyle, the proprietor of the nursing home Mom lived in. The matron states that my sister..."

The barrister for the estate jumped up. "Objection, Your Honour. This statement relates to something after the event and is therefore inadmissible."

"I agree," said the judge. He turned to Tim. "Have you anything else?"

"Your Honour, I have a letter from a neighbour of Mom's..."

Again the barrister stood up. "Objection. This letter doesn't name the person who is alleged to have had this conversation with the neighbour, who has since died."

The judge looked at Tim "Strike that," he said. "Have you anything else?"

Tim began to sweat. *They won't let me present my evidence*, he thought. He looked at his notes, trying to think.

Suddenly the background noise faded away. The wooden bar Tim was standing in front of became warm to his touch. Words came into his mind *"The medical notes have arrived. Ask for a recess."*

Tim was brought back to reality by the judge asking, "Is the plaintiff well enough to continue?"

"I wouldn't mind a break, Your Honour," Tim said.

The judge looked at his watch, then said, "It's getting late. This court is adjourned until 10 a.m. tomorrow."

The practice manager met Tim at his mother's doctor's surgery. "Mr Howell, I was about to phone you. The notes have arrived." Tim accepted an enormous wad of files, thanked her, and left.

He spent most of the night sorting through hundreds of entries. Having been seen or attended to by doctors 60 times during the previous 45 years, his mother had been attended by doctors 211 times during the last 4 years of her life. She was deaf, and wore thick spectacles because she was short-sighted. She complained of a myriad of things: headaches, stomach pains, breast pain, swollen ankles, memory loss, palpitations, asthma, depression. The list went on and on. She had had several falls, lacerating her legs in the process, but most important as far as he was concerned was an entry showing that Doreen had taken her to see a consultant psychiatrist, who diagnosed that his mother was suffering from Alzheimer's Disease.

No wonder Doreen wanted probate to go through quickly. She organised all Mom's psychiatric assessments, and never once corrected her when she said she never saw me, he thought.

Tim felt refreshed when the court was called to order the following morning. The barrister representing the estate, fed up with the uncomfortable time the memories were giving him, had brought a cushion with him.

Tim stood up, waiting until all eyes were on him before he began. Then he addressed the judge. "Your Honour, I have new evidence in the form of my mother's medical notes which I..." Tim paused. Inside him, it felt as if someone else had stood up, but a couple of seconds behind him. He opened his mouth to speak. But it was Sir Montague's memories that took over...

"...Which I will introduce in a moment. Firstly I would say this. The court—quite rightly I may add—supposes at the beginning of a case that the testator was of sound mind and judgement at the time of the execution of a Will. However, I intend to show, not only that the testator was *non compos mentis* at the time of the execution of the disputed Will, but that her free agency was compromised by her relationship with her daughter, who has since become the major beneficiary of the estate."

He paused to let the significance of this statement sink in. Then he continued. "I bring to the attention of the court the following judgements in Case Law: 'Persuasion is now unlawful, but pressure of *whatever character*, if so exerted as to overpower the volition, without convincing the judgement of the testator will constitute Undue Influence, though no force is used, or threatened.' Hall v Hall, 1868. Number 217 in the calendar. 'He (the propounder of the Will, in this case the executors) must dispel the strong suspicion which is created when the propounder is also a major beneficiary. Where the suspicion exists, there must be evidence to exclude *all reasonable doubt*, the testator knew and approved the contents of the Will.' Timlick Estate v Crawford, 1965. Number 2251."

A rustle of paper echoed round the courtroom as clerks attempted to find the relevant rulings. Tim hadn't a clue what he'd said. Still, it seemed to have got their attention. Then his mouth started again.

"'Where there is *some* evidence to show *some* mental incapacity, and also *some undue influence* has been exercised, in as much as the degree of influence needed to induce a person of strong mind, and in good health to do any act, is much stronger than that which would induce a person of feeble mind, and in a weak state.' Hamson v Gray, 1861. Number 2228."

Doreen's jaw dropped. Tim would have collapsed himself, but instead found his hand shooting up in the air with the proclamation; "Behold. The medical evidence.

"August 15th. Assessed by Dr Grewcott, a renowned consultant psychiatrist. And I quote; 'The most likely diagnosis is senile dementia in the form of Alzheimer's Disease.'"

Tim turned to the judge, and said, "Your Honour, this poor, aged, heroine of the Blitz is led, like A LAMB to...ahem. Sorry, m'lud. Is led in her confused state to a mental hospital to be assessed—behind my client's back."

Tim had enough control over his senses to realise that August 15th was months before his mother changed her Will. Then Sir Montague was off again: "January 6th. My client, extremely worried about the deterioration in his mother's mental capacities, goes to her doctor to disclose his concerns. He is fobbed off by being told his sister is already taking care of it.

"March 3rd. The testator is assessed again. This time a different consultant psychiatrist notices a further ten different symptoms of senile dementia.

"April 2nd. Daughter writes to doctors herself. 'Can you please bring my mother's appointment forward, as I am extremely worried at the rapid deterioration in my mother's capabilities to make judgements or decisions.'

"April 23rd. St George's Day. The testator is seen by another psychiatrist who notices further different symptoms of senile dementia."

Tim turned to the judge, and said solemnly: "Your Honour, all in all, the various assessments of my client's mother's ability to make considered judgements or decisions conclude that, and I quote, 'She is deaf, and wears heavy spectacles. She never knows the day, or date.'"

He paused to sip from a glass of water before continuing, thereby ensuring all eyes remained on him. "She very often cannot remember her words during conversations and cannot recognise people she knows. She lets people into her home inappropriately and is prone to stay in bed all day. She doesn't change her clothes. On at least one occasion she lost something in the house, and spent an inordinate amount of time looking for it."

At this point he turned away from the judge and gave his attention to the solicitors who had gone to Tim's mother's house, before continuing. "But the most damning report of all is contained in the report of Joan Slatterly, a psychiatric nurse who noted that, and I quote, 'Would appear to be independent, and able to care for herself when people first meet her, but the opposite is in fact the case.'"

Tim then pointed at the solicitors concerned, and repeated the words: "'Would *appear* to be able to care for herself.'" Then he turned to the judge, and said, "Your Honour, these lackeys, ever mindful of earning a few easy pounds, ignored one fundamental thing. It is the *duty* of any solicitor asked to execute a Will to first seek independent and professional opinion as to the mental capacity of a testator *before* accepting the commission."

Tim then closed with his submission. "Your Honour, I submit that in view of all this, and other evidence I have produced, that the propounder of this Will cannot dispel the grave suspicions which have been raised. I therefore entreat Your Honour to set this Will aside, in favour of the Will executed at a time when the lady's ability to make a Will is not in question." Then he sat down.

The silence in the court was palpable for a moment. Then uproar. As the judge raised the gavel Tim himself had presented to him at the opening ceremony, many years before, two things happened. The gavel gleamed as the judge brought it down, and Doreen fainted.

Tim could have sworn that the oak grain in the gavel opened into a smile as the judge looked at him and said, "I find this Will to be unsafe, and therefore order it to be set aside in favour of the previous Will, which states this fine woman's intention that both her first born and only son and his sister should inherit jointly should she predecease them. I find in favour of the plaintiff. That's all."

As the judge was speaking, Tim realised his own head was nodding up and down. He didn't know where the words had come from. All he knew was, he and his mom had won.

The clerk to the Magistrates called the court to order and brought proceedings to a close, leaving Tim to reflect. He looked round the courtroom for the first time. He recognised the oak panelling and benches, and smiled. A smile from deep inside. He spoke his words aloud. "Well it's all over now. It was never about money. Justice has been done."

"I agree."

The barrister who'd represented Tim's sister sat by Tim and held out his hand. "Congratulations," he said.

"You just tried to rob me in court. What are you after now?" said Tim.

"Nothing. Just doing my job. But I wanted to have a word with you. Will you just hear me out? Buy you a coffee? There's a canteen downstairs."

* * *

112

"Milk and sugar?"

"Yes, please," said Tim.

The two men settled down in a corner of the canteen. The barrister watched the white of the milk blend with the black of the coffee as he stirred the whirlpool in his coffee cup around for a moment. Then he said, "I don't always represent the estate, you know."

"I don't understand," said Tim.

The barrister took a sip, then looked at Tim. "I hope you don't mind me bringing this up, but I'm thinking long-term, now. It's about Doreen."

"Huh."

"I thought you'd say something like that. Look. You were both close before this matter, weren't you?"

"You could say that. We were like twins, emotionally. Well, I thought we were."

"Perhaps you can still be."

Tim stood up. "Look, you heard the evidence. She made her bed. Now she can lie in it."

"So then society will have another fractured family. Please hear me out."

Tim sat down. "OK. Go ahead."

"If you were to log on to the Home Office web site and look at records of contentious probate, which is what your case was about; look at records for, say 10 years ago, you'd find that about 500 cases went to court. The figure this year will be nearer 20,000."

"My God."

"Precisely. What I'm saying is that we live in a different society now. The days when who got what depended on who sneaked in first and pinched what they thought they were entitled to after someone died, are gone. Most of us own at least one house and have investments of some sort, so that estates of £500,000 plus are no longer a rarity. This means that there's a temptation for even the most law-abiding and Christian of people to pick up on the most innocuous of arguments between members of their family, and turn it to their own advantage. It's human nature. In my experience, these circumstances are splitting families apart more effectively than Thor's Hammer ever could."

"That's what my solicitor said, funnily enough. The point is, my own sister got me disinherited, and you want me to forgive her?"

"Doreen was executor of your mother's Will and, I think, persuaded herself that she was doing what your mother wanted. Even though she was in the grip of Alzheimer's. You might find that hard to believe at this moment, but I just wanted to say that you might find it beneficial to get together with Doreen sometime, and talk this through. We still have to go through complying with the order of the court to set the last Will aside, so what d'you say?"

"I don't know."

The barrister got up and held out his hand. "Must get going now, she'll be waiting for me, but, as I say, there'll be an opportunity to get round the table. I hope you'll attend."

Tim shook his hand. One small and seemingly insignificant gesture, but it was, in effect, another first step on the road back to common sense and empathy by a member of the population.

Chapter 19

Esther Returns Home

Esther wasn't sure how her mother would receive her. Her fears were confirmed when Joan opened the front door. "Where the hell have you been?" she said. "Your agent's been on the phone every hour for the last four days, and the studio's been going nuts."

Esther almost burst into tears as the smell of the house wafted unseen past her mother and embraced her. Almost immediately that feeling of being home and safe left her as Joan, unable to ignore the unspoken message in her daughter's eyes, took a step back. A brief, uneasy silence followed. The intangible bond between mother and daughter just wasn't there for Joan.

Being rejected in this way at the time she needed her mother most caused Esther to vow to never again show emotional weakness. She mentally shrugged, turned to Ricky and said, "Welcome to Dullsville." Then she turned smartly back to greet her mother with a smile. "Hi, Mom. This is Ricky. I met him on the plane coming back. Just thought I'd take a break, and see how you are."

The pain Esther was feeling soothed as she spotted Terry coming down the hall. The tension in her face disappeared and she blossomed, like a flower opening its petals at the first sight of the sun.

"Hi, Dad," she said. "Meet Ricky."

Terry beamed at her, took Ricky's hand, and said, "Come on in. I'll put the kettle on."

Ricky took his hand. "How d'you do?" he said.

"Yes, yes. How d'you do?" said Joan. "Look, Esther. You can't stay. Your Aunt Elizabeth is here. Alan died last month and she's staying with us for a while. You'll have to stop with

Sheila. Your friend can go up the road to The Swan. They'll have a room there. You really should've let me know you were coming, you know."

"I know, Mom. It was a spur of the moment thing. I'll go and see Sheila. Sorry about Alan."

"Come back for tea, if you want."

Esther didn't think so. Burger and fries were not her favourite things to eat. "We'll need time to settle in. P'raps we'll catch you at the club for a drink later," she said. "Where's Andrew, and Margaret?"

"Margaret had twins. She lives on the council estate up the road."

"That'll have made her happy. What did she call them?"

"Oh, I don't know, Esther. I've got enough on my plate with Andrew."

"What's the matter with Andrew?"

"Go and see Sheila. I'll tell you later."

Esther had been wondering how she could get out of staying at her mother's house, and was relieved the decision was taken out of her hands. "OK. See you later," she said, grabbing Ricky by the arm.

"Don't worry," she said, linking her arm through his as they walked to Sheila's house. "You'll like Sheila. She's my best pal."

Esther couldn't believe her eyes when she saw Sheila, who had matured into an attractive young woman herself. Sheila nearly knocked her over when she answered the front door to her.

"Esther. Ooh, you naughty girl. Why didn't you tell me you were coming? And who's the hunk?"

"Don't you start. Mom's just given me the once-over. My, how you've grown up. Blonde, too. This is Ricky. I met him on the flight back."

Sheila took Ricky's hand, and held it for a moment. "Hmm. Good handshake. Blue eyes, too. You're a lucky man, mister."

"Sheila, will you stop it. It's not like that. Ricky's a gentleman, and a friend."

"Aah. Friend is it? And where d'you live, mister nice guy?"

"Birmingham," said Ricky.

"Did you hear that? Bit of a detour, wouldn't you say?"

"Take no notice of her, Ricky. It's her hormones." Esther returned Sheila's hug. "It's lovely to see you. How's your mom and dad?"

"Fine. They just keep going, thank God. Where are you staying. Not at your mom's?"

"No. She told me about Alan."

"I know. It was awful. One minute he was fine. Next minute they're giving him six months. He lasted a year. Throat cancer. All that smoking, I suppose. Look, you can have my old room, if you want. We'll have to find somewhere else for you, lover boy."

"Sheila. Will you stop it," Esther said, although quite pleased Sheila approved.

"That's OK. I was only going to stay a few days after I'd seen Esther home," said Ricky.

Sheila kissed him on the cheek. "Come on in and sit down. I want to hear all about you."

Esther felt a little jealous as her friend fussed over Ricky. She decided to go to see Graham as soon as possible.

Sheila made up a bed while Esther and Ricky sat talking to Hilda and Norman, in the lounge. She tucked the bottom sheet under, then moved round to the other side of the bed. Her eyes lit on Billy, the rocking horse she and Esther had played on as children. When she pushed Billy's rump, his joints—dry and unused these days—squeaked, but what was left of his mane fluttered as he rocked back and forth a couple of times. And when his head came up it was if he was a foal again, let out into the paddock to play. Sheila looked at Billy again, and made a decision.

It didn't take long to walk the short distance to The Swan in Addington Road. After signing the register, Ricky patted his stomach. "Don't know about you two but my belly thinks my throat's been cut."

"What d'you fancy?" said Sheila. "Indian? Chinese? There's a McDonald's on the front."

"Well, the sea air's got to me already. Chinese'll do," he said.

"Chinese it is then," said Esther.

117

During the meal the conversation turned to family. "What's the matter with Andrew?" said Esther. "Mom said she's got a problem with him."

Sheila stopped trying to pick up a prawn with a pair of chopsticks. "He hasn't come out of his room for eighteen months. They've tried everything to get him out, but he just sits, playing games on that damned computer of his, apparently. Your mom takes his meals up, puts the tray on the floor outside his door, and goes back later to pick it up when he's finished. His owl starved to death."

"God. What about the authorities?" said Esther.

"He's left school. He's classed as an adult, now. They can't do anything."

"Well, somebody ought to do something. He can't stay in his room forever. Why haven't they pulled the plug on him, or something? What about Margaret?"

"She got pregnant before leaving school last year. Had twins, and got a council house."

Esther laughed. "That's her sorted, then. All she ever wanted to do was have kids." Then, more seriously, "Andrew's the one who needs help."

They finished their meals, and walked to the pub. The place was thumping when they got there. Terry was already on stage, doing his party piece. This involved him standing on one leg, wearing an eye patch. The owl, which he'd had stuffed, sat on one shoulder. Terry then recited a monologue while waving his arm around:

"The boy stood on the burning deck,
his back towards the mast;
He wouldn't move a flipping inch
till Montague had passed..."

Oh, God, thought Esther. She looked at Ricky, hoping he hadn't heard. He just shrugged his shoulders and clapped politely with the rest as Terry finished, and hopped down from the stage.

Esther looked at Sheila, who stuck her tongue out the side of her mouth and rolled her eyeballs. Esther's heart jumped as she realised how much she'd missed being girlish. Esther turned her attention to Aunt Elizabeth. Although she was older than Joan, the family resemblance was unmistakeable. Elizabeth had the same black hair and was slight in stature also, although a little heavier. Esther wasn't sure if it was from the effects of alcohol or music, but Elizabeth swayed in front of her. She didn't seem to be as distressed as Esther thought she'd be. "Sorry to hear about Alan," shouted Esther. "How'yer doing?"

The glass moved with Elizabeth as she answered. "I don't know why he did this to me. He had to go and leave me—after all those years."

I don't suppose he meant it, thought Esther. She did her best, and said "I know. It must've been a terrible shock. Are you getting on with Mom?"

"Yes, but I could do with a shag."

Esther didn't know what to say to that. She just hoped the remark got lost in the noise. She'd had enough by now and gave her excuses to Joan. "Mom, I'm tired. Jet lag must be setting in. I'm off now."

Joan raised her gin and tonic and looked somewhere in Esther's direction, "Here's to my little girl, who's a movie star," she said.

Elizabeth leaned across and breathed brandy fumes all over Esther. "Who's your friend? Wanna do a threesome later?" Esther grabbed Sheila's and Ricky's hands, and fled.

As the three waltzed along Station Road arm in arm, reciting "The boy stood on the burning deck" and hopping occasionally to mimic Terry, Esther felt some of the gloom lift. It was great to be back, and with friends. *Things will be alright. I'll go and see Graham. Everything will be great*, she thought.

Sheila and Esther exchanged gossip after seeing Ricky back to The Swan. Esther spoke first. "It's nice to be back in this room. We had such good times here. Where's the rocking horse?"

"Gave him to Margaret, for the kids. I've told her I want him back later, though. Been a bit broody myself lately."

"Anyone special?"

"No. Still looking. Now, tell me about Ricky."

"I just met him on the plane, that's all. He was celebrating and asked me to join him."

"Celebrating what?"

"He won two million dollars in a poker tournament."

"Wow! D'you love him?"

"Don't be silly. I just met him."

"Well I love him already. If you don't want him, I'll have him."

"I have to go to town, to see someone."

"Oh. So you've been holding out on me. Who is it?"

"Just someone I met, before I went to Hollywood."

Esther turned to Sheila quickly, and took her by both arms. "It was wonderful. But I don't know if he'll even remember me now."

"'Course he'll remember you. Did you keep in touch?"

"Not exactly. Just the odd phone call. I was so busy, and time flew by."

"Well, you'll have to phone him and go to town and see him then, won't you?"

"You're still my best friend."

"Don't worry. There's method in my madness. I'll have Ricky all to myself while you're gone. He likes you, you know. So, tell me all about it, Miss America. Did you meet Jack Nicholson? And what was it like, playing opposite Mimi Rogers in your first film?"

"It was great. I thought I'd really made it."

"So you have. What d'you mean, thought? That was the first of many, wasn't it?"

"Well. Something happened—I'm not sure. I just know I feel different inside now."

"You're not making sense. Come on. What happened?"

"I was introduced to the President and he asked me to go to Camp David for the weekend. That was only a couple of weeks ago. God, it seems like ages now. Anyway, I went and it was cool at first. He sent a limousine for me and I felt really important. I only had a couple of drinks, then I don't remember anything till I woke up in hospital."

"Perhaps he drugged you," said Sheila.

"Don't be daft. You've been watching too many late-night gangster films. I had a severe allergic reaction to some hors d'oeuvres, that's all. But I feel different now, as if something inside me has changed. I just can't remember."

"Well, it doesn't matter now. It'll come back to you if it's important. Phone your friend in London. Go to see him. You've still got friends on this side of the Atlantic, haven't you?"

"I suppose so. But I really wanted to make it there, and I don't know if I can go back now."

"And so you will make it. We'll sort you out. You just need a break, that's all."

Sheila thought about her friend later, as she dropped off to sleep. *So glad you came back. I've missed you. Mind you, looks like I'm going to be the only virgin left now.*

Connaught Square, London

Graham de Courcey wasn't at his best when Esther phoned him next morning. A brain full of champagne bubbles isn't exactly with it in the morning, after all. But he soon recovered his composure on hearing Esther's voice. "Esther, darling. How are you? Or should I say where are you? You've created quite a stink in the newspapers you know. Speculation is rife."

"Yes, I know. I'm coming up to London this afternoon. I'll make a statement, after I've seen my agent, probably. I was wondering if I could see you while I'm there."

Graham stopped tweaking the firm, round nipple belonging to the babe lying next to him, and leant on one elbow. "Look, I've just this minute woken up," he whispered. "Why don't you buzz me after you've checked in?"

"OK. I'll phone you when I get there."

Esther was disappointed he hadn't wanted to chat, but put it down to the fact she hadn't really kept in touch. Mind you, he hadn't phoned her at all while she'd been in America. She looked at her watch. *Just time for a bite to eat before taking the afternoon train,* she thought. Then, looking up the stairs, she shouted, "Will you help me pack before we go to pick Ricky up?"

"Down in a minute. D'you want breakfast before we go?"

"I thought I'd have coffee for now, and brunch at The

Swan. I wanted to have a word with Ricky before I went."

"Fine by me. Am I invited?"

"Of course you are. I want to talk to you as well."

Sheila poked her head over the bannister. "My, we are serious this morning, aren't we, Miss America?"

"I'm sorry. I was going to ask him if he'd do something for me while I'm away."

"Mysterious as well, huh? Of course I'll help, whatever it is. Be down in a minute. Put the kettle on will you?"

There was an eerie silence as the three ate in The Swan. Then Esther took a deep breath, and spoke. "You're going to think me a terrible hostess, but I have to go to London for a few days."

Ricky looked down at his toasted cheese and ham sandwich. "That's OK. I was going to take a look round Margate."

Sheila noticed his crestfallen look, and took over. "Yes, and I'm going to show him round. Don't worry, Delilah. Samson will still be here when you get back."

Esther blushed. "Of course I'm coming back. Will you do something for me while I'm away, Ricky? Will you try and get my brother Andrew to come out of his room? It's a cheek to ask you, but you could tell him you're into computers or something. Nobody else has had any luck. He might respond to someone he doesn't know, if you see what I mean."

This wasn't the strangest request Ricky had had as a taxi driver. Besides, he wanted to get to know Esther more. "Leave it to me. I'll have him out before you know it," he said.

Chapter 20

Andrew

Esther's natural confidence shrank a little, along with the figures of Sheila and Ricky waving goodbye to her, as the afternoon train left Margate Station. For the first time in her life, Esther felt utterly alone. Her stomach churned as her eyes locked with Ricky's for a moment. Somehow she knew that leaving him would be far more difficult from now on. *Still, it's only for a couple of days*, she thought.

She took her seat and looked out of the window, trying to decide if she was doing the right thing. She knew she had to find out if she really loved Graham, but Ricky was a complication now. *He's nice. Must mean something*, she thought.

The train rocked from side to side as it trundled through Herne Bay, then turned inland. Esther wondered what Graham would think of her now. She felt her eyes drooping as the motion of the train, and rain trickling down the window pane, sent her to sleep. Then she dreamt—of a man in a church. For the first time, Esther made a subconscious connection with Michael Jobson.

Ricky and Sheila waved goodbye to Esther at Margate Station and made their way to Terry's house. He opened the front door to them himself. "What ho. Come in both. I'll put the kettle on. Sorry about Elizabeth last night. You know what it's like when the drink takes hold. It's been a difficult few months for her, since Alan died."

Ricky said nothing.

Terry looked at him for a moment, then offered his hand. "Look, I like you, and I like the way you look at my Esther. She's got herself into the hardest game in the world. Plenty of people will want to have their hands in her pockets while she's famous, know what I mean? It would be nice for me to able to think someone like you is looking after her."

Ricky took his hand, but again said nothing.

They all sat and talked for a while. Terry was impressed to hear that Ricky had won the poker tournament. "Blimey. I sit and watch them, late at night. World Poker Tour, isn't it? Fancy winning that. I like a game myself, but it beats me how they stay so calm while they're playing for two million. I couldn't do it. Will it be on the telly?"

"Yes. But it's only just finished, so probably not till next year. I can give you a few tips, if you like. Perhaps Andrew would like to sit in."

Terry looked around to see if Joan was about. Seeing she wasn't, he leaned forward and lowered his voice. "Look, mate. There's a problem with Andrew. Don't get me wrong. There's nothing wrong with him. He just won't come out of his room."

"Perhaps we can go to him, then," said Ricky.

"You can try, but don't hold your breath."

Terry showed Ricky and Sheila to Andrew's bedroom. Terry knocked on the door. No reply. He knocked again. "Andrew, there's a friend of Esther's to see you. He plays poker," he said.

There was still no sign of movement from inside Andrew's room. Terry turned to Ricky and shrugged.

"Mind if I give it a try?" said Ricky.

"Carry on. Good luck to you."

Ricky put his ear close to the door and listened. Then he turned to Terry and Sheila and nodded. "Andrew, this is Ricky, a friend of Esther's. She says you're on the Internet. I do a bit of surfing myself and was wondering if you and I could have a chat before I go back to Brum."

Still no reply from Andrew, giving them no choice but to give up. They made their way back downstairs.

Andrew heard them. "So, Esther's back," he said to himself. "And it sounds as if she's got a boyfriend. I wonder if they've done *it*."

His mind went back to a Thursday morning, several years before.

Andrew's body and attitude changed just after his tenth

birthday, which was when his transformation from boy to man began. His body released massive amounts of testosterone into his bloodstream. Spots erupted on his face, along with the first signs of bristle. His pubic bone itched as hair began to grow. But he didn't know what was happening to him, and was embarrassed.

This alone might have set him back a year or so. Then he woke one morning to find his underpants wet with semen. He crept down the hall to the bathroom and went in. He could hear the shower going, but decided he'd enough time to clean himself and get out before whoever was in the cubicle finished. It was the urge to see who was inside the cubicle that led to his shame.

Esther had neglected to lock the bathroom door and didn't hear Andrew come in above the noise of streaming water. Leaving the bathroom door unlocked didn't concern her, as anyone coming in would hear that someone was in the shower and wait outside.

Andrew crawled over to the shower cubicle and peeped under the curtain. Esther was leaning back against the tiles as the exotic memories showed her what pleasures her body could experience by her own touch.

Andrew had never seen Esther like this. Steaming water trickled over beautiful breasts and down her lithe body. He'd never even seen breasts before. He knew about them, but as Esther caressed her special place a stirring in his own loins took him over. He masturbated. Urgently. Frantically. He'd no idea what he was doing, but the sight of his sister in an exotic pose compelled him. That spontaneous, boyish act later brought shame as he avoided looking at her at breakfast. Full of remorse he retired to his bedroom, vowing never to see the light of day again.

From that day on Andrew loved Esther in a different way. He adored her. His admiration for her knew no bounds. He read reports of her success in Hollywood after she left, and it was her he thought of when continuing to release sexual frustration on the occasions he found his penis to be inextricably, and painfully, erect. His imagination ran riot with erotic thoughts, and when he thought his brain would explode he trawled through soft-porn sites on the Internet. This led him to hack into all sorts of areas. Areas he'd become expert at hacking into.

But Esther had never written. He didn't like her for that. Perhaps she knew what he'd done, and didn't love him anymore. He desperately needed to see her, but didn't know if he could. And yet he had to find a way of telling her what he'd found out only that morning.

Downstairs, Terry, Ricky and Sheila were talking.

"Have you got time to show me the money hand, Ricky?" said Terry. He winked at Sheila to impress her with his knowledge of poker. "That's the hand that won him the two million," he said. "They call it the 'money hand'."

"Sure. Sheila's going to show me round Margate, but there's plenty of time for that. Got some cards? I already noticed you've got a card table."

"Yeah. Joan likes people to think we play bridge. Cards will be in the drawer underneath. I'll put the kettle on."

Rather than show Terry the final hand, which was a bit boring, Ricky showed him the earlier one which had been decisive. He dealt Terry the Ace and Queen he had held at the time, and the rubbish Johnson had had to himself. "I've seen Johnson," Terry said. "Did you beat him?"

"Yes. It came down to the two of us in the end."

"Blimey. You must be good, then. Mind you, an Ace and a Queen is a good starting hand."

"That's what I thought, so I bet it. Then the first three cards were dealt face up on..."

Terry grabbed Ricky's shoulder and put his finger to his lips. He pointed to the lounge door. They all heard a creaking of wood. Someone was coming down the stairs. Terry motioned Ricky to continue.

"The flop came King of Spades, King of Hearts, and Jack of Spades..." Ricky stopped again as the handle on the lounge door moved downwards. They all looked. The door opened and Andrew appeared. Sheila's hand flew to her mouth. The sight of him standing there sent her cold.

Andrew's confinement had resulted in his skin becoming pale white in colour. His sunken eyes had dark rings around them and his hair had obviously been cut with scissors. He stood, framed in the door, like Rip van Winkle. No one said a word. Sheila looked down at his feet. Bare ankles showed no spare flesh. Andrew was a mess. He looked at Ricky, and spoke: "Where's your stick?"

"It's — well, it's — back at the hotel. In my suitcase."

"Go and fetch it and bring it to me. On your own." Andrew turned on his heel and walked out.

"Well, I'll be blowed," said Terry, scratching his head. "He's come down. Just like that. What was he on about with the stick?"

"He must mean my nightstick. It's a lump of oak, in the shape of a policeman's truncheon. It's my lucky charm. Although quite how he knew about it I don't know."

"Perhaps they've shown highlights on the telly," said Sheila.

"Perhaps. Yes, that must be it. Anyway, I'd better go and fetch it. Back in a bit."

Ricky tapped on Andrew's door again. Andrew opened it and beckoned him to go in. It took Ricky a while to adjust his vision in the dim light. He was surprised to find the room tidy, imagining that if Andrew hadn't left his room for over twelve months it would be in a disgusting state. The well-worn chair in front of a computer gave a clue. Andrew didn't do anything other than sleep in the bed, and sit in front of the brightly-lit screen of his PC.

"You'll have to sit on the bed," said Andrew. "Show me the stick."

Ricky handed him the nightstick. Andrew's eyes lit up as he ran his hand over its smooth, oak surface. "I don't know how I knew you had this, but I did," he said. "It's warm."

"Yes. I feel it's warm to the touch. Must be the grain. Are you bleeding?"

Andrew turned his hand over, and licked the blood running down his finger. "It's not because of the grain. It is warm. Yes, I'm bleeding. I got a splinter in my thumb, ages ago."

"You should get it seen to. It could go septic."

Andrew looked at Ricky for a moment, then said, "No. It's OK. Besides, I like the taste."

Ricky knew Andrew needed help. "Look, there are some

great poker sites on the web. Let me show you some..."

"Forget the poker. Sit down and watch."

Andrew typed something into the computer and clicked Search. A web page came up. He typed again, putting numbers and letters in. Then he clicked again. The screen flickered, and something else came up. More letters, another page, more numbers—then the page flickered again, and another web page came up. This time, the screen showed a clear warning:

SECURE ACCESS. YOU RISK PROSECUTION IF YOU GO FURTHER.

"Andrew. You can't do that," said Ricky.

"Shut up and watch." Andrew typed again. The screen flickered and changed. This time he'd gained access to the file of CIA director Al Green. Ricky gasped.

Andrew turned to him. "Look," he said.

Ricky read the file. 'British starlet Esther Clayton invited to Camp David by President Jefferey. She's not the first young lady to have spent the weekend there alone. An aide took her to a hospital, off Highway One. She was in a coma. Upon her discharge she took a flight to the UK. On that flight she met a poker player by the name of Richmond Bates. He accompanied Miss Clayton to her home in Margate, southern England. Surveillance only at this time.'

Ricky was astonished. "What does this mean?"

"It means, my friend, that you and Esther are being watched. What we need to know is what happened at Camp David. Where's Esther?"

"She's gone to London, to see her agent. Sheila and I saw her off a couple of hours ago."

"Well, we'd better find her then."

Fortunately Esther had booked herself into the Connaught Hotel in her own name. Even so it took Andrew several hours to locate her. It was one o'clock in the morning before he found she was staying there.

"Right. Let's get after her," said Andrew.

"Hang on a minute. We've got to think this through. We'd better tell Terry first."

"No. The fewer people who know about this the better. If Terry and Joan start spouting off, the CIA will know we're on to them."

"What should we do, then?"

"We know they spotted you on the plane with her. But I haven't been out of this room for over twelve months. They can't have seen me. I'll go to London and warn Esther. You stay here with Sheila."

Ricky didn't like it, but he knew that Andrew was right. Andrew took the first train next morning, wondering what it was like for Ricky to know his sister.

If Andrew had been at his computer at nine o'clock that morning he would've seen the latest update in the CIA director's file.

Chapter 21

Graham de Courcey

A porter showed Esther to her suite at the Connaught Hotel, room 620, just after five o'clock. *A shower will freshen me up before I go to see Graham*, she decided.

Esther stripped off in a marble-covered bathroom and looked at herself in the mirror. *Might book myself in at Morrison's to have my hair done while I'm in town*, she thought. She tied her hair up with a towel and took another look. Esther wasn't a vain woman, but she liked what she saw. Getting onto the scales brought a pleasant surprise. *Haven't put an ounce on since I was eighteen*, she thought. Getting off the scales, she turned sideways.

Her complexion was rosy, and flawless. She turned the other way. Her full breasts had lost their teenage swelling round the areola of the nipples and taken on a look of ripeness. She still didn't need a brassière to hold them. They stood on their own, proud and bouncy.

Her flat stomach rose slightly before levelling off. She saw a perfectly shaped bottom and long, slender legs, tapering off to slim ankles and feet. *Feet are funny things. I'll do*, she decided.

The phone rang in Graham's apartment at 18.10. "Hello," he said.

"Hi. It's me," said Esther.

"Esther, darling. Have a nice trip?"

"Yes, thanks. I'm booked in at the Connaught. I was wondering if you're free tonight. It might get a bit hectic tomorrow."

"Tonight's fine. Kept it free, just in case. What d'you want to do?"

"Well, I'm sort of keeping my head down, at least until after tomorrow. How about you come and have dinner here?

Room six-twenty."

"About eight?"

"Eight's fine. Give me a ring from Reception when you get here, will you?"

"Will do. See you later."

Esther decided to phone Ricky. He wasn't at the Swan and she was diverted to his voicemail when she tried his mobile.

At 19.55 Graham de Courcey strode into the foyer at the Connaught, carrying flowers. A bunch always went down well with the ladies, he found. He took a look at himself in a mirror in Reception and straightened his grey and silver tie. "You dog," he growled, baring his teeth. Then he turned on his heels, and walked to the desk.

"Miss Clayton's room, please," he said to the desk clerk. "Tell her I'm here, and send a bottle of Krug to her room."

"Certainly, sir," said the desk clerk. "Miss Clayton's in room six-twenty. I'll tell her you're on your way. She did say she was expecting a gentleman."

"That's no business of yours, m'boy. Just tell her I'm here and send up the Krug."

"Yes, sir."

Esther answered Graham's tap on the door and welcomed him with a kiss on the cheek. "Come in. The flowers are gorgeous. You are thoughtful."

"You're more beautiful than ever," he said. "If there's a lovelier woman on the planet, I've yet to meet her." He returned her kiss, and went in.

Esther motioned him to a settee. "Martini?"

"Yes, please. Red. Pop a cherry in it, would you? And drown it with lemonade."

Esther made him his drink. "What have you been up to lately?" she said. "I read you had a fall from your horse."

"Yes. The damn thing fell at the last fence at Cheltenham when I was ten lengths clear in the amateurs' race. Won a race with him at Sandown last year, though. He's a nice prospect. Haven't done much else, lately. There's a party coming up at Fiona's place. Will you have time to go?"

Esther looked at him as she gave him his drink. Her heart wasn't beating any faster. "I hope to do something, but I've got to see my agent first. Try to calm him down a bit."

"You've created quite a stir in the press."

"I'll tell you all about it. Would you like to eat here, in case we get swamped downstairs?"

"Fine. I'll put some music on while you order."

There was a knock at the door as Esther picked up the phone. It was the wine waiter, bringing the Krug. "Ah, just what the doctor ordered," said Graham. "Put it on the table over there, will you?" The waiter put the champagne bucket on the table, and left.

"Did you order that? How lovely. It's a long time since I drank Krug." said Esther, hoping he remembered serving Krug at his party on *that* night. If he did he didn't show it.

Graham was much older than her, but she didn't mind. Men her own age never attracted her. Their juvenile behaviour turned her off. She'd seen enough people living off the state, too. She had decided long ago it was better to associate herself with men who'd grown up and made something of themselves first. But she was confused now. Alan's death brought home the realisation that even if she made the right decisions, Fate could ruin anything she did. *Perhaps I should just live for the day*, she thought. *Dad used to say he'd've been world champion if he hadn't lost his arm. But it doesn't seem to bother him. What if something happened to me, and I couldn't be an actress?*

Esther suddenly realised she wanted to be successful more than anything in the world, but that perhaps she ought to live for the moment as well. Perhaps she didn't need to love Graham. She needed to know though, and decided to see how he acted tonight. "What d'you want to eat?" she said.

Graham ordered asparagus and a steak from the menu, she sole meunière and a side salad. The mention of asparagus brought a smile to her face, and she thought of Ricky for a second.

"Penny for them?" said Graham.

"Oh, it's nothing. I just remembered a joke about asparagus."

"Come and sit down. I want to have a look at you."

Esther sat beside him on the settee. He put down his martini and looked at her. "Y'know, I've met a lot of women in my time, and I've led a privileged life. My wealth is inherited and my education reflected that. I've always socialised in the best circles and been able to afford virtually anything I ever wanted. But when I look at you, I realise nothing I can buy, or have, can give me the feeling I get when I look into your eyes."

He put his hands on her shoulders. "And you're a nice person, too. I've seen what fame and fortune can do to egos. You haven't changed at all. You're a good woman, Esther, and I love you very much."

She put both hands round his head and pulled him to her. "I was hoping you'd say that."

They kissed. Her lips were soft and inviting. Graham felt her breasts pressing against his chest and the quickening of her heartbeat. Her fragrance took him back to the night in his apartment two years before.

Esther, with Erato's memories gone, felt free and opened up her heart to him once again.

Graham laid her gently onto the settee and moved a hand to her special place. He felt the smoothness of the inside of her thigh, and moved his hand upwards.

Graham didn't get the expected reaction when he entered her. She pulled away sharply, and put her hands to her head as memories came flooding back. "I was raped."

"What d'you mean?"

"No, not you—the President. I was at Camp David. My head went fuzzy when I went to bed. He came in the middle of the night and raped me. I couldn't make him stop."

Panic gripped Esther and she jumped up from the settee. "Oh, my God," she said.

Graham held her. "Calm down. We'll sort this out. Have a drink and tell me what happened."

There was a knock at the door as Graham said this. It was the waiter, bringing their order. "Put it on the table over there," Graham said. He picked up a plate after the waiter left.

"I couldn't eat now," Esther said.

"I know you're confused, but it's best to go through the motions, believe me. We don't have to eat, but routine will help you sort things out in your head. I'll pour you another glass of champagne while you lay the table. Tell me about it while you're doing it."

Esther recounted events at Camp David while fiddling with her food. She even managed to eat something when she'd finished talking.

Then Graham spoke. "Can you carry on tomorrow? I have a contact or two at the Home Office. I don't exactly know what you want to do about it, but I promise I'll support you as best I can. You have to do it right, though."

"Yes, I suppose so. I don't know what to do. But he won't get away with it. I feel dirty. It's disgusting. A man in his position. I could kill him."

After finishing their meal they sat quietly watching television for a while, each with their own thoughts. Esther's mind was racing. Now she remembered everything that had happened she was angry beyond words. But she knew Graham was right. These were powerful people. As if reading her mind, Graham said, "Will you be alright if I go? I don't want to leave you, but the more I think about it the more I feel I can do something straight away. I happen to know the British Ambassador is attending a dinner in Washington soon. There are people I know who've contacts there. They might be useful."

"I'll be OK. I'm shattered now. Phone me tomorrow?"

Graham kissed her on the cheek. "I will. Don't worry, we'll sort this out."

After he'd gone Esther felt panicky and wished she'd asked him to stay while she sorted her head out. The events at Camp David kept coming back, over and over. *Him on top of me.* Then she remembered her reaction when Erato took over after he first touched her. "God," she said. "What was I doing? Why was I like that?"

With the oak splinter gone now, Esther got no answers from Erato, just pictures of *him,* and even worse, *her.* She felt dirty and knew she had to shower again.

The hot water calmed her a little, but brought more exhaustion. Afterwards she finished the Krug and abandoned herself to a fitful sleep.

Graham drove the Daimler to Whitehall himself. This was business he wanted to keep as low-profile as possible. Esther was about to find there was more to Graham than she thought.

He put his thumb on a button on the dashboard and waited. A red light began to flash in the rear-view mirror. He looked at it for a moment, then back to the road ahead. After a few seconds a message, blinking on the mirror, said "Identity of Commander de Courcey recognised." Then part of the dashboard opened up and a hands-free phone set rolled out. He pressed a button and waited.

Graham could trace his lineage back almost to when the Great Oak had been a seedling. The de Courceys came to Britain supporting William the Conqueror and settled after the defeat of the English King, Harold, in 1066. William gave his ancestor land in Cornwall, and the title Baron. The family motto was 'Defendum Coronam'—"I shall defend the Crown".

The following six hundred years saw much change in the way of life in Britain. The de Courceys showed their allegiance to the Crown by bending many times as the monarchy changed hands. They survived, somehow. It was a scourge of another kind which almost wiped them out. Smallpox raged throughout Britain and Europe in 1710. By the time the disease was overcome only one debt-ridden, profligate cousin, Richard de Courcey, remained alive.

A light on the button blinked green. Then the audio on the hands-free kicked in. Graham heard the sound of a phone ringing at the other end. The ringing stopped and a voice answered. "Graham, what can I do for you? I hope it's good. I had to cut short a conversation with you-know-who and find the nearest bathroom to answer this."

"Good evening, Prime Minister. Sorry to've disturbed you. A matter which may have serious consequences has come up. I could do with your advice. Can I see you tonight?"

"Well, I'm at a dinner at the Mansion House at the moment. Shall we say Downing Street, in an hour?"

"Thank you, sir. I'm on my way." The phone clicked, and the line went dead.

Richard de Courcey had to take a wife in order to take over the baronetcy. At least the plague of smallpox made his choice easier. There were plenty of traders—become rich by exploiting trade routes recently opened in the Indies and

Americas who wanted to further their ambitions in society by marrying into the aristocracy.

One such trader, George Wall, who brought in nutmeg and other spices from the Indies, approached Richard with the offer of an arrangement. He proposed that Richard marry his daughter Constance, thereby conferring on her, by marriage, the title Baroness. Mr Wall promised a dowry of £250,000 (a huge sum at the time) in return. The union was agreed and the nuptials arranged. The couple married in Exeter Cathedral in 1712.

The marriage produced three sons. The first, James, was born in 1712. He grew up to be a shifty character, who followed in his father's footsteps by running up a string of debts and being a menace to society in general. He was hanged in 1748 after being found guilty of forging a bond in his father's name. This despite the pleadings of his family in high places.

Their second son, Geoffrey, born in 1715, regained the family honour somewhat by performing the first of several feats of derring-do by members of subsequent generations of the family. Geoffrey invested heavily in the East India Company, which traded in America among other places, but became worried when relations between Britain and America soured in the 1770s. The British Government, wanting to protect its own interests in an increasingly Republican atmosphere, sent a fleet to blockade New York. At the age of sixty, and at his own expense, Geoffrey sailed to New York to help the Admiralty in its mission. Once there and finding the sailors low food and ammunition, he took it upon himself to organise a series of moonlight raids on enemy positions and nearby settlements. The provisions he plundered gave renewed hope, and stimulated the sailors to a sturdy defence of their position.

The war was eventually lost and America became a republic, but Geoffrey returned a hero. George III, hearing of his exploits, restored all honour to the de Courcey family and insisted that a member of the de Courcey family be at his side at all times. Geoffrey had the office of 'Silver Stick In Waiting' conferred on him, which entailed carrying a heavy, silver-tipped staff, with which he protected the monarch night and day.

Geoffrey had fallen in love with America, however, and soon left a son to manage the Cornwall estate while he went back and settled in Virginia. While there he sired two more sons, but never lost contact with home. The family kept up this tradition of closeness after his death in 1790.

A great-great-grandson, Colonel Harry de Courcey, led his brigade, which included the 16th Ohio Volunteer Infantry, over the bayou and across 100 yards of open ground, between the bayou and the first line of rifle pits defended by federal troops. This action took place at Chicksaw Bluffs in 1862 during the American Civil War.

From then on, both sides of the family worked in positions of importance within respective governments on either side of the Atlantic.

After the Second World War both governments wanted to improve the gathering of intelligence and information, which until then had been unco-ordinated. America set up the CIA Britain MI5, of which Graham was now top man. The Parker-Bowles family took over the office of 'Silver Stick In Waiting'.

To the likes of Graham and Al Green, this was like giving them the keys to their country's coffers. As governments either side of the Atlantic came and went, they remained in power. A power they used to cut through the red tape of convention.

Educated at Eton and the military college at Sandhurst, Graham showed the same devotion to duty as his forebears. *But*, the President of the United States had raped Esther, and all loyalty was about to be set aside in her defence. The special relationship didn't include this situation. *This* was a matter of honour. Besides, the information could be invaluable to British security forces.

Next Morning

Andrew almost fell out of the train at Waterloo Station. Two years of inactivity had left him totally unfit. He hadn't eaten for hours, either, which made things worse. He didn't care. All he knew was he had to hail a cab and get to Esther.

"The Connaught Hotel please, as quick as you can."

"Having a laugh aren't you, mister?" the cabbie said. "At this time of day you'll be lucky to get there in time to turn round and catch the last train back to where you've just come from."

"Please, do your best." The cabbie looked at Andrew through his rear-view mirror. He decided he'd better, before the geezer who was speaking croaked. "OK, guvnor, but it's on the other side of town, so make yourself comfortable."

Esther answered a knock, thinking it would be her agent. Andrew stood swaying in front of her.

"Andrew. What on earth? ..." He fell into her arms.

"I had to come. I... You're being watched."

Esther supported him while he staggered to the settee and flopped down. "Have you eaten?" she said.

"No. I came straight away. Ricky's with Sheila. I found out on the Internet..."

Esther stopped him. "Sit there. I'll get you a warm drink. What's happened?"

After Andrew had pulled himself together he told her about the CIA involvement, and that she was being watched.

"I know," she said. "Well, I know that something happened. I didn't know I was being watched, though. I'll try Graham."

Esther got no reply from Graham's apartment. She phoned Ricky, and Terry's house, without getting an answer from either. Then she tried the Watsons, but Norman knew only that Sheila was out with Ricky.

Chapter 22
Mistaken Identity

Margaret had kept to herself after being given a council house, but decided to show her face when she heard Esther was in town. There might be something in it for her, now Esther was rich and famous. She was her sister, after all.

Margaret strapped the twins into her £400 buggy, and made her way quickly to her mother's house. Joan opened the door.

"Oh, it's you," she said.

"Come on, Mom. Don't be like that. Just thought you'd like to see the kids, that's all."

"You're too late. You've missed her."

"Missed who?"

Joan sneered. "You know exactly who. Esther, that's who. She's gone to London."

"Esther. How nice. When did she come home?"

"Cut the crap, Margaret. You'd better come in. Your father's in the lounge."

Margaret squeezed the buggy down the hall, and into the lounge. Joan noticed one of the twins drawing a snotty line down the wallpaper, and made a mental note to get the Flash liquid out after Margaret had gone. *Is there a funny smell as well?* she wondered.

"Helloh," drawled Terry in his usual manner. "Come in and sit yourself down." He struggled with the buckles on the buggy. "Put the kettle on, Joan," he said.

Terry was endearingly English in this department. Putting the kettle on was the first thing to do when people came to visit. He was a kind man despite his faults, and had a generous heart.

"Hi, Margaret," said Elizabeth, who was sitting on a side chair, twiddling her fingers nervously as dehydration blotted her energy away. "How are you?"

139

"OK, thanks. Sorry to hear about Alan."

"I know. Why he did this to me, I don't know. I'm OK. Could do with a shag, though."

Unlike Esther, Margaret didn't flinch at this. She knew what Elizabeth meant, in a way. Her plan to have babies. But she didn't realise she'd get to like sex for its own sake. She'd almost been in love with the father of the twins, and was confused now. He hadn't ignored them like he was supposed to, and wanted to be a real father to them. And to make things worse, he was working. That situation wasn't what Margaret had had in mind. If she wasn't careful she'd lose some of her benefits. Trouble was, having sex with him was different from having sex with the others. He'd only to touch her and she'd start to orgasm.

They came to an arrangement—that he could stay at weekends, but not in the week. That way the benefits people would be less likely to be working, therefore less likely to catch them cohabiting.

"Yeah. I know what you mean," she said. "Here, hold one of the kids."

"Oh—do I have to? You know they dribble all over the place."

"Well, kids do that. Offer her up a tit, if you like. That'll help your cravings."

Joan brought in tea, and sat down. "What's new with you, Margaret?" she said.

"Oh, not much. Bloody kids are driving me crazy, what with birthdays coming up and all. Still, we should get something off Esther now she's back."

"Don't be disgusting," said Joan (who was privately hoping the same thing). "Besides, I've already told you you've missed her."

The twin Elizabeth was holding squirmed in her lap. "Margaret, put the television on. I think it wants to watch *The Simpsons* or something."

"Here, give her to me," said Terry. "What d'you think about Andrew? Esther's friend got him to come down. He's a poker player. Won two million dollars in a tournament."

"Where's he now?" said Margaret.

"Sheila's showing him round Margate."

Margaret thought for a second, then said, "Mom, I've got some shopping to do. Got to go now."

With that, she piled the twins back into the buggy and went in search of Sheila.

"You haven't finished your tea," Joan shouted as Margaret disappeared down the path.

Margaret surmised that Sheila would show Ricky the seafront first. She pushed the buggy down Queens Drive and Eaton Road, before turning onto Marine Drive. As she rounded the corner, she glanced through the darkened windows of a large, black car parked in a lay-by. Three men, wearing raincoats and trilbies sat inside, like statues. Seeing Sheila and Ricky sitting talking on a bench on the front, Margaret made her way towards them.

"Seriously, Rick," Sheila was saying. "Why did you see Esther home? It's a long way out of your way."

"Don't know really. She just took my breath away. When I spoke to her on the plane, it was as if I'd known her all my life."

Sheila put her arm through his. "Look. You're a nice guy, but you've only known her a few days. I've known her all my life. She's my best friend. I hope you don't hurt her. Are you married?"

"No. I think I fell in love with her the moment I set eyes on her."

"Good boy. Come on, I think it's going to rain. Let's go back to the Swan."

Margaret picked up the pace as the pair got up and walked across the road. She was about to shout to them when one of the men she'd seen brushed past her.

The nightstick in Ricky's pocket grew warm, as the man in the trilby approached, fast, from behind. Ricky, feeling something behind him, began to turn; but before he did so, the man drew alongside and prodded Sheila with an umbrella. The nightstick became red-hot.

Margaret raised her hand to protest. Ricky opened his mouth to say something, but Sheila staggered and fell to the ground. The man broke into a run.

Ricky instinctively pulled out the nightstick and threw it at him in one movement. The man fell in a heap as it hit him behind his left ear. PC Kitchen, watching all this from a patrol car, gave a short blast from its siren and switched on the blue lights. As Ricky retrieved the nightstick, he took the man's wallet from an inside pocket. Then he ran back to Sheila.

The patrol car pulled up with a screech of brakes, and PC Kitchen jumped out. "What's going on?" he said.

"That man. He hit Sheila with an umbrella. I saw him," said Margaret. The constable looked in the direction where the man lay.

The black car pulled up silently while the man was regaining his senses. He jumped up as its door opened, and got in. Then the car sped off round the corner. PC Kitchen looked at the car, then at Sheila. He'd a decision to make. Once that car got to Hawley Street, he wouldn't know which way it had gone. But this woman's breathing was shallow. Her needs were more important. He made a note of the car's number plate instead. PC Kitchen called for an ambulance on his shoulder radio, and covered Sheila with a blanket.

Within minutes she was on her way to Ramsgate Hospital. Ricky went with her, escorted by the policeman and a wail of sirens. Sheila seemed to be feverish now, and her blood pressure was dropping. Ricky told the crew that Sheila had collapsed. The nightstick, warm in his pocket, reminded him about the man, and he added: "A chap prodded her out of the way with an umbrella. Then she fell on the floor. She's been like this ever since."

A paramedic looked at him. "Prodded her with an umbrella?"

"Yes. Well, he appeared to."

"Hook her up to an intravenous drip, Joe," the medic said. "There's no sign of trauma, but I fancy we might find a small puncture wound somewhere when we get her to A&E."

A doctor ordered Sheila's clothes to be cut off, and a thorough medical examination of her was made. Breathing was becoming difficult for Sheila now as fluid built up on her lungs. She was also sweating profusely.

The examination revealed one tiny puncture mark, just

above her left hip. The doctor found a small pellet lodged in the belt round her trousers. The position of the pellet corresponded to the mark on Sheila's hip. The doctor called PC Kitchen in.

"I'm treating this woman as having been poisoned. Probably by this pellet, which was supposed to be injected into her when she was prodded with the umbrella. The pellet would then have dissolved."

He showed the pellet to PC Kitchen, who scratched his head. The doctor continued, "It looks as if the tip of the umbrella came into contact with the belt first, and lodged there. I just hope she hasn't received the full dose. It's an old fashioned method of assassination, but most effective. I recall..." He broke off as Sheila began to choke, leaving PC Kitchen to wander off in disbelief. "Assassination. In Margate?" he muttered. Spotting Ricky waiting in the corridor, PC Kitchen approached him. "You'll have to come to the station and make a statement, sir," he said.

Ricky, his mind in a whirl, had a feeling he ought to follow Andrew to London as quickly as he could. "It's important I get to London, officer."

"Look, I could arrest you, but I'm asking you to co-operate, the young lady with the pushchair as well. I need you both to make statements, then you'll be free to go."

Ricky looked at his watch. *Looks like I've got no choice*, he thought. "OK, let's make it quick."

Ricky gave a statement and tried to sort his mind out as he walked back to the Swan. *What on earth's going on?* he thought. He took out the wallet and opened it. A business card for American Investments was the only thing inside. He wondered if PC Kitchen had made a note of the number plate, and decided to give him a call. The constable wasn't very forthcoming with answers. "I'm afraid I can't release that information, Mister Bates. We can't have you running around vigilante-fashion, can we?"

Ricky wondered if all policemen talked like that. "Look, officer," he said. "I understand, but there's more to it than you think. Like I told you at the station, there's no reason for Sheila Watson to have been attacked. What you don't know is, from behind she looks a lot like her friend Esther Clayton, the movie actress. It might be a case of mistaken identity. Miss Clayton went to London yesterday, on business. I'm worried she might be at risk from a deranged fan. Remember John Lennon? If I could go to London and brief her security people, it might prevent something worse happening."

Ricky crossed his fingers, then added: "It wouldn't reflect well if it became known at a later date, that we could've prevented something happening, would it?"

PC Kitchen took his point and decided he'd better cover his back. "What I can tell you is, the number plate is registered to a company in London called American Investments. That's all we know at the moment."

"Great, thanks. How's Miss Watson doing?"

"She's stable. We've got a man at her bedside, waiting for her to regain consciousness."

"OK, thanks. I'll tell Miss Clayton."

Ricky put the phone down. *American Investments again,* he thought. *Wonder if I could find out anything about them on the Internet. Should I phone Esther? Better not. It might spook her. She'll probably be back tomorrow. How am I going to tell her about Sheila? Oh, well. Computer first.*

Terry answered Ricky's knock. "Helloh. Come on in. I've just put the kettle on," he said.

"Have you heard? Sheila collapsed on the front. She's in hospital." Ricky said.

"No. I hadn't heard. What happened?"

"Don't know yet, they're waiting for her to come round. D'you mind if I surf the Net? There's a firm I want to look up."

"Course you can. Blimey. There's a lot going on, today."

Ricky switched Andrew's computer on. Fortunately he hadn't entered a password. Nobody else ever went in his room, so Andrew didn't think it necessary. Ricky typed in *American Investments,* and pressed Search.

Several addresses around the world came up. The London office was in Soho. *Not very high-profile for an investment company,* he thought. Then another address caught his eye. Langley, Virginia. Headquarters of the CIA.

He went back to the menu, and considered for a moment. His eyes settled on Andrew's notepad, by the side of the computer. He picked it up, and held it to the light. He could make out writing, and the letters *www* but that was all. There were numbers, and words, then more numbers, and more words. Then two words. *Two words. That's what Andrew used to get the CIA file up.*

He ripped the top sheet of paper off, and held it to the light. It was a website address. Spotting a pencil, he began to trace lightly over the paper. Slowly the address became clear. Going back into the Internet, Ricky went through the same sequence that Andrew had. A chill ran down his spine as he read an update in the director's file:

April 2nd 1991.
Agents obtained files of UK surveillance target. They confirm the hospital tests show her to be pregnant. Message to UK operatives authorising termination of target with extreme prejudice sent June 17th, 14.00 E.S.T. First reports are that agents made the hit, but wrongly identified the target. Further message sent to London office, telling them to make sure this time.

"My God," said Ricky. He knew now that he *must* get to Esther. He decided he couldn't risk panic by phoning the hotel. "Never know who might be listening." He shut the computer down, and considered his options.

It would take hours to get to London, whichever way he went. Unless...

"I'm going to London." he shouted, nearly knocking Terry over as he came out of the kitchen with a pot of tea in his hand.

"Well, don't mind me, will you?" Terry shouted after him.

Ricky scanned the row of leaflets in Reception at the Swan Hotel. Sure enough, there was one advertising pleasure trips round Margate Bay. He grabbed one, ordered a taxi, then went to his room. He was slipping the nightstick in his pocket as Reception rang to say that the taxi had arrived.

While Ricky was getting into the taxi, a black car pulled up outside Terry's house. Two men wearing raincoats and trilbies got out, walked down the path and knocked on the front door. Joan opened it.

"Mrs Clayton? We're investigating the incident on the front this afternoon. May we come in?"

Joan glanced at what, to her, looked like a warrant card, then at the man who flourished it, and let them in.

"Helloh," said Terry. "Come on in, I'll put the kettle on."

Once inside, the man who'd spoken to Joan punched Terry full on the jaw, knocking him to the floor. As Joan raised her hand to protest, the other man hit her in the solar plexus. She slumped, open-mouthed, against the sideboard and slid to the floor. The other man hit Terry again, "Where's Esther Clayton?" he said.

"Get stuffed," said Terry. The man took out a silenced revolver and pointed it at Joan.

"Where's Esther Clayton?" As the man turned to ask him again, Terry caught him flush on the jaw with a right hook. The other man shot Terry in the knee as his partner collapsed in a heap.

Neither Terry nor Joan knew anything, other than that Esther had gone to London. The man Terry had punched sat, holding his swollen jaw, keeping watch through the lounge window, while the other one had a look round upstairs. It took him over an hour to work it all out from the computer. By then Ricky was halfway up the Thames in a motorboat, heading for London.

Margaret and Elizabeth had been out shopping with the twins. They walked down the path to Terry's house. Elizabeth put her key in the door. She turned to Margaret. "It's open," she said.

"Let me have a look." Margaret gently pushed the door open. "Mom. Dad. Have you left the front door open?" she called. Getting no reply, they made their way inside. Margaret pushed the lounge door open with the buggy, and looked in. There on the floor lay her parents. Margaret fainted.

Chapter 23

Rachel Jefferey Intervenes

In Langley, Virginia, the telephone console on the desk of CIA supremo Al Green flashed. He flicked the switch. "What?" he snapped.

"Mister Green, it's the First Lady," said his secretary.

"Put her through."

"No, sir—I mean, she's here, and wants to see you."

Goddammit. What the hell does she want? he thought. "OK. Send her in."

President Jeffery's wife stalked into his office, and plonked herself down in a chair even as Green was opening his mouth to offer her a seat. She'd got a bee in her bonnet about something, and he reckoned he could guess what. Better be careful, though. He knew she held her husband in contempt, and also that she had considerable influence over him.

"Rachel. How nice..."

"Cut the bull. What's that idiot been up to now? And watch what you say to me. I've got my own sources, don't forget."

Al sighed, and decided he'd better tell her what her philandering husband had been up to at Camp David. "Are you sure you want to know?" he asked.

"Why d'you think I'm here? Get on with it, before I twist your balls off and shove them where the sun don't shine. You men make me sick. All you ever think about is money and pussy. Why is it that you all think the road to happiness lies between a woman's thighs?"

"I'm sure the President loves you very much. He just takes advantage of silly girls who throw themselves at him from time to time..."

"If you don't..."

"However," he continued. "This time things are more serious."

"Serious? How serious?"

"Well, looks like his aide gave Esther Clayton, an actress, a very stiff cocktail while they were at Camp David. It knocked her out. I can only tell it straight, Rachel. Your husband then raped Miss Clayton. Hospital tests show that she's pregnant."

Rachel Jefferey jumped from her seat. "Jesus, mother and Joseph. The stupid fool. I'll have him killed. I'll have his balls cut off and fed to him in a McDonald's. That'll stop him. Who else knows about this?"

"Fortunately the aide had the presence of mind to bundle her off to hospital anonymously, before she came to. When asked the reason for her admission, he implied that she might be suffering from a drugs overdose. She doesn't remember a thing."

Green paused before continuing. "Look, I know how you feel. My advice is to consider his position before you act. Think of his office. There are other ways."

"What d'you mean?"

"You and I are the only ones who know about it, apart from him. One thing's for sure, we can't take the chance of her suddenly remembering anything. To that end I've ordered operatives in the field to eliminate her."

Rachel Jefferey considered this. Green didn't know it, but she had her own agenda. After a pause, she spoke. "Call off your dogs for a while. He'll keep till I decide what to do with him. I want to meet this woman. What can she do, even if she does remember?"

"These things are precise these days. What if she had a DNA test done?"

"It's been barely a month since she was at Camp David. She can't make that sort of test for a while yet. I only need a week. You can do whatever you want after that."

"OK. But she's in England now. I don't know if I can get in touch with the agents in time to stop them."

"Al. If you don't, the order at McDonald's will be for a double-decker."

"OK. I get your drift. Leave it to me. I'll see you out."

"That'll take time. I'll see myself out. Just make the call."

The phone rang at the offices of American Investments. Agent Hill answered it.

"Who's that?" said the voice at the other end.

"Agent Hill, sir."

"Where's Agent Cainer?"

"In the field, sir. Carrying out your orders."

"Has he got a radio?"

"Yes, sir."

"Call him, and tell him to stand down. Has the mission been accomplished?"

"No, sir. But the whereabouts of the target has been verified. She booked into the Connaught Hotel yesterday. Agent Cainer and two operatives are on their way. I'm sure they'll accomplish the mission this time."

"Did you not hear me, Agent Hill? I said *stand them down.* If they kill that woman, I'll hang your guts on a flagpole on the White House lawn. D'you understand me, Agent Hill?"

Agent Hill jumped out of his chair, and saluted. "Sir. Yes, sir," he said.

Agent Hill tried to contact Cainer on the short-wave set, with no luck. He tried again. All he got was crackling from the speaker. He looked at his watch. 19.45. Then he tried the personal radios. Same result. He began to sweat, and looked at his watch again. 19.46. *The Connaught's not far away. Maybe I can get there before anything happens. I can keep trying to get hold of Cainer on short-wave while I'm driving*, he thought. Agent Hill grabbed his car keys and a radio set, and ran to the underground car park.

Chapter 24

The Connaught Hotel

Andrew was exhausted and went straight to bed. Frightened to call anyone, Esther fretted the time away, waiting for the phone to ring. Her words rushed out when Graham phoned, just after two o'clock. "My brother Andrew's turned up out of the blue. He found something on the Internet, to do with the CIA. They're watching me, apparently. What shall I do? I can't ring home, and I just don't know what to do."

"Whoa. Slow down," said Graham. "Above all, you must stay calm."

The pitch of Esther's voice raised now as she approached hysteria. "What d'you mean, stay calm?"

"I told you. I've contacts at the Home Office. I won't be long."

"Please hurry."

Graham tried to reassure her. "You're inside a suite, in a hotel, a hundred miles away from where they think you are. It's not likely they know where you are, but I do. I'm on my way. Just don't answer the door until you know it's me, OK?"

"OK. But please hurry."

Esther put the phone down and went to check on Andrew. He was sleeping peacefully. She sat on the side of the bed, and watched him. She almost burst into tears at the bedraggled state of him, then smiled as she realised how brave he'd been to come after her. She felt his forehead, and ran her fingers lightly through his hair. *He's a bit too warm*, she decided.

She went back into the lounge, thinking she'd open a window. Looking out, she couldn't decide who could be friend or assassin. *Crazy*, she thought.

Returning to Andrew, she lay down beside him, and cuddled him. The steady beat of his heart calmed her, and she slept. Her last thoughts as she dozed off were of Ricky. *Well, you certainly got Andrew to come out of his room. Where are you now? What are you doing?*

Esther woke to the sound of the phone ringing. Andrew stirred as she jumped up to answer it. "Hello," she said.

"Where are you?" Graham asked.

"In the suite, where are you?"

"If you'd open the door, you'd find out."

Esther's giggle as she opened the door to find Graham, leaning against the corridor wall with a mobile in his hand, released a little of the tension. "Sorry, I just nodded off," she said.

"Well you had me worried for a moment. Where's this brother of yours?"

While Andrew was telling Graham what he knew, Ricky was disembarking at Hammersmith Bridge. He flagged a cab down, telling the cabbie he'd get double fare if he made it to the hotel within thirty minutes.

While Ricky was in the cab, a large black car pulled up outside the Connaught Hotel. Two men got out, went inside and sat in the foyer. Meanwhile, Agent Hill was banging the steering wheel of his car in frustration, a mile away. "Agent Hill to Cainer—come in."

In Esther's suite, Graham took her to one side while Andrew went to the bathroom. "Something's going on. D'you know a woman by the name of Sheila Watson?"

"She's my best friend."

"I'm sorry, Esther. Sheila died an hour ago. She was poisoned."

Esther's face went white. Graham eased her to a chair as the strength drained from her body. She began to shake. "What's happening?" she whispered. "Why is all this happening?"

"I don't know, but we have to assume they were after you. Now it's too late to move you from here. My contacts have been keeping an eye on a firm in Soho. It might be a front for the CIA. One of them came out of that office a while ago. He was in a hurry. They're following him. It looks as if he's on his way here."

"Oh, God, he's coming here to get me," said Esther.

"*Don't worry*. Have you eaten?"

Esther jumped up. "How the hell d'you expect me to eat?" she shouted.

"An army marches on its stomach, Esther. Play is about to start, by the look of it. It's a sticky wicket, but *nil desperandum*, what?"

"This isn't a game of bloody cricket."

Graham turned the light down, walked to the window, and lifted one corner of the net as Andrew came into the room, and sat on a chair. Graham went back to Esther. He took her hands gently in his. "Discipline. Tactics and discipline are what helped this dot in the ocean rule the world for several centuries. A playboy you may think me. Well, that's what I like people to think. But this sort of thing is going on all over the world, and men like me are fighting against it."

Esther pulled her hands from his. "The world's gone mad," she said.

Graham looked at the woman in front of him for a moment. *She's even more lovely, now she's scared*, he thought. *And feisty.* He knew all about the adrenaline rush when danger threatens. And about how people reacted differently under stress. Seeing Esther, flattened one minute by devastating news and back on her feet, fighting mad, the next, excited him.

"This island may not be at the centre of things any more," he said. "But it still has a vital role to play. The SAS are the finest fighting men in the world. We'll get you out of this."

Esther flopped onto the settee and put her head in her hands. She looked up at him.

"Mad," she said. "SAS? What d'you mean, *we* will get me out of this? Are you SAS?"

Graham didn't speak for a moment. His eyes turned a cold, icy grey. She'd no doubt he was serious. He *would* kill for her.

Ricky flung a twenty-pound note at the driver, and leapt out, while the cab was still pulling up outside the Connaught Hotel. "Keep the change," he said.

"Esther Clayton. Which room's she in?" he asked at Reception.

"Room 620, sir. Third floor." Ricky ran to the lift. The two men in trilbies, sitting opposite each other, exchanged a look.

One shook his head. Better to let Ricky lead them to Esther.

In the suite, Graham answered Esther while ushering her to the bedroom. Andrew sat on a chair in the lounge. "No, I'm MI5. Now, I want you to stay in your bedroom. There are no windows in there..."

A knock at the door interrupted Graham. He pushed Esther inside the bedroom, and shut the door. "Just sit there, Andrew," he said, taking a Browning automatic pistol from his shoulder holster. He eased off the safety catch. Then he took out a dentist's mirror and poked it slowly under the door. He didn't recognise the man standing there. "Yes," he said.

"It's Ricky, Esther's friend."

"That's the man I told you about," said Andrew.

Graham opened the door, and looked down the corridor. "Come in," he said.

"Where's Esther?" said Ricky, nodding to Andrew.

"She's in the bedroom. Why are you here?" said Graham.

"The CIA are trying to get to her. Her friend has been attacked."

"Yes, I know. Her friend, Sheila Watson?"

"Yes."

"I'm afraid she's dead. Died a while ago."

"Ricky. What are you doing here?"

Graham turned to see Esther at the bedroom door. He ushered her back inside. "Will you stay in the bedroom, please?"

At that moment the door to Esther's suite crashed open, and in walked the two men, pointing the same kind of silenced revolvers Terry's attackers had used. Graham froze. The Browning was back in its shoulder holster. Ricky was between him and them. He'd have to wait.

One of the men pointed his gun at Graham. "Where's Esther Clayton?"

The nightstick in Ricky's pocket grew hot as a shadow outside the bay window caught his eye. "Do you mind if I sit down? I feel faint," he said, drawing attention to himself.

The two men turned their pistols towards him. As they did so, the window disintegrated and a stun bomb exploded. The shadow materialised as a dark-clad, masked SAS figure, carrying a sub-machine gun.

The men turned their pistols towards the sound, then, confused, began to turn back towards Graham as he shouted and dropped to one knee, drawing his Browning. He fired. It jammed. The sub-machine gun spluttered, cutting one of the men down, but the other agent was about to fire.

"Here," shouted Ricky. The man fired just as Ricky threw the nightstick at him. He too was shot by the soldier, but too late to stop the heavy duty round hitting Ricky in the chest. It tore though bone, and muscle, and a lung, before exiting through his back. Ricky fell back against the wall, and slid to the floor. The soldier shouted, "Down on the floor. Spread your arms." Then he turned to Graham. "Where's the girl, sir?"

"In the bedroom, Major."

"Good. Are you hurt?"

"No, I'm fine."

The Major knelt down to look at the CIA agents. He blinked, as the perfect emblem of the letter Y sizzled on the forehead of the man Ricky's nightstick had hit. He put it down to heightened senses, as the emblem disappeared after he'd looked at the other agent. He felt Ricky's pulse, then spoke into a shoulder mike. "Able Two. This is Able One. All secure. Two perps down and out. One friendly has a chest wound. Medic required. Repeat, medic required."

His radio crackled. "Roger, Able One. Medic on the way. Well done, Able One."

Esther appeared at the bedroom door, took one look at Graham and Andrew, and ran to Ricky. He coughed as she lifted his head. Blood trickled from his mouth. He smiled at her. "Hi, you alright?" He coughed again.

"Shush, don't speak," she said. She threw a look of desperation at Graham. He shrugged.

Tears rolled down Esther's face as Ricky coughed blood again. Feeling her tears, Ricky said, "You know, I fell in love with you the minute I saw you." His face contorted in pain, but he carried on. "In all my life, I've never met a woman as beautiful as you. Don't forget me."

Esther sobbed as Ricky stopped talking. His head fell back.

Graham went to her, and put a hand on her shoulder. But she wouldn't get up. She cradled Ricky's head in her arms, and kissed him. "No, I'll never forget you. I love you, too. Thank you for being my friend. I'm sorry I got you into this."

Graham touched her arm. "The medic's here. Let him do his job." She got up, and fell, shoulders convulsing, into Graham's arms. The Major's radio crackled again. He called to Graham.

"Commander. We've got to get going. One other agent's unaccounted for. He's on his way here."

"OK, back stairs?"

"Yes, sir."

Graham moved Esther and Andrew out of the suite, and through fire-safety doors by the side of the lift. The doors opened, and a medic appeared. The Major pointed to Ricky. "That one's the friendly. I think he's dead, now," he said. The medic nodded, and went to do what he could.

Esther pulled away from Graham, and ran to where Ricky lay. She kissed him again, on the lips this time. Then, spotting the nightstick on the floor, she ran over and picked it up. It grew warm in her hands. She felt, then looked at a rough edge that caught her fingers as they ran down the back stairs.

Ricky had been too late to stop the agent firing, but the disturbance of air as the bullet grazed the nightstick was enough to cause it to miss his vital organs. He had something else going for him, too. Shards of oak, containing memories of the dead, were left in his wounds. Blood stopped seeping into his lung, as the oak had a cauterising effect. There was still a flicker of life in Ricky as Esther ran down the back stairs.

Chapter 25

Esther Plans Revenge

Agent Hill sighed with relief as Graham, Esther and Andrew emerged from the Connaught Hotel unscathed, and got into a waiting car. Two out-riders accompanied it as it sped off, motorbike sirens wailing and lights flashing.

Then the major came out, together with two stretcher-bearers carrying Ricky. Hill watched as the stretcher was put into an ambulance. It too sped off. "Thank God for the SAS," he said.

Inside the car, Graham was talking. "I'm taking you to a safe place. We can get ourselves cleaned up, and our thoughts together. There'll be a de-briefing later. I'll stall that as long as I can..." The driver cut Graham off in mid-sentence.

"Excuse me, sir, there's a phone call for you."

Graham took the receiver. His lips tightened as he listened. "OK, thanks," he said.

Esther noticed. "What now?" she said, as he handed the phone back.

Graham looked at Andrew, then Esther. "I'm so sorry, Esther. They attacked your mom and dad, too. Earlier today."

Andrew began to cry. Esther just stared at Graham, then lowered her gaze. "Why? Why is all this happening? What have I done? The CIA are supposed to be on our side, aren't they?"

"They shot your dad, but he's OK. Your mom's just shaken up."

Graham took Esther by the shoulders, and turned her towards him. "There's something else. You're pregnant," he said.

Esther's mouth fell open. She stared at him for a moment, her mind in a whirl. "I... How?"

"You stopped taking the Pill, didn't you?"

"Yes, but that was because I wasn't in a relationship. I haven't had...sex?" Then she remembered. "Oh, God. The President."

"Yes, the President. You're going to have his baby, that's why they tried to kill you."

"Oh no I'm not. We'll soon see about that. And I want him dead."

She grabbed the nightstick. "Here, take this. I want you to make me a gun. Use the oak for its stock. Make me the most powerful sniper gun in the world. And I want bullets that explode on impact. Then I want you to show me how to fire it." Esther put her head in her hands and said, "And I want to go home."

Graham put a hand on Andrew's shoulder. *She's serious*, he thought. *Can I take a chance by sending her home, though? It would probably be OK. They daren't make another move, now they've shown their hand. And they don't know about me. Well, they didn't before this. That bloody Green. Why the hell wasn't I told? I'm going to give him such a bollocking.*

"I'll take the nightstick," he said. "And I'll have you taken home. The driver is one of my best men. His name's Peter. He'll watch over you. I'll stay in London, and sort the Home Office out. You go home and do what you have to, OK? I'll try to smooth the way. You can phone me when you feel the need. I'll give you a number."

Esther sat by Andrew. "OK. And thanks, by the way. I shouldn't have doubted you. If you hadn't helped us, we'd all be dead. Let me know about Ricky. I don't know if he had any family."

"Don't worry. I'll sort everything." Graham pressed a button to open the compartment divider. "Peter, pull over, and turn the lights off, please."

"Yes, sir," said Peter. Graham got out, and spoke to the out-riders for a moment. They left.

Graham had a word with Peter, then opened the door. Esther sat, holding Andrew and looking through the rear window.

"I've told the out-riders to leave," said Graham. "Less conspicuous if they're not around. Can you put Peter up?"

"I expect so."

"Good. I know all of this has been a shock, but don't worry."

"I'll phone you at the apartment, later."

Graham kissed her goodbye, shut the door, tapped the roof, and began to look for a cab.

Graham was busy while Peter drove Esther and Andrew back to Margate. He ensured that the local constabulary were relieved of their responsibilities, and MI5 personnel made only a cursory investigation at Terry's house. Esther found just one man keeping an eye on the place when they arrived. Peter left them in his care while he went to check in at the police station.

Esther's head was spinning as she put her key into the front door. When she opened it, memories of Terry being there saying, "Come on in. I'll just put the kettle on," came flooding back, together with tears.

The police had done a good job of cleaning the house, but seeing the exactness of everything in its place seemed to make it look more empty than it was. She flopped in the lounge, while Andrew went upstairs.

Looking round the room, Esther saw the stuffed owl on top of the drinks cabinet. The tears came again, but now they were tears of frustration and anger. She *would* avenge herself, and get rid of this—thing inside her. At that moment she made a solemn vow. Nothing would stop her, "So help me, God," she said. She laughed. A short, cynical laugh. "Huh. God. Where was he? No matter. I'll do without God."

Audeus' memories, aware of Esther's distress, put thoughts of Ricky, who might still be her support, into her brain. She realised his blood was dry and caked on her hands. She kissed it. "Yes. I'll have revenge."

What she needed now, though, was a shower. She switched on the boiler, then shouted up the stairs. This was a different Esther talking. "Andrew. D'you want tea? Don't hide yourself away in your room again. I've got too much to do without having you to worry about."

Andrew heard her, but didn't reply. He'd fired up the computer. He typed in the letters SAS, and clicked Search. He wanted to know everything about the SAS. He had a plan of his own.

The phone rang downstairs. Esther answered it. "Esther? It's Elizabeth."

"Hello, Aunt. You alright?"

"Yes. I'm with Margaret, at the hospital. Are you coming?"

"We'll be over in a bit. How are they?"

"Terry's still in surgery, but Joan's in shock, I think."

"OK. I've got to shower. Be over, after."

Peter came back as Esther put the phone down. "Come in," she said. She couldn't bring herself to say she'd put the kettle on, so merely said, "Make yourself at home."

While undressing, it occurred to her that she'd have to get her clothes from Sheila's house. She hadn't thought of Sheila, till now. *I'll have to see the Watsons, as well. What on earth am I going to tell them? When will this nightmare end?* she thought. Feeling the tightness in her muscles, she decided to soak in the bath instead of showering.

Esther eased herself gratefully into water which was a little too warm. She lay back, and closed her eyes, letting the soothing liquid envelop her. Instantly, her aching muscles responded, and she relaxed. The only sound was the drip of hot water from the tap. This, together with its movement, rising and falling over her chest as she breathed, almost sent her to sleep.

After a while she opened her eyes, and pulled herself up. The sight of a tiny insect sitting, legs splayed out on the water's film, as if frightened to move in case the tenuous barrier be broken, and it be sucked under and drowned, made her tense up again. Normally, such a sight would have seen her jump out, but somehow, all fear seemed to have left her. She gently lifted it up with her finger. "Know how you feel, mister, I'm on the edge myself," she said. As she laid it down on the side of the bath, it dropped to the floor, then scuttled away.

Esther broke the news about Sheila. "Scum." said Terry. "Why were they after you?"

"I don't know, but I've a friend in London who's going to help me find out. Don't speak now, Dad. Just get better."

"Well, I hung a right hook on one of them. Why's your mother looking like that?"

"She's OK. A bit shook up, but OK."

Joan wasn't OK. Not the most extrovert of people at the best of times, she was deeply traumatised by what had happened, and retreated to an inner place. A place of such inner torment that even the memories couldn't help.

Esther spent time with her at the hospital, but needed to see the Watsons.

They were inconsolable at the loss of their only daughter. A post-mortem showed she had died of Ricin poisoning. She was just twenty years old—the same age as Esther. Sheila had never had a bad word to say about anyone. All who knew her, loved her, and her infectious enthusiasm for life. Esther felt the upset rise inside her, and made an excuse to leave.

"There's a parcel for you upstairs, in her room," said Norman. "She wrapped it for you the day you came home. I think she was going to give it to you on your birthday."

Esther saw a large—something, covered with wrapping paper, standing in the corner of Sheila's room. An envelope sat on top. She opened it, and took out a card, which read: "Happy Birthday. I told you a little fib. As soon as I saw you and Ricky together, I knew he'd be the one for you. We had a lot of fun on Billy, you and I. He's yours, now. For your children to play on. Happy Birthday."

Esther pulled off the wrapping paper. The sight of the rocking horse, swaying gently in front of her, broke her heart. The guilt came with a rush. She fell on Sheila's bed, sobbing. "It's my fault. If I hadn't gone to London, I would've been here. It's my fault."

Downstairs, Hilda heard her. "She's crying. Should I go to her?"

"No, dear. Let her be. She feels she's got a terrible burden to carry. We know Sheila wouldn't want that. But now's not the time."

Upstairs, Esther lay on Sheila's bed, staring at the wallpaper. Solitary tears quivered on her eyelashes like dewdrops on a strand of spider's silk. Wearied through grief she finally gave in to the pearly weight pulling her eyelids together, and slept.

When she woke an hour later she raised herself up to see Billy, gently rocking back and forth. Esther felt a warmth in the fine oak grain as she ran the palm of her hand over his withers. She read Sheila's note again. This time there were no tears. It was as if being in Sheila's room, surrounded by her still lingering fragrance, invoked her presence. Esther remembered their conversations about boys; the laughter, and how she'd always been her best friend. Then she realised that she'd never see her again. Esther kissed Sheila's note. "I love you," she said. "And I'll keep you in my heart, forever."

The phone rang early in the evening. It was Graham. "How'yer doing?" he said.

"OK, I suppose."

"When's the funeral?"

"Couple of days, I guess. Thanks for smoothing things over."

"That's OK. We picked up the last agent, and the driver of the other car. That's all of them now. They're being interrogated. I'll find out what happened."

Esther didn't reply straight away. Her despondency showed when she then said, "That won't bring Sheila back."

Graham felt he'd better change the subject. "Is Peter there? I'd like a word if he is."

"Yes. He can stay with me." She handed the phone to Peter, who merely nodded while Graham spoke. "Leave it to me," he said finally, and handed the phone back to Esther.

"I want to see you after the funeral's over," she said. Then she replaced the receiver.

Esther wrestled with her conscience the next day. Her parents needed her, now. She realised at last that she had no real relationship with her mother. She knew it wasn't her fault, which seemed to make it even more important she do her best. But she had to do something about her pregnancy.

After a while, Andrew spoke. "Who was that man?"

"What man?" she said.

"Graham."

"Oh, he's just a man I met in London, a couple of years ago. He's a friend. Why?"

"Is he SAS?"

"Sort of. I didn't know that before yesterday, though."

"D'you think he's James Bond?"

Esther laughed. For a second it felt good to laugh. Then she felt shame. She went to Andrew and hugged him close. "I'm sorry I was short with you when we came home yesterday. Thank you for coming to warn me. You're a brave boy, you know. And I love you very much. We're all going to need each other even more now."

Inside, Andrew was churning as Esther hugged him. The feel of her breasts against him brought thoughts of his mother, but then the smell of Esther's sweet personal fragrance brought a reminder of his imaginings. His shame would have over-whelmed him, but Esther said, "No, he's not James Bond, but he could've been, couldn't he?" This brought Andrew back, and he lightened up.

"Yes. and did you see that soldier? He came crashing through the window and shot that man in a second, Pow. Pow. Pow. He was all in black."

Esther hugged him again. *He's just sixteen*, she thought. *Such a young boy to have seen such things. Perhaps he'll develop now he's out of that room.*

Her thoughts returned to her own problems again. The sooner she could get back to London, the sooner she could talk to Graham. She needed to get rid of what was inside her, as soon as possible. But how could she leave her parents so soon? *Perhaps Elizabeth might help*, she thought. *I could help out Margaret, and Andrew too. If I know they're alright, I can get on with what I have to do.* She determined to talk to them, after the funeral.

The service and laying to rest of Sheila passed Esther by. Norman Watson was distraught, and couldn't control his emotions. Even Margaret sat in a daze, while Elizabeth sobbed uncontrollably.

Esther knew she had to be strong, but it was difficult; and to tell the truth, she was glad when it was over. She kept Andrew, who she thought might faint at any second, close to her, and made sure she gave him plenty of attention. Andrew withdrew to his room again when the party returned home.

At the first opportunity, Esther took Elizabeth to one side. "I have to go to London," she said. "I don't know for how long, but in any case, Terry, Joan and Andrew will need looking after. I'm thinking long-term now. Will you stay here and look after them? At least for a while. I'll pay the mortgage off, and put enough money aside for you to manage on. I don't want Andrew to return to his old ways, either."

"Of course I'll stay. As long as they need me."

"Good. The excitement of what Andrew saw in London didn't seem real to him. If you're here with him, in his own home, he'll find it easier to cope. And he'll be close to Margaret."

Esther found Margaret sitting on the patio in the back garden. The glint of red glass, set in a cheap seaside novelty ring on Margaret's wedding finger as she pushed the buggy back and forth drew Esther's attention.

"Can I have a word?" she said. "I want to ask you something." Margaret shrugged.

"That chap. The one you're seeing. I don't know his name. Is he the twins' father?"

"Yes, why?"

"D'you love him?"

"Don't know. Maybe."

"D'you love him enough to marry him?"

"What are you getting at?"

"Look. This has hit us all hard. There's no getting away from it, it's going to change our lives. Elizabeth has agreed to stay in the house and look after Mom, Dad and Andrew. I've told her I'll pay the mortgage off and provide enough money for them to live on."

Margaret looked at the floor while Esther continued.

"I can't do any less for you, and the children. I'm prepared to settle the equivalent amount on you, and them. They need a father, and the money would enable you to send them to school early. Then you could do something for yourself. What d'you say?"

"Let me think about it."

"Don't take too long, Margaret. I have to be in London the day after tomorrow."

Margaret decided that if Esther was in such a hurry, she could settle on her terms. "How much have you decided to give Mom, Dad and Andrew?"

"About eighty thousand, why?"

"So you'd need to set aside about one hundred and thirty thousand for me, bearing in mind that you haven't got to buy them a house."

Esther thought that Margaret lived in a council house, but took her point. "I suppose so, why?"

"Wouldn't it be better if you just gave me the money? You've enough to think about at the moment." Esther said nothing, giving Margaret the opportunity to tell the biggest whopper of her grasping life so far. She reached for a tissue, and let her bottom lip quiver a little, before telling it.

"I've been sitting here, thinking. What with Mom and Dad, it's been a terrible shock." She sniffed. "I've been a bad mother, and a selfish woman. The children deserve to have their father around all the time. But I don't know if I can stay around here after all this. If you could transfer the money to my account, I could move nearer to Canterbury. The schools there are better, and there's more work about. I could go to college, and finish my education. This is so kind of you."

Esther fell for it. She'd no choice if she wanted the freedom to pursue her plans.

Chapter 26

The Queen Elizabeth Hospital

Peter drove Esther to Graham's London apartment two days later. He welcomed her with a hug.

"You OK? Everything go alright?"

"As far as it could, thanks. There was so much to do. Things like Ricky's bill at The Swan. D'you have his effects? Credit card, or something? Where did they take him?"

"I'll tell you about it later. I'm afraid the Ministry *must* be our first call."

"Alright. But the second will be to a clinic. I need to get rid of this—thing inside me. D'you know anybody?"

Graham regarded Esther for a moment. He'd have given much to spare this woman, who enchanted him above all others, the trauma of what she'd been exposed to. But she was coping, admirably, as far as he could see. *Some chap is going to be very lucky, one day*, he thought. First, he'd a surprise for her, though. "I can do better than that. The top man at the Queen Elizabeth is my personal friend. We'll call in and see him on the way back."

The debriefing wasn't as bad as Esther had expected. She simply related events as she remembered them.

Thirty minutes later, Graham's Daimler pulled up in front of the Queen Elizabeth Hospital. "This chap's office is on the second floor," he said. "We have to go up in the lift and through the private wards to get there."

Graham ushered Esther out of the lift and down a corridor. As they walked through the private wards, he stopped and opened a door. "Here we are," he said.

The light inside was dim, but Esther could see a figure lying on a bed in the corner of the room. Drips seemed to be attached everywhere. An oxygen pump, wheezing air through a mask, obscured the face, but she knew who it was. She put her hands to her face, and slowly sank to her knees. "Oh, Ricky," she said.

Graham helped her up. "I'll leave you alone with him," he said softly. "He can't talk, so you'll have to manage the best you can. I'll be outside the door if you want me."

Esther sat on the side of the bed, and looked at Ricky. She took the one hand that didn't have a drip in it, and held it, gently. His eyes flickered open, then closed. When he opened them again, a tear ran down his cheek.

"Hello, mister," she said. "You didn't think you'd get away from me that easy, did you?"

Ricky smiled with his eyes.

"You're my hero, you know," she said. "Everything's going to be alright, and when you get better, I'll never let you out of my sight again. D'you hear me?"

Ricky slowly nodded.

"I've got to go now, but I'll be back later, OK?"

He nodded again. She kissed his cheek, and left.

Graham was waiting in the corridor. Esther kissed him on the lips. "I owe you so much. You really are the best friend a woman could have, and I love you. Now, where's this surgeon fellah?"

"Well he doesn't actually practise from here. That was all about Ricky. But, if you're sure you want to go ahead with it, I know just the man."

"If I want—Graham, What are you up to? What d'you know that I don't? I think I'd better have some tests done, quickly."

"Nothing. I know nothing more than you. Well, almost nothing. There is something I want to talk to you about, though. I'll tell you in the car."

Graham pushed a button bringing up the compartment divider, and turned the radio on. Then he spoke. "You remember I told you about the British Ambassador being at The White House next week?"

"Yes."

"You've been invited. Actually, Rachel Jefferey, the President's wife, has asked to meet you."

Esther looked at him with stunned amazement. Then she became angry. "What for? Why the hell should I want to meet the President's wife?"

Graham hunched his shoulders.

"Haven't a clue, but the suggestion intrigues me. It's inconceivable that she isn't aware of her husband's infidelities. We know for sure the CIA is involved. This could be a massive opportunity for our country to get to know what's going on inside their heads."

"Don't you dare give me that king and country bunk. Let me think." She turned the proposition over in her mind. *What about Ricky? How would he feel if I went to America and killed the President? What would Mom and Dad think? I'll check on Ricky first.*

"What chance has Ricky got?" she said.

"Better than fifty-fifty."

"Have you made me a gun?"

"Not yet, but it would be a great chance to size up the situation. Plus you can show the Yanks how we breed the loveliest girls in the world."

Esther looked at Graham, pointedly. "Since when do I fall for flattery? Why does she want to see me?"

"I'm not sure, but seriously, if you're to get revenge, you need to check things out."

Esther wrestled with the proposition. *What was Graham up to? What did her going to see Jefferey's wife have to do with her not having an abortion?* Finally, for some reason, she felt she ought to go. And wait. To see how things turned out, before taking her revenge.

"OK, I'll go, but make me the gun," she said.

"Good. Now, what did you want to talk to me about?"

"Our relationship. When I came to town, I wanted to know if you loved me. Enough to marry me, I mean. Do you?"

She looked at him, waiting for a reply. Graham returned her gaze for a moment, then said, "I love you more than any woman I've known. But I won't ask you to marry me. I'm much older than you; not that that would stop me. I've dedicated my life to the defence of my country, and I enjoy being a bachelor. But most of all, I'm selfish."

He paused for a moment, then continued.

"You're a beautiful woman. You have your whole life ahead of you. I never know if I'm coming home at night. Your children should have no such uncertainty about their father hanging over them. I don't mean the child you're carrying. I mean the ones you should have with Ricky."

"Ricky?"

"He loves you. *Really* loves you. More to the point, I think you love him. What I just witnessed in that hospital confirms that. In any case, you should give yourself more time. Your friendship and our relationship is dear to me. It will keep me warm when I'm cold."

Graham seemed to remember something. "I've been in situations where it would've been easier to give up, believe me. If I'm unlucky enough to be in those situations again, thoughts of you will keep me going. I'm not just a king and country man, you know."

Then he turned Esther towards him, and said, "I want you to know, I'll be here for you if ever you need me. Now, go back to Ricky. Look after him for a few days, before you go to Washington. I'll take care of the details."

Esther put her arm through his, and laid her head on his shoulder. "You're a strange man. You seem to know me better than I do myself."

Only the memories knew of the intolerable strain future events would put on their relationship.

Graham took Esther back to the hospital. As they approached Ricky's room, they met a nurse coming out. "Any change?" Graham asked.

"If there is, it's for the better. Since you were here before, his attitude seems to have become more positive."

"Good," said Graham, turning to Esther. "Fancy some hospital food? I can recommend it. Then you can fuss over Ricky for a few days."

* * *

Ricky's progress gathered pace with the extra attention Esther gave him. The memories strengthened him, but seeing her, alive, gave him the will to recover. His lung healed to the extent that he didn't need oxygen by the time she was preparing to leave for America. This meant he could speak to her, for the first time since he'd been shot. "All I remember is a loud bang, and a soldier crashing in through the window. I flung the nightstick at one of the men, and that's it. Don't remember a thing after that. When I woke here, all I could think of was that you and Andrew might be dead. Nobody told me you were alright. Is he OK?"

"You very nearly died yourself. You didn't wake up till I came, three days after you were shot. Andrew's fine, and as you can see, so am I. It's you who's got to get well now."

Esther considered whether she should tell him everything, then realising she'd be away, decided it would be better if she told him now, rather than let someone else do it.

"They shot Dad."

Neither spoke again for a while. Then Ricky said, "What's it all about? Why is all this happening? Something was bothering you when I met you on the plane. What was it?"

"It's a long story. I'll tell you everything, but I've got to go to America tomorrow. I hope to find answers there. I'm pregnant."

Ricky was speechless.

"Do you trust me, Ricky?"

"Yes, but look, you don't have to tell me anything, unless you want to."

"I didn't want this baby. I was raped."

"Well, I can understand if you're angry. You probably want to lash out."

"Does it show that much?"

"Yep, 'fraid so. But it's a natural reaction. If you can give yourself time, what goes around, comes around. Know what I mean?"

"No, I don't."

Ricky didn't answer for a moment, then said, "I don't know why I said that. I was thinking about the old man in my dream."

"What dream? What old man?"

"The old man in the dream I had while we were on the plane."

Esther's blood ran cold. "Was he a brave old man who had to leave his son, and memories kept him safe, and eased his pain as he was dying? And did they take him somewhere after he died?"

"Yes, but they weren't just his memories. I don't know how to explain this, I think they were *all* of our memories."

Esther held his hand. She put the warmth coming from them down to a high temperature. Still, it didn't feel like a feverish type of heat. More a comforting heat. "I had the exact same dream, while we were on the plane. Did you mean what you said?"

"When?"

"When I held you, after you were shot. You said you loved me."

The answer almost gushed from him. But he couldn't say it. Neither knew how much they would come to rely on each other in the future, but with recollections of the dream they shared fresh in his mind, Ricky had the feeling this moment was important—for him. *Here I am. A woman, who I love more than life itself, is asking me if I love her. And I know she's really saying, "Will you marry me?" I can see it in her eyes. I know what she's going to say after I answer. Can I be so lucky? If only this moment could last forever.* But it couldn't.

"Yes. I love you. From the moment I saw you, sitting by yourself, on that plane. I knew, even if you said no—remember when I asked you if you'd join me in a glass of champagne?"

Esther laughed. "Yes, I remember."

"Well, I knew that if you said no, I'd be really disappointed. And wonder about you for the rest of my life."

Esther melted inside while Ricky was talking. After he finished, she kissed him. "And I meant it when I said I loved you, too. It's been quite a day for surprises. Now, you get better. I'll see you when I get back. We'd better put up the banns then, or whatever we're supposed to do, hadn't we?"

Chapter 27

The Proposition

As far as she knew, her entry into America for the meeting was to be incognito. Esther assumed, therefore, that the Lear jet which took off from Heathrow was laid on for her convenience. She watched the ground fall away beneath her, and remembered the day an ordinary chartered flight had taken her and her agent across the Atlantic a little over two years before.

She recalled the collywobbles in her stomach as Hollywood beckoned. The frightening but exhilarating experience of flying away into the unknown, with possible fame and fortune before her. Or failure.

For the only time in her life, Esther saw her father cry. After she got into the taxi waiting to take her to Heathrow, Terry knocked the window and said, "Try to keep in touch. And don't forget, if things get rough, just put the kettle on, and have a nice cup of tea. I hope they have tea in America."

Esther smiled as she remembered. "OK, Dad. I will," she'd said. But she hadn't, and realised she too had been very lucky. They might both be dead now, as well as Sheila.

Then she remembered forcing herself to think of it as just another modelling job. *Well, I was younger then,* she thought. *I'll look after number one from now on.*

Esther didn't notice that the Lear jet only climbed to 15,000 feet. After it levelled out, she undid her seat belt, and closed her eyes. There was a long flight ahead.

The phone was ringing as Graham opened the door to his apartment. He looked at his watch and picked up the phone.

"Hello," he said.

"Hello. Is that Graham?"

"Yes. Who am I speaking to?"

"It's Andrew. Esther's brother."

"Hello Andrew. How are you?"

"Fine, sir. I was wondering if I could come and see you—in London, I mean. There's something I want to ask you."

Graham wondered what he could want. Still, he was Esther's brother. That made him almost family. "Certainly, my boy. When d'you want to come up?"

"Well, I've called you now because I don't want Esther to know about me phoning you. Could we keep this to ourselves?"

"Don't see why not. I'm leaving straight away, but I'll be back in a couple of days. Call me then. I'll have my man pick you up at Waterloo."

"Yes, sir. Thank you."

The Lear Jet had only been in the air a few minutes when Esther felt a tap on her shoulder. She opened her eyes, and looked at the woman standing in front of her. This was no stewardess. The designer suit said that much. She was around 5' 6", slim and brunette. She wasn't as old as she looked, Esther reckoned. *Probably in her forties. Pretty, though.*

The woman held out her hand. Esther took it. The handshake told Esther this woman was confident and powerful, without being overly crushing. Just the right balance.

"I'm Rachel Jefferey, Miss Clayton. My husband is the President of the United States. Please excuse this subterfuge. I wanted our meeting to be private. May I call you Esther?"

"Sure. Why not?"

Rachel Jefferey sat down. "Thanks. I must apologise for the behaviour of my husband. The arsehole's been at it like a rutting stag ever since he got elected."

"You know about that?"

"Yes. I'm afraid you weren't the first. Please don't be offended. I don't mean to imply that you were a willing participant. I know you weren't. I'm on your side. This time he's gone too far. I'm wondering if we could strike a deal that would be to our mutual advantage."

She paused, waiting for a reaction. Getting none, she continued, "I understand you're having a baby."

"Not for long."

"That's what I wanted to talk to you about. The most

natural reaction is to want to destroy it, and I wouldn't blame you if you did get rid of it. I've a proposition that will, I hope, change your mind. I assume you'd like him to suffer in some way for the distress he's caused you?"

Rachel Jefferey tapped her fingers on the arm of her seat. Esther picked up on it and wondered, *Is that a sign of nerves? Or impatience? I do believe she's intimidated by me. She's got a damn cheek, anyway.*

Esther turned her head away from Jefferey and looked out the window. "I can take care of that myself, thank you."

"I've no doubt. You've a useful ally in Graham de Courcey."

That response surprised Esther. "Is there anything you don't know?"

"In my position, I have to know as much as I can. You must understand that."

Esther turned her attention back to Jefferey. "I suppose so. Please get to the point."

"Firstly, I'm offering you a million dollars to carry the baby to term. Now you know this has nothing to do with getting payback for my husband's philandering. My goals are much higher than that. I'm sick and tired of the way men are running my country, and ruining the planet. I intend putting a stop to it by getting into the White House myself. The President is up for re-election next year. Whether or not he returns to office is of no concern to me, although it would have its benefits."

"I agree with you about the mess they're making, but what's that to do with me?"

"The baby. I intend running for Mayor of New York next year. I *will* win that election. Four years later I'll run for the Presidency. I expect to win that too. Between us, my friends and I have several hundred million dollars of disposable assets. Moreover, their husbands hold key seats in states across America."

"Yes, but where does the baby come in?"

"If you agree to carry the baby to term, the money will be paid into your account immediately. I'll announce myself to be pregnant, and take steps to show that physically. Six weeks before the baby is due, I'll go into seclusion."

"Why don't you just get pregnant by him yourself? You don't need me."

"I'm forty-two years old. It's by no means certain I could get pregnant, and if I did, the gestation could be difficult. On top of that, the child would stand an increased chance of being retarded in some way. Besides, I can't stand the thought of having that heaving lump on top of me on the off-chance. It's worth a million for us to have a child with his DNA in it. The fact you provided the other DNA would be of no consequence."

"So I assume you'll groom the child to take over from you at a later date. He'd be under your control. Clever. What if you don't become President? And what if this baby's a she?"

"There's nothing in the constitution preventing a woman becoming President. Let me worry about that. Look, this will have come as a surprise to you. We own an island in the Atlantic. The weather's nice at this time of the year. Why don't I drop you off there for a couple of days? Think it over. It's fully staffed and completely self-contained. There'll be no one else to bother you, and the steward will stay with you. What d'you say?"

Rachel Jefferey was no different from many other people in positions of influence. She assumed that her plan would succeed simply because it was what she wanted. And that Esther, as a naïve young woman, would show the same deference to her that the wives of prominent politicians who sought favours from the President showed. In this she was mistaken. Esther had grown up quickly, and, prompted by the memories, wasn't about to give in that easily. She could barely contain herself. *Who the hell does this woman think she is? Well two can play this game*, she thought.

"I'd say it depends on your politics."

"What d'you mean?" said Rachel.

"Well. You're hoping to take power in your country. I need to know where you stand on certain things. We've already agreed that your husband's disgusting behaviour towards me is unacceptable. D'you think rapists like your husband and murderers get what they deserve? What d'you think of the fact that white men get treated differently to black men? What's your position on the Israel/Palestine question? What will you do about third world debt?"

Jefferey smiled. "Very astute, Esther. I can see you're a woman after my own heart. What's your price?"

"No. We're not the same. In fact we're as opposite as two women can be. I've had to do a lot of growing up recently, remember? And I'll be doing a little campaigning myself after this is all over. I'll need much more than a million dollars. I'll take you up on your offer of a holiday. While I'm there please consider another figure—say ten million."

"I won't bargain with you. Ten million it is. Five immediately, and five after the baby's born. OK?"

"OK. Two days it is."

"Good. Now, I've things to discuss with the pilot, and orders to give the steward. If you'll excuse me, I'll be back in a moment."

Rachel Jefferey left Esther, and went forward. She found Carter in the galley. "She's gone for it," she said. "But find out what she's thinking. If it looks as if she's going to change her mind, kill her. Then phone me. I'll arrange for the jet to pick you up. Then you can dump her somewhere in the Atlantic. That'll throw her man off the scent."

"Leave it to me, ma'am," said Carter.

*　*　*

President Jefferey was enjoying himself. Rachel was at a fund-raising event, as far as he knew. A good opportunity to have a quickie with his secretary, Pamela Livesey. During this, particularly energetic, session of lovemaking the tiny sliver of oak in Jefferey transferred itself to Pamela. Inside, thirsty memories waited. Fed up with the thrustings of a sweaty, middle-aged man, they wanted something different. Something sweeter.

At Connaught Square, Graham sat drumming his fingers on the arm of a chair in his apartment. He looked at his watch. Eight-thirty. Esther had been gone for over two hours now. He almost leapt out of the chair to lift the receiver when a light on the phone flashed. "Yes," he said.

"It's Jock, sir."

"Have you traced that jet?"

Jock, standing on the deck of the operations room on one of Her Majesty's Carriers patrolling the Atlantic, looked at the figure peering intently at the screen in front of him.

"Yes, sir. They passed over us thirty minutes ago. It's headed NNW, at 500 knots. Doesn't look as if it's on course for the USA."

"What d'you reckon?"

"It looks as if it's heading for a group of small islands off the east coast of Canada."

Graham looked at his watch. 20.45. "Keep your eyes on it. You know what you have to do. You can download the reconnaissance files on all those islands from the ship's computer."

"Yes, sir."

Graham replaced the receiver. All he could do now was wait. He had every confidence in Jock, one of his best men. Still...

The Lear jet landed on a small, remote island. At midnight, a Sea King helicopter hovered above a clearing. Jock, dressed in typical SAS garb and carrying an attaché case, was lowered by winch, then ran to conceal himself in vegetation. He lay for a moment, allowing his hearing to adjust to the sounds of crashing surf. Then he moved off in the direction of the chalets which he knew to be on the opposite side of the island.

Jock calculated that the occupants of the four chalets would be asleep by the time he got there. A full moon didn't offer him any cover, but he had no control over that. There was no reason for anyone to expect an intruder, so the odds were in his favour. There was only one agent stationed there. At least the weather was fine. Two hours later, he arrived.

When it became obvious where the jet was going to land, Jock pulled a reconnaissance report from SAS files. He read it now:

'Vegetation, surrounding three sides of a runway, excluding the flight path, which is south facing and approximately 150 metres from the sea-shore. Fifty metres in from the edge of the runway, on the west side, and clustered together, are: one store room, containing a large fridge; one brick construction, in which one diesel generator is housed, together with a short-wave radio set.'

That checks out, thought Jock. He looked to his right, then down at the report.

'Four chalets in a clearing, eighty metres off the north-west side.' Jock looked at an update to the file. 'One chalet set apart from the others. This used as staff quarters. Of the other three, one is used by an agent on permanent security duty. The other two are for guests.'

Jock scanned the area. *Yep. All checks out.*

His only problem was finding which chalet the man he was looking for was sleeping in. He put the map back into the attaché case and looked at the moon. Waiting until cloud moved across it he broke cover, moving as a shadow among gently swaying trees. He approached the first chalet.

Looking for loose floorboards on the verandah, he carefully skirted the edge until he could see through its shore-facing window. He saw a man lying on a four-poster bed. A US service revolver hung in a holster from the bedpost. *That's the agent*, he thought. Jock knelt down and eased the attaché case open. He took out a glass phial and cotton wool. Then he eased the door open, and went inside.

The agent was breathing deeply as Jock approached him. At the bed, he took the top off the phial, held it under the agent's nose and let him inhale the fumes. The agent never suspected that the headache he suffered next morning was anything other than the result of being hung over.

Jock moved to the next chalet. Esther was lying on her back, breathing gently. Moonlight, shining on her face, lit her more naturally than a camera ever could. Jock took a photograph from a pocket and looked at it. *The boss was right*, he thought. *Looks better in the flesh, though.*

Jock moved on. In the last chalet, Carter was snoring. *Good*, thought Jock. There would be no gentle holding of the phial under *his* nose. Jock poured half the remaining ether onto the cotton wool, took out a six-inch, army-issue dagger, which he gripped in his teeth, just in case, and opened the door. Carter snorted and turned over, leaving him facing the other way. Jock stopped, like a lioness stalking, paw raised.

Carter snorted again and turned onto his back. *Perfect,*

thought Jock. In one movement he slid his hand under the back of Carter's head, tilted it back, and smothered his face with the cotton wool. Carter struggled for a moment, then went limp.

Jock retraced his steps, putting the cotton wool back into the attaché case. From a tube he took out a syringe, and a fine needle.

The sudden cry of a seagull stopped him in his tracks. Nothing moved. He heard no other sound. He checked his watch. *OK for time.* He returned to the chalet. Carter hadn't moved. Jock lifted Carter's right foot and inserted the syringe under its big toenail. It took a full two minutes for Jock to inject the 0.2 milligrams of Ricin poison which killed Carter.

Jock reflected on the irony of it as he made his way back to Esther's chalet. *Died of a heart attack, in his sleep. Nice trick, that Ricin.*

Jock looked at Esther for a moment, then took his balaclava off. He covered her mouth with his right hand and put a finger to his mouth. She woke with a start, eyes wide with terror.

"It's alright, Miss. Commander de Courcey sent me," he said, releasing her.

"What for?" she whispered.

"I haven't long. Everything's fine, but the Commander needs to know what Rachel Jefferey had in mind."

"Graham knew they weren't taking me to America?"

"It pays to keep one step ahead of them, friend or foe. Now, tell me what she said."

Esther told him about the offer, and what Rachel Jefferey had in mind after the birth. Jock whistled between his teeth. "Wow! That would be a good trick, if they could pull it off. Can you do it?"

"Does he want me to?"

"Ask him yourself. I'll hook you up."

Jock proceeded to open up a Satellite Receiver-Transmitter, and dialled Graham's number. He gave a headset to Esther.

Graham answered immediately: "Esther?" he said.

"Yes, it's me."

"Hi, you OK? What's happening?"

"Well, let's put it this way—I guess I know what life's all about, now."

"What d'you mean? Tell me what Rachel Jefferey had to

say."

"Basically, she showed me that money can buy anything. And that I have power. She wants to buy the child."

Esther reiterated what she'd told Jock.

"Will you do it?"

"Why should I?"

"There'd be definite advantages if you could. Let's face it, ten million. Seriously though, I know you're not interested in the king and country bit, but could you do it for yourself?"

"For myself? No. Not for myself. I've already accepted her offer, but—you might not understand this—I'm so angry that people like her, and Jefferey—and you Graham—you all just think that you can do anything. My best friend has been killed, I've been raped, and you lot think that you can just buy me off."

Graham had no answer. "I know" was all he could muster.

Graham's silence was, to Esther, a kind of acknowledgement that what she'd said could not be refuted. That, powerful as these people were, in the end they had no real justification for their actions.

"I've told you I'll do it, but on my terms."

"Good girl. Now put me onto Jock."

Jock listened, nodded, then said, "Yes, I've disposed of him." Then he handed the headset back to Esther.

"Rachel Jefferey will come back to the island tomorrow. Tell her of your decision then. OK? I'll see you when you get back," said Graham.

"What did this man mean, when he said he'd disposed of him?"

"Carter was a killer. I couldn't take a chance on you refusing them. He would've killed you, if you hadn't gone along with them."

"You just had a man killed, for me?"

"I'm sorry, it's a dirty business."

"Well, when this is over I'm going to buy myself a place as far away from people as I can. Tomorrow I'll tell them I accept, then they can take me home. By the way, I'm in love."

"Well, well. Told you so. No need to ask who the lucky man is."

"No. You were right."

"I'm very happy for you. Now, be natural. Take the two days. It'll be alright. They'll think he died of a heart attack. I promise. Jock will stay around until you're safely on your way back."

Esther, unable to sleep after Jock had gone, thought of Ricky, and Andrew, so far away. And of her parents, and Sheila. Her eyes became heavy and she felt herself being taken back across the sea on a cloud of blue as she dreamed again. This time she was in the hospital room. There was no sound as her subconscious looked down at Ricky, sleeping peacefully. She reached out a hand to touch him, but felt no flesh. Then the scene faded, as the cloud took her swirling away into the peace of the Universe.

Rachel Jefferey arrived four hours after Carter's body was found. As Graham said, it was assumed he had died of a heart attack. Esther breathed a sigh of relief, as did Jock, watching nearby.

Esther told Rachel of her decision. "I'll need a husband to make the whole thing look normal. I've got somebody in mind."

"OK," said Rachel Jefferey. "The five million will be in your account before you get back to Heathrow. I won't come with you, but I'll give you a number. Only call if there's a problem, otherwise I'll be in touch."

Chapter 28
Margaret Makes Plans

Esther and Ricky married at the same church where Sheila was buried. Terry gave Esther away from a wheelchair, before being returned to hospital. Joan, in a world of her own, was making little progress.

Ricky, trim and handsome after a month on hospital food, showed no sign of his close encounter with death. Esther looked stunning in a modest, pearl-coloured outfit. She wore a lace veil and carried three lucky horseshoes. One each from Elizabeth, Margaret and Andrew. She was really pleased with Andrew. He seemed to be fitter and more confident now, and shaping up to be something. She put the reason for his improvement down to his having come out of his room.

* * *

A sense of fusion came over Ricky as his lips met Esther's after the minister told him, "You may now kiss the bride."

With his eyes closed it was, at first, as if the moment Esther's lips parted to receive his kiss was sexual; in the way that penetration is emotional as well as physical. But then he felt her body relax, almost collapse, in the same way that his much-loved whippet, Jenny, had done when the vet injected into her vein the anaesthetic that would send her to sleep forever.

He opened his eyes to find Esther looking at him, and realised she was offering herself to him completely.

Instantly, Ricky's soul poured out of him and joined with hers. He just knew, as the minister began to say, "Those whom God has joined, let no man put asunder," that the commitment he was taking part in was more than a marriage between a man

and a woman. He knew he loved Esther, more than life itself—
that was why he was marrying her—but something sublime
and wonderful from deep within them had expressed itself too,
and become a part of the world itself, in a profound way.
Something they would never need to talk about, but would
each know was there, in and around them.

* * *

It was a nerve-wracking experience for all concerned, but the
memories were with them, bringing an atmosphere of coming
together to the proceedings. The Watsons wanted to be there.

Most of the tears cried that day were not for the bride and
groom.

* * *

While on a short honeymoon Esther and Ricky discussed
Rachel Jefferey's offer, and her acceptance of it. Although she'd
agreed, Esther was uneasy at the prospect of carrying the baby,
and, wanting her first union with Ricky to be pure, suggested
they put off the consummation of their marriage until after she
gave birth. Ricky agreed.

On their return Esther fulfilled her wish for solitude. They
bought Uplands Park, a forty-acre estate in Haslemere, about
twelve miles from Guildford, Surrey. A Tudor-style, six-
bedroomed house stood on a plateau, affording them stunning
views of the leafy village three miles or so behind. Hurt Hill
and Gibbet Hill lay to the south, in the direction of
Portsmouth, and the Devil's Punchbowl (part of Hindhead
Common) to the west. Esther finally settled down to endure
the remainder of her pregnancy.

Esther managed, with Elizabeth's help. Joan made further
progress, gradually remembering more, so that Esther began to
look again to her own future. She set up her own fashion
house, which she ran from home, producing wonderful, inno-
vative designs—an irony not lost on Ricky, who told her about
Rosie. Esther was true to her word. He was constantly by her
side. Best of all, though, her true character returned, so that the

need for revenge began to haunt her less.

Margaret had also been busy. Her beau, Thomas, whose lacquered, Teddy-Boy and Brylcream looks seduced Elizabeth, spent most of his time with her, and Andrew spent the week away. Elizabeth, who looked on Thomas as the son she had never had, didn't much mind where.

The first thing Margaret did with her money was buy the council house she lived in, at the discounted price of £40,000. She soon realised that men's heads could be more easily turned, and their pockets more easily emptied, if she presented an attractive front.

She did go to Canterbury, to buy designer outfits three sizes smaller than her figure. Then she lost two stone in weight so she could fit into them, and had her hair permed. At the end of it Margaret's transformation from slut to business woman was complete. Then she turned her attention to the owner of the bingo hall Joan so often frequented.

He was easy to snare, and when he was completely besotted with her, Margaret turned the screw. First, she got the manager the sack, saying she could do a much better job. Then she began to syphon off the profits. When the reduction showed up in the accounts she fiddled the attendance figures, convincing the old boy that the age of the bingo hall was almost at an end. The owner's wife was no problem. Margaret simply made friends with her. After a while, Margaret suggested it was about time her husband spent more time with her. They could "make me a partner, and retire to sunnier climes," she suggested. "You could buy a villa in Spain. I'll send your share of the profits to you every month."

The owner's wife thought this a wonderful idea, and readily agreed when Margaret suggested they ratify the agreement through a solicitor—"So you needn't worry," Margaret said. "I'll have my solicitor draw up a copy, and send it to you in Spain."

The old girl fell for it, but neglected to read the small print. When the company went bankrupt, six months later, they found Margaret had a controlling interest, and was the main creditor. This meant she could accept offers for the business.

Eventually, they accepted her offer of £10,000 in full settlement and gave up. Margaret took full responsibility, of course.

She'd been unable to stem the outflow of customers, who "prefer the video-machine arcades these days," she had said.

Margaret was now sole owner and knew exactly where she was going. Having foreseen the relaxation of gaming laws, she applied for planning permission to turn it into Margate's first casino. After that was passed (with the help of cash sweeteners to the most influential members of the Planning Committee) she applied for a licence. She got that too, and after a month's closure for renovation, the place was re-opened. She was on her way. And no-one knew she owned the place.

Esther's difficult moments during the pregnancy came when she had to make an excuse for losing the baby. "There's a problem, Dad. A scan shows the baby's not doing so good. I'm going to America, to see a specialist."

Early in January 1992, Esther and Ricky boarded a flight bound for America, with one of Graham's best operatives keeping tabs on them while they were there.

Rachel Jefferey made sure the medical personnel who attended Esther were qualified to cope with any eventuality, but she had no problems during the birth. Although relieved to get rid of what she saw as an alien thing, Esther felt no animosity towards the baby—a boy—but that didn't prevent her from giving him up at the point of birth. This pleased Ricky, who privately had had concerns in that area.

Esther recovered quickly from her labour, but there was still the difficulty of having to tell Terry and Joan another lie. Even though she'd prepared her ground, Esther felt ashamed. She sent a message from Washington, telling them the baby was stillborn, and they were taking a couple of weeks to recuperate before coming home to Surrey, and Margate, a few days after.

She sat in the lounge, holding her father's hand. "How are you?" she said.

"I'm OK. But how are you?"

"Oh, y'know. Could be better, but I can have more children, so it's not the end of the world."

Terry looked at Ricky, who nodded when he said, "Well, that's something. Look after her."

Esther went to Joan, who was crying. "Don't cry, Mom. It's OK. I'm fine. I'll put the kettle on."

Esther found Elizabeth in the kitchen, making the tea. "How are things?" she asked.

"They're OK, but they don't do much. Terry watches telly a lot. Joan doesn't say much."

"Does Margaret come round?"

"Sometimes. You know Margaret."

"Well, I'll be in and out every day. I'm only just up the road if you need me."

Esther returned to her business, which went from strength to strength. The freshness of her creations was the envy of all and she quickly found herself invited to give private exhibitions for A-list celebrities. Being back on the road again gave her an opportunity to get involved in various charities. She soon had a shock, though.

"Have you got a fan club or something?" said Ricky, as Esther opened her post at breakfast.

"Well, remember I said I'd get involved with charity work? Probably in Sheila's name?"

"Yes. Have you found something?"

"Look at this," said Esther, handing him a list of names. "There's thirty-four *categories*, before you even get to individual charities."

"Good God." said Ricky. "There are thousands. From A to Z. From AIDS, Age Concern, children's charities with subsections for them, education, all the way through mental health and overseas aid, to voluntary work. How can you possibly decide?"

"I've already decided to support an AIDS charity. And before you start, I don't disagree with you. But how people get it doesn't matter. The point is, it's a condition anybody can get, and it threatens everybody. It has to be beaten. I'll set up something special for Sheila. Something to do with children. We talked about having children. She was convinced you were right for me, and was so looking forward to finding someone special herself. She'd've made a great moth..."

Esther's voice cracked, the loss of her friend too painful to recall. She put down her letters and went to the kitchen window. Ricky followed her and put his arms round her. She laid her left hand on his forearm, and took a tissue from a pocket. They stood looking through the window for a while. Then Esther shared her secret, at last. "It's all my fault. If I hadn't gone to London, Sheila would still be alive."

Ricky turned her round, and brushed a couple of strands of hair away from her eyes. He held her close. Tall sycamore trees, swaying in a balmy breeze at the edge of the top paddock, caught his eye. *So that's the problem*, he thought. *Guilt. What about me? What would I do if you were dead?*

He cast the thought from his mind. "I know," he said. "But it's not your fault, and you mustn't think it is. Those people were evil. There are terrible things going on in the world. Things we can't prevent. All we can do is carry on. Sheila was happy for us, you know. She gave me a right going over just before it happened. Her only concern was that I didn't hurt you."

"What did she say?"

"She said I'd only just met you, but she'd been your best friend all your lives. Then she asked me if I was married. I said no, and that I fell in love with you the minute I saw you on the plane."

Esther smiled. "Good boy."

"She said that, too."

Esther felt better now she'd shared her burden with Ricky. He supported her in everything she did, which gave her the opportunity to forgive herself. When he became bored with fashion, he played a little poker for fun, enjoying the status the winner of a World Poker Tour event commands. Without the nightstick he couldn't read players like he'd used to, but he revelled in the mind games a player needs to use in order to be successful. The pressure was off, and he became a decent player in his own right. He never missed a charity function, though.

While on a short break at home several months later, Esther had a question for him. "D'you think the spare room would look nice if we decorated it in pastel shades of blue and pink?"

Ricky, about to reply, suddenly realised the significance of the question. He stopped what he was doing, and looked at her. She was grinning. "D'you mean?" he said.

"I certainly do. You're going to be a father."

Ricky whooped, picked her up, and swung her round. Then

he carried her to the bedroom. He laid her gently on the bed, and kissed her. Esther put her hand up, and with a stern look, said, "You wouldn't take advantage of a pregnant woman would you, sir?" Laughter filled their lives.

Two days later, they travelled to Margate to break the good news. "Dad, you're going to be a grandad. Mom, you're going to be a grandma."

Terry smiled, and held out his hand. He looked tired now. Esther sat beside him and clasped his fingers. "Hey. In a couple of years you'll be on the seafront again, remember? Telling your grandkid all about when you boxed for the title. Just like you did me. Remember?"

"Yes, I remember," he said. Terry did a lot of remembering while he sat in that chair.

* * *

Esther and Ricky spent their time between Surrey and Margate. Terry, Joan, Elizabeth and the twins stayed often, bringing the house to life. Esther had it in mind that they should all live there together, some day. The house and its 90 acres of paddocks and grazing land, overlooking swathes of Surrey, now became an idyllic place in which Esther hoped they could put their horrors behind them. She had mixed feelings about Margate, but came up with a plan to ensure Sheila's name would always be spoken in her household.

Also, she converted a spare room to an office, installed a bank of computers, and employed a secretary, experienced in the fashion business, and let her take over a little. Then she set about spending more time with Terry and Joan, and preparing for the birth of her baby.

Esther was delighted when Andrew came to visit in the summer. They walked for hours, pushing Terry and Joan in wheelchairs along winding pathways throughout the estate. They paused now and then to sit and rest on one of several benches, set here and there. On one such occasion, Esther took the opportunity to quiz Andrew.

"You look tremendous. What are you doing?" she said.

Andrew shielded his eyes from the sun, and peered over

trees and lanes, into the distance. He felt good. Fit. Confident. He knew where he was going. If he could put the demons to rest. *If only you knew*, he thought.

"I feel great, sis. I've joined up. What's that expanse of forest over there?"

Esther looked in the direction he was pointing. "That's the Devil's Punchbowl, at Hindhead. It's about five miles away. There's miles of it. It's beautiful. Quiet, and untouched. And there's the barracks at Aldershot, behind."

Andrew walked to the Devil's Punchbowl, after taking leave of Esther and the family. No-one thought anything of the gunfire they heard. They were in the countryside, after all.

Chapter 29

The Reckoning

Andrew stretched his aching limbs and cradled a matt black Mannlicher-Carcano sniper rifle lovingly in his arms. He'd been holed up in vegetation surrounding the tenth hole at Augusta Golf Course for three days, while ex-President Jefferey's security men swept the area. Twice they moved to within feet of him, but passed by as he lay motionless.

It seemed longer than five years since he'd phoned Graham, asking him to train him—to kill. Andrew wanted revenge for the attack on his parents—he said. That was true, but Andrew also saw an opportunity to purge himself of some of the guilt he felt. A chance to do something for his beloved Esther. If he could kill the man who'd raped her, he'd be paying something off his own account.

The shame Andrew felt conflicted with the overwhelming pleasure and fulfilment he got from thinking about her, and his admiration for her. Here he was at last, about to accomplish his mission. Jefferey and his party made their way to the tenth hole. Andrew, two hundred metres away, squinted down the sights of the rifle. Tailored for him, its barrel was the same as the US equivalent; the bullet he was about to fire was the .45 calibre favoured by the Mafia. The stock had been fashioned using the nightstick, and was warm and comfortable in his grip. Andrew licked his lips in anticipation of the adrenaline rush.

Graham had agreed to train Andrew, but he'd seen something else in him, too. Andrew had the motivation, undoubtably. What Graham saw was somebody he could mould into anything he wanted. Andrew was young, and basically knew nothing. He'd done well in training, and was completely under Graham's control—he thought. There would be other missions for Andrew, if this one was a success. Graham didn't know of Andrew's problems.

Andrew looked through the sights again. He checked the sun. It was high, and behind him. A problem for anyone looking in his direction from the tenth hole.

Ex-President Jefferey was enjoying his retirement. His wife had provided him with a son when she was forty-three years of age, and had completed a landside victory in her quest to fill the office he'd vacated. Today was his birthday. His son, now four years of age, was with him, and he was two up on his playing partner. They had the course to themselves, and the weather was glorious. There wasn't even a breeze to deflect the flight of his golf ball. It felt good to be alive.

Andrew eased a round into the chamber as Jefferey completed his approach shot. The rifle was perfectly balanced, even with a silencer on it. The sights were an innovation of Graham's, taking wind and rising heat into consideration automatically. The weapon was accurate to a millimetre from half a mile away.

Jefferey walked onto the green, and was pleased to find his ball ten feet or so from the pin. He was confident of getting down in two from there, maybe even holing out. Then he'd be three up. He sized up his putt, then knelt down to look along the line, using his putter as a sighter.

Andrew, through the drill, followed his every move. He took a deep breath, and covered the trigger with the forefinger of his right hand. Then he exhaled. Jefferey stood up and addressed the ball. Like every good golf player, he stood stock still, making an even better target. Andrew took one last, deep breath, exhaled, and held it.

As Jefferey turned his head towards Andrew he was aware of a red beam in his peripheral vision. Looking along it, he saw Andrew at the moment he pulled the trigger. A thin wisp of smoke rising from the barrel of the rifle was the only sign a shot had been fired.

In the split second between seeing the red beam, far away in the vegetation, and his head disintegrating, Jefferey knew he was going to die. All at once he saw trees swaying in a breeze, and smelt the flowery perfume of magnolia. The warmth of the sun on his face reminded him of the caresses of a thousand nubile women. The lush, green grass felt soft beneath his feet. Then he shat himself as the missile struck home.

The boy, standing behind his father, opened his mouth to say something as blood and matter splattered his face. The bullet diverted course as it addled Jefferey's brain, exited just above his right ear, and went straight through the boy's mouth, blowing his head off. What was left of him and his father fell to the ground.

"Huh, a cannon," said Andrew. "A billiard player would be proud of that shot. Happy birthday, mister. That's from me, and Esther."

Andrew made his escape, easing into a ground-devouring lope. He headed north to where a helicopter with USAF markings on waited, half a mile away. Its engine began to whine and its blades turn as he approached, some ninety seconds later. Andrew had picked his spot well. Augusta golf course is one of the most lush in the world, providing perfect cover. Even the security man, who didn't give in to instinct and rush towards the stricken President, missed Andrew, who blended in with the swaying vegetation. He rushed, pistol drawn, to where he *thought* the shot had been fired from, but found nothing. He stopped and listened. He could hear the faint whine of a helicopter, but took it to be a SWAT team vehicle. Eventually he had to accept that there was just nothing to shoot at.

A door opened in the helicopter. Andrew handed the rifle to Graham, who stretched out a hand to help him aboard.

"Mission accomplished," said Andrew.

"Good. Give me five," said Graham.

Andrew gave him a *high* five.

Chapter 30

Pam and Jo

Rachel Jefferey was livid when the news of her son's death broke. She couldn't care less about her husband, but Johnathan—it was just too much. And yet she had to be careful. She was under the care of Al Green now. She held herself together admirably when he phoned to report.

"I assure you Rachel, the whole thing was a tragic accident. Both your son and husband were just in the wrong place at the wrong time. Agents at the scene have positively identified an amateur hunter, who fired one round from a high-powered rifle in the forest next to the tenth green. He was a little loose with his aim and the bullet ricocheted through the trees."

Rachel Jefferey didn't believe him for a second, but had no option other than to accept what he said. It took great control to stop herself from slamming the receiver down. "Thank you. Please keep me informed," she said. Then she did slam the receiver down.

She looked at her secretary, Joanne Amin. "Every goddam thing I've tried to do has gone wrong, somehow. It's as if that Green is one step in front of me all the time. He's got an excuse for everything."

"What's happened now?"

"He's given me some bull about a hunter who can't hit an elephant from six inches, firing off a bullet that bounced off a tree and killed them both."

"D'you think he knows more than he's saying?"

"I'm bloody sure he does."

Rachel Jefferey would have to try a different strategy.

Another less prominent, but no less seething, person mourned the death of President Jefferey. His lover, Pamela Livesey. Their affair had been a clandestine one, and she knew she hadn't been the only one. But she had loved him. She wouldn't have been surprised if Rachel Jefferey had had something to do with his murder. She'd already heard the rumours in the ladies' room—about Rachel Jefferey being part of a clique of powerful women. Pamela chose to start with Joanne Amin in her quest to find out who killed her lover.

Joanne, an Asian girl, was twenty-six years old. Small, and very pretty, with her long, black hair that was usually fastened discreetly in a bun during office hours. The night Pamela chose to follow her, she had let it fall as free as her spirit. It was Saturday.

Pamela followed Joanne's Corvette through the streets of downtown Washington. It was past midnight. When Joanne pulled into an underground car park on the corner of Washington and Ninth Streets, Pamela followed her in and parked up. She sat and watched as Joanne got out of her car and tossed her hair. As she swung her purse over her shoulder, Joanne dropped her keys, and in bending down, gave Pamela a view of perfectly rounded breasts inside a white, Sara Berman camisole. Pam's eyes dropped to Joanne's knee-length skirt. Pam thought for a moment she caught a glimpse of pubic hair. *This is no promised bride*, she thought.

Pamela jumped out of her car and shouted, "Hi, Joanne. Fancy seeing you here. Off on the town?"

Joanne turned, and recognising her, said, "Yes, I'm going to the Bailey Club."

"What a coincidence, so am I. Got a date?"

"Haven't arranged to meet anyone, you?"

"No. Come on, I'll buy you a drink."

The two women clattered down the back stairs together, and out onto Ninth Street. Pamela hadn't a clue what the Bailey Club was, never mind where it was. She just followed Joanne's lead. They exited the car park, and walked a block. Then Joanne stopped, and rummaged around in her bag. "Got your membership card?" she said.

Pamela made a fair show of looking for it, then said, "Dammit. Must've left it behind."

"Too bad. It's a good job you ran into me. I'll get you in on mine."

It took a moment for Pamela to adjust her sight to the dim light in Reception at the Bailey Club. Sounds of soft music wafted up from downstairs. After paying her entrance fee, she tottered down the stairs behind Joanne, who obviously knew her way around. At the bottom was a double door, which opened easily to a comparatively small lounge. Around the edges of three sides were booths, interspersed with low tables, plush settees, and chairs. Fairy lights flickered among the torsos of figures painted on the wall behind the bar on the other side. In the middle of the room was a small dance floor. Vibrations from the music swept over them as they walked in. Pamela noticed couples dancing. They were all female.

"What's your pleasure, Pam?" said Joanne.

Pamela looked quizzically at this shortening of her name. Strobe lights, reflecting off dark, sultry eyes, glinted back at her. Pam was drawn in as their pupils opened wide. For a moment she didn't mind. But she averted her gaze as lush, red lips smiled invitingly at her.

Pam quickly scanned the back of the bar. "Um, spritzer, please," she said. She was annoyed at having ordered alcohol, but it was too late to change her mind. *What the heck*, she thought. *I'll just stay an hour, have a chat, and arrange to lunch with her tomorrow, or something.*

Inside Pam, Erato's memories stirred. In a few hours' time, Pam would wish that tomorrow would never come.

Jo led the way to where two white girls and a black girl sat, chatting. "Hi, Marie," said Jo. "This is Pam. She works in the same place I do. Pam, meet Marie."

Jo then pointed to the others. "This is Sharon, and this is Chelsea. We call her Chav." The girls laughed as Pam waved and said, "Hi."

"Hi, Pam," they said in unison.

Pam watched the girls talk, and sipped her spritzer. She sat slightly behind Jo, and to one side of her. A deep yellow gold earring, swaying from side to side, threatened to send Pam to sleep. She noticed a thin layer of perspiration on Jo's neck. Pam turned her head away, embarrassed at the thought which crossed her mind. The memories were hungry.

She was brought out of her musings by Jo saying, "Wanna dance?" and felt more than a little stupid as she heard herself saying, "You asking?"

Jo took her hand and led her to the dance floor. Pam suddenly realised she'd didn't know what to do. She'd never danced with another woman. Jo, sensing her nervousness, took control by putting both hands on Pam's hips. They swayed to the rhythm for a few minutes. Then Jo broke off as the beat changed to an oriental theme. She stood still, and lowered her eyes.

Jo began to gyrate her hips. She pushed her long, hypnotising fingers through dark, flowing tresses, which shimmered as the light caught them. Jo cast a glance in Pam's direction with eyes come alive. Then she lowered her chin again. Pam was transfixed. Her heart beat a little faster as Jo moved her hands down, lightly covering her breasts. The hands moved further down, smoothing the hips. Then Jo brought them back up again, caressing the insides of her thighs. Pam's tongue flicked over her drying lips. "No," said a voice in her brain. "Yes," whispered Erato's memories.

As if reading her mind, Jo took her hand. "Come on. We'll go to my place," she said.

"No," said the voice. But Pam didn't say the word.

"Looks as if Jo's scored," said Marie, as the pair left the dance-floor and walked away.

"Hmm. Nice arse," said Chelsea.

"She's got lovely tits, as well," said Sharon. "Plenty for Jo to get her gob round. Bet Pam's a virgin."

Laughter followed Jo and Pam, through the doors and up the stairs.

A cool night air caused Pam to catch her breath as they emerged outside. Jo quickly flagged down a cab. She told the cabbie their destination, then opened the door for Pam. The cabbie pursed his lips. He'd picked up from the Bailey Club before.

Jo smiled confidently, then leaned over and kissed Pam lightly on the lips. Pam felt herself drawn into beautiful, liquid, Asian eyes. She couldn't break away. Her legs went weak, and her heart thumped loudly as Jo's tongue gently prised open her teeth. Pam groaned, and gave in. Her legs twitched. Jo put a hand on a knee, and left it there.

Jo pulled away as the cab arrived outside her apartment block. She swivelled round, and opened the cab door. Her exit was more elegant than Pam's. Jo paid the driver, who smiled as Pam fell out onto the sidewalk, then got up and wobbled away. "Have a good night, girls," he leered.

Jo turned, and gave him the finger.

"Yeah. Wonder how many of those the other one will be getting in a minute," he muttered as he drove off.

The next few minutes were a blur to Pam as Jo showed her the way to her apartment on the third floor. The door opened directly into a large sitting room. As they went in, Jo, still holding Pam's hand, threw her purse onto a huge, cream-coloured leather settee, and led her to a large shower room. There, she slowly stripped for Pam.

The sight of Jo taking off her jewellery, and crossing both arms before lifting off her top to reveal naked breasts, mesmerised Pam. A faint, intoxicating fragrance infused her brain. Jo slipped off her skirt. *I was right*, thought Pam. She closed her eyes and leaned back against the tiles. Then she let the mood take her.

Jo's skin glistened as Pam took in every inch of her with a glance. Jo then turned her attention to Pam. First, she kissed her again, putting a hand over a breast. Pam gasped. She melted as Jo pushed her jacket off her shoulders. Then Jo undid the buttons on her blouse. A tingling sensation spread throughout Pam's body as Jo snapped her bra, revealing her voluptuousness. Swiftly, Jo put both hands inside Pam's trousers, and pushed everything to the floor.

Then she stood back and leaned against the tiled wall, stretching out a hand to turn on the water. They stood, enjoying each other's beauty for a moment, as warm water flowed over them. Pam watched Jo pick up a bar of soap, and lather up. Bubbles ran down Jo's body, and trickled into the shower pan, before swirling round and disappearing down the plug hole.

Jo washed Pam. She tilted her head back, and leant against the tiles again, under gentle pressure from Jo's smoothing hands. They seemed to have a magical touch in them. She began to tremble. *Oh, God*, she thought. Jo turned her round, and started on her back. Pam's breasts pressed against the wall as Jo's hands began a rotating, downward motion on her shoulders. Pam instinctively opened her legs, as water trickled off her head, down the middle of her back, and under her bottom. She was sure she would've orgasmed then, but Jo took a shower rose and sprayed the soap away.

Pam swayed with the pleasure of it. When her back was done, Jo turned her round, and repeated the process.

Pam closed her eyes, and drifted away. It was as if she was alone under a waterfall, in a beautiful, tropical forest. She imagined the humming of insects, and sunlight bursting through a swaying canopy, as Erato's memories took her on a telepathic journey back to the beginning of time. Then Jo sprayed her clitoris with the shower rose.

Pam froze, and held her breath. "Ooh. Oh, my God." She began to shudder uncontrollably, as her body reacted with climax after climax. If she hadn't put out her hands, she was sure she would've fallen in a heap. She was still shaking when Jo turned the water off, took a towel off the rail, and wrapped it around her. Jo then took a smaller one, and fluffed up Pam's hair. "Go and lie down on my bed," she said softly. "I'll be back in a minute."

Pam flopped onto a king-size bed, closed her eyes, and went back to the forest. Presently, Jo came back, carrying a lighted candle, and a bowl of hot water. These she put on a bedside cabinet. She took from a pocket a small bottle of fragrant massaging oil. "Turn onto your front," she said. Pam obeyed. She would've done anything Jo asked at that moment.

Pam felt a dribble of warm oil between her shoulder blades. Jo massaged the muscles in her back. Pam just knew she'd done it before. Jo worked every muscle in Pam's back, neck and shoulders, then said, "Turn over again."

The look Jo gave her as the towel fell away, as she turned over, made Pam blush. *She's quite pretty, really*, thought Jo. *Her tousled hair makes her look like a boy. You think this has been good. In a moment, I'll make you fly.*

She dribbled oil onto Pam's breastbone, and spread her fingers. Pam closed her eyes as Jo moved them round and down, over her breasts and stomach. No sound could've perforated the mood as the memories took Pam back to a time when similar acts were part of daily ritual.

Monkeys groom members of their family, she thought. *We're all just animals, really.* Her eyes flickered open, as Jo moved her hands over her stomach, and further down. This was her last chance to stop. "*No*," said a voice, inside. "*Yes, Yes,*" said Erato's memories. They could wait no longer. Pam drew Jo down, and kissed her. This time it was her tongue that probed, and flicked, inside Jo's mouth, bringing emotional urges which couldn't be denied. Jo moaned, and moved a finger to press the button that would send Pam into raptures of ecstasy.

Pam began to tingle, as Jo worked her tiny pleasure spot. Their moist skins glowed; beads of perspiration formed on their bodies. Way past the point of no return herself, now, Jo took Pam's right hand, and placed it on her clitoris. Pam closed her eyes again and, feeling herself coming to passion, arched her back. "Don't stop. Don't stop," she cried.

As they orgasmed together, Pam's eyes flew open. She stopped breathing for a second, then made a noise, something between a growl and a purr. Pam was sure she could've died from it.

President Jefferey had never made her feel this way.

Inside the oak splinter, the erotic memory's frustrations ebbed away in one continuous, swooning release. When Pam could take no more, she put her hand on Jo's. Slowly, she laid her head on Pam's stomach. Both women clung to the moment, not wanting to let it go. The only way was to take it with them, into sublime sleep.

Erato's memories were content—for now.

Chapter 31

Andrew Finds His Vocation

Graham and Andrew returned to London for debriefing. Afterwards, Graham cracked a bottle of Krug at his apartment, and raised a glass. "Congratulations on your first, m'boy."

Andrew said nothing.

"Someday I hope you'll tell me about it, Andrew. I mean, tell me about what you didn't say to the debriefing officer."

"What d'you mean, sir?" Andrew said.

"Come off it. I've been in this game a long time. Not that it's any of my business, but if I send you on any more missions, I have to be sure you're up to it. It's all very well being fired up for revenge, although you controlled your emotions in the field, but are you cold-blooded enough to blow a man's head off just because I tell you to?"

"That remains to be seen, sir."

The phone rang, interrupting the conversation. It was Esther. "Have you heard? Well, I suppose I should ask you straight out, did you do the job for me, after all? Jefferey?" she said.

Graham swerved that one. He wanted Andrew to field any of those questions. "Esther, dear. Are you in the city?"

"Not yet, but we're on our way."

"OK. Andrew's here. He's staying with me for a few days. D'you want to talk to him?"

"What've you been up to, Graham?"

"Can't think what you mean, darling."

"I'll be there in an hour."

Graham replaced the receiver. "Whoops. Better take cover, m'boy. Hurricane Esther's on the way," he said. Then, taking a good look at Andrew, he decided to press the question of Andrew's commitment, and get an answer, once and for all.

"Seriously," he said. "I need to know where you stand. It's cost a lot of money to train you. You've done well, and I think you could do a lot more to help your country, and yourself. It's a very well-paid job. I realise you asked me to train you for one mission. I did so for Esther's sake. Now I'm offering you a job. D'you want it?"

Andrew looked at his hands for a while. He felt excited inside. The same sort of excitement he'd felt when he squeezed the trigger on the Mannlicher. The memories in the oak splinter in his thumb wanted this. *He* wanted it.

"I don't care about money. I'll blow anybody's head off. Just tell me where and when," he said.

Graham was shocked at this controlled outburst, and for a moment wondered if he should reconsider his offer. Then he realised Andrew had shown absolutely no emotion at all when he spoke. *My God. I've unearthed a natural*, he thought. *I've never seen anyone as cold and calculating as him.* "Good," he said. "There's a lot of inactivity between assignments, so you'll have to keep on top of your game. I'll send you to Hereford. You'll enjoy training with the boys. They're preparing for next year's Olympics, in Atlanta, at the moment."

Andrew's heart missed a beat. He knew about Hereford from surfing the Internet. That was where the SAS barracks were. Now he was *really* someone. The best of the best. "When can I go?" he said.

"No rush. In a week or so," said Graham. "Let's enjoy Esther's company for a few days. She's bringing the boy with her."

In Solihull, Michael Jobson went into a trance-like state. Audeus' mind was searching. His master, Pythagoras, had taught him that mankind had to be allowed to rule the Earth, and he could not interfere unless a great evil was abroad. Audeus witnessed this conversation between Andrew and Graham, and saw evil personified in Andrew. He would have to act.

Margate — Same Day

Margaret, now a wealthy woman in her own right with a dozen holiday homes she'd acquired in Margate bringing in rent (including her first council house), was ready to spread her wings. She sat in the penthouse above her casino, watching play at the tables on a bank of television screens. She mulled over what had gone on during the past four years.

First Esther came home, after being all over the press as a drug addict. Then she shot off to London, followed by Andrew, who came out of his room for no reason. Then I see Sheila killed on the same day Mom and Dad get attacked. I don't know what's going on.

Margaret looked at one punter in particular on one of the screens. Then she went back to her thoughts. *That bloke, Ricky, shoots off to London. Then, when they all come back, Esther pays me and Andrew off. She must've been nearly skint after that, but twelve months later, she's got a mansion in Surrey and a designer-wear business. She hasn't made a film, so what's going on?*

Margaret picked up the phone and pressed a button. Downstairs a red light flashed on the floor manager's hot-line. He picked it up. "Yes, Miss," he said.

"Change the dealer on table four. That chap in the black jacket's winning too much. Put Clare on. Tell her to skin him."

"Yes, Miss. Straight away."

An hour later, the punter was enjoying a glass of cheap champagne in Margaret's office. "Relax," she said. "Better luck next time. You play Blackjack well. We were lucky tonight. By the way, I can extend you credit now you're a member. If you introduce a friend, you'll be credited with a thousand pounds worth of chips the first time you bring him in to play."

The hapless punter left—minus £3,000—thinking what a nice woman she was. After closing, Margaret sat down to plan her next move. It would be on Esther.

London—Same Day

Esther arrived with Ricky and their four-year-old son, Paul, at Graham's apartment exactly one hour later. Graham checked the CT screen to see who was calling, and buzzed them in. "Prepare yourself for a rollicking, m'boy," he said. He couldn't have been more wrong. Esther threw her arms around Graham's neck, and planted the noisiest, sloppiest kiss on his cheek she could. Then she made straight for Andrew.

"Gerroff," he said, swatting her away. She turned her attention to Paul.

"Say good evening to your uncles Andrew and Graham, Paul."

"Good evening, Uncle," the boy said politely to each in turn. Both men shook his hand. Paul sat on Graham's lap while Andrew went to greet Ricky. "How'ya doin?" he said.

"OK, mate. Yourself?"

"Yeah, I'm fine. How's the dressmaking?"

Ricky laughed, and gave him a hug. As he did so he whispered in Andrew's ear. "I get the feeling you evened the score. Thanks." Andrew said nothing. Ricky then went to Graham. He held Graham's hand longer, and when Graham looked at him, just nodded and said, "Thanks."

Paul held out his hand and said, "Thanks, Dad."

"What for, son?" Ricky said.

"Just thanks. Can we play I-Spy, Dad?" The boy yawned. Esther smiled at the sight of all the people she loved most in one room together. She wished she had a camera, and thought of Sheila. *She'd have loved him to death*, she thought.

Stifling the tears, Esther scooped Paul up, "Never mind I-Spy, young man, it's time you went to dreamland." She looked at Graham, "You don't mind, do you?"

"I'll be cross if you don't stay at least a week. I'll show you the guest room."

This gave Esther the chance to quiz Graham after she'd put Paul to bed. "Did Andrew do it?" she said.

"Yes, he did it. He's a natural..."

"Natural what? Killer?"

Graham studied Esther for a moment, then said, "Andrew has problems."

Esther's eyes widened. "What problems?"

Graham struggled. "Well, sometimes, if a person spends a lot of time on their own, like Andrew did, they lose the perspective of reality. They see the world as an alien place, with no useful place in it for them. Andrew's quite deep, you know. The training helped him, but he still has problems. I think he's found a role in society."

"Killing people?"

"Better that aggression be channelled to good use than be left to find its own lightning rod. Come on, let's go back to the lounge."

Graham began to give his reasons for keeping quiet about Andrew's involvement. "I couldn't let you destroy yourself with bitterness and hate, Esther. After the events in Margate and at the Connaught, you weren't thinking straight. Tempers ran high, naturally. But this sort of thing has to be done with reasoning." Graham sat down, glanced at Andrew, then continued:

"When Andrew came to me, I saw a way to settle all scores at a time of our choosing. But I had to be sure he could do the job. He's been a model pupil, and my best marksman. You can be proud of him. By the way, I have something for you, Ricky."

Graham went to a drawer in his desk. From it he took out a mini-version of Ricky's nightstick. He gave it to him. "There was a little left. I thought you might like it."

Ricky took the lump of oak and stared at it. Immediately, the oak became warm to his touch.

"Thanks," he said, and slipped the wood into his pocket.

Graham continued, "Esther gave me Ricky's nightstick when she thought he was dead. You asked me to incorporate it into a gun to kill Jefferey with. I had a gun made. In fact it was a sniper rifle. The nightstick was built into its stock. D'you want to show it to them, Andrew?"

Andrew fetched a case, and sat down in a chair. He opened the case and spread the two halves wide on the carpet. The sinister, matt black barrel of the Mannlicher soaked up the light. The swirling grain of the oak stock, perfectly tailored to the geometry of Andrew's shoulder, mesmerised all present except him. The huge, but lightweight, aluminium sight lay dull in its pocket, as if sleeping. Four, slim, pointed .45 calibre bullets sat snugly in a clip, waiting to be sent as the harbingers of doom. A small aluminium rifle support, shaped in a perfect emblem of the letter Y, stood upright, seeming to be a communication from within.

Esther shivered at the sight of it. Andrew unclipped the stock, and offered it to her. She shook her head. Graham was right. She wouldn't have been able to use the rifle. Andrew quickly assembled the rifle and handed it to Ricky. The light weight and balance of the thing surprised him. It stayed perfectly still while sitting in the palm of his hand. He put it to his shoulder, and looked down the sight.

"You won't be able to see anything in this room," Andrew said. "It's far-sighted, so to speak. For long range, from under cover." Andrew looked at Esther. "After I read what was in the CIA files, I knew I had to do something. My mind was made up when Sheila was killed, and Mom and Dad were attacked. I asked Graham to train me. I did it for you."

Esther went to his side, and sat down. She took his hands in hers. Andrew breathed in her fragrance, and looked down at her fingers. The memories came. *God, how I love you*, he thought.

Esther put her right hand under his chin, and lifted his head. "You were my little brother for so long. I was worried to death about you, stuck in that room on your own. Now, you're my big brother, and I love you very much. But I don't want you to do it any more. That little boy was only twelve months older than Paul. He was innocent."

What Andrew said next chilled her to the bone. "But I liked it," he said.

Andrew lay in bed later, unable to sleep. He knew he had to carry on. Each time he nuzzled the oak stock; got that warm feeling when he looked through the sight; he could almost taste the adrenaline rush as he pulled the trigger. Each time, a little bit of the shame and anger went away. *This* was his escape from the memories.

Andrew thought of Esther in the shower. Afterwards, he dozed—for as long as he was allowed. Andrew was on the edge of the abyss.

Around 1 a.m. Paul stirred, waking Esther. "You alright, honey? Want a drink?" she said.

"Yes, please, Mummy."

She got up and made her way, bleary-eyed from the bedroom. When she opened the door to the lounge, she found

Andrew, cleaning his rifle. "It has to be done every day," he said.

"At one o'clock in the morning?"

"I don't sleep very well. Never have, really."

"Is something troubling you, Andrew?"

He looked down at the oak stock. Its fine, whirly grain shimmered back at him. *She doesn't know what I'm going through*, he thought. *I bet she never lies awake at night, breaking her heart. I wouldn't want her to. But she's never had to worry about getting a man. No girl's ever even looked at me.* "I'm going for a drive," he said.

Esther kissed him on the cheek. "Take care. Talk to me, if you want to."

He laid the oak stock across his lap, securing it with a seat belt. The stock warmed him. Memories inside were his comfort as he drove through the night, leaving London far behind. He didn't know where he was going, and didn't care. He just drove.

Square signs, triangular signs, fluorescent lights, hanging above a people-less, tarmacked canvas tapering away in front of Andrew, drew him to a point in the distance. It was as if the car itself was taking him—not away from something, but *towards* something.

Margate—Same Night
Darren

The time was 4 a.m. A cavernous black, moonless night provided perfect cover for his task. All was still as Darren, Margaret's head of security, deftly turned a glass cutter in a circle. He applied a strip of tape to the wound, being careful to overlap the cut. Then he tapped the middle. The glass fell free, but didn't drop. He took it out, and put his hand inside the hole. He felt a key.

Looking once over his shoulder, he turned it, and opened the door. Once inside he switched on a pencil torch, and found himself to be in a kitchen. Darren put the torch in his mouth, and shone it on a rough drawing. "Out through the kitchen door, along the hallway, turn left, and go upstairs. Left at the top, second door on the right," he muttered to himself.

He reduced the chance of a squeaky floorboard giving him away by staying close to the skirting board as he crept along the hallway. The pencil beam showed him to be at the bottom of the stairs. He stopped, and listened. The only sound he heard was that of the fridge in the kitchen behind him. He'd propped the door open, in case he needed a quick exit. This man was a professional, and proud of it.

Darren walked slowly upstairs, again keeping to the sides. At the top, he paused. No sound. He shone the torch down the landing and, seeing the door, tiptoed to it. He tried the handle. Locked. Putting the torch back in his mouth, he took out a wallet containing a set of skeleton keys. Selecting one, he tried it. No luck.

Success came at the third attempt. Darren entered Andrew's bedroom, and locked the door behind him. He walked to the window and looked out. Seeing nothing, he opened it. From an inside pocket he took a knotted rope, and tied one end to a central heating radiator under the window sill. The rest he left coiled up on the window ledge: another exit route, if needed. Then he closed the curtains, and switched on the light.

Darren looked around the room. Spotting the computer in the corner, he sat down and pressed the On switch. *Fingers crossed*, he thought. The screen lit up, showing a meadow scene, with a tree in the middle and clouds in a sky.

Yes, he thought. He pressed Start. A full menu showed up on the screen. He clicked on Coral Word Perfect and " 'My Files'. Not knowing what he was looking for, he clicked on the last file to have been opened. Darren gasped as he read Andrew's last entry:

'Dad shot. Sheila dead. Ricky dead. Esther raped by President of United States. I'm going to kill the President.'

"Jesus," said Darren, out loud. "The price for this job just went up. I'll have to take a chance on the printer."

Pleased to find the printer wasn't a bubble jet, Darren selected one copy, then changed his mind and amended it to two. "Insurance," he muttered. The printer whirred, virtually silently, and spewed out two copies. He checked they were readable and dry, then put each in a separate pocket, and retraced his steps. On his way out, Darren went into the lounge, opened all the drawers, and helped himself to whatever took his fancy. Some gold. Some money. Then he opened a cocktail cabinet standing in the corner of the room. *That's a favourite place*, he thought. He took the roll of twenty-pound notes Elizabeth had stuffed into a pint pot, then tried the kitchen.

First, he opened all the jars with loose lids on, and looked inside. Then he ran his fingers along the top of the cupboards. He smiled when he touched a wallet-like object. *What mugs people are*, he thought. *And so predictable.* The wallet was stuffed with fifty pound notes. *Nice bonus*, he thought. Then he left.

Margaret was checking that night's take in the penthouse when the intercom buzzed. She pressed the button. "Yes," she said.

"It's me."

Margaret pressed the release button. Darren took the stairs two at a time, with the grace of a panther. The door to Margaret's apartment was open. She was pouring a drink when he let himself in. She looked in his direction. His face portrayed nothing.

"Well?" she said, turning away from the drinks cabinet. She sat on a cream-coloured, leather settee, and crossed her legs.

"Not much," he lied. "A few quid lying about, here and there."

"What about the computer?"

"I had a bit of trouble with that. Took me a while to work out the password."

"So? You worked it out. What did you find?"

"That's what I need to talk to you about. I'm not sure you'd want to know what I found."

"Let me be the judge of that."

"It's like this. Certain things are likely to happen after you get this information. Now, I'm not afraid of anybody, but the CIA, that's another matter."

Margaret's ears pricked up at this. "CIA?"

"Exactly. If you get involved in anything, and then squeal,

I'm likely to get it as well." Darren put his hand inside his jacket pocket, and withdrew one of the copies. "This will cost you another ten thousand."

Margaret got up slowly, and walked away from him, glass in hand. "Want a drink?" *I've got no choice but to pay him, but I'll get it back later*, she thought. "Scotch on the rocks, isn't it?" she said.

"Yeah, make it a stiff one. My mouth's as dry as President Jefferey's tongue after they found it up a tree."

"What's that got to do with what's on the paper?"

"You read the papers. Fifteen grand, lady."

"Yes, of course. Drink your scotch. I have to go to the safe." Margaret gave him his malt, and left the room. When she got back, she counted out fifteen thousand pounds, in cash.

Darren gave her the paper, finished his drink in one gulp, and held out his other hand. "Nice doing business with you, lady," he said.

Margaret turned away from him. "Get out," she said.

"Suit yourself, lady. I'll let myself out."

Darren found the stairs unlit as he left Margaret's room. *Sure the lights were on when I came up*, he thought. *Must be on a timer*. He fiddled his way halfway down the stairs, then stopped to let his eyes get used to the dim light. As he did so, a dark figure came from the shadows and threw a garotte round his head.

Darren's hands flew to his neck, scrabbling to get his fingers under the wire. The figure jerked back and sat down, pulling Darren to the floor. The wire cut into his windpipe as he tried, desperately, to shake off his attacker. But he tired with every twist and turn, and it was only the last, futile attempt of a dying man that caused them both to career down the stairs.

The end came quickly, with blood pouring into Darren's bulging eyes. The last thing he saw as his pupils drowned in blood was the face of his killer. "You..." he whispered. Then the darkness came.

The door to the penthouse opened slowly. The air around Margaret seemed to cool as she looked out the window to make sure Darren had left. Then a voice she knew well said, "Hi, sis."

She spun round. "Andrew. Where did you come from? How did you get in?"

"Followed your man in. It's a good job I came home for a few days. I very often sit in the bathroom when I can't sleep. That's where I was when your man broke in."

Margaret flew across the room. "I can explain. It's lovely to see you. I've missed you. Where've you been?"

Andrew grabbed her by the throat. "Listen, you whore. Start talking. What are you up to? What were you going to do with this?" He took out a copy of the computer printout, and rammed it into her mouth. She read it, and dropped to her knees.

"Yes, he had a spare," said Andrew. "If you get into this business, you've got to know what you're doing."

"I was only trying to find out what was going on. Nobody ever tells me anything."

She thought quickly. She felt her life depended on it. "I saw Sheila get killed. Then Dad got shot. It was horrible. You came out of your room, and disappeared. I didn't know where to, or why. I thought you'd gone mad, and were going around killing everybody." She sniffed as Andrew sat down. He said nothing.

Encouraged, Margaret carried on. "I didn't know what was on that piece of paper. I haven't read it yet. I thought I might be next."

Andrew considered this. *Either she's telling the truth, or Esther isn't the only actress in this family. Still, I've scared her witless, and she might be useful in the future. Besides, one killing a night is enough. Esther wouldn't like it if I killed our sister.* He looked at Margaret, then round the room. She held her breath.

"You seem to be doing alright for yourself," he said.

Margaret, who'd wet herself, struggled to her feet. She relaxed when she saw that cruel look gone from his face.

"Yes. Thanks. Casino's doing well. I'm sorry, but now you're here you can tell me what's going on. I only want to be included."

"I'm going home for some kip. You still have a busy night ahead of you."

"What d'you mean?"

"You've got some rubbish on the stairs to clean up."

Andrew took out a business card and threw it at her. Turning on his heel, he said, "Call them. They'll get rid of it." Margaret looked at the card, it read:

A1 Dry Cleaners.
Free Quotes For Every Job.
Carpets, Furniture and Upholstery.
Phone/Fax 0902 683 4000.

"I don't understand," she said.

Andrew's eyes froze over again. "Your man's on the stairs," he said, walking to the door.

Margaret shuddered, then raised the card. "Thanks, Andrew. I'll see you in the morning. I was going to see Elizab..."

The door closed behind him.

"Goodnight, Andr..." The door clicked shut.

Margaret flopped onto the settee, and put her head in her hands. She shook uncontrollably for several moments, then sat up, downed her brandy in one swallow, then spread her arms along the settee. "Phew, that was close. Hope the fifteen grand's still there," she said.

Washington — Next Morning

Sunlight streamed in through the window in Jo's apartment as Pam woke to the sound of birds singing. She breathed in deeply and snuggled closer to her lover, entwining the toes of her right foot with the tendon on Jo's heel. Pam gently squeezed the breast nestling in her hand.

Jo murmured something and turned towards her, tossing her hair. Pam breathed in her sweet scent, and blew the tresses away. Dark, fathomless eyes twinkled wickedly back at her.

"Hi," Pam said.

Jo yawned, turned on her back, and stretched her long, slim, almost half-caste coloured arms. The satin sheets fell away to reveal her beauty. "Hmm, hi. Want coffee?" she said.

Pam leaned across and slid a hand between Jo's legs. A smouldering look from her met Jo's questioning gaze. "Later. Now it's my turn."

Jo lowered her arms, and pulled Pam's head down. She whispered, coquettish, in Pam's ear, and began to writhe beneath her. "Be gentle. I'm a virgin." This drove Pam wild. She grasped Jo's hair, and pulled her head up. It was Sunday. No need to hurry.

Afterwards, the pair showered, drank coffee and ate toast, while sitting on pine stools in Jo's kitchen. Jo spoke first. "Terrible about President Jefferey, wasn't it?"

Now's my chance, thought Pam. "Dreadful. How's Rachel taking it?"

What Jo said next surprised Pam. "The bitch couldn't care less. If the boy hadn't been killed as well, I'd have said she probably had him shot."

"What makes you say that?"

"You must've heard the rumours. I mean, how is it she all of a sudden announces she's pregnant? Never mind she was forty-three at the time. She wasn't sleeping with him. Everybody knows he was sleeping with you, along with half the White House Staff." Jo shrugged. "Sorry. No offence. Anyway, she hated him."

"So you think there's more to it?"

"Stands to reason. I'm no shooter, but surely whoever fired that shot didn't expect the boy to die as well. Some say the Mafia were involved. What d'you think?"

They ate and drank for a moment, then Pam said, "What's security like for Rachel?"

"She has regular meetings with Al Green. She sneaks off and thinks I don't notice. I had to fetch her from the Pink Room one day, when she was supposed to be with Jefferey."

"Wow!" said Pam. "So you think Rachel's got something different on her mind?"

"I dunno," said Jo. "Seemed a bit fishy at the time. Now it looks worse. Come on, let's go back to bed."

Chapter 32

On the Edge

Esther and Ricky settled down to the realities of running her business and looking after Paul. They mapped out his long-term education, sending him as a day boy to nearby Charterhouse, partly so that Graham, who along with Andrew was godfather to Paul, could keep an eye on him while they were away.

Esther never made another film. She threw herself into her business, which thrived. Many of her customers were extremely wealthy and moved in the highest circles. Esther's fame and beauty plus Ricky's notoriety as a fearless gambler meant they were high on the list of party invites amongst the A-list clique in America. She had to go on the road again, but bought an apartment in New York to make things easier.

When she'd conquered the bitchy world of fashion Esther moved into fundraising for the AIDS Foundation. Rachel Jefferey was also involved in this organisation, but Esther managed to avoid direct contact with her. Then Esther became pregnant, and they returned to Surrey. The birth of a daughter gave Esther the opportunity to keep her promise. She named the baby Sheila.

The birth of Paul had been, for Ricky, an amazing thing. Even though he and his family were living in a society which lionised those who had money and possessions, his sense at the time was that the tiny creature, his son, was a most precious thing. Something which could not be bought. It was a time for pushing out his chest, like a puffin with a beak full of sand-eels, and proclaiming to the world that he'd played his part in securing the future of mankind. But when he held Sheila in his arms, he was overwhelmed.

"What's the matter?" said Esther.

Mesmerised, Ricky couldn't answer straight away. An energy from Sheila's as yet unseeing eyes seemed to bore into him, as if searching for his soul. Under this gaze, with the five little fingers clinging to his thumb, Ricky made the same, solemn, unspoken promise he had made when he married Esther. He had a feeling of holding the creation of the Universe in his hands. It was as if he had dipped his hands into the well of everlasting life and pulled from it the juice of the gods. "Nothing. There's nothing the matter," he whispered.

* * *

When Sheila was two years old Esther and Ricky employed a local girl, Mary, as a nanny. This enabled them to ease themselves back into the swing of things.

Andrew revelled in the discipline of Army life, and the camaraderie of the SAS soldiers at Hereford. His inner demons were kept under control, expressing themselves well in that testosterone-fuelled environment. But a repentant sinner has to have a means to dispose of shame and guilt. The opportunity to relieve the pressure came when Andrew's skills as a marksman were needed again. Rachel Jefferey had crossed the line drawn between Al Green and herself once too often.

A fund-raiser at the Hilton Hotel in Washington, early in 1999, saw everyone of note attending. Esther was surprised to see Graham and Andrew there. She kissed them both, and whispered in Graham's ear, "Why didn't you tell me you were coming?"

"Esther, darling. Didn't know you were going to be here," he lied. "How are the children? You look gorgeous, by the way."

She looked at Andrew, then back to Graham. Neither spoke. "Now I know you're up to something," she said.

"Just having a look around."

"Well look then, don't touch. At least while we're here. Come on, buy us a drink."

Graham monitored the dance floor to see who was with who, and tried to get a hint of their conversations. Andrew appeared to be taking no notice, but one woman in particular gained his attention when she brushed past him. A tingling sensation began in his thumb, and went on to cover his whole body. He felt alive.

The memories in the tiny oak splinter inside Pamela Livesey also reacted. She turned to see who she'd brushed against. She saw Andrew, smiling at her. Tossing her head, she walked away.

Graham frowned. They were supposed to be keeping their heads down.

Andrew managed to get hold of Pam on the dance floor later. Their bodies seemed to fuse together as they danced a waltz. When the dance was over, Pam whispered in Andrew's ear, "Room 1270. I'll be back around two o'clock." Andrew nodded as they clapped. Then they went their separate ways.

The sound of Andrew's footsteps were cushioned by deep pile carpet as he made his way along the tenth-floor corridor. When he found room 1270 he stopped and looked around. Then he tapped the door. Pam opened it and motioned him to enter. Not a word was spoken as they grabbed each other. Pam kissed him hard, then broke off. "Not here. Too many prying eyes. One of Green's men followed me up."

"Where, then?"

"There's an all-night Turkish called Ibrahim's. It's down the block. Go down the back stairs. I'll come to you."

The attendant at Ibrahim's was half asleep when Andrew paid and took a towel. He would later be unable to say whether or not the man who gave him ten dollars was tall or short. He did remember he might have had an Italian accent, but he wasn't sure. In any case, the woman came in alone.

Andrew took his towel and made his way to the men's changing room. He wasn't there for a sauna, so sat propping the door open with his foot. Presently Pam Livesey came in. She'd dressed down into jeans and was wearing a floppy hat, which covered one side of her face. She too paid, and took a towel. Andrew watched as she passed by on her way to the ladies' changing room. He waited a minute, then followed her. Pam was walking towards him when he cracked the door open. She had a bath towel wrapped round her otherwise naked body.

"Where?" he said. She took his hand and led him to a storeroom. Her insides were on fire. The memories *really* wanted this one. Andrew closed the door behind them, and locked it. Pam swept aside everything cluttering up the floor with her foot. She spread towels in the space she'd made, then let her towel drop, and faced him.

Andrew ripped his clothes off. Semen was already dripping from him as they met. He took her head in his hands, and kissed her, hard. She ripped his back with bared fingernails. This prompted brutal passion in Andrew. He smothered her body with nipping, biting kisses. She cried out, and lay down on the towels.

Andrew was already ejaculating as he entered her. Soon he was spent, but still he thrust in and out. Her vaginal muscles closed around him, keeping him erect. Andrew tried to pull away, but she wouldn't let him. Then she stopped.

The look that had come over Esther's face when Jefferey had raped her now leered back at Andrew. Two savage, sexual forces joined together in a crescendo of violent coupling.

Andrew, helpless, couldn't resist. Then, to his eyes, Pam's face took on Esther's visage. "No," he cried. *Yes,* a voice in his brain screamed.

Esther writhed and moaned underneath him. "Nooo," he screamed, but the memories wouldn't let him go. He could speak no more. He began to sob as Esther's sensuous look dissolved what little respect for himself he'd regained. "Make love to me," she said. "I love you. Love me, love me, love me."

Andrew whimpered as his penis rose again. Then his attitude changed as he let years of suppressed feelings for Esther go. He took Pam's buttocks in a vice-like grip, and slammed into her. "Yes, I'll make love to you. I've always loved you. I've always wanted to. I love you, I love you. I watched you in the shower. I saw you. Ohh, how I love you. I killed them for you. I killed them all for you."

The memories inside Pam realised they were no longer in charge. *She* now tried to pull away. Andrew wouldn't let her. Then, when she opened her mouth to speak, Andrew put his hands round her throat.

Even as Pam was dying, the diminishing amount of oxygen

in her brain brought on a feeling of euphoria as Andrew's pelvis ground against hers. Again and again he thrust deep into her. Finally, the force of one last, shuddering climax split them apart. Andrew flopped onto the floor, pulling the oak splinter free, as Pamela Livesey's muscles relaxed their grip on life.

Andrew sat with a glazed look in his eyes, his mind gradually blocking out the devastating scene. Then he realised where he was. He looked at Pam. She was obviously dead. He jumped to his feet, and put his clothes on. Then he unlocked the door, and took a look outside. *Nobody about.*

Unnoticed by Andrew as he dragged her body to the ladies' changing room, the splinter slid down Pam's thigh, dropped off, and lodged in the grouted recess of a tile on the floor. He laid Pam's body in one of the cubicles, thinking as he went. Graham's training had been thorough. Andrew now put it to good use.

Andrew went back to the store-room and took dry towels, and a bottle of massaging oil before returning to the changing room. There, he made sure Pam's body was free of moisture. The next step was to soak the towels in oil, leaving one corner dry. Then he carefully wrapped her in them, pausing only briefly when he came to her head. Even the hideous look of derangement on her face brought no emotion from him. He quickly closed her eyes. *Ready.*

Lighting the dry end of one towel, he stepped back and watched. He stopped long enough to make sure the oil-soaked parts began to smoulder, then locked the door from the inside and climbed over the top of the cubicle.

On his way out, Andrew switched on an extractor fan, turned the light off, then walked calmly past the sleeping attendant and down the alleyway by the side of the sauna.

Inside the cubicle, and under the towel—now glowing like a gauze element—Pam's blackened skin split as sizzling fat expanded and oozed out, adding further fuel to her cremation.

Andrew whistled calmly as he walked back to the hotel. Nobody had seen him. *With a bit of luck, whoever finds her will come to the only conclusion the facts present*, he thought. *In a few hours' time, all that will be left will be a pile of ashes. Even the bones will be reduced to ash. Pretty slick idea, my son.*

The lads would be proud of you. You really are 'the best of the best'. Sharp as knapped flint. Must tell the sergeant his idea works. "Oil-soaked rags act like the wick in a candle," he said. "But from outside. Under the rags, the temperature will rise to over one thousand degrees centigrade. And yet nothing outside the body will even be singed." *Wow!*

A snigger from Andrew's lips caused rats, scuttling across the alleyway, to pause. "She spontaneously combusted."

*   *   *

As Andrew went into his room, Graham peered down the corridor on the sixth floor. He shook his head, turned away, and went through what he'd just witnessed. *Andrew hasn't slipped over the edge, he's plunged over, head first.*

Graham let the door close behind him, took off his hat and coat, and threw them on the bed with a sigh. *Hope he can hold himself together till after the fund-raiser*, he thought.

Chapter 33

Dramatic Events at the Hilton

Margaret had been busy since her narrow escape from Andrew. She'd put herself about, leaving the raising of her children more and more to Elizabeth, who didn't mind as Margaret was paying. In fact she enjoyed acting as a mother to them. Something she'd been denied herself.

Acting on the bare information the copied paper supplied, and needing to see what was going on, Margaret flew to America. First she visited the White House as a tourist, to get the feel of the place. Then she went to the main library to find out more about the CIA, and how it worked.

While there she brought up back copies of American newspapers, to see what Esther was up to in the gossip columns. They were saying plenty.

"Esther Clayton
Ex Movie Star & Fashion Icon
Gives Generously To AIDS Foundation."

Esther this. Esther that, thought Margaret. *Well, I could spread a few quid about myself.* During the rest of her visit, Margaret hatched her plan. Then she returned to Margate.

When Margaret got back, she donated £100,000 to Rachel Jefferey's political fighting fund, and £100,000 to the AIDS Foundation. *One of them should bite*, she reckoned.

In Washington, Joanne Amin watched a fax come through. She read the contents, and handed it to Rachel Jefferey. "Looks like Esther Clayton has a sister. She lives in Margate. Look."

Rachel took the fax. "Two donations made by Margaret Clayton. One to the fighting fund, one to the AIDS Foundation." She looked at Jo. *God, you're pretty,* she thought.

Might have you myself, one of these days. "Hmm. Wonder what she's up to," she said. "D'you think she knows anything?"

"Maybe. Sisters talk to each other."

"Invite her to a fund-raiser. Not the ball. Just the dinner and auction."

Margaret duly got her invitation, and set about buying a suitable outfit. Something to show off her now trim figure. She settled for a black, knee length Chanel dress, with a neckline that would expose her chest a little, and a matching bag and shoes. Then she set off for the States.

Margaret booked into the Hilton on the morning of the auction dinner, and was given a room on the floor below Andrew and Graham. Wanting to bring herself up to date with recent events, she then took a cab to the library. Flicking through the pages of the *Washington Times*, she noticed a distinguished-looking man sitting at a study desk opposite. She couldn't quite make out what he was reading, but smelled an opportunity. It took two attempts to get his attention.

"Excuse me. Excuse me."

"Sorry," the man said. "What can I do for you?"

"I'm looking for the section on American Home Affairs, and was wondering if you could direct me."

"Not sure. There's a very helpful young lady at the Information Desk. She might be able to help you. You sound as if you're a long way from home."

Margaret smiled, and put out a hand. "Margaret Clayton. English. Over for a fund-raiser, at the Hilton tonight."

"Colin Cattell. American. That's a coincidence. I'm attending that function myself, with a client. Maybe we'll meet there."

"I'm sure we will. In fact, I look forward to it."

With that Margaret said goodbye, and walked away in her best toes-out, hip-dropping fashion, making sure Colin Cattell had a good view of her backside as she went.

Colin Cattell, a surgeon, had been deep in thought. He'd met his client—J.P. Branston, a sixty-eight-year-old billionaire computer wholesaler from Detroit, a fortnight before in Central Park, New York. The operation Branston had asked him to perform had never previously been attempted, but it was life or death for him. His doctor had diagnosed him as having a cancer from which he would die. He gave him two years at most. Colin Cattell was as certain as he could be that he was able to do what was being asked, but needed to find out as much as he could about the surgical procedure before making a final decision.

He closed his medical book, and watched Margaret's bottom sashay away. He felt a twitch in his groin. *I've just been hit on*, he thought.

Rachel Jefferey made provision for Margaret to be close to her at dinner. She wanted her on the top table, with her biggest benefactor, J.P. Branston, on her other side. Colin Cattell sat next to him. Margaret managed to overhear snippets of conversation, and realised the extent of Branston's wealth. By the time the auction was about to begin she'd made sure the places were changed so that she now sat next to Branston.

Esther, also attending with Ricky, was amazed to see Margaret there. *She's talking to Jefferey as if she knows her. Must get hold of her, later.*

In fact, the only person missing was Andrew. He was in a cubby-hole above an enormous chandelier that hovered in the middle of the ceiling. Looking round the room, he spotted Margaret. "What the hell is she doing here?" he said to himself, "I've a good mind to take the two of them out. There's Esther and Ricky. God, she's so beautiful." He began to weep as the memories haunted him again. "I'm sorry," he said. "It'll be alright soon. I love you."

Esther turned to Graham. "How's Andrew?" she said.

"He's here."

Esther looked directly at Graham, then said, "I'll never forgive you, Graham. You heard me tell him I didn't want him to do it any more. Come on, Ricky. I want to go home." The time was eleven o'clock.

"Sure. I'll get the coats," said Ricky.

"D'you want my car?" said Graham.

Esther ignored him. She got up and walked away, devastated by the feeling she had inside.

Ricky held Esther's coat open to make it easier for her to

put her arms in the sleeves. In an effort to lighten the mood, he kissed the back of her neck. "You look very beautiful tonight, Mrs Bates," he said.

Esther scrunched up her shoulders, and looked at the man she loved. The man who'd almost lost his life trying to protect her. She felt an overwhelming urge to draw her family close. "I want to be at home, Ricky," she said.

"I know. The driver will take us straight to the airport."

"I mean, I want to be with you and the children."

"OK. We'll get a flight to the UK."

Ricky regarded Esther as the car pulled onto the Dwight D. Eisenhower Memorial Freeway on its thirty-minute journey to Washington Dulles airport. Street lights flashing by, casting light and shade onto her face, brought an old-time movie atmosphere to the scene. "What's the matter?" he said.

"Did you feel anything in there?"

"Well, I wasn't very warm, even though there must've been a couple of hundred people in there, at least."

"I felt cold, too. But it was more than that. It was as if we were in a different time. A dark, dank time. I felt like an animal, when it knows something in nature is about to happen. You know—they find cover before a storm comes, and things like that. I just didn't want to be there any more."

Esther looked at Ricky for a moment, then said, "I don't want to be where Graham and Andrew are any more, either."

The car pulled up at Dulles airport at 11.40. Passengers were about to board a Jumbo jet bound for Heathrow as the couple walked into Departures, hand in hand.

At midnight, the Jumbo heaved its massive bulk into the air, and climbed to 36,000 feet. Then the pilot levelled off, and set course for the UK.

At twenty-five minutes past midnight, on the morning of February 10th 1999, all outward-bound flights from America were cancelled. Forty minutes into the flight, the pilot's earphones crackled as a message from the tower came over the airwaves.

"Jeez," he exclaimed.

"What's up?" said the co-pilot.

"Looks like we're the last flight out tonight. Hang on."

The co-pilot waited impatiently to get the rest of the message. Finally, the pilot turned to him and eased the earphones down onto his shoulders. "They're not diverting us, but the FBI will be at the other end to interview everybody when we get there," he said.

"What's it all about?"

"Dunno, but it must be big."

Twenty Minutes Before Midnight

Andrew pulled himself together. He'd seen Esther and Ricky leave. *Just as well*, he thought. He eased a bullet into the Mannlicher. No need to check the sights. They weren't needed for a shot at this close range. He looked round the room. Graham would be going to the roof soon, to fetch the gun they'd leave behind to throw investigators off the scent.

At 11.40, when the guests had drunk enough free wine and spirits to loosen their wallets, organisers began to set the auction up. While all eyes were focussed on the clearing of Rachel Jefferey's table, Graham slipped away and made his way to the roof. A cool breeze, mixing with heat coming out of large-finned extraction vents, ruffled Graham's hair as he gazed up at the stars. *They look so close*, he thought.

The Jumbo carrying Esther and Ricky passed gracefully through his line of vision. Graham thought he saw a shooting star. He looked at his watch. 11.50. As he turned and nodded at a CIA agent standing by a helicopter, the shooting star in the sky altered its trajectory, and slowly came towards where Graham stood. Audeus, seeking out evil, came in a Y-shaped, blue mist, and fused into Graham's body from behind. Graham paused, then said to the agent, "Come with me."

Visions of his youth came to Graham as he went to where Andrew lay. He remembered his father shooting his favourite hound. It had bitten a neighbour's child, and drawn blood. There was no hesitation, he simply took the dog behind a shed and blew its brains out.

Andrew looked at his watch. Thirty seconds to go. He checked the back-up piece on his other wrist, and looked at the clock on the wall behind Rachel Jefferey's head. All matched. Then he went through the routine. Andrew watched the second hand click down to midnight through the corner of his eye. As it signalled the hour, he gently squeezed the trigger.

Andrew didn't move as Rachel Jefferey's head disintegrated. He lay motionless, blood trickling from a neat hole in the back of his head, made by a round from the pistol Graham had fired.

For a moment Graham stood, as if unsure of what he'd done. Words came into his mind: *"Then shall the rabid be put to death. Even so by his own master's hand."* Graham looked at the gun he had fired, and found himself nodding helplessly. Then the whole episode faded from his senses, as Audeus left him. Graham took one look at Andrew, then sprang into action, exchanging the Mannlicher for a US weapon of the same calibre he'd fired earlier. Then he looped a strand of fishing line round Andrew's thumb. Next, he placed a packet of American cigarettes in Andrew's pocket, together with a book of matches. The book had 'Gino's Place' printed on its cover. Deftly, he played out the fishing line, and tied the other end loosely to the door handle. Then he carefully closed the door, and ran to the bottom of a flight of stairs. He handed the Mannlicher to the agent, who returned to the roof. Graham then ducked into a recess in the wall and knelt down, drawing his Browning as he did so. All this took him fifty seconds to accomplish.

Downstairs, the ticking of the brain-splattered clock on the wall behind Rachel Jefferey's seat echoed in a stunned silence for a moment. Then chaos. Graham had counted on that. Agents appeared from all directions. Women screamed. Margaret, as quick-thinking as ever, lurched to her feet, and fainted into J.P. Branston's arms, ripping the dress and exposing a breast as she did so.

Graham, kneeling in the recess, heard the patter of many footsteps. He made himself more visible, and held out his warrant card. As SWAT team members rounded the corner, he pointed to the cubby-hole and said, "I think he's in there."

The SWAT team leader looked at the warrant card, and nodded. He signed to his colleagues, then to a soldier who followed him to the cubby-hole. When outside, the leader stopped, and signed to the soldier. At the leader's signal, he kicked the door in, and rushed inside.

When the door jerked open, the fishing line pulled back Andrew's hand, then fell on the floor. The soldiers, thinking they were about to be shot at, opened fire. Andrew's body jerked as bullets ripped into it, each leaving a hole the size of the one Graham's bullet had made.

While the SWAT team members were firing, Graham—right behind them at every stage—quickly gathered up the fishing line, put it into his pocket and said, "Good show, men. Jolly good show. I'll go and liaise with Al Green to see if anything can be done for the President."

The SWAT team leader turned, and pointed his smoking gun at Graham. He held his breath. The soldier looked through a haze of cordite for a moment. Then he smiled and said, "You'd better take a bucket and spade with you then, hadn't you—old boy?"

Chapter 34

The Struggle for Margaret's Soul

Margaret produced a performance Esther would have been proud of, and when Branston suggested Colin take her outside for a breath of fresh air, saw her chance to consolidate her meeting with them. When they left the hotel, she ran off screaming.

She came to a hysterical stop when Colin caught up with her outside Ibrahim's Sauna.

"Margaret. Margaret," he said, shaking her. "Stop it." Margaret fell into his arms, sobbing.

Colin saw Ibrahim's and ushered her inside. "Look, the place will be teeming with cops soon. We'll calm down, and clean ourselves up in here, before we go back." Margaret nodded. She'd no intention of going back.

Colin paid the attendant double after seeing his quizzical look. They'd been accosted outside a takeaway, and the woman with him had had spaghetti and sauce thrown at her, he explained. They just wanted to clean themselves up. "Ten minutes in the sauna will freshen us up," he said.

Margaret congratulated herself as she took off the now ruined Chanel dress in a cubicle. *If nobody's about, I'll have him in here*, she thought.

She wrapped a towel round herself and left, looking at herself in a mirror on an opposite wall on the way out. She felt nothing as her right foot picked up the splinter, and remained unaware of its presence as she plucked at her cheeks until the rosy colour came back. Then she made her way to the sauna.

Colin was already there, dripping with sweat, head slung low. They spent a few minutes letting dirt, and matter, seep out. Colin was in no mood for sex.

The cabbie Colin flagged down thought he'd seen everything, but a man and woman standing outside a sauna wearing nothing but towels, and carrying their clothes in black bin liners, was a first. He just had time to pull away before the entire four-block area was sealed off.

Colin insisted she stay at his hotel while their clothes were laundered.

"Where are you staying?" she asked.

"The Hotel Crystal City. It's just across the Potomac River, about ten minutes from here. Not far from the Pentagon."

Margaret flicked through the pages of a catalogue in Colin's room, choosing something from the boutique downstairs. She sipped her coffee, and leant forward to put the cup on a table. The crossed-over edges of the dressing gown she was wearing buckled, giving Colin a view of a pert nipple. His heart beat a little stronger. Blood, rushing to his loins, produced movement. He was quite taken with this young, blonde Englishwoman. She was pretty, confident, without being too pushy, and obviously resourceful. Looking at her reminded him of a brief dalliance he had had with a nurse, at medical college, many years before. *Too many years*, he reckoned. He looked at Margaret's hand. *No wedding ring*.

Margaret brought him out of his fantasy. "Right. I've chosen. If I order it, will they bring it up?"

"Just write the catalogue number on the order form, along with your size. Room Service will take care of everything. Don't forget, US sizes are smaller, so if you're, say, a ten, you'll have to put down size eight."

There was a knock at the door while Colin gave Margaret's order to room service. It was a bell-boy with a note for him. He read it. "It looks as if JP's one step ahead of everybody."

"Oh. Why's that?" said Margaret.

"I quote. 'Have explained my situation to Al Green. He's given me leave to travel back to Detroit by private charter. A plane will be waiting for you at Dulles airport. It has clearance to bring you to Detroit. I expect Miss Clayton will be with you. She's welcome to come, too. My car will be waiting for you both at the other end.'"

"Why are you going to Detroit?"

"JP has a problem, and has asked me to operate."

"What a coincidence. My next stop's Detroit. I'm tracing my family tree. My father died. That's what stopped me finishing my nursing studies in England. I'm trying to trace my distant relatives."

"Sorry to hear about your father. So, you were training to be a nurse."

"Yes. But when Dad died, I had to take over the family business. That's been a success, and now I'm involved in charity work. But I'm still fascinated by surgery. Tell me more."

"Well, last year I performed an operation on a woman. She had an aneurism deep in her brain. After surgery she told me every step of the operation."

"An out of body experience?"

"Yes. But this was no ordinary experience. I'd drained the blood from her body, and stopped her heart. I'd also cooled her brain to lessen the possibility of brain damage. There was no cognitive functioning. Clinically, she was dead."

Even Margaret realised the significance of this. "Wow! That means her mind separated from her body while she was on the operating table."

"Quite so. I don't want to get too technical, but you might be surprised to know that the human brain, particularly a woman's brain, is the most complex arrangement of matter in the universe."

"Why a woman's brain particularly?"

"Because a woman's brain makes up 2.5% of her body weight, whereas a man's brain only contributes 2% of his body weight."

Margaret, about to make a smug remark about how she always knew women were smarter than men, caught sight of Colin grinning at her. "You're having me on," she said.

"No, the math is correct. It's just what you were thinking that I find amusing."

Margaret smiled sweetly, and fluttered her eyelashes. "And what was I thinking, mister clever clogs?"

"Well, to quote from Kipling, 'The silliest woman can manage the cleverest man.'"

"Kip, who?"

Colin drank a mouthful of coffee and let his eyes drop to Margaret's knees as she uncrossed her legs, then crossed them again. Their eyes met briefly. "You shouldn't sit with your legs crossed. Prevents the blood circulating—to other parts of your body—if you know what I mean," he said.

I know exactly what you mean, mister, she thought. *But Kip whatsisname was right, women are brainier than men. That's why you ain't getting any till I find out what's going on.*

She smiled seductively, and said, "You were saying, about Mr Branston?"

Colin, his unspoken invitation rejected, put down his coffee cup and sighed. "He's been diagnosed as having a cancer in his digestive system. It's terminal. His medical researchers in Detroit think they've isolated the site in the human brain where memories are stored. He wants me to transfer his memory bank to the brain of a clone he's produced, thereby saving his life."

Room service bringing in Margaret's clothes from the boutique interrupted the conversation at this point. She took them into Colin's bedroom to try them on while he dressed in the lounge.

Her mind worked like lightning. *If he can do this, the implications for cosmetic surgery are tremendous. If they'll pay forty grand for a nip and tuck, God only knows what they'll pay for a brain transplant to a new, younger body if they're terminally ill*, she thought. *I'll have to play this one at both ends, though. Just in case.*

"Colin. Could I watch you work?" she called from the bedroom.

"Well, that would be up to him. I've no objection."

Margaret smiled. "Got him," she muttered. "Great. Are you married, Colin?"

"What was that?" he said.

"I said, are you decent? Are you ready?"

"Yes, I'm ready."

Margaret emerged from the bedroom wearing a pastel-blue blouse with a high collar, and matching trousers which tapered to her ankles. A small slit at the bottom, with a pair of buttons on either side, finished them off. She knew the open-toed shoes she was wearing, similar to those Joan wore, wouldn't give her feet much protection in the cold weather, but she wanted to make an impression on JP when she got to Detroit.

She walked over to Colin, and kissed him on the cheek. "Thanks for looking after me," she said.

Colin breathed in her sweet, young body odour. "That's mah pleasure," he drawled.

"D'you think JP will have gotten away yet?" she said.

Colin looked at his watch. It was 3 a.m. "With the clout he's got, he'll be long gone."

Margaret put her arm through his. "Let's get going, then," she said.

As they waited for the lift, Margaret reflected on how cool she'd sounded when she'd said "Gotten." She fancied her English accent would charm both Colin and J.P. Branston. *Might even have the pair of them*, she decided. *P'raps not at the same time, though.*

* * *

Inside Margaret, a struggle between memories was taking place. The sexually vortacious memories anticipated having sex with two men at the same time with relish. But the road she was taking appalled another memory. Donations of organs by people in stressful situations was one thing. But no "father" was entitled to kill his child in order to save his own life. Clone or no clone. A message had to be sent to the bench.

Chapter 35

Ricky and Esther Fly Home

Esther was dozing with her head on Ricky's shoulder as Margaret and Colin Cattell waited to board the plane at Dulles airport. Ricky was thinking about Paul and Sheila, and how much he missed them. Neither he nor Esther had seen much of their children since Sheila's birth. His thoughts turned to the series of fantastic events that had changed his life forever when he met Esther.

She groaned, and shifted position. Ricky wondered if she was dreaming again. He looked out of the porthole, as the giant plane flew on, taking them ever closer to home, and the children. The blackness of the night outside became a screen for his mind to project his memories onto. He saw himself lying on a hospital bed, after the shooting at the Connaught Hotel. He'd no motivation to live. Nobody came to him, and he thought Esther was dead. He felt no pain. The memories inside healed his wounds, and tried to comfort him. But he thought his heart would break. Then Esther came to him, as if in a dream, and put her hand in his. He knew then he *would* live.

The revelation that she was pregnant by Jefferey had only strengthened his bond with her. His commitment to her was unconditional. In fact, it meant so much to him, he'd had difficulty getting the words out, when asked, at their wedding. He smiled as the scene changed.

"Do you take this woman to be your lawful wedded wife?" the vicar asked.

Ricky had no problem with that. "I do," he said.

It was when the vicar said, "Repeat after me, I, Richmond Edward Bates, take thee, Esther Joan Clayton, to have and to hold..." Ricky just couldn't say the words. He breathed in too deeply, bringing the danger of hyperventilating. Then, when he exhaled to have another go at it, his insides got all knotted up. Esther squeezed his hand, and the vicar leaned forward in anticipation, but nothing happened. The congregation nearest to them nodded slowly up and down, as if willing him to say the words.

After he'd finally got them out, the vicar said, "Thank God for that. I was thinking I'd have to do it myself."

Laughter broke the tension, but Ricky had been making a solemn vow to himself—that he'd always be there for Esther, and try to make her happy. His last thought as Esther stirred, and brought him back to reality, was that when they got back, he'd be a proper father to his children.

Mumblings and gesticulations by passengers in seats around them caused Ricky to look round. They were pointing at a television screen. This disturbed Esther, who shook the cobwebs away. "What's going on?" she said. Ricky pointed to the screen. It was showing the aftermath of events at the Hilton. Esther jumped up. "Let me out. I must see."

She ran to the nearest screen, looking for any sign of Andrew, Margaret or Graham. An air hostess tried to make her sit down. "Please, Miss Clayton, return to your seat. There are headphones there."

Esther was frantic. "My brother's there. I must see what's happened." Then she turned to Ricky. "Ricky, go and speak to the captain, please." Then she burst into tears. She knew her premonition had been correct. Something bad had happened. Now the feelings of panic, and guilt for not being there for Andrew, overwhelmed her. The blood seemed to drain from her legs as she stared at the screen, and a feeling of emptiness she'd never fill took its place. She slumped into her seat, and put on a pair of headphones.

Suddenly, the Jumbo lost height sharply, causing panic amongst some of the passengers. Ricky felt a tangible atmosphere of fear pervade the plane. Then the co-pilot appeared from the flight deck, a service revolver in a holster hanging from his hip. He raised his arms. "OK folks, don't be alarmed. There's been an incident at the Hilton Hotel in Washington. President Jefferey's been assassinated." A stunned silence greeted this statement, followed by uproar.

Ricky was almost at the cabin door when the co-pilot appeared. "Can I have a word with the Captain, please? We came from the Hilton to get this flight. Relatives of my wife, the actress Esther Clayton, were also at that function. She's worried."

The co-pilot looked at Ricky for a moment, then said, "You'd better be quick. They'll all want to go in soon."

"Thanks. I won't be long."

"You'll get more information from television screens than I can give you, Mister Bates," said the pilot. "I've been instructed to reduce height, but that's just a precaution. We're continuing our flight, and will be landing at Heathrow in about four and a half hours. I should warn you, there'll be a long delay after we land."

Ricky thanked the pilot, and returned to his seat.

The Jumbo banked hard right and began its approach to Heathrow. Ricky peered through the window at the new day dawning and wondered what lay ahead for them after they landed. The giant plane swooped down, as if it were a bird of prey sighting its target. Wing flaps, opening to slow it down, produced a scream which could have been a death knell. Ricky turned to Esther and said, "There'll be chaos when we get off. Before it starts, I want to tell you this. I know what you meant when you said you wanted to be with me and the children. When this is over, we're going to be a proper family. No more travelling the world, not until they've grown up, at least."

Esther, wiping mascara away, started crying again as he continued. "You and the children are the most important things in the world to me. Paul and Sheila are going to come home from school each day to find their mother and father waiting for them. If you want to do something in business, you can do it from home."

Esther realised she'd been terribly selfish. She remembered once thinking she wanted to conquer Hollywood more than anything. Now this man, the father of her children, was showing her the way to ultimate happiness. Bursting with emotion, she said, "I'm going to be the best wife in the world to you. Will you marry me again?"

"Yes. I'll marry you again. And to do it, I'll take you to my church, back in Solihull. The vicar there's a good man. He'll bless us."

Ricky was interrupted by an air hostess as the plane came to a standstill. "Ladies and gentlemen, please keep your seats. Don't be alarmed by the sight of armed men boarding the plane. They're policemen who will be asking for your details before you leave. With respect, this is not optional. Please remain seated until they say you're free to go."

An hour later, Esther and Ricky still hadn't been interviewed. Then Esther recognised one of a fresh batch of soldiers boarding the plane. It was the SAS Major who had saved their lives at the Connaught Hotel. She waved to him. The major noticed her, and nodded. He brought his hand up, then lowered it slowly, turning his palm downwards as he did so. Esther sat down. The major first said something to the man behind him, who spoke into a radio, then made his way to where Esther and Ricky were sitting. "Hello, Miss," then "Sir," acknowledging Ricky. "I've ordered my colleague to get in touch with Commander de Courcey. He'll be here to see you later. In the meantime, please remain seated while we interview the other passengers."

"What's happened?" said Esther. "Is my brother alright? What about my sister? She was there, as well."

"D'you mean you were at the Hilton, Miss?"

"Yes. We were at a fundraising dinner, but left early."

The Major thought it suspicious that they'd left early, and stranger still that they'd gone straight to the airport and left the country minutes before the President was assassinated. Still, that was no concern of his. The Commander would sort them out. "You probably know at least as much as me, Miss. The Commander will tell you what you want to know."

Graham was drinking champagne from a flute with one hand, and running his fingers through the fine, blonde hair of a Swedish beauty with the other, six hours after leaving the Hilton. The helicopter waiting on the roof took him to rendezvous with a USAF fighter, which landed him at Lakenheath five hours later. He needed to be in London when the phones started ringing, as his did now. He put his glass down, and said to Agnetha, "Take a shower while I answer this, will you, my dear?" He watched the girl slip from under satin bedsheets, and bounce across the room. "I do love blondes," he sighed. He lifted the receiver, and looked at the front page headline in *The Times*, already reporting the bad news. The date of the bulletin was February 12th 1999.

MURDER OF PRESIDENT STUNS US
SECOND TRAGEDY IN JEFFEREY FAMILY
BRINGS COMPARISONS WITH PRESIDENT
KENNEDY AND BOBBY KENNEDY
OUR SPECIAL REPORTER ASKS—IS THE
MAFIA INVOLVED?

"Hello, Al. How are you?"

"Great, thanks. You?"

"Tired, but OK."

"Does the British Government suspect anything?"

"Not a thing, old boy. Everything's hunky dory, as they say in Virginia."

"Well done. Stupid woman. Thinking she could run a man's world. And her even more stupid husband. He had it made, and he shagged himself into an early grave. Nearly spoiled it for all of us."

"I don't know about him, but I'm all for women's lib."

"Haven't a clue what you're talking about. Whatever. Did you cover your tracks?"

"Yes, they'll think the Mafia did it."

"Good. You know what you're doing. Leaving your man, I mean. Have you got anything for me?"

Graham ignored the mention of Andrew. "The Cabinet is meeting tomorrow. My contact will have the minutes an hour after it closes. I'll send the details via the usual route," he said.

"Great. The hundred grand will be in your Swiss account by mid-morning your time. Goodnight, or should I say good afternoon where you are?"

"Goodnight, Al."

Graham didn't replace the receiver, but pressed another number. The line clicked at the other end.

"Good morning, Prime Minister," said Graham. "Green's

none the wiser. I've told him I'll leak the details of the Cabinet meeting. Probably later in the afternoon. That'll give your men time to decide what to feed him."

"Well done. You'll get a knighthood for this. Shame about your man. Did he have family?"

"Just sisters, and an aunt, I think." A cold, slithering feeling started in the back of Graham's head, and made its way down his spine and the outsides of his legs, before exiting through his feet. He shuddered.

"Well. Damn good man," said the Prime Minister. "I'll mention him to Her Majesty at the next honours meeting. Can you make up a four at bridge tonight?"

"Thank you, sir. I don't know, yet. Can I phone later, to confirm?"

There would be no bridge for Graham that day.

Graham was uneasy as he replaced the receiver. There were questions he needed answers to. *What caused Andrew to go insane? Why did I suddenly decide to kill him? Why did Andrew shout Esther's name as he had sex with Pamela Livesey? And why were they so drawn to each other? As far as I know they didn't even know each other. How am I going to tell Esther? What am I supposed to say? "I'm sorry Esther. I don't know what made me do it. Andrew was insane, you see. He strangled this woman in a sauna while he was having sex with her. He was calling your name out, by the way. Then he wrapped her body in towels, and set light to it. I had to do it..."*

Two firm breasts, pressing into his back, took Graham away from his post-mortem. "Are you coming back to bed?" Agnetha said.

"Yes, my dear, you warm my side, I'll be with you in a minute."

As Graham slid back into bed, he'd a feeling of déjà vu. He wasn't alone.

When a murder is committed close up, the victim and killer exchange something. Body fluids, DNA, or in Graham's and Andrew's case, skin. At the point of his death, in circumstances of neglect and betrayal, Andrew's memories left his body. Audeus would've taken them, but as Graham manhandled Andrew, his memories transmigrated to a flake of skin on the rifle stock. The attraction of static electricity from Graham saw the skin transferred to him. Graham could enjoy the fruits of life, something Andrew could never now do. *But his memories knew.*

As soon as Graham had settled down again the phone rang. He was wanted at Heathrow.

Esther spotted Graham, and waved, as he entered the plane. He motioned her to go to him.

"Hi," said Graham as they approached. Esther looked at him, but said nothing. Ricky returned his greeting.

Graham led them away from the Jumbo, and into the terminal building. He took them to an interview room, and sat them down. Esther thought the air hung—not dank or primeval as in the Hilton, though. This time she felt a void surrounding her. It was as if she and Ricky were separate from Graham now. A barrier was between them.

Esther's eyes traversed the table in front of her. She noticed a blonde hair on Graham's shoulder. When their eyes met, she was drawn in, but not with trust and love as on the night she'd given herself to him. A picture of the blonde hair flashed into her mind, together with words: *'When there's contact between people, something's exchanged.'*

Esther felt nervous. Audeus' energy, sensing Esther's distress, now linked with hers. She stood, transfixed, as she looked at Graham. The atmosphere in the room became heavy with emotion. Graham's eyes widened as Esther concentrated all her mental energy on him. For the first time, she began to use that sixth sense. That feeling of just *knowing* something. All stress faded from her, to be replaced by a feeling. A feeling of death.

The mind cannot run when the eyes tell it danger threatens. If the eyes cannot see the missile or blow which kills it, instinct takes over at the moment of impact. An animal such as a cat will jump straight up in the air when it's startled. This is an instantaneous reaction, stimulated by the brain using all its senses to assess information and send a signal to act, in a billionth of a second.

As the bullet from Graham's gun smashed through the back of Andrew's head, his brain was instantly aware of all things around him, through sight, sound and smell. Esther smelled *Graham*.

She flew across the table at him, screaming, "You *killed* him."

The table overturned as Esther tried to get at Graham. Pencils, papers, an ashtray, pens and a coffee cup, which Ricky noticed in *his* peripheral vision had mould round the inside of its rim, went flying.

Graham lurched back, open-mouthed, as Esther went for him. Ricky froze for a second, then leapt forward and got between them. She was hysterical. "You killed him," she screamed again, scrabbling with bared fingernails. Graham's mouth shut, then fell open again, as Esther ranted.

"Esther," shouted Ricky, putting his arms round her. She whirled him round, still trying to get to Graham. Her strength was superhuman, and Ricky was having difficulty holding her. He turned towards Graham. "Get out. Go, now," he shouted.

Graham, ashen-faced, slowly sidled away. As he approached the door, he turned and looked at Esther, who was drooping, utterly defeated, in Ricky's arms. *What have I done?* he thought. *What have I done?*

* * *

Esther and Ricky wandered out of the interview room, and looked for a taxi.

"It's about a hundred quid to Surrey, Guv. You OK for that?"

Ricky smiled, realising how scruffy they must look to the taxi-driver, and recalled an occasion he'd said much the same thing to a punter who'd flagged him down, in Birmingham. *How long ago* was *that? Can't remember, now. Seems a life-time ago.* He opened the door, and took Esther's hand.

"That's OK," he said.

Exhausted, she laid her head in Ricky's lap, and dozed. Bewildered by what he'd seen, and disturbed by Esther's outburst, Ricky stroked her hair and tried to make sense of it all. *What did she mean when she screamed, "You killed him" at Graham? The President was a woman. And what happened to Margaret?*

Esther stirred and sat up as the taxi pulled off the M3 and took the road for Guildford. She fluffed up her hair, and rummaged about in her bag for a wet-wipe.

"You OK?" said Ricky.

"Andrew's dead," she said.

"How d'you know? It was the President who got killed."

"Andrew did it. Then Graham killed him. I can't explain it, but I felt it. Like the dreams."

"You're not making sense."

Esther found a wet-wipe, and her powder compact. She flipped it open, and looked in its mirror. Smudged tear marks had replaced the rosy complexion. Dark shadows under her eyes underlined the misery pouring from her soul through bloodshot pupils staring back at her. She wiped her face, took one quick look, and closed the tiny case. "Andrew's dead," she repeated.

The taxi driver half-turned as he drove into Guildford. "Which road now, Guv?" he said.

"Take the Godalming road, please. You go through Godalming, and head for Haslemere. It's not far."

"OK, Guv."

Ricky looked at Esther, now staring through the window. Her hands were shaking. He moved across the seat, and pulled her to him. Her shoulders convulsed within his embrace. She let it all go in silence.

Twenty minutes later Ricky directed the driver through the lodge gate and along the winding, uphill driveway. It was late afternoon. The driver noticed the paddocks, once filled with yearlings, and an outdoor swimming pool. The tarmac petered out and became shale-covered dirt, before reappearing as the car reached the plateau. He saw a house with a separate garage and a mature, enclosed rear garden. Tall, frost-covered conifers protected the house from the side.

Esther went to the house while Ricky sorted the driver out.

"Nice place, like a Christmas card," he said.

"Thanks," said Ricky. He would've agreed, but somehow felt the cold in his bones this day. He pushed both hands into his pockets, and looked around. "Yeah. Like a Christmas card. Thanks, g'bye."

Sheila met Ricky at the front door. She ran to him. "Daddy. Daddy."

"Hi ho, what's this, then? How's my girl?" said Ricky, sweeping Sheila into the air. Sheila touched his forehead. "Daddy. Your face is dirty. Mary will tell you off."

"Well then, I'll have to shower, won't I? Ask Mary to make a cup of tea. You can help. Where's your brother?"

"Don't know."

"Well, go and find him, please."

Ricky hunched his daughter up, carried her into the house, then put her down. Sheila ran off as Mary appeared.

"Hi, Mary. Where's my wife?" said Ricky.

"I think she went straight to her room, sir."

"OK. Take Sheila to the kitchen, will you? And keep her occupied for a moment, please."

"Yes, sir."

Ricky found Esther sitting in front of her dressing table in their bedroom, speaking on the phone. He sat on the bed, and watched her. She smiled a wan smile.

"Dad, we came back early. Yes, we had a nice time. How are you? How's Mom?"

Ricky put a hand on her knee. She covered it, and squeezed. She nodded as Terry spoke. Ricky was amazed at the transformation. *This woman would get up and walk away five minutes after a nuclear explosion,* he thought.

The misery Esther felt inside seeped from the corners of her eyes again as she said, "Dad, Andrew won't be coming home for a while. You know he was working away? Well, he's been posted overseas, now. No, I don't know where, but it's a very important job. He said he'll only be able to phone me sometimes."

Ricky put his hands on her shoulders. He kissed the top of her head while she finished.

"OK, Dad. I'll phone. Bye."

Esther pulled a Kleenex out of a box on the dressing table and wiped her eyes. "That's all I could think of to say. I couldn't tell him," she said.

"But you don't know..."

"Believe me, I know—he's dead, and Graham killed him."

Ricky put his arms round her. "Well, at least it'll buy us some time."

"Thank God I've got you. Make love to me."

"The children."

"Make love to me quickly, then."

Ricky locked the door.

Terry put the phone down and looked at Joan. She sat in a lounge chair, wide-eyed and open-mouthed, as if gasping for breath. He hopped the couple of paces between them and put his arm round her. "That was Esther, sweetheart. Andrew won't be coming home for a while."

Joan closed her mouth, then whispered something he couldn't understand. Terry patted her shoulder, then hopped back and plonked himself down in his seat. *She's getting worse again,* he thought, turning up the sound on the television. He looked at her again. "I expect Esther will bring the children soon. You'd like to see them, wouldn't you?"

Joan said nothing.

Terry rubbed his left knee and looked at the stump on the other side, sticking straight out. He could feel his other leg, even though it wasn't there. He imagined the stump being in the middle. *Could be a massive, sheathed penis,* he thought. Then he closed his eyes, and tried to doze. Thoughts of Andrew came to him. And of Esther as a little girl, dangling her legs under the bench on the seafront. And of Margaret. *What's she doing?* he wondered.

Margaret was still on the other side of the Atlantic.

Chapter 36

J.P. Branston

Colin Cattell seemed to Margaret to have retreated into the preoccupied state she'd found him in when she'd first met him in Washington Library. He didn't utter a word throughout the whole flight. She didn't mind. He was no longer number one on her list.

Colin was considering the proposed surgery. He didn't yet know if the facilities at Branston's medical centre would even be suitable. He'd have to take that on trust. The main problem, as far as he was concerned, was detaching the minute piece of Branston's brain safely, never mind attaching it to the clone. *Rejection shouldn't be a problem*, he thought. *Branston and the clone share the same DNA. Perhaps I could transplant the whole brain.* He was still mulling this over when Margaret nudged him, two hours later. "The plane's about to land," she said.

"Oh. Right. Thanks."

They only had hand luggage, so progress was swift at Detroit Metropolitan, Wayne County Airport, eighteen miles southwest from downtown Detroit. Branston's chauffeur was waiting on the runway with a limousine, as promised. A bitingly cold wind, blowing as she disembarked from the plane scantily dressed, reminded Margaret to do a little shopping at the first opportunity.

Margaret supposed Detroit to be boring. The only thing she knew about the place was that cars were made there. Sitting in the plush interior of the limousine reminded her that she couldn't remember when she'd last slept. She dozed as the car glided out of the airport and began the remainder of their journey to the youthful, upmarket suburb of Royal Oak, some ten miles north of downtown Detroit.

Colin took much more notice of the surroundings. He also knew cars were made there, but seeing the place again brought back memories.

The legend that is Tamla Motown started in 1959 when Henry Ford and part-time songwriter Berry Gordy Jr borrowed eight hundred dollars to set up a studio in Detroit's West Grand Boulevard.

Three miles east of the Renaissance Center, Belle Island is an inner-city island retreat, with twenty miles of walkways, sports facilities, a marina, and attractions such as elaborate gardens and the Great Lakes Museum. Colin had seen them all. He'd attended the Detroit Grand Prix Indy Race when studying at Wayne County University. He remembered "digging" the music at the annual free Ford Detroit International Jazz Festival in his sophomore year, almost twenty-five years before. He knew the place well.

The limousine passed the Henry Ford Museum and manu-facturing plant on Oakwood Drive, where Henry Ford employed 78,000 workers in the 1930s, and skirted Detroit City, as it made its way to pick up the freeway. Colin dozed.

The crunching of tyres on gravel woke Margaret. She yawned and stretched, even more drowsy now, and looked at the scene.

The limousine made its way slowly up a long, tree-lined avenue, before pulling up outside a wide, two-storey wooden mansion. Margaret was impressed; even more so when a servant opened the door of the car, and offered an arm to help her out. "Good morning, Miss," he said. "Mister Branston's expecting you."

"What's your name?" said Margaret.

"Henry, Miss."

"Thank you, Henry," said Margaret, taking his arm.

J.P. Branston met Colin and Margaret in a large reception hall. He took Margaret's hand, and bowed slightly. "Good morning, my dear. I trust you've recovered from the traumas you were forced to witness?"

"Yes, thank you," said Margaret, impressed again. This time by the old boy's style.

Branston then addressed Colin. "Good morning, Doctor. I

hope the exertions of the last twenty-four hours haven't diminished your capabilities."

"I'm OK," said Colin, shaking Branston's hand.

Margaret felt as if she'd been transported back to a time of gracious living and manners. Indeed she had, in a way. The old colonial house echoed with those kind of memories.

"I expect jet lag is setting in after her change of continents," said Branston. "I've had a light snack prepared. After that, perhaps she'd like to rest."

Margaret was afraid to open her mouth. *It'll take time to adjust. Don't want to put the old boy off with any lack of manners*, she thought.

She decided to make sure he'd a good view of her cleavage when she replied, so turned full-on towards him before saying, "Thank you. Yes, I expect you've things to discuss with Colin."

Branston showed them to a lounge-reception room just off the entrance hall, and sat them down. Then he pressed a button on the wall.

Margaret let the plush, damson-coloured leather settee envelop her, as if Heaven's clouds themselves were wrapping around her. *I've never seen such poshness*, she thought. *This lounge is as big as my house.*

Henry appeared, carrying two silver salvers of hors d'oeuvres, which he placed on a knee-high table in front of Margaret. A girl, suitably dressed in a white blouse and black skirt, around which a frilly white apron was tied, followed him in carrying a tray of sandwiches—*with the crusts cut off,* Margaret noticed.

Henry opened a drawer in a sideboard which occupied one corner of the room, and took out three napkins. From another drawer he took three side salad plates, one of which he gave to each of Branston and his guests. The girl supplied the cutlery to go with them.

I'm definitely having some of this, thought Margaret.

"Ahem," said Henry, offering a tray of hors d'oeuvres to Margaret.

Margaret realised both Colin and Branston were looking at her, waiting for her to choose first. She scanned the tray, looking for something she recognised.

Realising the small, round tin full of little black balls must be caviar, Margaret took the silver spoon resting on the rim's edge and scooped out a portion. Then, spotting brown, curled-up toast in a lattice-like pile on a plate, she smeared the caviar on a slice, and took a bite. *Fishy,* she thought. *Nice, though. Reminds me of Sago.*

Margaret glanced at Branston, who was talking to Colin. Even though the men were ten feet or so away from her, the layout of the room prevented her from feeling isolated in any way. She gave a distinctly uninterested appearance as she gazed round the room, nibbling on her toast. But Margaret heard everything.

"How are your symptoms?" Colin said.

"No change," said Branston.

"I'd like to check your blood pressure and vitals at the earliest opportunity. Is your medical complex in Detroit?"

"No. It's nearer than that," said Branston. "Don't you want to rest first?"

"I'd rather give you the once-over, and familiarise myself with the layout."

"OK."

Branston turned his attention to Margaret. "Would you excuse us, my dear? The doctor needs to examine me. I'm sure you understand."

"Of course, Mister Branston."

"Henry will show you to your room when you're ready. Dinner is at eight. In the meantime, feel free to browse round the house. And please call me James."

"Fine. Thank you, James, and the caviar was delicious."

Branston smiled at her, rose to his feet and motioned Colin to follow him.

Colin expected to travel to Branston's medical centre, and was surprised when he produced a key and unlocked a door in the reception hall. Colin saw a pair of lift doors about three feet in front of them, which opened smoothly after Branston pressed a button on the wall. Colin's eyes needed a moment to adjust to a pink-tinged light, illuminating a long corridor facing the men, after the doors opened.

"Follow me," said Branston.

This place must go on for miles, thought Colin as Branston led him past room after room. In fact, the only thing that would give anyone an idea of the size of Branston's underground complex was a barn, situated in a field about two hundred yards away from the house. This vent-covered structure concealed equipment necessary to keep air circulating below.

Presently, Branston stopped and opened one of the doors. Inside was a consulting room containing everything Colin would need to complete his examination.

For a man of his age Branston appeared unusually fit and healthy. Tallish and broad-shouldered, with a thick set of dark hair, he gave no outward signs of the monster within slowly invading his life-support system.

Born in 1931, James Philip Branston was the third son of wealthy Jewish immigrants who, like hundreds of thousands before them, had emigrated to what had become known as 'the Land of the Free' in the hope they could make a better life. His father, Binjamin, a jeweller, had fifty dollars in his pocket when he disembarked at New York in 1925. He met Elisha, the woman who was to become his wife, on the ship. The physical attraction was instant and mutual, but it was with solemn purpose they travelled separately from Amsterdam.

The euphoria that being in love brings was tempered by that purpose. After clearing immigration they set out, hand in hand. He with his fifty dollars, a few watches, and two small diamonds, sewn into a pouch under his armpit. She with a suitcase containing underwear, a spare petticoat, a set of silver cutlery, and a dog-eared picture of her parents.

First, they married. The dingy room in which they were united bore none of the Byzantine trappings of nuptial celebrations their faith usually demanded. Just a parlour, in a house owned by the nearest rabbi they could find. But all five of them, Binjamin, Elisha, the rabbi and two witnesses, shared the same ethnic bond.

After a week in lodgings, and a lot of asking about, Binjamin made several contacts and set up business. The couple scrimped along during the years which followed, with Elisha saving a few cents here and there as best she could.

Branston's elder brothers were born, and as the business flourished, Binjamin put down a deposit on a shop and moved his growing family into the flat above. Through their hard work the situation changed so radically they began to plan for a future they had hardly dared think possible before. Elisha loved her sons, but they'd come in difficult times. She looked forward to James's birth. As she nursed him, Elisha talked to him. "Yes, my son. I'm your mother. No-one will ever love you as I do."

James gazed into his mother's eyes while suckling. Her tone of voice and gaze first triggered, then cemented, the bond innate in both. "You'll grow up tall and strong in this land of opportunity. You'll never know the pangs of hunger, or fear the sound of a human voice."

Binjamin, sitting, smoking his pipe and watching this, later confided to a friend at Elisha's funeral that this moment was the only time in his life he doubted his faith. "For a second, I was convinced of the truth of Christianity," he said. "I sometimes feel that there has to be more than a book. It just came to me. Then I saw the creation of the Universe. And I knew that watching Elisha was seeing the manifestation of the Universe evolved in a woman. I know my son couldn't be alive without me, but I felt, more strongly, that Elisha, and all women, are the true givers of life. Each time a child is born, it's the creation of the Universe all over again."

"She was quite a woman, your Elisha."

While James was growing up, Europe descended into war. Binjamin was fearful of American involvement, despite the general feeling of detachment from Europe and President Roosevelt's assurances that America would stay out of it. He moved his family inland, and settled in the bustling manufacturing city of Detroit.

His fears were realised when America was forced to declare war on Japan in 1941, following that country's cowardly attack on the American fleet docked in Pearl Harbour. Binjamin had his hopes of his sons taking over the business dashed during this period. James's brothers went to work at the Henry Ford plant as soon as they could. Elisha was just relieved they were too young to be included in the slaughter.

Priorities changed immediately war broke out. Production of cars was put aside. James sat, mesmerised, in a field on a hill overlooking the plant, watching a seemingly never-ending stream of vehicles of every sort disgorge from the factory.

As James followed the progress of the war, he absorbed information about new things that technology invented. By the time hostilities ended, his mind was filled with scenes of code-breaking, jet engines, and what we now know to have been the invention of the computer. He too joined the Henry Ford Motor plant when he was old enough.

James flourished in an environment of forward thinking, and soon transferred to a department researching braking systems and the early use of electricity within the car. Windows that raised at the touch of a button, and such like.

As the years passed by, basic computers became smaller, and the idea that they could be incorporated into the motor car was investigated. Some knew the future for computers wasn't in cars, or in being used to calculate mathematical tables and equations for wage-slips in offices.

Cottage industries abounded in garages all over the country. James was involved, but realised competition was so intense that making money from it would be difficult, especially as egos had to be contended with. He saw the different factions come up with a new advancement each month or so, and decided to get out.

James quietly made contracts with each faction to supply the finished product to what he saw was going to become a massive private market. He also contracted to deliver, by hand, any replacement computer part to anywhere in America within twenty-four hours. This was a stroke of genius, and the foundation of his fortune.

But running such an empire, and fending off competition, left no time for socialising. Elisha did her best, arranging for him to meet nice girls from good Jewish families. But James always had a deadline to meet, or a deal to broker. The most he managed these days was an occasional midnight tryst with Carrie, the maid.

Then, in the early 1970s, James sensed that advances in medical science were about to take off at the same rate that earlier advances in computers and transport had, after the success of an experiment to fertilize a human egg inside a test-tube, was announced. Determined to be in on it from the beginning, James bought his house, and the grounds it stood in, with the building of an underground research centre in mind. He wanted no prying eyes stealing his thunder. He chose his staff himself, and paid them well. But he took no chances. None of them knew what the research in any other part of the complex had to do with what they themselves were doing. He alone knew the possibilities his research promised.

Even James hadn't seen the possibility of cancer, though. As Colin examined him, he lay thinking: *What am I left with, after all these years? A death sentence. I own a billion-dollar business. My parents are entombed in a vault on a huge estate, which I own outright, and I've millions in spare cash. Yet I've no-one to say I love you to, or to say it to me. I must have more time.*

Chapter 37

J.P. Branston Jr

Margaret subconsciously took in every aspect of Henry's taut bottom as she followed him up the stairs to the first floor. She was thinking about the future. Her own future. *The first thing I'm going to do is shop. But next is a phone call to Elizabeth. I'll sell off everything back there. It's peanuts, compared to what's going down here. I'll pay her off to look after the kids. Then I'll be free.*

Henry opened the door to Margaret's room. "The Pink Room, Miss. The maid, Carrie, will help you to unpack. If you need anything, press the button on the wall by the bed."

"Thank you, Henry," Margaret said. She just loved being called "Miss".

Carrie took an instant dislike to Margaret, and had a good look at the few bits and pieces of travelling attire she put away in a drawer. "White trash," she muttered. Carrie was white herself, and from the same lowly background as Margaret, but considered being in service a vocation, and herself above anyone who hadn't acquired the status James had. *I'll have to watch her*, she thought.

Margaret showered, then crashed. As she drifted off to sleep, the memories took over, with her more usual dreams of greed and avarice.

The conversation at dinner revolved around the forthcoming surgery. Colin had compared the findings of his examination with previous results, and found there was a slight deterioration in Branston's condition. Just a little weight loss, but it was enough to prompt Colin to want to get on with it while Branston was still strong enough.

Branston spoke to Margaret. "Doctor Cattell tells me you've an interest in surgery. Your youthful beauty tells me it will be many years before you feel the need to turn to cosmetic surgery, so you won't understand what I'm talking about. But you will understand when I tell you this. What we're about to do is a kind of cosmetic surgery. Would you like to watch as Colin transforms me from what I am to a virile young man of twenty?"

Margaret didn't really know what he was talking about, but detected the underlying inference that Branston wanted her to be there after he'd taken on this new lease of life.

"I'd love to, James. In fact I'd like to help in any way I can," she said.

"Good. Will you come with us, then?"

Branston took them down in the lift. Margaret, like Colin, took time to adjust her vision as he led them down the corridor. Finally, he stopped in a more secluded part of the complex. If Margaret had been impressed by what she'd seen up till now, she was stunned when the voice-activated door Branston spoke to swung effortlessly open on dampened hinges. They went inside.

The first thing Margaret was aware of was a low humming noise. Then, through the same pink-tinged light, she saw a line of glass tubes, standing upright. Like Colin, she couldn't prevent her mouth from falling open. Each tube was the size of a human being. And each was occupied.

Branston beamed. "This is what you might call my nursery," he said. "The result of over twenty years of research by my scientists."

Colin was amazed. Any doubts he'd had previously disappeared. He was going to be famous as the first surgeon to attempt this surgery. It didn't matter if he failed. Branston wouldn't be around to complain. Besides, the million dollars Branston was paying him had already cleared in his account.

As Branston was talking, a man about Colin's age approached. "This is the surgeon who will assist you, Colin. Meet Brian Curley. Brian, this is Colin Cattell." Then, turning to Margaret, he said, "And this is the lovely Miss Margaret Clayton."

This was Branston's way of marking Margaret with his scent. He'd shown his interest in her with this introduction.

They'd all defer to him where she was concerned from now on.

The party walked along the line of tubes. Margaret realised there were several lines of these things behind the ones they were looking at. *My God. There must be dozens of them. There must be millions of dollars worth of these things. They must've come on since the eighties. They'll be able to produce them quicker now, for sure. If Colin can do it, I'll make a fortune.*

Branston was talking. "In the 1970s, I took eggs donated by a beautiful and intelligent woman, and fertilized them using my own sperm. I paid plenty, but my scientists quickly discovered how to nurture the eggs in these tubes. Today, I've many clones at different stages of life. These tubes contain a sort of amniotic fluid, which feeds and sustains them, much as they would've been in the womb of their mother. They are the wombs of my creation, so to speak." He stopped and pointed to a tube. "This is James Branston Jr. He was my first, twenty years ago. He's ready, and so am I."

Colin and Margaret stared at the human being swaying in the fluid-filled tube. Margaret blinked in disbelief. It had the same dark hair Branston had, and the genitals of a fully-grown man. Its penis seemed to wave at her. A thin tube protruded from its nostrils, and another, wider one from its rectum. It seemed to be sleeping.

"How on earth did you achieve this?" said Colin. "The muscle tone is that of an athlete, and his fingernails could've been manicured this morning."

"I have to tell you, Doc, I'm pretty proud of myself. It's straightforward, really. As he grew, we introduced food supplements and calcium, and all the ingredients needed to promote his growth, through the tube you see in his nostril. Waste products are disposed of through the tube in his rectum."

"He's breathing, isn't he?" said Margaret.

"Sort of. The fluid transports oxygen to his lungs faster than blood. When he's released, he'll take his first breath with fully-inflated lungs. Superficial maintenance such as you mentioned, Doc, is performed through the access portholes. We can reach any part of his body using the rubber gloves. Natural growth has been stimulated using ultrasonic sound waves. He's as fit as an Olympic runner. All you have to do is transfer the site of my memories from my brain to his. Then you can dispose of my old body."

"I suppose it's possible," said Colin.

"Sure it's possible, and there's no risk to anyone but me. I've every confidence in you; besides, you'll have Brian to show you where the memory bank is situated. You can do a trial run on one of the others, if you want to."

"That's a good idea. How soon can we do it?" said Colin.

"Straight away. I'll take Margaret and show her round the place."

Colin discussed the procedure with Brian while he dissected a brain from one of the clones. "D'you think we can do it?" he said. Brian's answer surprised him.

"Well, we're about to find out. I've successfully taken memory banks from clones before, but the tissue died after a few minutes because of the lack of a recipient for them. Strangely, the clones didn't die. They lived on in a zombie-like state."

Colin hadn't considered this, or the moral implications of what he was contemplating. It took about ten seconds for him to decide, like many before him, that he could attempt the operation with no restraint or obligation. He remembered Robert Oppenheimer saying when watching the first atom bomb explode in trials: "I am become death, the destroyer of worlds."

He made the Hiroshima bomb anyway.

As far as Colin was concerned, *his* science would ultimately save lives. Besides, one million dollars was a lot of money. He did wonder whether he should've asked for more, now the time to fulfil his part of the deal had come.

"I was wondering if it would be safer to transplant the whole brain," he said.

"Trouble is, I haven't found out how to remove the entire spinal cord with it," Brian said. "I've sewn spinal cords together, but there hasn't been a complete recovery of bodily functions by those I've tried it on yet. Don't worry. The surgery to remove the memory bank is straightforward. You're apprehensive because you haven't done it before, that's all. I know how to remove the memory bank, and you know how to work deep in the brain without killing it. We'll be a good team."

"OK. Let's do it."

Carrie looked through an upstairs window to see Branston driving Margaret through the estate in his buggy. She drew back her lips in seething hate.

After what Margaret had witnessed so far, she wasn't at all surprised that James had a buggy. But she still didn't understand how Henry just appeared at the press of a button on the wall.

The grounds looked lovely in the frosty February setting. Margaret looked magnificent, wrapped in winter warmers, blonde hair fluttering in a biting wind. Branston saw her as a free spirit, majestically mistress of all she surveyed. He noticed her complexion change to a ruddy pink colour, and wondered if that was how she looked when in the throes of passion. He was falling in love.

Margaret knew he was looking at her. She said nothing as the driver brought the buggy to a halt outside a grey-brick building, about twelve feet high and twenty feet long, seemingly in the middle of nowhere. Branston offered an arm. She didn't let it go after getting out of the buggy, but slid her hand under his elbow as they walked to an oak bench in front of the building. She cuddled up close, and peeped at crunchy-looking grass stretching away from them. White, frosty branches of leafless trees swayed gently in front of her. For a moment they seemed to be pointing at her. Then James spoke.

"My parents are here. This is their shrine. They came to this country in the twenties, to get away from oppression in Europe. They raised themselves up, and gave me the good life I've had."

Margaret knew instantly how to snare him after he said that. She lowered her head, and opened her purse. She withdrew a tissue and looked up. A tear trickled down her cheek. Branston took her hand. "My dear. I'm so sorry. I didn't think. Please forgive me. You've got memories too, possibly not as happy as mine. What can I do to make amends?"

"It's alright, James. It's just, well, my mother and father

were murdered by the CIA. I don't know why. I think it was a case of mistaken identity. I don't know. They were part Jewish."

"Monstrous," Branston cried. "Come on. I'm going to make it up to you. I'm falling in love with you, you know. In a few days, I'll be the sort of man who'll be able to win your hand."

Words flooded Margaret's mind. *You've got him. But get it right. Not yet.* She turned to him, put a hand to the side of his face, and said, "James, I've never thought of you as an old man. I only met you two days ago, but I saw in you a man I could trust. My father was a good man, too. I looked up to him, and loved him, very much. But I never had the chance to fulfil my relationship with him."

She broke off for a second to wipe her eyes, then continued. "When I met you, I saw in you the qualities he had. I was drawn to you as you are, not as you might be."

"I want to marry you," said Branston. "Today. I'll shower you with all you've ever dreamed of. And tomorrow I'll be a young man. How's that for a proposal? You must say yes."

Steady. Not yet. "James, you might feel differently when you come round from the anaesthetic. You'll be able to have any woman you want." She paused, before delivering the punch that floored him. She looked up at the inscription on the wall of his parents' tomb, and said, "Like a good Jewish woman."

That clinched it for Branston. He leapt to his feet. "Have you got your passport?"

"Yes, why?"

Branston called to the driver of the buggy. "We're going straight back. When we get to the house, get the limousine out. Bring it round the front." Branston grabbed Margaret, and bundled her into the buggy.

"James, what are you doing? Where are we going?"

"We're going to be married, that's what."

Inside Margaret, wedding bells had been clanging for several minutes. She did a great job of keeping him focussed, and on his high. "You're mad," she said. "It's nine o'clock at night. Where can we get married?"

"This is America. The land of opportunity. We can do anything."

"I thought you needed blood tests, and things."

"Let me worry about that. I'll take care of it. First, I'm going to buy you the biggest diamond ring in Detroit. Then we're going shopping for wedding outfits."

The limousine brought James and Margaret back just after one o'clock the next morning. A large diamond ring sat next to a twenty-four carat gold wedding ring on Margaret's finger. She clasped a bouquet of red and pink roses in her hands—the licence safe in her pocket.

All was quiet when they went into the house. Colin had gone to bed; Brian, home. They'd agreed to begin surgery first thing in the morning, and left a note for Branston on a table in the reception hall to that effect. After reading it, he said, "We'll have to postpone our first night together, dear."

She kissed him on the cheek, and said, "I can wait." Then the memories prompted her, and as a second thought she said, "Take me to James Junior, please."

Margaret held him close as the motor in the lift whirred. Minute vibrations helped stir passion inside, but they held back. The lift stopped, and they walked along the corridor leading to the nursery. Their footsteps, patting soft tiles together, seemed to Branston to confirm their union.

Margaret looked at James Jr. She now thought of him as a person, somehow. She put her hand on the tube, and looked at Branston. He seemed to know her thoughts. "You can touch him," he said.

Margaret put her arm into one of the rubber gloves, and reversed it into the warm fluid. It gave her a feeling of buoyancy. She felt the firmness of the chest muscles, and smoothed her hand down and over the hips. Then, as if drawn to it, she stroked the penis hanging between his legs.

Branston put his arms round Margaret from behind, and felt her breasts. She closed her eyes as he nuzzled her ear, then gasped as he found her special place. Her hand worked in unison with his as he brought her to passion. She withdrew it as she climaxed, and turned to him, unaware of the memories flowing out of her fingertips, through the rubber gloves, and into the fluid. They kissed passionately, but held back.

Chapter 38

Success for Branston—Salvation for Margaret

Telepathic pathways of communication were alive with news of only one subject. All over the world, the memories of the dead cried out for Branston's experiment to be stopped.

Branston saw the operation as the only way for him to continue living, whereas Colin agreed to do it for money in the first instance. Having justified it by allying the procedure to the growing ability of mankind to regenerate parts of the human body, he now saw it as a step forward. *His* science would eventually save lives.

Leprosy was fast becoming controllable with drugs but that aside, millions of people who'd lost limbs were, unknown to them, about to be given new hope. A release only those trapped within paralysed bodies could appreciate would be given them, if James Branston could survive. The need to take medication in order to avoid the rejection of a whole-body transplant would be a minor inconvenience to millions of sufferers all over the world.

And yet the memories were uneasy. They knew the prospect of helping the living was more important than the egos of dead people. Nevertheless, the moral issue was a massive one.

Pythagoras would have to speak.

Finally, Audeus brought a message from his master. "Evil will always be sought out, and the perpetrators receive justice, before or after death. Those with selfish reason in their hearts will never truly find peace, and their gains, like them, will crumble to dust. Mankind, in his ignorance, fears death, and will forever try to find ways of preventing it. This is not evil. Events must be allowed to run their course."

Colin and Brian were up early the next morning, preparing for their ground-breaking surgery. Selecting the correct surgical instruments and sterilising them correctly was vital, and couldn't be rushed. Colin carefully opened a stainless steel case, and took out the saw he would use. The patient with the aneurism described it as looking "like an electric toothbrush" when she recounted the events she'd seen. Colin laid it alongside other instruments in a stainless steel tray, which he then put into a steam oven. Levels of anaesthesia, he discussed with the technician who'd be responsible for keeping Branston sedated.

Branston hadn't eaten since midnight the night before, and could only fidget while Margaret ate breakfast. She felt sorry for the old boy in a way. Usually, she had no problem in ruthlessly exploiting weakness. As far as she was concerned, life was about getting the most out of it, without minding who she abused on the way. She had been brought up in a society that idolised the getters of things, even if that society didn't consciously know it.

What Margaret didn't know was, her character was changing. Seeing the lifeless bodies of Sheila and Darren—eyes bulging and filled with blood and her shattered parents triggered a reaction. She had never seen a dead body before then. Now she was confused. If Colin was able to do this, she wouldn't have to worry about dying. But what if he failed? What if there was life after death?

She couldn't work it out. But it niggled her. Whatever, she decided to take Branston's mind off food for a while. "What exactly are they going to do?" she said.

"First, Brian and his team will take James Junior out of the tube, disconnecting the pipes as they go. They'll drain the fluid away, introduce my blood to him, and start his heart. Then they'll sedate him, and bring him to lie alongside me in the theatre. While they're doing that, Colin will begin the tricky part. He has to drain the blood from my body, and stop my heart beating. Then he'll take the top of my skull off with an electrically powered saw, and cool my brain."

Margaret was pushing a fork into an egg, fried over easy, as Branston said this. She gulped, and pushed the plate to one side. "How interesting," she said.

Branston continued. "Brian will watch this part of the procedure. Then Colin will watch as Brian shows him the site of my memory bank. After that it's just a case of making the switch, and reviving me."

"You make it all sound so easy."

"It's straightforward surgery, really. I've every confidence in them, otherwise I'd accept my fate with as much grace as I could muster. Besides, I have no choice."

"I'm still nervous for you."

"I know. But think what this would mean if we could do it. The possibilities for countless people would be endless."

Margaret was thinking of the countless bank accounts she could empty. Of the functions she'd be invited to, and the dignitaries she'd meet: kings and queens. *The Queen. I'll be presented to the Queen, at Buckingham Palace.*

"Yes, James. The possibilities are endless," she said.

Branston looked at his watch. His lawyer would be in his office, and settled, by now. No-one would reap any benefit if Branston died on the operating table. He hadn't built a business empire on ifs and buts, though. There'd been many a gamble along the way, but always with insurance. This time, no underwriter could take his bet. The odds were in favour of him being dead this time tomorrow. This time he'd have to cater for the buts himself.

"Would you excuse me, my dear? Just a couple of calls to make. I'll be back before you've finished."

Margaret watched Branston walk wearily away. *Hope the wife gets the money in this state,* she thought.

Branston's rough, dry tongue flicked the envelope. Eventually, he summoned up enough saliva to seal it. He took off his wedding ring, and kissed it. Then he opened a small wall-safe, put the ring in its box, and propped the letter against it. He closed the safe, twiddled the dial, and returned to his desk.

Branston dialled a number, and settled into a black leather chair. He looked at the wall to his left, and saw a yellow-edged, black and white photograph of his proud parents, painstakingly mounted and framed so as to iron out the creases. Next to it, a view of their first shop, in which hopes and dreams came to fruition—slowly, through a dogged routine of work, and sleep, and praying; tired eyes, and broken fingernails; the sweat of childbirth, the washing and the tears, and scrimping along through the 1920s, while the rest of society roared on. They survived—just—on unleavened bread, and fish, and bitter salt. And love.

His gaze traversed along the collage. After his brothers were born, laughter came. And later, a bicycle, a baseball bat, a radio, new clothes, a bigger shop. And him.

Branston's eyes, continuing their pictorial sweep of his life, settled on a photograph, in colour now, of him and his brothers, taken to celebrate—he couldn't remember what, now—but they were all smiling. Branston's grin disappeared as his gaze took in the office door, and came to a stop. The brilliant white wall on the other side was empty.

The ring of the telephone stopped, his call answered. "Good morning. Hadgkiss, Hughes and Bealle. Can I help you?"

"Hadgkiss, please. Branston here."

"Yes, sir. I'll put you through."

"Good morning, James. How'ya doin?"

"Morning, Cord. Fine, thanks. Mary, and the kids?"

"She's fine. They're all fine. Those papers came, first thing. You're in a hurry, aren't you?"

"We already talked about this, months ago. You know I've arranged to take a back seat in the running of the company. I've done my shift. Now I have other plans."

"Yes, I know, but changing things from a board of trustees back to a solely-owned, private business is, with respect, taking a bit of a chance. Have I been introduced to the lady?"

"No, but she's a very successful businesswoman. And she's my wife."

Hadgkiss dropped his pencil, then quickly picked it up and scribbled a note on his blotter, reminding him to get a bill for his services over to Branston by the end of business that day.

"Well, that's different. I'll actuate proceedings immediately. I saw you signed everything right. Going away?"

"Thanks, Cord. Thanks for everything. Just make sure I can change my mind next month, if I want to."

259

Hadgkiss put the receiver down, and frowned. "Next month? Better call my analyst, and tell him to keep an eye on the market. Slippery, these rabbis. Might be anything."

Margaret was pretending to be reading the *New York Times* (Financial Section), and drinking tea in the lounge, when Branston rejoined her. He kissed the top of her head.

"Everything OK?" she said.

"Don't worry. Everything's fine."

Colin and Brian came into the room at this juncture. "We're ready," said Colin. "Just need to take your blood pressure first."

The reading was a little higher, but Colin had expected that. Even though he'd organised his expedition into the unknown himself, Branston had no control over his body. The subconscious anticipation of danger triggered a release of massive amounts of adrenaline and testosterone into his bloodstream. Levels that wouldn't drop until he'd been sedated. Besides, this brave man was hungry and irritable. "Come on. Let's get on with it," he said.

Colin and Brian exchanged a look. Colin nodded, and opened the door.

Margaret almost said "Good luck" or something, but decided she'd better not.

The party made their way underground, and into a room adjoining the theatre. Margaret helped Branston to undress and get into a hospital gown, while Colin and Brian scrubbed up.

Presently, a nurse came to sedate Branston, which was the signal for Margaret to leave. She kissed him on the forehead, squeezed his hand, and said, "I'll be waiting for you."

Branston nodded to the nurse, and winked at Margaret. "And then I'll fly you to the moon, honey," he said.

The whole thing seemed to Margaret to be bizarre. She couldn't quite get her head round the fact that someone she knew as an old man was going into an operating theatre, expecting to be a young man when he came out. *Unbelievable, and yet it's happening*, she thought.

Something made Margaret turn and look back as she made to leave the room. An ice-cold, damp shiver ran down her spine as Branston's parting words echoed in her brain. *"And then I'll fly you to the moon, honey."*

Margaret sat in an observation gallery, looking into the theatre. Branston, his body covered in a green sheet, was under general anaesthetic. Only his head was visible to her as James Jr was brought in on another trolley, which was set alongside the operating table. She stayed when an enormous needle was inserted into a vein in order to drain Branston's blood. She stayed when his heart was stopped. But when Colin produced the electric drill, and began to saw into the top of his shaven skull, she decided she wouldn't watch any more after all.

Margaret knew it was to be a long operation, so made her way back upstairs, and into the lounge. She stood, looking through wide, patio-type windows, for what seemed an hour. Snow, falling outside, produced a hypnotic effect, reminding her of other Christmases, long ago.

"Christmas. Goodwill towards men," she said, out loud. Memories of Christmas spent as a little girl in Margate came. A tree—tinsel—Terry, with a party hat on, hopping about, waving his arm around, pretending to be a pirate. The laughter. And the frantic opening of presents. Margaret thought of her own children, and began to cry. Real tears.

She wept for a while, then pulled herself together. Spotting the button on the wall, she pressed it. A couple of minutes later, Henry knocked and entered. "Yes, Miss," he said.

"Good morning, Henry."

"Good afternoon, Miss."

Margaret looked at her watch, which showed 14.30. Feeling foolish, she smiled at him. "Bit behind myself today."

"Indeed, Miss. Can I get you anything?"

"Some coffee, please. And a phone."

"Would you like milk or cream, Miss?"

Margaret had never even drunk coffee before, with or without cream, but decided it would be posher if she said, "Cream, please."

＊ ＊ ＊

Margaret's conversation with Elizabeth didn't go the way she'd thought it would. After the preliminaries were over, she asked, "And how are the kids?"

Margaret thought that the following silence was a delay in the transmission of her words, caused by the fact that Elizabeth was several thousand miles away. She knew when Elizabeth next spoke that it was not. "I've something to tell you," Elizabeth said.

For the first time in her life, Margaret experienced an emotion she had no control over. An emotion all parents feel, even if prompted, as in her case, by the possibility of being told that they can no longer exercise their parental rights. All was well with Margaret while she was in charge. But in between Elizabeth finishing that sentence and her asking, "Oh. What's that?" Margaret felt as if all her blood had turned cold and was draining out of her body. In that moment of silence, Margaret was afraid. A million questions flashed through her mind, and all were prefixed by one thought: *What have I overlooked?* Even Margaret's carefully catalogued brain didn't come up with the possibility of "Sivean called me mother the other day."

Instead of feeling that this fitted perfectly into her plans, Margaret found that she didn't like it. In her mind, this was something she hadn't instigated and which would have been bad enough in Margate; but now, having been exposed to the character-building environment of owning, albeit via marriage, a large estate and the virtually unlimited funds she expected to go with it—and also her every whim indulged by servants, this was impossible. This was something she had not given her consent to, and for that reason it could not be allowed.

Margaret ignored the statement and talked about the family as a whole instead, meaning to take steps to regain control of her children as soon as she put the phone down.

* * *

Colin and Brian had prepared well. Their meticulous planning of every step of the operation meant that a rhythm was soon established. The whole thing took a little over seven hours to complete. When they had finished they shook hands. All they could do then was wait.

Margaret, curled up and asleep on the settee, didn't hear

Colin come in, and he, not seeing her, walked across the lounge to the window. The movement of air as he passed caused her to slowly come round. "Oo-er," she groaned, raising herself onto one elbow. Then she noticed Colin. Their eyes met. He smiled, and nodded.

Margaret jumped up and ran, barefoot, out of the lounge. She cursed the lift doors, pressing the button repeatedly, like a girl having an epileptic fit on the check-out at Sainsbury's. "Come on. Come on—work you stupid thing," she said.

She hurtled out of the lift at the bottom, ran down the corridor, and came to a stop outside the ante-room. It was empty. She ran to the theatre—again, empty. Turning to run out, she bumped into Colin, who'd followed her down. He held her close.

"Let me go, where is he?" she said, shoving him away. For a second, she thought he wasn't going to answer, then felt him relax as Brian turned the corner.

"Where *is* he, Brian?" she said.

Brian's eyes locked with Colin's for a second, then dropped to his fingers, which slowly regained their red colour as his grip on Margaret eased. "This way," said Brian.

Brian showed Margaret to a recovery room. There, lying on a hospital bed, was James Branston Jr. An oxygen mask covered his mouth and nose. The monotone of the pump, beating at regular intervals, sounded like the echo of an ancient drumbeat. A blipping sound drew her attention to a heart monitor.

She walked to the bedside, and looked at him. She'd only seen him swaying in the amniotic fluid before. Now, the introduction of blood to his veins had given a healthy pink colour to his face and electrical activity was stimulating his facial muscles, giving expression. *He's quite handsome, really*, she thought.

She turned to Brian, and said, "What happens now?"

"We just wait."

"Can't you tell what's happening?"

"No. We know there's brain activity, that's all. In a couple of days, after we're sure he's stable, we'll decrease the sedation and start to bring him round. But it has to be done slowly."

Margaret felt weak at the knees. Two days sounded like an eternity. "OK. I'll stay with him," she said.

"There's another room next door. You can rest in there when you need to," said Brian. "I'll be in and out all the time, so don't worry." Then, pointing at the wall, he said, "Press that red button if you have any problems."

Margaret was beginning to like Brian. He was OK. She sat with James, hardly leaving his side. Mostly, she gazed at his face, looking for a sign. She held his hand, hoping for a reaction to her gentle squeezing of it. There was nothing. At one point the voracious memory put coarse thoughts in her mind. *Offer him up a tit, if you like. That'll help your cravings.* This thought, coming at the precise moment that Margaret, in her intense concentration, imagined a muscle twitch in James's face, brought with it a picture of her saying much the same thing to Elizabeth in Margate when she held one of the twins. Margaret frowned, not understanding the feeling now inside her, nor why that picture was quickly followed by one of Christmas spent with her family.

Margaret was not yet lost to selfishness. These rememberings of shared emotions, although alien to her, meant that Margaret was still capable of empathising with other human beings. This common bond would be further enhanced during James's battle for life.

On the third day, Brian began to reduce James's sedation. During the night of the next day, Branston stirred. Margaret first felt a twitch in his fingers. She shook herself awake, and listened. *What's happened?* she thought, looking around the room. Nothing moved in the soft, pink-tinged light. The only sounds she could hear were those of an oxygen pump and a heart monitor. She yawned. Another twitch. Margaret stared at his fingers, entwined with hers, then looked at his face. Her wait was over.

James's eyes flickered, then opened wide. He looked from one side of the room to the other, eyes rolling, not seeming to recognise anything. "James," she said, softly. His eyes rolled again, and closed. "James." She said it a little louder this time. Then she remembered the button.

Margaret jumped up, ran to the wall, and pressed the

button. Still in bare feet she ran to the door, flung it open, and shouted down the empty corridor. "Help, he's awake."

The sound of her voice, ricocheting off walls, brought Colin and Brian running into the room.

Colin looked at the heart monitor: 115 over 85. Brian checked James's pulse. "Both normal," said Brian. "In fact, he's as fit as a footballer."

"But can he speak? He didn't recognise me. Is it him?" said Margaret.

Brian shrugged. "We're in completely unknown territory there. Just have to wait and see."

James was sleeping again now. Margaret, emotionally exhausted but refusing to give in to tiredness, sat, holding his hand and talking to him. Sometimes her maternal instinct came, and she mothered him. Then Elisha's words came to her. *"Yes, my son. I'm your mother. Nobody will ever love you like I do."*

Margaret was overwhelmed by this. She knew she wouldn't think that. *Where have all these big words and high thoughts come from?* Then Elisha spoke to her again. "This is my son. Beloved in his conception, and borne in pain by me. Do not betray him."

In her weakened state, Margaret nearly fainted. There was more to this than she thought. That *was* his mother talking. She knew it.

James squeezed her hand again. She squeezed back, and looked at his face. He opened his eyes and smiled at her, his dark eyes flickering in recognition of her. He nodded, slowly. She put her head on his hands, and wept, "Oh, James—James." Real tears again.

Weary now, Margaret got up, and pressed the button on the wall. She didn't leave the room this time. Just went back, and sat down beside him.

"Can you talk?" she said. James tried, then shook his head. Margaret put a hand on his penis, and said, "Can you feel that?"

His eyes sparkled. "Well, that's alright, then," she said. "So long as you can love me."

Branston's planning paid further dividends in the weeks that followed. The fitness level of his new body enabled him to make rapid progress as he underwent comprehensive physio-therapy. It took longer for him to start talking, though. But he had to have his new-found fitness explained to his staff—including Carrie, who nearly fainted when confronted by an employer who appeared to have shed fifty pounds and fifty years. She accepted the explanation that he couldn't speak because the skin on his cheeks was tight, having undergone a face lift.

Henry, with his African roots, was uneasy. He too accepted the same explanation, but smelled *Witch Doctor* and *Voodoo stuff*, and quickly made a visit to a poulterer.

Branston's plans for the future were given in detail to his scientists and researchers, who, now sworn to secrecy, threw themselves into the task of eliminating rejection and producing female clones. Colin and Brian were particularly pleased to find themselves years ahead when the disclosure that the Chinese were approaching success in their attempts to introduce human DNA to animals was announced.

Margaret instructed her solicitor in Margate to discreetly sell off everything and forward the proceeds to her. Then she had to decide what the next step should be. *I'll keep quiet about my money till I find out what he invests in*, she thought.

Thereafter, Margaret spent every available moment in the swimming pool with James, or in the gym. And when he rested, she sat alone on the bench by his parents' shrine.

A hint of early spring boosted this magical change in Margaret. Fresh blossom; clean, crisp air. The short, melodious song of a North American robin, fluttering in the trees, welcoming a new season, all inspired her to feel hope for the future. Only one thing constantly nagged at her. Her children.

Again Elisha's memories came to Margaret, this time giving her an insight into Jewish tradition in family life. Elisha constantly fed scenes of the early days into Margaret's mind, and of her struggle to bring up her children. Within a week, Margaret was determined to attempt a reconciliation with the twins. Her only problem was how to invent an excuse to bring their existence to Branston's attention. *I'll think of something later*, she thought. In the meantime Margaret was fearful of rejection, and wasn't even sure that the girls would recognise her. So she phoned Elizabeth and asked her to bring them to New York for a visit. She agreed. Margaret booked the flight in her maiden name.

Margaret's transformation from selfish to selfless was complete.

Three weeks later, Margaret looked down at the flatlands, moving slowly by underneath Flight 401. After the seat belt sign went off, she settled back, and thought about the twins. *How will they react to me? How much have they changed? How much have they grown?* A feeling of panic came over her. *Will they give me another chance?* She realised she desperately wanted them to. She opened her purse and rummaged about, putting the thoughts from her mind. Her fingers touched her little red wallet, containing the marriage licence. She took it out and looked at it. *Amazing. I only met him a few weeks ago.*

Paula Lane, a businesswoman from Liverpool, sitting several rows behind Margaret, was on her way to New York for a couple of days' shopping before flying back home. In the seat next to her was Graham de Courcey.

When terrorists, about to blow up Flight 401, gave passengers one minute to call loved ones on their mobile phones, neither Margaret nor Graham had anyone they could ring up and speak to.

In the moments before they died, memories flooded passengers' minds. Graham sat, transfixed, as visions of murder, and betrayal, and the hedonism he'd indulged in were made clear to him. He died in abject misery.

After the initial shock, the sounds of chaos around Margaret faded away. Elisha's memories came to her with words of comfort. Margaret heard the matriarchal chorus, speaking the *Kaddish*—the prayer for the dead—and knew at last that family is everything. In the final seconds of her life, she reflected on the irony of it all, but gave thanks for the opportunity she'd had to be, at the last, part of a greater, selfless ideal.

In Liverpool, Malcolm Lane answered his phone. "Hello," he said.

"Malcolm. I haven't got long. I love you, darl..." The phone went dead. Malcolm looked at it. Nothing. That was when his world fell apart.

Chapter 39

Malcolm Lane

Malcolm and Paula Lane ran a successful wholesale business near Liverpool city centre. Their son, Cliff, had been born five months after their wedding in 1979, twenty years before. A daughter, Christine, had come along the following year.

Malcolm and Paula worked together, except when Paula travelled the world scouting for next year's lines. This time Paula was off to America. Malcolm drove her to the airport as usual, but today felt uneasy. He thought about asking her to cancel, and go another time, but the moment passed, and he thought no more about it.

When the time for Paula to board came, they cuddled, and Malcolm kissed her on the cheek.

"Take care, darling. Give me a ring when you get to the hotel," he said.

"I will. Now give me a proper kiss," said Paula. Malcolm laughed, and kissed her on the lips.

"That's better. Now, look after yourself, and the dogs. I'll speak to you later." With that, Paula walked through the gate and was gone. Malcolm never saw her again.

Eight hours later Paula phoned to say she'd arrived, and was having an early night. She had a tight schedule to keep to, taking in Chicago, Michigan and Detroit before spending her last day shopping in New York. Paula spoke to Malcolm on the phone at each stop, and was on the last leg of her journey.

Then came the call from Flight 401.

Malcolm pressed dial-back. No response. Paula's number was unobtainable. He phoned Christine to see if she'd heard anything. She hadn't. Then he tried Cliff. He hadn't heard, either.

Then he phoned the police.

"When did you see your wife last, sir?" asked the despatcher.

"Three days ago. I saw her off at the airport. She went to America."

"And did you part on the best of terms, sir?"

"Of course we bloody well did. What sort of a question's that?"

"I'm sorry, sir. I have to ask. Did you say America?"

"Yes."

"Would she have been on an internal flight today?"

"Yes. She left Detroit to go shopping in New York. Then she was coming home." Malcolm's phone bleeped to show someone else was trying to get through. "Why?" he said.

The despatcher continued, using the monotone people use when trying to distance themselves from the bad news they're about to give out. "There's no need to be alarmed, sir. There's been an incident involving an internal flight on that route. I'll give you another number. They'll be able to give you all the information you need."

Malcolm wrote down the number and replaced the receiver, his mind in a whirl. The phone rang again immediately. It was Christine. "Dad. Turn the telly on," she said.

Malcolm was dismayed when he turned on the television. All he could see was flames, and wreckage. He didn't hear what the reporter was saying. He just knew Paula was dead.

"Dad. Dad?" Malcolm wasn't on the line anymore. He was staring at words moving slowly across the bottom of the screen. "Terrorists down plane bound for New York. All feared dead."

Malcolm was still staring at the television when Christine and Cliff arrived. They tried to help him, but Malcolm was inconsolable. They put up a notice at the warehouse: "Closed Till Further Notice", and left it at that. Christine stayed with him. She tried to talk to him; make him eat. He wouldn't respond.

His doctor sedated him, and tried to reassure Christine. "He's in shock. I can't say how long it will be before he comes out of it, but he will, don't worry."

Christine and Cliff did worry. Malcolm was lethargic, and

didn't want to get out of bed in the mornings. Two nights later, Christine was woken at 2 a.m. by the phone ringing. It was the police.

"I knew there was something wrong immediately I saw him climb onto the bridge, officer. Then he just dived off," said the man who'd been driving his car behind the lorry Malcolm had missed. "Don't know how he landed on his feet. Should've been his head."

Malcolm, dressed only in pyjamas, *had* dived off, but somehow somersaulted in mid-air and landed on his feet, breaking his ankle in the process.

The driver of the lorry, twenty stones of testosterone-fuelled anger, approached Malcolm—now sitting in the inside lane, nursing his ankle in the glare of a police patrol car's headlights. Malcolm was sure somebody or something had got under his back as he fell and turned him over. *Must've been my imagination*, he thought.

The lorry driver glared at him, fists clenched. "Are you dead?" he said.

"No."

"Well, you soon will be."

"Come on then, you fat slob. I wanna die," screamed Malcolm. At least he was talking now. Malcolm was taken by ambulance to Liverpool General Hospital, where his ankle was X-rayed and set. He was then transported by wheelchair to Ward C, where emotionally disturbed patients were cared for.

Huge, round lights on the ceiling, floating by like UFOs, mesmerised Malcolm as a porter pushed the chair down seemingly endless, pastel-painted corridors. "Keep your arms in," he said at one point, before unlocking a heavy metal door. Malcolm didn't notice as the doors became more frequent.

After arriving at Ward C, the porter wheeled Malcolm into an office just inside reception. He positioned the wheelchair in front of a desk, and put the brake on. "I'll tell the doctor you're here," he said.

Malcolm saw a sparsely furnished room. Two chairs and a bookcase, besides the desk. A round tin bucket sat on the floor on his side of the desk. Cigarette stub-out marks lining the inside of its rim competed with flaking enamel to draw his attention.

Presently, Malcolm heard the door behind him open. The caress of expensive, flowery perfume soothed stale air as a smartly-dressed woman brushed past. She sat on the other side of the desk. Malcolm saw metal bars on the windows behind her. *I'm in a nut-house*, he thought.

Suddenly, the woman jumped up, marched over to where Malcolm sat, hitched up her dress, pulled down her panties, and peed in the bucket.

Malcolm looked—first at her face, then her stoop. Steam wafted out from the gap between white, stocking-topped thighs and the bucket. Then he heard urine rattling around inside, and saw it dribble out through tiny holes in its base.

The door opened again, and in walked Doctor Kumar. "Come, Judy. That's not a nice way to welcome Malcolm now, is it?" he said.

Judy finished what she was doing, pulled up her panties, and strode out.

Doctor Kumar offered his hand. "Doctor Kumar. That was Judy, a patient."

＊　＊　＊

Malcolm had supposed Judith Richardson to be a doctor when she entered the room. Impeccably dressed, Judy had oozed confidence and given Malcolm the impression that she'd every right to be there. But Judy had been a patient of Doctor Kumar's for almost two months by the time Malcolm met her.

As an owner of three highly-successful retail outlets selling high-class designer wear in Liverpool, Judy, at thirty-eight years of age, felt that she'd finally made it. She'd worked and battled for fifteen years to achieve her goal of owning her own shop, and the future seemed to hold unlimited prospects for her on the night she raised a glass of champagne to toast herself, outside her new premises in the heart of Manchester.

Judy looked up at the sign bearing her name. The sacrifices she'd made along the way, including her rejection of an offer of marriage from Robert, the man she'd loved to distraction, but whom she'd let go because the relationship was interfering with business, now seemed to have been totally justified.

Having reached her goal, Judy began to ease off a little by delegating the day-to-day responsibility for running her outlets to managers. She installed herself in an office above the frontage in Manchester and entertained only her best customers. Then she heard that Robert had married.

Judy was sincere in her thoughts about Robert at first. She was truly happy for him, until she could no longer deny what her body was telling her—she needed to be a mother.

Mornings were fine for Judy. Routine, in fact. Rise at 6 a.m. Hang up her outfit for the day on the wardrobe door. Select a pair of shoes. Have a quick shower. Go downstairs and put the kettle on, switching on the radio at the same time. Make coffee. Drink coffee and put on her make-up while sitting on a high stool in front of a long pine table. Go back upstairs to do her hair and dress.

At 7.30 a.m. Judy would ease herself into the driver's seat of her two-door Merc and press a button on her remote. The garage doors would open. By 8 a.m., not having had an original thought, Judy would become part of a daily migration of people going to work in Lancashire which is staggering in its proportions. But having visited each shop in turn to make sure all was in order, Judy would be in her Manchester office by 11 a.m. Then she'd look after her customers.

Judy couldn't remember the last time she'd socialised, never mind made love. She certainly hadn't had time for a boyfriend. Nor was she a drinker. Nevertheless, one of the facilities she incorporated into her new office was a small drinks cabinet. This led to her preparing pre-lunch cocktails for herself and customers. She wouldn't drink during lunch, but got into the habit of pouring herself a scotch and dry in the mid-afternoon, which she enjoyed while keeping an eye on her portfolio of shares via teletext. Occasionally she'd have a mobile hairdresser or manicurist call in and settle down to be pampered. And this led to conversation.

When Doctor Kumar interviewed Judy two days later, the only thing she could remember was that after the manicurist had left she'd poured herself a drink and switched on the television. Police, however, established that Judy was at least eight times over the legal limit for drivers when she walked into a branch of Mothercare in Stockport later that same afternoon and attempted to walk out with a two-year-old child under her coat.

Judy, having detached herself emotionally from the rest of society while on her single-minded quest, had lost her social skills in the process and was unable now to see how she could establish even a friendship, never mind find a man whose child she could bear. She'd simply gone to pieces.

＊　＊　＊

Malcolm ignored the hand, his thoughts returning to Paula. *Didn't even have time to say "goodbye" or "I love you"*, he thought.

The doctor sat on the other side of the desk, reading a report.

"How's the ankle?" said Doctor Kumar.

"I love you," said Malcolm.

"Pardon me?"

Malcolm said nothing, but was brought back to reality when Doctor Kumar, seeing the gesticulations of a colleague telling him Malcolm's children had arrived, said, "Ah, your children. Perhaps you'll introduce me to them."

Malcolm was no more responsive during that conversation, either.

"I blame myself," said Christine. "Should've seen it coming. He's been getting more and more depressed ever since Mom died."

Doctor Kumar tried to convince Christine and Cliff that Malcolm had simply suffered a temporary breakdown in his ability to sift information. "The shock of seeing the crash on television, then the telephone call, followed by confirmation that his wife was dead, was just too much to take all at once. He's confused now, but in time he'll work it out."

"But why does he have to stay in here?" said Cliff.

"For his own safety, really. Besides, if we don't look after him for a while, the police might press charges. Can you bring some clothes in for him?"

They left, unconvinced.

Malcolm was placed in a queue of patients, waiting to be

served breakfast in the ward. *Wonder why they always play Mantovani music in these places?* he thought.

A young man in front of him shifted nervously from side to side, reminding Malcolm of a penguin, each time the queue moved forward. Malcolm took his food and looked for a place to eat. A man holding a stainless steel ashtray close to his chest sat on one of several armchairs, dotted amongst coffee tables. Spotting a table by a window, which ran across the entire length of the ward, Malcolm made his way to it. *More bars.*

Malcolm sat, but didn't eat. He wasn't left alone for long. A pretty young nurse, instructed to keep an eye on him, sat beside him. "You OK?" she said.

Malcolm turned away, and looked out through the bars. He saw a garden and an oak bench on the other side.

The nurse took his hand as tears streamed down his face. He saw himself and Paula, sitting on the bench. Paula laughed. He did too—now, recalling the moment he knew he loved her.

It was summer. Paula was sitting on a hammock in Malcolm's back garden, reading a book and humming softly. Her white cotton, gypsy-style skirt hung down from one side, brushing the ground, as the hammock swung lazily in a balmy June breeze.

Malcolm watched her from an upstairs window for a while. Then he whistled, softly.

The sun lit Paula's face from behind as the floppy summer hat she was wearing tilted his way.

She looked up at Malcolm and said, "Hi. What you doin'?"

This was, for Malcolm, a moment of sublime purity. The moment he knew he loved this woman more than anything.

The nurse put her arm round Malcolm, and led him away to be sedated and put to bed.

Christine called into Malcolm's house to check the post after dropping Cliff off. There was an assortment of letters, condolence cards and bills, which she sorted through. Creditors wanted payment. A letter from one of her parents' suppliers asked if Paula was calling on them this year. Christine sighed, and looked around the lounge. There on the wall was her mother's picture. Christine had given her a make-over and photoshoot for a Christmas present, only months before. *She looks beautiful in that. She'd've loved the surprise trip to London for the Millennium*, she thought.

Christine's tears began to fall as the front doorbell sounded. It was the pools man.

"Hello, Missus," he said. "Is Malcolm in?"

"No, I'm afraid not. But why are you here now? I haven't seen you before."

"I only come once a year. His numbers run out next week."

"Oh, well. How much is it?"

"Ten full perms, any eight from ten, fifty-two weeks, comes to eighty-six pounds for the year."

"I'll have to give you a cheque. Does it matter if it's in my name?"

"No, missus. How are they both?"

"You haven't heard? Mom was in that plane that got crashed."

"Oh, I'm sorry. Stupid question, but how's your Dad?"

"He's OK. It's difficult."

"Yes. Give him a nod for me. And tell him not to worry about the pools. Have you got a number I can reach you on, if there's any good news?"

Christine gave him her number, then set about filling a suitcase with some clothes for Malcolm, wondering at the same time how a win on the pools could possibly make up for the loss of her mother, and possibly her father as well, now.

Chapter 40

Malcolm's Rehabilitation

The incident that helped Malcolm to come out of himself occurred on April 15th 1999. After breakfast the patients went off to do their own things. Malcolm wasn't interested in the group therapy session, or lying on his back in a room, listening to tapes of dolphins squeaking, with his eyes closed. He sat in the lounge, looking at the oak bench in the garden, instead.

Joe, a Rastafarian, was standing in his usual position—dead centre of the room, dreadlocks swaying as he rocked from side to side, in time to the Mantovani music. Another patient, with his nose pressed against a wall, murmured to himself. Others played cards. Clive, the boy Malcolm had seen in the breakfast queue, was walking across the room to join them.

Suddenly Joe threw his arms out and shouted, "Riot. Riot. Liverpool 1999."

This frightened Clive so much, he jumped two feet in the air. When he came down, he flew at Joe, and the two fell to the floor. Chaos broke out as the pair rolled around, with Joe still screaming "Riot" and Clive trying to gouge his eyes out.

The man facing the wall began to mess himself, the results of which he smeared on the wall. Norton Jones, a barrister and one of the men playing cards, jumped up and shouted, "I haven't dismissed this case yet. The judge can't leave until he's said goodbye."

Mike, a patient and schoolteacher, pointed at the two figures grappling on the floor. "Quiet," he shouted. "You two. Go to the headmaster's office. I'll give you six of the best."

Malcolm, shocked out of his stupor, reacted quickest to separate Joe and Clive as male nurses ran in, followed by Doctor Kumar.

After it was all over, another patient approached Malcolm

and held out a hand. "The name's Frank. Well done. Fancy a walk?"

Malcolm looked at Frank for a moment, then said: "Don't know if I can."

Frank turned his head. "Can Malcolm come with me, Doc?" Doctor Kumar nodded. Frank was allowed to walk once a day round the hospital complex, which was adjacent to a prison. The total distance was about one mile. "Why do they let you go out walking?" Malcolm asked.

"It's sort of therapy, I guess. I killed my wife and her lover when I found them in bed together. The judge gave me seven years, but said I could serve my time here because of extenuating circumstances. Stops me becoming institutionalised, I suppose."

Joe didn't return to the ward, but Malcolm fancied he saw him, peering through barred windows in a block behind the garden wall one morning while he and Frank were walking. He asked Frank if he knew what that block was. "That's where they keep the long-term patients. Padded cells, electric shock therapy, and all that. Some of them in there are soldiers. They've been there since the war."

"But that's over fifty years ago," said Malcolm.

"I know, it's disgusting, but what can they do? They brought one chap to Ward C, but the first time he heard a noise, he dived under a coffee table, screaming 'Bomb'. By the way, that nurse fancies you, you know."

"Which nurse?"

"The one who sat beside you when you first came in. Nicky's her name."

"But she's no older than my kids."

"Well, I'm telling you, she does."

Everyone liked Nicky Hutchens. She was young, good at her job, attentive and caring. She always carried out her duties meticulously, and wasn't a clock watcher.

Later that afternoon, Nicky found Malcolm in his usual position, sitting on the oak bench in the garden. This was a bench Tim Howell had sold. Memories inside sent a telepathic message to Audeus, who gave them a task.

Nicky sat down beside Malcolm. Neither felt the force

277

emanating from the bench, fusing them together. It was the warmth of the sun — they thought.

"Are you a local girl?" Malcolm asked.

"Yes. I live in my parents' house. I was going to move into nurses' accommodation after I qualified, but I haven't got round to it yet."

"Sorry. I didn't mean to pry."

"That's OK. You and I have something in common."

"Oh. What?"

"My parents and brother were on the same flight as your wife."

Malcolm was stunned. He realised he wasn't the only one to lose loved ones in that tragedy. He felt ashamed. "I'm so sorry," he said. "I didn't know. It must be awful for you."

"That's OK. Why would you know? I guess it hasn't really sunk in yet. It's difficult to get used to an empty house."

"You live alone?"

"Yep. All on me tod. Mind you, there's been so much attention from the media, it's good to have a door I can close behind me every night."

Christine and Cliff, arriving to visit, interrupted their conversation, so Nicky went back to her duties.

Christine brought with her a letter which all relatives of victims of Flight 401 had received. Malcolm read it, then gave it back to her to read:

Dear Mr Lane,

Please accept my sincere condolences for your tragic loss. The prayers of the people of my country are with you.

My wife and I would be honored if you, and your family, would join us in a service commemorating the lives of those lost on Flight 401. This to be held at the White House on July 6th 1999.

The letter was signed by the President of the United States.

Malcolm realised he had to go on. He looked at his children for a moment, then said, "I love you both very much, you know, and I'm sorry I've not supported you through this.

Your mother and I never spoke about what we'd do if..." He trailed off for a second, then gathered them together in his arms, and said, "It's time for me to leave this place."

Next Day

"Doc. I want to sign myself out. The ankle's fine."

"That's a nice surprise, Malcolm," said Doctor Kumar. "Could it have anything to do with a certain nurse?"

"Everything. She showed me how selfish I'd been. I've found a way to carry on."

"Good. Now, what about your medication? I think I'll give you a prescription that'll tide you over until you can see your own doctor."

"That's OK, doc. I wasn't taking it, anyway."

"You haven't been pulling the wool over my eyes, have you, Malcolm?"

"No. Absolutely not. I guess I always knew I'd have to pull myself together, know what I mean?"

"And did you pull yourself together on your own?"

"Sorry, doc. Pretty good idea of yours. Making sure Nicky and I would meet."

"Not so. Nicky's new to Ward C. Transferred the same day you arrived. I knew nothing about her family being on the same plane as your wife. I was thinking more about her."

"Oh, well. Can I see Nicky before I go?"

"Of course. I think she's on the ward, somewhere."

Malcolm shook Doctor Kumar's hand. "Thanks for everything, doc."

Malcolm found Nicky in the kitchen, and told her he was leaving.

"I'm glad. You didn't belong here," she said. "Did our little talk help? I'd like to think it did."

Malcolm looked at his hands, then said, "Look, I'm older than you. A lot older. I... er... erm. Oh God. I'm hopeless. I don't know how to put this. I don't want you to be offended. What I'm trying to say is..."

"Take a big breath, and start again. Don't worry."

279

The words came this time. "You told me you were living on your own, in a big house. Well, I have a big house, too. It's quite close to the hospital. There's plenty of room. You could have a whole floor to yourself—if you wanted to."

He stood, feeling bashful, looking into lovely, hazel-coloured eyes, which lowered. When they returned his gaze, Malcolm knew the meaning of one solitary tear, rolling, silently, down a woman's cheek. "I was hoping you might ask me that," she said. "Yes, I'd like to."

Nicky moved in with Malcolm straight away. He insisted she have the main bedroom. They agreed to share the chores, but he wouldn't let her pay anything towards the costs of running the place. "After all, you've got to save for your future, and they don't pay nurses a lot," he said.

A fortnight later, Nicky went to Malcolm in the night. "Hold me, please," she said.

Malcolm held her until she dropped off to sleep. Her soft breathing, and her smooth, silky hair caressing his shoulder, brought memories. Moonlight, shining in through the window and bouncing off the chromium-plated ashtray he'd taken from Ward C as a keepsake, caused him to reflect on the things he'd seen there.

He didn't even know the name of the man found frozen to death in the garden one morning, still holding the ashtray. Malcolm thought of Judy, and Joe, and all the others. And the inner place to which he and they had retreated, each in their own private, living Hell. *Clive. So young to be in such a place,* he thought. Then he looked down at Nicky. *She can't be much older than twenty.*

Malcolm looked through the window, and considered the families of all those who'd perished on Flight 401. *Why?* he wondered.

The moon appeared to blink in agreement as a cloud covered it for a second. Sounds of trees, rustling in the wind, seemed to Malcolm to let him know he wasn't alone. He drifted off to sleep, breathing in Nicky's sweet fragrance.

In his dreams, Paula came and spoke to him, letting him know it was alright.

The next morning, Malcolm and Nicky made love.

After breakfast, Doctor Kumar, writing up Malcolm's medical notes while sitting on the oak bench, read the police report and the accompanying witness statement "He just dived off. Definitely tried to kill himself, but as he fell, a figure in blue came underneath him, and turned him over. He landed on his feet."

The doctor put down the report, and looked up. Fluffy clouds drifted by in an overcast sky.

Hmm, he thought. *Figure in blue.*

Unlike Malcolm, the doctor didn't dismiss the witness's report. He'd seen many things in his time. He looked at his watch. *Time to go back in*, he thought. *Good luck, Malcolm.*

A wispy, blue spectre rose with the doctor, then disappeared. The telepathic energy of Audeus' memories winged its way back to rejoin that of his master.

Chapter 41

Armageddon

On the day Margaret and Paula boarded Flight 401, Ricky and Esther renewed their marriage vows in St Mary's Church.

As Ricky drove up the M40, his thoughts turned to the day he met Esther. Of sharing a meal of asparagus tips and Tournedos Rossini with her on the plane. It was still his favourite meal. He recalled the day she came to him when he was in hospital. That was when he knew she loved him.

"Bored, Rick?" she said, bringing him back to reality.

He didn't take his eyes off the motorway, just smiled and said, "I was thinking."

"Have you spoken to the vicar in the last few days? What's his name? Michael..."

"Phoned him a fortnight ago, and confirmed with him yesterday. His name's Michael Jobson."

On Paul Andrew Bates's sixth birthday, Reverend Michael Jobson blessed the renewed marital commitment of his parents. To complete the congregation, Ricky had asked that the choir be present. Among the dozen or so members who attended, eight-and-a-half-year-old Clare Black dug the boy next to her in the ribs.

After the blessing, the congregation sang a hymn. The now deeper, but no less dulcet, tone in Michael's voice echoed throughout the church and the hollowed-out roots of the Great Oak tree.

St Mary's Church is hexagonal. As Michael sang, he looked up and out of one of a line of oblong windows, high up on the walls above the Stations of the Cross. He felt as if the host of heaven were watching as puffs of white clouds, looking like curls of angel's hair, drifted by.

But inside him, the memories of Pythagoras and Audeus

were troubled. Their empathy with Nature, and human beings, made them aware of the drama about to unfold on Flight 401. Fanatical men, having prepared plans to cause death and destruction, were about to let loose squads of suicide bombers in order to destabilise major countries in the western hemisphere. And the most evil of memories, hosted by a shrouded man, were getting stronger. Time was short. Although they couldn't stop these outrages, Pythagoras and Audeus would have to warn mankind.

Clare caught her breath. She was looking at Michael as the spectres of Pythagoras and Audeus left him. She nudged the boy again.

"Whaatt?" he said.

"Can't you see it?"

"See what?"

Only Clare saw the shades of Pythagoras and Audeus leave Michael and drift up through the window on their mission to save mankind. But Ricky noticed Michael Jobson stagger.

After the service, Ricky asked him if he was alright. "Oh, I'm fine. All this kneeling and getting up over the years has taken its toll, I expect. But thank you for asking. I'm particularly pleased to conduct this service for you and your wife. I like to think that people still want to marry in church, because even if they don't come to Communion, or attend church regularly, when it comes to marrying, something inside them tells them it's the right thing to do."

"Well, I love this place, and Esther will come to love it too. I used to walk my dog in the field behind the church, and the woods. I always had a good feeling. We live a long way away, now, as you know, but it's as if—well, occasionally, I need a top-up of that feeling of community. I don't know if you can understand that."

"I understand completely. And that's why some people might think me to be like Emperor Franz Joseph, propping up a tottering edifice, but I have to be here, and this place has to remain open. Faith is fundamental to this church. I believe that people are bound to feel the need of that faith and community again, some time."

Esther and Ricky strolled up the incline, and into the

woods behind the church, before going home. They held hands, and ambled round the perimeter while the children played. Something they'd do many times in the future.

Paul chased Sheila up and down the dried-out moat, and swung on the ropes. They frolicked about in a warm breeze, on bluebell-covered earth. Esther and Ricky watched them play, unaware of the tragic news waiting for them when they returned home.

Michael Jobson was getting weaker, too.

* * *

The shroud-covered man whom Audeus and Pythagoras searched for had once had a name. Walter Jackson. Walt travelled the vastness which is the United States for over twenty years, after being demobbed. Everywhere he went, someone ignited the rage he struggled unsuccessfully to control. Then, in 1996, in Chicago, a USAF man half his size insulted the Marines, who, like Walt, had served in Vietnam. Walt, listening to this while sitting in a corner of a two-bit bar, began to sweat. The glass he was holding shook as flashbacks came. The noise increased, till he thought his head would burst. When, finally, a fight broke out, he let go. He got up from his seat, walked slowly over to the man, picked him up by his collar and trousers, and lifted him in the air. Then Walt brought him swiftly down over his knee. The crack as the man's spine broke brought silence to the room.

Walt bolted like a hare, screaming with fright as the pack bore down on him.

* * *

A screeching of wheels woke Walt as the goods train he had hitched a ride on began to slow. Sliding the door open, he peered into the gloom. When the train passed a sign saying Detroit 325, he jumped off and rolled down an embankment. Then he began to walk.

Two hours later, Walt found himself in Royal Oak, where he bought the last bottle of Jack Daniels he'd ever drink.

At 03.00 Walt lifted the bottle, and downed the dregs. He threw the bottle down, his look transferring from its hollow emptiness to the sky beyond. He smiled at the dark, rippling-starred universe, and brought his arms—outstretched—in front of him. Lurching forward, he ran in circles, gulping in air and moving his arms, as if swimming in Heaven's firmament.

After a while, Walt's alcohol-sodden brain became disorientated, and he careered into the woods behind. As he did so he bumped his head against a tree, and crumpled slowly to the ground. He smiled again as the rustling of dry leaves reminded him of a crisp, clean petticoat caressing white, stocking-topped thighs.

He closed his eyes, and stretched his arms forward again, singing: "Ohhh, the yellow rose of Texas, is the only one for me..." Walt opened his eyes then, seeing the world swirling in front of him, shut them again. He'd found the oblivion he so desired.

In his short-lived state of euphoria, Walt's dulled senses didn't register the sharp pain caused by a splinter entering his flesh when he bumped his head. From that day onwards, Walt never ate or drank. His appearance changed as the splinter took root. The evil force spread an aura round his head, then took form in filthy, lank hair surrounding his head. By the time Clare saw the spectres of Pythagoras and Audeus leave Michael Jobson, in the summer of 1999, Walt didn't exist anymore. Only his shroud-covered shell remained. The force within also searched telepathic airwaves, looking for the opposition it knew it would soon have to overcome in its bid for power.

Two days after Esther and Ricky returned from renewing their vows, they watched the television, along with the rest of the world. Reaction to the downing of Flight 401 was swift. America lashed out, obliterating the parts of Arabia inhabited by those sworn to wage the holy war of Jihad. Mankind stood on the brink.

An official letter from the British Government to Esther stated that Margaret was named on the passenger list of Flight 401, and therefore presumed dead. The letter also recommended that Esther wait for the return of Margaret's effects, as final confirmation.

Esther already knew. Probably before the Government. Within an hour of the explosion, Elizabeth, in a hysterical phone call from John F. Kennedy Airport, had asked her what she should do. Esther told her to get on a plane as soon as possible, and bring the children to her.

Esther felt numb. Pregnant again, she worried for her baby, and for them all. Turning to Ricky, she said, "D'you feel it?"

He did, but he wasn't letting on. He took her hand. "Hey. It's nothing. We're just panicking, that's all. Fools they are. You don't think they'll get away with it, do you?"

"Suppose not."

"Well, then. I'll put the kettle on."

Memories of Terry flooded Esther's mind.

Ricky watched the children through the kitchen window as he filled the kettle. Paul was sitting on the swing, dragging his feet in the dust, as boys do. Sheila was running around with Margaret's girls, as girls do. The nightstick in Ricky's pocket grew warm. By now he'd realised that wasn't necessarily a good sign. He was sure he said the words, "Come in children, it's getting cold," but wasn't sure. Everything around him seemed to be happening in slow motion.

After tea, Esther and Ricky watched the television with the sound off. Paul sat on the floor, behind the settee, reading a book about magic and wizards—with his back to the wall, just in case.

Ricky felt the nightstick warmer in his pocket. He reached out, and took Esther's hand. This time, he was sure something was about to happen. And felt helpless.

All over the world, people of every race, colour and creed who had come into contact with remnants of trees struck by lightning had the same feeling of empathy with something unknown.

After setting the Communion table at St Mary's, Michael Jobson returned to the vicarage for a few minutes, totally unprepared for the scene he'd witness on his return. People were coming to his church from every direction.

Time was getting on. Michael hurried to the rear of the church and let himself in through the vestry door. After quickly dressing in Communion robes, he entered from behind the pews where the choir would sit, and made as if to check the Communion table.

Thanks be to God, he thought, as the church filled. People of all races and colours came in quietly, and sat down. Young people and the old. Families sat together, some on the front row, the children between their parents. Couples came, holding hands, sometimes one helping the other.

When Michael addressed his congregation he was convinced that the tide had turned, at last.

Realising what had brought such a turnout, Michael broke from the norm slightly by beginning the service with a prayer for all the victims of recent terrorist atrocities and their families. The mood in church that morning was tangible, so much so that when the time came for Michael to administer Holy Communion, he was finding it difficult to remain composed. The altar rail became full. Still people came, heads bowed in silence, to form a queue. As Michael served the first of the congregation, the air became charged with the energy of their personalities.

It was at this moment that Michael knew it would be alright. *The bombers can't win*, he thought. *These people have come to show a sense of community. They'll quietly bury their dead, not with bitterness, but like they've come today. Sadly, and with dignity. They won't seek revenge, not because they'll forget, but in the sure knowledge that they're united: ready to take the place of those who died in the fight against evil, just like their forefathers.*

Chapter 41

July 6th 1999

Carrie, rummaging around in Margaret's things in her bedroom, was in the act of discovering a key, wrapped in a receipt and taped to the underside of a drawer. She jumped when Branston, now able to speak, shouted up, "Carrie. I'm going to New York. Relay any messages to the limousine."

Carrie quickly stuffed the key in her apron and ran to the top of the stairs, hoping JP had a good view of her as she said, "Yes, sir."

He could, and did. There was a twitch in his groin, prompted by Erato's memories. The Muse relished the prospect of inhabiting Branston, after transmigrating from Margaret through the rubber gloves. Now she'd know the pleasure of sex from a young, virile male's point of view.

Carrie listened until the sound of the limo faded. Then she took out the key and looked at it again. It had the number 28 punched into it. The receipt was for payment of three months' rent, in advance, from Spaces, a Detroit company specialising in storage. It also had on it Margaret's passport number and name. Carrie's jaw dropped. *Branston. He married her.*

JP had attended the Washington service, wondering why he hadn't been notified as next of kin. The only clues he had were that Margaret had gone to New York, and that she had a sister. *I'll find her, and introduce myself*, he decided.

Esther and Ricky represented Terry and Joan. Audeus, having searched out Esther's energy, was with her.

As in Margate, for Sheila, Esther remembered little of the memorial service. All she could think of was Margaret, Andrew and her parents. And the CIA. *After this, I'm never coming back to this lousy country*, she thought.

"Esther." Ricky touched her arm. "It's time to get the coach," he said.

Echoes of Gregorio Allegri's chilling but beautiful plea *Miserere*, ringing round the church, brought a cold shiver crawling over her skin. Ricky saw the pain in her eyes as she laid her head on his shoulder. "Can we stay—just for a while?" she said.

Esther didn't see people leaving, or notice Branston looking at her. But that music, those words: "Make me a clean heart, and renew a right spirit within me. Give me the comfort of your help again." Amid the words she heard a name. *It's my name. What does it mean?* she thought.

Too quietly spoken to be heard above the choir, a whisper crept over her lips; "Am I going to die, too?"—and like an Arctic wind looking for a warm place, it found every nook and cranny in the church.

As the huge doors were opened to let the congregation out, a unifying mood seemed to sweep in on a ripple of noise, and rays of sunshine from outside. In that moment Esther knew that within their grief, everybody was feeling the same thing. *This isn't just a service for the dead,* she thought. *This is a statement. People will always come together to fight a common enemy.*

Ricky touched her arm again. "Come on, love. We're the last."

Photographers had been kept a discreet distance away, but she heard the cameras and the distant shouts, although she couldn't quite hear what they were saying. "Miss Clayton. Is it true... married one of Amer...'s richest men?", "... pregnant?", "Miss Clayton ... you be ... movie?"

Her head swam as they ran to get the coach. *What do they mean? Who pregnant? Who married?*

Relatives had been invited to congregate after the service, for refreshments. This would provide an opportunity for victims' property mixed up in the crash to be returned. Anything that wasn't recognised would be pinned to the noticeboards provided. Relatives could write their name on a label and attach it to the item.

Esther, still confused and irritated by the Press, wanted to get away. She stayed outside, while Ricky went inside, where Malcolm was also searching for anything of Paula's.

289

Paula's handbag contained her passport, and photographs of her family, and the dogs. There were also two photographs Malcolm didn't recognise. These he put on the noticeboard. The first was a picture of Esther, receiving her Oscar. On the back of it was her phone number. The second was a picture of Esther, Andrew and Margaret, taken when they were young, but unmistakeably them. Both had transferred from Graham, who'd been tailing Margaret and Branston.

The jostling crowd made it difficult for Ricky to stand in one place for long, but he finally found a spot from which he could have a good look. As he did so, a shadow occupied the area immediately around him. Only a shadow. But this shadow was different. It seemed to Ricky to be tangible, and able to exclude all other things surrounding it. Except him. A handbag—Margaret's handbag—was thrust in front of him.

As in the poker tournament when, in his concentration, he had ceased to notice background noise and movement, or the features of the bellboy who had returned the nightstick at a critical point in the poker hand, all Ricky's senses honed in on the handbag and the smooth-skinned fingers holding it. They were long and mesmerising in their elegance Ricky couldn't take his eyes off them, even when his mind began to search for the name of the person who had said, "Excuse me, sir, I believe this belongs to your wife."

Ricky looked into the soft brown eyes of the man who had given Terry the book at the car-boot sale in Margate. The bag hovered closer and higher. Ricky took it, opened it, and looked inside. Then he remembered. "Look, I know you..."

The eyes were green this time, and the accent American. "Hey, buddy. If you're done, can I get to the board?"

Ricky looked sharply left and right, then at the serviceman who'd spoken. "Sorry. Did you see another man, just now?"

The serviceman spread his arms. "Look, mister. This is a hard time for all of us. But you gotta take your stuff and move away."

Ricky moved away. "Yes, I'm sorry."

* * *

In Margaret's handbag, amongst other things, was a picture

of Elisha and Binjamin. On the back was J.P. Branston's address in Royal Oak. Esther gave it to Ricky to pin on the noticeboard. The rest of the contents she recognised, including Margaret's red wallet. She shut the bag and sat, fidgeting, for a short time. She *needed* to get away. "Can we go now?" she said when Ricky returned.

"Well, I had a good look. There's nothing else I can see."

J.P. Branston looked for Esther, but couldn't find her. He was drawn to her, but had the feeling something was keeping them apart. Audeus knew Erato, the force he couldn't defeat alone when she was at the height of her passion, was inside Branston. This time he kept Esther and Branston apart.

When Branston, impelled by Erato, finally connected with Esther, it was too late. She'd gone. But, he had the photographs, taken from the noticeboards.

The Warning

Outside the limits of gravity, memories in the universe were aware of an awesome, all-knowing presence. The memories of the greatest and most revered Druid of all, Pythagoras, had come amongst them. Using telepathy, he spoke. "Violence is escalating on Earth. Man seems bent on destroying himself. He cannot help himself, therefore we must show him the way."

"Why should we concern ourselves?" another said.

The presence of Pythagoras quivered slightly. "Didn't you learn at the time of Jesus Christ? The evolution of mankind must continue."

"But what can we do? They're about to obliterate each other. There isn't time," said another.

"Time. What is time? You are what you are—and know the way."

"We don't understand."

"Are you not the collective memories of mankind? Do you not have, between you, all the understanding and knowledge man has learned since time began? And haven't you become part of the universe? All there is."

"Of course." The memories of the most intelligent and far-seeing minds that had ever lived in the minds of men and women got it as one. To Aristotle, Ptolemy, Copernicus, Galileo, Newton and Einstein, all was revealed.

"We are what we are. Memories. We can be wherever we want to be. And in whatever we want to be in, by transmigration."

"Come. Concentrate," said Pythagoras. "I've prepared for this moment. I remind you that many memories are trapped on Earth. In people. In trees struck by lightning. All memory must be united against this evil. The transmigration of memories into the minds of men and women everywhere is the only way."

An ominous hush descended in the universe as the apparitions of Pythagoras and Audeus, like silent supernovas forming the perfect emblem of the letter Y, rose in Heaven's vault. From them emanated an ancient incantation. Ricky grasped Esther's hand tightly as the telepathic message came into their minds, and those of men and women everywhere. They fell immediately into a deep sleep.

People like Esther and Ricky slept untroubled by the message. To others, there was no doubting the warning in the words, and the chilling scenes portrayed:

"For spirits freed from mortal laws
with ease assume what sexes and
shapes they please;
We do not trifle with divinity,
but are the heirs of customs and memories
hallowed by age, and handed down to us
by our fathers;
No quibbling logic can topple them,
whatever subtleties *this* age invents;
that which man has made
in time will surely crumble and fade.
See now the journey's end for those
whose evil pollutes the world."

Then they came. Apparitions of every evil person who'd lived appeared, like ragged ghosts, emerging through a mist from the depths of eternal purgatory, answering Pythagoras' command. In the dreams of mankind, the parade went on and on. Semi-clothed skeletons, wailing open-jawed and pointing stick-like, fleshless fingers, taunted them.

In the minds of the martyrs of Jihad, unimaginable horrors of the bitterness of the food of the damned were shown, via the words of the Koran: "How will it be for him whose food is Zakkum?", as the reward for continuing their murderous ways. Scenes of Audeus cutting swathes through their ranks, like a reaper's blade, left no doubt. They could not win. Mankind drew back from Armageddon, unaware of the evil force waiting to take control of minds, not countries.

* * *

Michael Jobson's body, now weakened by illness, could not withstand the mental battle to come. Pythagoras and Audeus needed to transmigrate. It would be to Esther.

Michael's problems had begun before Ricky saw him lose his balance in church. No amount of water would quench his thirst. Then he became unsteady, and it was only dedication to his faith that enabled him to carry on. The day after Ricky and Esther renewed their vows he collapsed, and was taken to a hospital where it was discovered he had diabetes. Part of Michael's out-patient treatment involved a visit to an optician, to assess how much damage, if any, this condition had caused in his eyes.

Chapter 43

The Transmigration

The optician's assistant, Annie, sat Michael in front of a Fields Test apparatus and made sure everything was calibrated. Then she went through the routine.

"Now, Father, look through the binocular type viewer, please. You'll see a white screen with a black spot in the centre. Keep looking at the spot and press the button each time you see a flash. That's all there is to it, OK?"

"OK."

Annie waited to see that the machine was working, then left him to it. She returned after a buzzer let her know the sequence had been completed. "All done? Now I'll show you to the consulting room for the rest of the test. The optician will be with you in a minute or two," she said, ripping the results sheet from the printer.

The consulting room was dimly lit. Annie showed Michael to a large, high-backed leather chair, in which he sat. Next to him was an oblong desk. She put the sheet on the desk, and left. On the walls hung the usual charts, and others, showing the inner eye and its workings in detail. In the middle of the room was a trial lens machine, in which the optician would put different-strength lenses to assess whether or not Michael needed glasses.

The optician, a young Asian man, came in and held out a hand. "Hi, Mister Jobson. I'm Ravi. How are you?"

Michael took the hand, and shook it. "Fine, thanks, your-self?"

"Yes, thanks. Now, let's have a look."

Ravi sat down behind the desk and picked up the results sheet. His mind was fifty per cent on what he was doing, and fifty per cent on his stomach, which was a little bloated: the result of eating too many samosas at lunch. He soon became focused. Ravi looked at the Fields Test results. "Good," he said. "Now, do you see the letters on the chart, on the wall?"

"Yes."

"Read the lowest line you can most easily identify, from the left, please."

Michael read the bottom line without a pause.

"Very good. Now, let me have a look at the back of your eyes."

Michael tilted his head back to afford Ravi the best angle to shine his ophthalmoscope.

"Look straight ahead, please."

Ravi couldn't believe what he was seeing. *This isn't possible*, he thought. *The man's almost blind. He shouldn't even be able to read the top line.*

Ravi sat, and looked at the results sheet again. He turned it over, and looked at the other side. He shook his head, then looked at Michael. "Won't be a minute," he said.

Ravi left the consulting room, looking for Annie. Spotting her dusting sample spectacles lined up in a display stand, he raised his hand and snapped his fingers to get her attention. "Annie. Annie, come," he whispered.

Annie caught sight of him and stopped what she was doing. "Yes, Mister Waheed. I'm free," she said in her best drama queen's voice. Then holding her hands under her chin, she said, "Woof, Woof." Then, imitating a dog, Annie panted and shook her bottom enthusiastically.

"Stop it," whispered Ravi.

"Well don't treat me like a dog, then. One of these days I'm gonna bark. Will I see you tonight? I've got something special for you."

"Maybe. Look, this is important. Is the machine working?"

"Yes. Checked it, and waited while it started the sequence. Why?"

"Well, is there toner in the printer?"

"Yes. I checked it this morning," said Annie. Then added, testily, "Like I always do."

"Only asking," said Ravi.

Annie put her tongue out at his back as he walked away.

"You don't pay me enough, mister," she said.

Ravi went back into the treatment room. He knew that blindness can come gradually, and that a person's other senses could compensate. *This is impossible. The man shouldn't be able to see any of the flashes, never mind score 100%,* he thought. He decided to stall. "Did you say you were a clergyman?" he said.

"Yes. I'm vicar at St Mary's, just up the road."

Ravi shook his head as Michael left the shop and walked out onto the street. The damage to Michael's retina was such that he shouldn't have been able to see at all. Ravi hadn't known what to say, so had said nothing. *A mystery.* Then he caught sight of his partner, John Rai, coming to take over the afternoon shift. "John, I've something to show you."

John Rai studied the results of Ravi's tests, and looked at him. "Doesn't make sense," he said. "Was he safe?"

"Yeah. Walked in under his own steam. He's a holy man."

"What? a fakir?"

"No, he's Christian."

"Oh, well. The machine must be wrong. What did you do?"

"Nothing. What could I do? I'm not going to sell him a prescription for glasses that he doesn't need, and he's not a danger to himself. I'll send a report to his doctor and let him sort it out."

In fact, the telepathic vision of the memories of Pythagoras and Audeus had become such a part of his own thinking, Michael was permanently in a virtual state of grace and needed very little mechanical vision.

＊　＊　＊

The church was full when Michael next administered Communion. He felt at last that people wanted to share in the communion and empathy the church offers. Roy Marshall, and Ricky, and their families also attended that day.

After the service ended, Michael clasped Esther's hands as the congregation left. He knew immediately. *This is the one*

I've waited for, he thought.

No-one noticed the transmigration take place. No words were spoken as the power flowed. Emotionally tangible in its depth, they were swept away as Pythagoras and Audeus joined minds with them. Esther was shown the creation, and fundamental workings of the universe, which explained her dreams.

'Your Father.'

The words came, as if on a wind—impossible in a void. Unfolding before her, she saw the magnificence of the birth of creation. Of matter, spreading out and away, then coming back together to form things. Rock, ice, gases.

'Your Mother.'

A brilliant kaleidoscope of green and blue, red and yellow swirled in front of her. Headlong, she went through it, becoming part of a phenomenon repeated time and again. She saw the Earth; the evolvement of its seas and land as the molten orb cooled. The spawning of life flashed through her mind. And the coming of man.

Mankind separated into tribes, using force to protect what they needed. Then she saw single-minded men manipulating nations, using political means and financial power to get, not what they needed, but what they wanted.

For an instant she glimpsed a blissful existence. It was not physical. This was the future. A time when the evolution of man was complete.

In this state she recognised nothing. Knew no human traits. Had no sense of right or wrong, or need for judgement of any kind. Then Esther felt herself coming back. Not to gravitational reality, though. Her inner self seemed enlightened. Impervious to any human foible. Audeus showed her the truth of the Harmony of the Spheres, and that the universe is unending, and man's soul the crowning achievement of creation.

'You are what you are.' This came next as an echo, both from outside and from inside. She was aware of being at the heart of everything. At the centre of a black hole, the gravitational pull of which was so strong the whole universe could be swallowed by it.

But she knew *she* could escape. The inspired revelation that man's mind is separate from his body came to her. She realised that even if all matter vanished, all magnetic fields and influences ceased to exist, the spirit of mankind—their spirit—would remain unrestrained. Free.

Finally, she saw a great army pouring out from deep underground, in such numbers as to block out the sun. An army of almost unimaginable evil; its release timed to coincide with the reincarnation of a force whose entire being was cold hate and lust for power. And she saw the shrouded man.

Michael, eyes closed, swayed as Esther's spirit rushed back towards him and the church. Esther's descent slowed. Sweet scents of flowers infused her brain, and fresh clean air filled her lungs. An awareness of Ricky and her family brought love flooding into her, together with the certain knowledge that if mankind has faith and love, is unconquerable.

Esther inhaled sharply as she burst through Michael's subconscious and back into herself, at which point Michael relaxed his grip and sank gracefully to the floor.

My God. He's had a diabetic fit or something, thought Esther, remembering nothing.

* * *

Ricky and Esther stayed until Michael had recovered. Very weak now, and bed-ridden, he took her hands once again. "Did you feel it?" he said.

"You held onto my hands as you fainted."

Michael, feeling the power within her, studied Esther for a moment. "You are a special person. God has great work for you. Do you feel it now?" he said.

Esther blushed, and took her hands away. It was difficult for her. *Should I tell such a lovely man what I feel?* she thought.

Deciding she shouldn't, she said, "Well, they say He works in mysterious ways, don't they?"

Michael took her hands again. "Do you believe me?"

For a moment, emotions of terrible anger and hurt rushed into Esther's mind. "I don't believe in God, I believe in people," she said.

Michael smiled. "You've suffered a lot. But you mustn't be angry with God for man's sins. He loves you and will not fail you. Why do you come to church?"

Esther didn't know why. "Because my husband likes to come, I suppose. I do feel something while I'm here, though."

"Do you have dreams you don't understand? Did you feel something pass between us, in church?"

Relieved that a man she trusted should ask about her dreams, the answer came quickly. "Yes, I felt it, and I have *very* strange dreams."

"All I ask is that you keep an open mind. I cannot explain your dreams, but I do know you will soon have a task of great importance to complete. What you feel in church is the unity of souls. You wouldn't feel that if you only came because your husband likes to. When the time comes, draw on that unity of common purpose between human beings. Will you promise me that?"

Esther's hands were almost numb by now. She could see in his eyes he was sincere. She looked at the tips of her fingers, which were turning white. Michael let go of Esther's hands. "I'm sorry. When you go from here will you remember what I said, and keep faith?"

"Well, whatever I believe about a God doesn't seem to matter. All I know is I feel I have the power within me to over-come anything. But it's just what I've always had to do. You know?"

"Yes, but not all people have that power. That's why you're special. Now, off you go, and please thank your husband for me."

Michael made the sign of the cross. "Bless you. And remember, be strong and have faith."

"I will, and I hope you're better soon."

❊   ❊   ❊

Esther found herself more accepting of the dreams she'd been having. She now felt that there would be an end product and that she'd be a part of that end, whatever it was. *Perhaps Sheila and Andrew and Margaret will forgive me if I do this work for charity*, she thought.

More importantly, Esther wasn't frightened. She believed the words repeated occasionally in her dreams. Audeus was preparing her.

Esther found Terry to be very low when she next visited, however.

Chapter 44

Esther Brings the Family Together—July 1999

"I'm cursed and this place is cursed," said Terry, quietly. "Leave, and don't come back."

Esther looked at the top of her father's balding head. Memories of him dancing on the sea-front, ginger hair flowing like a cornfield rippling in a summer's breeze, came. She leaned forward and took his hand. "Nonsense," she said. "You and Mom are coming to stay with us. We've bought a big house. There's plenty of room. This place is getting worse anyway. Drunks smashing cars and urinating all over the place every night after closing. Elizabeth told me about the cans in the front garden. In fact she's coming too, if she wants to. I'll tell Ricky later."

* * *

"Well, this place is plenty big enough, and having Elizabeth around to help with all the kids would be a great help," said Ricky. "Will she come? And what about Margaret's children's father?"

Esther hadn't considered him, and realised that her plan to bring the family together needed thinking through. She had a shock when she spoke to Elizabeth, who got in first when Esther next visited.

"I need to have a chat with you," she said, ushering Esther into the kitchen. For a moment her courage failed at Esther's quizzical look and she turned towards the sink. "I'll put the kettle on," she said.

Feeling better now there wasn't any eye contact, Elizabeth told Esther her news. "I'm in love," she said, filling the kettle.

Esther was stunned. "Who with?" she said.

Elizabeth paused, turned off the tap, and plugged the kettle in. "Thomas," she said, pressing the On switch.

Esther couldn't think who she meant for a moment. Then Elizabeth whirled round. "I wouldn't have said anything. It's very soon after Margaret..." A feeling of guilt strangled the words for a moment; but remembering that Margaret had virtually abandoned them all, Elizabeth felt she could continue. "She phoned, and said she wanted to see the children. You know that's why I took them to New York. She didn't say anything about wanting to see Thomas. She hadn't seen him for ages. In fact, it was me he was having s..."

Elizabeth couldn't bring herself to admit straight out that she and Thomas had been lovers almost from the day Margaret had left the children with her.

The kettle came to the boil, giving Elizabeth the opportunity for relief, and she turned away. Esther was shaking as she got up and left the kitchen. She went into the lounge and sat down. Terry peered at her from across the room.

Although Elizabeth's outburst had come as a complete shock, Esther quickly adjusted as Audeus guided her. A tray, with a teapot, mugs and spoons clattering on it, appeared first from the kitchen, followed by an equally unstable, and nervous Elizabeth. Avoiding Esther's gaze, she put the tray down on the coffee table and touched Terry's arm. "Let it stand for a minute," she said.

Esther caught her eye, and jerked her head. Elizabeth followed her into the kitchen.

"Does he love you?" asked Esther.

"He said he does."

"Look, I was going to ask you if you wanted to come with the children and live with us, now Margaret's... Now she's..." She couldn't say the word, either.

Audeus helped, reminding Esther that devastating as the deaths of her only sister and brother were, she had to carry on. That along with their father, *she* was responsible for and in a position to help, not only the children, but her parents also. "D'you want to come? Will you talk to him and ask him if he'll come?" she said.

"Yes, I do want to come. I'll speak to Thomas."

Terry broke the conversation up. "Stop nattering like a couple of fishwives, will you?. This tea'll be as soggy as Margate sands in a minute."

Esther and Elizabeth hugged, then joined Terry, who said, "And don't think I didn't hear what you were talking about." His stump twitched as he pointed at Elizabeth. "The walls in this house aren't as thick as you think, you know. I had to put two pillows behind me head while you and him were bonking. Thought you'd come through the wall, I did."

Then he chuckled. The first time Esther had seen him laugh for a long time. Both she and Elizabeth blushed as he then said, "Must admit, it brought back memories of your mom and me. We had some good times on that bed, you know. Good luck to you."

Esther had to make provision for Joan to be well catered for, employing a full-time nurse to look after her at the estate, and also indemnifying the authorities from responsibility. But the vision she had of them all living together came to fruition, at last.

Chapter 45

Royal Oak

J.P. Branston sat at his desk, looking at the photographs. First, the picture of Esther receiving her Oscar. His gaze lowered from her hair to take in round, ocean-blue eyes sparkling with life and vitality, lips then as soft and lovely as a summer sunset, then gathered pace along the thin, black track-line strap of a three-quarter length dress, appearing from behind her shoulder, all turned half towards the camera, before free-wheeling on down, drawn inexorably to the curve of her bosom.

His head didn't move as he glanced a couple of inches to the right. The sight of Margaret, aged about ten, face tilted to one side, tongue pointing at the picture taker, didn't move him. But Esther, at fourteen years old, was blossoming. Her pose, hand on hip, one knee raised and crossing the other leg, causing her toe to touch the ground, held him in awe.

The spell wasn't broken by the telephone ringing. Branston reached out a hand to pick up the receiver, and glanced back at the first photograph. Esther's open-mouthed expression of joy and delight while standing on the podium was drawing him in.

"Hello. Hello. Branston?"

"Hell—o."

"What the hell? You smoking a joint or something? You sound as if you're far out, man. You're too old for that shit."

"Oh. Green. It's you. Well, I ain't too old any more."

"Ain't? Why the hell are you talking like a teenage bum? Don't tell me—you haven't...?"

"Yes. It's over. I've done it. The operation went ahead, three months ago. And I'm fine."

Al Green whistled. "Well, congratulations, I guess. I'd like to come and see you. Buy you dinner," he said.

Can't very well deny him, thought Branston. *He's the one man who has an inkling of what's going on. If I hadn't told him, I'd never have gotten out of Washington the night Jefferey got shot. The Chinese are on the same case. I'll need him when the story breaks. Better agree.* "Sure," he said. "When?"

"Tomorrow? Around midday?"

"I'll have the limousine waiting at the airport."

"Haven't you got a wide open space on that spread of yours?"

"It'll have to be a 'copter. Too much uneven ground."

"Just paint a big old white cross on the ground. We'll hit the bullseye."

"You got it. Bye."

Branston returned to the photographs. He looked at the telephone number, and, urged on by Erato's whispers of *"Isn't she beautiful? Wouldn't you just love to? Why don't you phone her?"* reached out a finger to dial the number.

A little moisture formed on Branston's forehead. His heart beat more quickly as he considered it. *I've got the perfect reason. I was married to her sister.* The telephone hovered for a moment, but clattered back into its cradle as he found himself answering, aloud. "No. She wouldn't. I couldn't. She's..."

He didn't know what Esther was, or wasn't. But at that moment he felt she was unobtainable. His desire was also tempered by the memory of seeing her in the church with Ricky. Branston's upbringing had been strictly Jewish. To pursue a married woman would be an affront to the memory of his parents. For the moment, Branston's faith was Erato's barrier.

Colin knocked at the door, interrupting him. "Time for your check-up, JP."

Branston lay on the couch, thinking as Colin took his blood pressure and checked his pulse: *Well, I've got my reprieve. And yet I've had love taken away. She was so young. So looking forward to a new life here, with me. After struggling to run a business alone.*

"You're fine, JP," said Colin. "All your tests have been consistent for over a month, now. I think I can give you a clean bill of health."

Branston sat up. "Good. Now, what's happening with those tubes?"

"First phase is going well. The double-sized tubes allow the clones to exercise each day after we've drained the fluid. And they're responding well to the educational tapes. They like the music, too."

"What about when you refill the tubes at night?"

"A few of them struggled at first, so we added a tranquilliser to the fluid and warmed it up a bit. Just like training an animal, really. Once they realised that they could breathe in the fluid, they got used to the routine. In fact, taking in the fluid gets oxygen to their lungs much quicker than air."

"Good. I'll have a look at them in the morning. Green is flying in around lunchtime. I'm off to the gym."

While exercising, Branston wondered why he couldn't phone Esther. He'd looked at those photographs every day since the memorial service and each time the same thing happened. He wanted her so badly it hurt. Yet he broke into a sweat every time he picked up the phone.

The answer came suddenly. *I've the testosterone-fuelled body of a young man, but my mature character allows me to think these situations through. I know what I would be doing. I can make responsible decisions. This really is having the best of both worlds.* It wasn't, for Erato.

* * *

As Branston showered he reasoned that he could suppress these conflicting emotions; but like many a man before him who had sex on his mind, he talked himself into it. *I'll definitely call her tomorrow*, he decided.

It was past midnight when Branston left his en-suite and turned down the bedroom lights. He was about to slide between the sheets when a light tap on the door startled him. He opened it to find Carrie standing there, light shining through from behind a flimsy, full-length nightie. Her lips parted slightly as she moved towards him. She put a hand on his breast, and smiled. "Will there be anything else tonight, sir?" she said.

His body answered with instincts too powerful to deny, even before Erato's memories screamed *"Yes"* in his brain. His control vanished as quickly as it had been attained. Branston took Carrie's hand, and led her in.

Next Day

Branston didn't know the man Al Green had brought with him. A dour, upright man with a pale, indoor complexion, who said nothing and made no observations while Branston showed them round the complex. *Could've come straight from Belsen*, he thought.

Green showed much more interest, and surprised Branston with one particular question as their tour neared its end. "Have you checked this place for bugs?" he asked.

"There are special anti-contamination filters on all the air vents. Nothing can get in, and all personnel are screened in and out."

"I meant listening devices."

"Oh. No, I haven't."

"Well it's time you did. Don't worry about it. I'll have my men give the place the once-over."

"Thanks for bringing that up. What I meant to say was that I haven't yet. But I've got a note reminding me to make arrangements for men to come in and take care of that."

"Is there somewhere outside we can talk?" said Green.

"Well, there's a bench up at my parents' tomb."

"Okay. Let's go."

Haslemere

Esther turned over in bed as consciousness approached. She peered, bleary-eyed, at the clock on her bedside cabinet. This disturbed Ricky. "You OK? What's the time?" he said.

"Six-thirty."

Ricky turned towards her and slipped an arm under hers. "Time for another hour, then."

Audeus left her and searched. In her dreams, Esther heard men talking.

"This is Doctor Jankl," said Green. "He's got some interesting news. Go ahead, Doc."

Jankl, sitting on the other end of the bench, leaned forward to make better eye contact with Branston, then stood up when he couldn't. He looked at Branston and began. "I've been researching progeria for several years. There's been a breakthrough..."

Jankl stopped as Branston raised his hand. "I'm no scientist. You'll have to make it easy for me."

Jankl stood a little more upright and flexed his shoulderblades. "It's commonly known as Hutchinson-Gilford Syndrome. Premature ageing caused by the mutation of a single gene, bringing connective tissue disease."

Jankl looked at Branston, who showed a brief recognition of what he was talking about. Jankl continued. "You may have seen pictures of children who appear much older than their years. This is because their bodies are ageing at an abnormally quick rate. It's rare for a person so afflicted to live beyond the age of thirty. I've halted that ageing process."

Green broke in. "Yeah, but when he stops the medication the ageing rate quickens up again. That means he can stop and start it when he likes. This means we can introduce the defective gene at the test-tube stage of production. That'll speed up the growth process of the clones."

"Do the military know about all this?" said Branston.

"Look, JP. This won't affect your business. You can still sell body parts to the cosmetics industry."

Branston jumped up. "How dare you? This was about giving quality of life back to countless people. The chance to live a full and happy life. This isn't about producing automatons for the bloody army. I won't do it."

Incandescent with rage, Branston walked off, shouting: "I'll destroy the whole lot, and all the research files."

Green took out a two-way radio. "Go," he said.

A window in the helicopter glinted as it was opened. The muzzle of a rifle slid through, and lined up on the figure several hundred yards away. A virtually silent *phutt* brought Branston to a halt, and he slumped to the ground.

Jankl staggered back, then froze. "What's happening?" he gasped.

"Don't worry. He'll be out for a few minutes, but he'll be alright. He'll come round and he *will* agree—when he's cooled off."

Chapter 46

Family Life

Esther stretched out an arm and killed the alarm. Ricky heaved himself up and swivelled round to put on his slippers. "Morning," he said, scratching as far round his back as he could. This would normally be a sign for Esther to take over as back-scratcher, followed by a kiss and a cuddle.

Today, though, she lay back, not moving. He turned and looked at her. "You OK?" he said.

"D'you dream any more?" she asked.

Ricky yawned, stood up, and walked to the bedroom wall. *Thank God for rough wallpaper*, he thought, rubbing his shoulders against the stipple. "Of course."

"No. I meant like the dream we had on the plane. About the old man."

"Well, if I do I don't remember them."

"I had another one, last night. They keep coming. I don't understand what's happening."

"Oh, well. Eating before you come to bed, probably. D'you want the bathroom first?"

She shook her head.

*   *   *

The sound of running water almost broke Esther's dream. But nothing came, so she jumped out of bed and ran into the bathroom. Ricky almost swallowed the toothpaste as she scratched his back furiously. When he gulped and turned round Esther planted a smacker of a kiss straight on top of the toothpaste, then ran back into the bedroom. "Oi. Come here, you," he said, chasing after her.

He caught up with her as she jumped onto the bed. They

both collapsed onto the duvet, laughing. She squirmed beneath him, then turned on her back, eyes alight with mischief. Neither spoke for a moment. Then she reached out and wiped the toothpaste away from his mouth.

"Morning," she said, and grinning at him, ran her tongue over her own lips, smoothing away the taste of peppermint.

God, how I love you, he thought. "I love your... your tongue," he said.

Esther wriggled out from underneath him and ran for the shower. "Prove it," she shouted, casting a glance over her shoulder to see how close he was. Sometimes, making love in the shower, with warm water caressing her body and his, was *the* most sensual experience for Esther.

The family ate breakfast together as usual, round a long pine table which ran down the centre of the kitchen. Afterwards, Ricky picked up his car keys and faced Terry. "You ready?" he said.

Terry turned the wheelchair away from the table. "Just about," he said. Then, looking at Esther, "You won't know me when I've had me new prosth- pros- you know, me peg-leg fitted. Thanks."

Esther kissed the top of his head. "That's OK, Dad. You deserve it."

She stopped helping to feed Joan when she heard Ricky's car door shut. Her eyes grew moist as she watched his car disappear over the hill in a cloud of dust. But this time there was a smile to go with the tears. Terry was getting better.

Elizabeth was too busy to notice Joan's eyes flicker as, over her shoulder, a shimmering ray of sunlight burst in through the window. Audeus returned to Esther in a twinkling of snowflake-like purity.

Esther was subconsciously making the decision to have a proper look through Margaret's things after breakfast. "Come on, Mom. Let's get you sorted," she said, turning from the window.

"Be careful, Esther," Joan whispered.

Esther stopped and looked at Joan, then at Elizabeth who was bringing the plates to the sink. "What did you say?"

"Me? Nothing. D'you want another cup of tea before we start?"

"Did Mom say something?"

Elizabeth looked at Joan. "I didn't hear anything," she said, turning the volume down on the radio.

"You can't hear anything above the *1812 Overture.*"

Esther sat beside Joan. Her once jet-black hair was flecked with white. Esther pushed her fingers under limp, cold hands. "Shall we go for a walk today, Mom?" she said.

Esther sat for several moments without blinking, hoping for a response. There was none. She squeezed Joan's hand. Nothing. *Wishful thinking.*

* * *

Joan, isolated within her own mental prison, screamed. *What's the matter with me? If I did it then, why can't I do it all the time? Something bad's happened. Why can't I remember? I know something worse is coming. Why can't I warn her?* A cold, dank shiver spread over her body as, over Elizabeth's shoulder and through the window, she saw evil personified in the same dark shadow she'd seen time and time again since the shooting.

Leave me alone, she screamed, wordlessly. The shadow paused, as if looking in. Two holes where eyes should have been appeared near its top. Joan screamed again, then felt herself being sucked into a blast furnace. But there was no heat. Joan was in a maelstrom of tortured souls, and couldn't get out. The feeling only left her when the shadow faded.

Esther shook Joan's hand. "Mom. What's the matter? You're sweating." Esther felt a mighty power rise within her as she turned in the direction of Joan's gaze. Twin bolts of blue fire appeared in Esther's eyes as Audeus' telepathic power rose within her to meet the danger.

As quickly as it had come, the shadow vanished. The force inside Walt Jackson had found what it was looking for. Its evil threat trailed behind it as a vapour when it left.

Joan fainted into Esther's arms. She was as cold as the heart of the one she'd seen.

Dust billowed up behind Ricky's car on its way down the hill. It slewed across the dirt track at an angle, brakes locked on. "What the flip..." said Terry, his body slamming against his seat-belt.

"Something's wrong. We've gotta go back," said Ricky.

Ricky entered through the back door. "Esther. Elizabeth. Mary." No answer. The only sound, a single violin reaching the final, anaesthetic-like climax to Massenet's *Meditation from Thais*. He turned off the radio and walked across the hallway and into the lounge. Esther sat with Margaret's handbag in her lap. She looked at him, and smiled. "Hi. You're back soon."

Ricky saw Joan sitting, facing away from him, and looking through closed windows. The setting seemed to be so peaceful. "Just forgot something. You OK?" he said.

"Fine. We're fine," said Esther, the memories of what had happened blanked from her mind. Audeus could only once allow her to face what was to come.

Ricky kissed her. He didn't close his eyes, but looked directly into hers. She smiled—a faintly amused smile, and touched the side of his face. "Mind how you go," she said.

Satisfied, Ricky straightened himself and said, "OK. See you later."

Chapter 47

Carrie Strikes Gold

Carrie pushed lightly against the pool wall, brought her legs forward, turned, and propelled herself effortlessly in the opposite direction. She drew her feet to her bottom, then kicked against the warm water. Raising her eyes, she watched Branston vigorously punch his way down the pool in front of her. *He was fantastic last night*, she thought. *I was fantastic. Something's got into him today, though. I need to find out what's going on. They don't think I notice them. Him and the doctors sneaking off through that door he keeps locked in reception. First, I'm gonna see what's in that storage.*

Carrie walked to Spaces. Less conspicuous than arriving in a car. She'd already had a chat with the purple- and black-haired, floozie on the desk a few days before.

"You gotta get your own key," the girl had said. Then she'd paused, and tilted her head to one side while transferring gum to the other cheek. "And you pick your own number. It's twenny dollars a week. Suit yourself."

Carrie had told her she'd think about it.

If the girl recognised her today (unlikely, as she'd only briefly glanced at Carrie while she went through the routine), she would think she'd taken up the option during another shift. Carrie stooped under a roller shutter and walked up a concrete incline, sectioned off with yellow-painted lines. She looked straight ahead, making sure she passed a parked vehicle on the side that prevented anyone in the office seeing her. When out of sight, she stood reading posters on the wall. After a couple of minutes she heard a clicking sound coming from the door by her side. She stuck out a hand and caught hold of it, as if preventing it from hitting her.

"Oh. Sorry," said a man struggling with a case under each

arm. Carrie, still looking at the posters, held the door open for him. "Thanks," he said, squeezing by.

"You're welcome. Have a nice day," she said.

Carrie slipped inside and looked around. The corridors went both ways. She took out the key and checked the number. Then she looked up at the walls. 'One Through Thirty' was printed on a sign.

Units of different sizes lined either side of the corridor, but she wasn't sure what she was looking for. The signs read "Seventy-five square feet", "One hundred square feet". Panic set in when she came to the end. *The numbers finish at twenty-seven. Where's number twenty-eight?* she thought. *I'm sure I came the right way.*

She swivelled round and looked back down the corridor. She turned back and walked the last few feet. Then she saw it. The last three units sat, one on top of the other, in a section no more than two feet wide. Carrie looked round. Her heart thumped loudly. She wiped her forehead, and licked her lips. *Where's that key?* she thought. "Huh," she said, dropping her bag. Then she took a deep breath, picked it up, and said to herself, "Calm down."

The lock turned easily, and the door swung open. A red light on a digital security panel winked at her, advertising its challenge. *Numbers. The stupid cow put in numbers.* Her mind raced. *What do I know about her? Nothing. What's her birthday? Goddammit. How the hell should I know? Think. Think.*

Finally, she began to think logically. *She must've done it soon after she arrived. She didn't know anyone, except Branston. What's his birthday? What's his phone number? Goddamn. Her mobile? No. That went down with the plane. What year is it?*

As she was considering what Margaret might have done, she fiddled with the receipt. She paused and held her breath as she heard the door behind her open. She closed her eyes, then sighed with relief as a sound of footsteps going the other way echoed down the corridor. When she opened her eyes she saw Margaret's passport number on the receipt. She looked at the security panel. *Four numbers.* She looked at the passport, counting the numbers, then stamped her foot. "Seven. That's no good. I need four," she said.

Then her eyes caught sight of the receipt number in the top right-hand corner. *1945. Surely it's not going to be that easy*, she thought. Shaking fingers caused her to make several mistakes as she pressed the numbers. Finally she pressed the correct ones. The door swung open. Carrie bent down, and peeped in. She saw a shoebox.

* * *

The helicopter still sat in the field, moth-like, with feelers drooping, as Carrie got back. Nobody was at the front of the house, but Henry saw her go in. Lapsing into the vernacular of his forefathers, he raised a cheek, put his tongue between his teeth, and drew in a sharp breath. "Aw, Jeez, man. You sure is something, now." He shook his head and polished the silver dish he was holding a little faster, and a little harder.

Carrie walked into the lounge, pulling up short when she saw a man sitting in the chesterfield. *Cop*, she thought. "Where's the master?" she said.

Al Green's man gave her the once-over. "Resting," he said.

"Aren't you warm in a raincoat and trilby?" she said.

The agent looked straight ahead.

"Bloody spic cop," she said as she flounced out.

Branston had come round and was sitting, holding his head in his hands. Green was speaking. "Sorry, James. But you have to understand. I can't let you run this as a business. The bloody Commies are on the same track."

"I'm years ahead of them, even more so now Jankl's come up with a way to accelerate the maturing of the clones."

"This is too big. Look. I've been your buddy right along. OK, in the beginning it was business." Green prodded himself in the chest while continuing, "*My* business. I have to know who's who, and what they're up to. The buck stops with me. But we got on alright, didn't we? Now, we can do this two ways. With or without you. Are you in or out?"

Green knew Branston couldn't be bought, and couldn't really be successfully threatened. The easy way would be to arrange for him to suffer a relapse and die, but that might compromise the work on the clones. Better to make him an offer he couldn't turn down. He worked on that now. Branston didn't need to know what his real plans were.

"James, you haven't thought this through. But you musta reckoned what my angle is."

Branston, having regained his senses, sat up. "Well, what *are* you after?"

"Just think. Apart from the benefit to those in the same situation as you, there are patients with terminal illnesses and the like, and people in need of new limbs or whatever. There's the future to think about."

Green, as a diversion, now brought family into the argument. "Your folks lying up on that hill must be mighty proud of you, boy. You could be the saviour of humanity."

"What d'you mean?"

"What you don't know is our boys are trying to find ways of exploring deep space. Some time in the future—I'm not saying soon, but everybody knows that we're going to have to leave this planet. We've gotta do some serious research between now and then. And somebody is gonna have to pilot the spacecraft to do it. We gotta beat the Chinese." Then, as a second thought, "And the Ruskies. Now you don't want to shame your folks by being unpatriotic, d'you?"

Branston sighed. Being a Jew in America was still only one step above being black. "OK. Now let me sleep," he said.

Green thumped him on the back. "That's m'boy. Knew you'd see sense. Now I'm due back in Langley. Call you tomorrow."

Branston turned his back, and lay down on the sofa. "OK, so long," he said.

Green shook Jankl's hand as the helicopter raised itself off the ground and banked away. "Congratulations, Doc. We'll soon have you in there. Then you can mass-produce them sons of bitches."

Jankl's facial muscles twitched and formed a weak smile, but his eyes remained cold.

Carrie watched the helicopter fly away, drew the bedroom curtains, and locked the door. She looked at the shoebox sitting on her vanity table. A picture of a pink and blue broken-heeled shoe, lying on its side beside a stricken aircraft, flickered in her brain. She ignored it, rolled off the rubber bands holding the lid down, and looked inside. "Wow!" Her eyes opened wide. Visions of lying on sun-kissed beaches in California, and driving an open-topped Cabriolet with Dior sunglasses perched on the bridge of her nose, flashed into her mind. She stretched out a hand and touched the top of a deep pile of dollar bills.

She briefly noticed an envelope underneath the money, and the little ring Margaret had got in Margate. "Oh. That's nice, I'll wear that," she said. She put the envelope to one side and picked up the ring, which slid easily onto her finger.

She counted the bills—all hundreds—into piles with one thousand dollars in each. There were twenty piles. "Wow! I'm rich. Thanks, Margaret. White trash you might've been. But you had class, babe," she said.

She put the cash back into the box, then picked up the envelope. It had Margaret's name and Branston's address on it. The date on the envelope, posted in London, was the week before Margaret had died on Flight 401. The envelope fluttered to the floor, followed by the letter, after the words Carrie read had sunk in.

> Dear Miss Clayton,
> Please find enclosed our cheque for £1,000,000 in full and final settlement of the purchase of Margate Casino and properties listed in the contract. This is net of tax, as assessed.
>
> I would like to take this opportunity to wish you a happy and prosperous new life in America.
>
> Yours sincerely,

The letter was signed by a solicitor representing a dot com company buying up premises in the UK, in anticipation of a surge of gambling, following their investment in online betting.

Carrie picked up the letter and turned it over. The cheque was stapled to the back. "She didn't have time to open an account. I've got her passport number, and her signature. Wow! Las Vegas, here I come."

Haslemere—Same Day

Esther's attention returned to Margaret's bag after Ricky had left. She gently folded back the frayed strap's end. Pictures of the bag being ripped from Margaret's grasp in the debacle of Flight 401 filled her brain. She closed the bag, as if doing so would stop the projection. She looked at it as it lay flat and motionless in her lap. It wouldn't be slung onto a settee, or a bed, or be used to whack some cheeky man playfully. Or hide a secret in, or carry dreams in. It was lifeless now. Like her sister. The sister she had not really known, but wished she had.

Esther picked up the bag and opened it, drawing in a deep sniff as she did so, hoping to get a whiff of Margaret. *Funny what people do when someone's dead,* she thought. *I wonder if people keep their partner's clothes and things, and smell them occasionally, just when they miss them most. I wonder if it does any good, when all you've got left are memories.*

Esther reached over and turned Joan round, so she could see what she was doing. She took out Margaret's things, one by one. A hairbrush and a couple of tissues lay on the top. She looked to see if there were any marks to suggest they'd been in contact with Margaret's face, or eyes. They unfurled like pink, crumpled roses in her hand. She put them, and the brush, to one side.

"Oh, look, Mom. Here's a picture of the twins." There was no reaction from Joan. Esther delved about a bit, then decided to make it easy and gently tipped the contents into her lap. Margaret's red wallet caught her eye. She smiled and brushed her finger over the words written in biro on the cover. "Margaret Clayton. Class 6C 1986."

Esther looked up and through the window. *She would've been eleve, then*, she thought. Two jackdaws circled in the sky in one of the top paddocks. *Waiting to pick over the remains of some dead animal, I suppose*, she thought.

When memories of Andrew came too, Esther banished the

thoughts. "Not going down that road," she said to herself.

One of the jackdaws peeled away and glided over to the topmost branch of a beech tree. It landed, flapping its huge wings for a moment as it balanced itself. Then it nodded its black, grey-flecked head up and down, and pecked the branch beneath its talons. Its squawk echoed throughout the countryside, like the sound of a lone church-bell on a Sunday morning.

As Esther looked down at the items in her lap, the bird fixed its eyes on her. Eyes not refracting light but bottomless, black-holed voids from which nothing could escape once taken in. The mental force behind this apparition studied her. It knew of the power inside her. The power it would have to defeat in the coming battle for control of people's thoughts, and souls.

A bit of paper with sums of money on it, giving no indication of what they referred to, was the first thing Esther took out of the wallet. Then a Washington Library ticket (with Colin Cattell's name written on the back) and the Hotel Crystal City receipt, which Margaret had signed for clothing.

On the reverse was Branston's name, and the Detroit district of Royal Oak.

Esther looked at Joan. "You alright, Mom?"

Another receipt dropped out of the wallet. Esther didn't see Joan's eyes flicker, nor the beads of perspiration beginning to form on her forehead when she bent down to pick it up. The receipt referred to several items of jewellery bought from a shop in the Renaissance Center, Detroit, in March 1999. It listed:

One Lady's Solitaire Diamond Engagement Ring	$35,000
One Lady's 24c Gold Wedding Ring	$18,000
One Gentleman's 24c Gold Wedding Ring	<u>$23,000</u>
Sub Total	$76,000
Sales Tax @ 5.067%	<u>$ 3,850.92</u>
Total	$79,850.92

"What on earth?" said Esther.

"Hello, there. What d'you make of me now, then?"

Esther hadn't heard the car come back, or Terry and Ricky come in. She looked at her watch. "Oh, my goodness. Twelve o'clock. You haven't..." She turned to see Terry, supported by crutches but upright, wobbling about in the doorway. A bird-like false leg with a brown plastic foot at the end stuck out, like a railway signal at five o'clock underneath his trousers. A big grin lit up his face. A cigarette dangled from the side of his mouth.

Esther smiled. "I think you look great. All you need now is a dog, and an empty tin. You'll earn a fortune sitting outside Guildford Station."

Paul, arriving home from school on a half-day, heard this conversation as he entered the room. A worried look appeared on his face as Esther finished speaking and turned to greet him.

"Grandad can't sit on the pavement. The 'Swallowers of Space' will tread on him," he said.

"What do you mean, darling?" said Esther.

"People. They just walk straight at you, and if you don't move, you know they'll just walk over you. Mr Gallagher calls them the Swallowers of Space." An uneasy silence followed. Ricky sighed—acknowledging the significance of his younger son's observation—that passers-by are, in the main, indifferent to one another these days.

Terry, in an effort to brighten the mood again, said, "Haaa. Right. You sit there. I can make a cuppa again, now."

Esther, emotion bursting from her like a genie uncorked from a bottle, went to him with arms open wide. "Oh, Dad. No. You sit by Mom. I'll make you both one." She caught sight of Ricky, gesticulating behind Terry, telling her to let him make the tea. "Second thoughts, Dad. You haven't made one for ages. You know where the kettle is."

Esther took Ricky's hand and led him in. "You know. I think we ought to organise something special. We're going to celebrate the Millennium as a family. What d'you say?"

"OK. What have you got in mind?"

"Oh, I dunno. We'll think of something."

Outside, the jackdaw spread its wings, lifted from the tree, and wheeled away on an updraft. No-one heard Joan hiss.

Chapter 48

Production Is Stepped Up

"Come on, honey, we gotta get back. I'm cold, and it's almost midnight." The stifling midsummer heat that lingers, even through the night in Royal Oak suddenly chilled. A light breeze, teasing leaves on the tree next to Elisha's tomb, covered sounds of clothing being adjusted, before it too relaxed.

The girl sat up and pulled pink- and blue-spotted knickers over her white Bobby Sox. She got up, trailing a coat of many colours, laid down on the concrete for her protection, behind her. Fluffing up her hair, she tucked one corner of the coat under an arm while snapping the clips on her front-loading brassiere with the other hand. She fastened the buttons on her top, then kissed him quickly on the lips before running off down the field. "Race you," she shouted.

The leaves drooped, as if in resignation, when the breeze stilled. Air in the suburb of Royal Oak cooled and gave way in the face of an energy which gradually took shape, becoming a shroud-covered figure resembling a man. Passing the tomb, it grew large in the moonlight and, like a spirit come alive, made its way to the tree.

The gaunt-featured, malnourished body hosting these memories stretched out a stick-like finger from inside a deep sleeve, and touched the tree for a moment. Then it pushed back a cowl covering its head. A pallid, pock-marked face lowered, and turned to put an ear against the trunk. A person looking into its eyes would have seen nothing before being drawn in, to be enslaved forever.

The figure moved on to visit other lightning-scarred trees.

In the house, Carrie lay in her bed, struggling to sleep. She was thinking about the wonderful time she'd have after she'd banked Margaret's cheque.

Branston sat in his office, staring at Esther's photograph. He looked at his watch. "Can't call her now. Too early. I'll do it later."

Not sleepy, he decided to check how progress downstairs was going. It had been Green's idea to step up production to a twenty-four-hour operation. Branston didn't care any more. But he'd keep an eye on them.

He stepped out of the lift and walked along the corridor, pausing to look into each room that he passed. All available space had been turned over to housing the tubes. He stopped outside what had been his consulting room. *Requisitioned by a bloody fascist*, he thought.

He walked on until he arrived at one of the largest rooms. Inside, mature clones who'd been sidetracked for undergoing more advanced activities ("educating", as Green put it) were housed in the double-sectioned tubes. He looked into a glass-fronted box placed halfway up the door, and said, "Branston". Recognising his voice and iris, the door swung open and he entered. Two men holding sub-machine guns briefly acknowledged him.

Branston's pupils shrank as bright light poured into them, instead of the pink-tinged light he was accustomed to seeing. He switched a speaker on to allow him to hear what the hundreds of clones were listening to, and cringed as pre-recorded anti-communist propaganda echoed round the room.

The sound of Muster, being played by a bugler, interrupted the rhetoric for a moment. Then came the words, "Now hear this."

The clones came to attention as one, in response to a rendition of *The Star-Spangled Banner*, and remained so when the music faded. Presently, a voice spoke in solemn tones. "This is the President, speaking to you from the White House. Today, this country faces its greatest threat since the Japanese invaded Pearl Harbour. Once again we have been called to defend our way of life. This time in response to terrorists whose murderous deeds, which they claim to be a part of Jihad—a holy war—have cost the lives of many Americans."

A pause followed before the President continued. "During the coming months and years, I will be calling upon you,

America's finest soldiers, to do your duty in the defence of our country. Are you ready to do your duty?"

The clones replied in unison, "Sir, yes sir."

"God speed. Long live America."

Branston turned on his heel. "Bloody fascists," he shouted.

Upstairs, faint sounds, coming from the vents outside, wafted in through the window in Carrie's bedroom. "The sooner I get out of here, the better," she said.

Henry, wide-eyed and limbs trembling, crossed his heart and pulled the duvet over his head. "I's gonna quit, boss," he mumbled. "Quit. I will."

Haslemere — Same Day

Paul loved weekends. He and his friends could run free. They'd lie on straw in the barn, and wait to see if a mouse would come and sniff out their cheese-baited traps. When they got fed up with that they'd explore the far corners of the estate, where adults never went. He even let his sister go with him. Not for noble reasons, though. Sheila was much braver than he, and only too willing to go first into dark, gloomy places. He wasn't scared, but — well, "Ladies before Gentlemen," he'd say. Another reason was she'd always play goalkeeper so that he could score goals. Sheila was always the one who was most dirty when they got home.

But today was special. It was his ninth birthday and a party was being held in his honour. Later on all of his friends (and some of Sheila's, whom Esther would sneak in) were invited. First, though, he had to help his mother push Grandma Joan in the wheelchair.

It was a glorious morning. As he pushed the wheelchair he noticed different species of birds darting in and out of the trees. Paul very soon got tired, though, so he parked Grandma by a bench on the pathway by the top paddock and sat, shying pebbles at the gateposts. Esther breathed in the balmy air, and relaxed.

When he ran out of pebbles, Paul wandered over to the paddock fence. He put one foot on a rail and laid his head in his hands. As he tilted his head a blue tit fluttered by and disappeared into a tree somewhere to his left. He squinted in the sunlight and watched the space, waiting for it to reappear. When the blue tit came out another one flew in straight away, so he decided to see how long he could not blink while counting how many times they went in and out. His eyes grew wider and wider and his mouth more open as he tried to prevent his eyes closing. But only seconds went by before nature overcame his willpower.

Kicking the rail, Paul turned to Esther. "Mo-om," he whined.

"Ye-es," she replied.

"How many times do those birds go in and out in an hour?"

A darkening of the sky beyond the trees and the Devil's Punchbowl caught Esther's eye. "Go in and out of what, darling?" she said.

"Of a nest, silly?"

Esther felt uneasy. She smelled that same dank, primeval atmosphere she'd felt in the Hilton Hotel. She stood up, shielding her eyes from the sun with a hand while she looked. "I don't know. About fifty. It's time to go back now. Let's go."

Paul knocked the brake off and swung Joan round. Esther was too busy with her thoughts to notice Joan sweating profusely.

"Mom."

"Yes."

Paul, eager to show he'd worked it out, said, "That means they only get ten minutes off every hour, then."

Esther was too engrossed to reply. *Not again, surely*, she thought. Audeus knew the time had come. Esther, subconsciously, decided to call Branston.

Terry staggered drunkenly on his crutches to meet them as they approached the house. "I'll come with you next time, sweetheart," he said, looking at Joan. He wobbled the last twenty yards. "See, I'm getting good, now." His peg-leg knocked over a plant pot as he hauled it round to show them. He looked at Esther, who'd put her hands over her face to stifle a laugh and hunched up her shoulders. She raised her eyebrows and put her arms out wide. "Well, we could do with a scare-crow in the bottom paddock."

Terry looked down at the shattered pot, then back at her. He gave her a hurt look, then threw his head back, almost falling over in the process, and laughed. "Haa. What about me shift at Guildford Station?"

Paul ran to him. "Grandad. You've got a dandelion on your foot."

Terry looked at his plastic foot and laughed again. "Come on. I'll put the kettle on."

After Paul's friends had arrived and the man from the joke shop in Guildford started his magic show, Terry disappeared. Just as the magician finished there was a knock at the door. "Listen, children. Who d'you think that could be?" said Ricky.

All eyes studied the door, which creaked open.

The stuffed owl sitting on a shoulder appeared first, closely followed by an ear, then an eyepatch. "Be any o' you shipmates know where me treasure is?" said Terry, gradually becoming visible.

Some of the children didn't know what to make of it at first, but they all laughed together when Terry purposely fell the rest of the way in. Esther ran to him and helped him up. "Don't you dare do that monologue. You'll get me hung."

"Don't worry," he said. Then, turning to the children, repeated, louder this time, "Be any o' you shipmates know where me treasure is?"

"No" they cried in unison.

Terry turned on his one leg, making sure the door was there to support him, and shouted, "Come on, then. There's a present for everybody. But they're all hidden, so you've got to find 'em."

By the end of the afternoon the whole family was shattered, but happy. After the last cheerio had been said, they all congregated in the kitchen. "I'll take the kids up for their baths. You lot can take the weight off and have a cuppa," said Elizabeth.

Esther kissed her on the cheek. "Thanks. You're an angel."

"I'll do it," said Ricky. "Haven't done much this after-noon."

"Them tricks with the poker chips were good," said Terry,

eyepatch round his head, owl leaning precariously off his shoulder.

"Don't, Esther," whispered Joan.

Ricky, stunned by the silence which followed, stopped filling the kettle.

"Mom?" said Esther. She ran, tears streaming down her face, to Joan. "Mom. What did you say?"

Joan sat looking straight ahead. Esther put both hands on her shoulders. "Mom. I didn't hear you. Say it again."

They all held their breath as one of Joan's fingers twitched. She began to sweat, and almost imperceptibly, her head moved. At last Joan had made the connection with her firstborn and realised how much she loved her. Somehow she knew Esther was in danger. *It's too late now*, she thought. A withering feeling of being unable to do anything swept over Joan. Then came a feeling of guilt for all the wasted years.

This was quickly replaced by a surge of emotion, as her eyes met with Esther's. The warmth coming from Esther's hands, still resting on her shoulders, slowly filled each vein in her body; the body she'd thought useless, until now. She looked deep into Esther's eyes and straight away felt the strength of character within her daughter: the pureness of her heart and the power inside her.

Joan's inner self rose, like ichor flowing through the veins of the gods, and joined with Esther's. Joan was immediately aware of the indomitable spirit her daughter possessed.

The elation this revelation brought Joan was short-lived. A strong feeling that Esther had been chosen for something—*because* she was so different—overcame the warning Joan was trying to communicate. Still she drew in air through clenched teeth. Not a sound could be heard as the family watched, and waited.

When Joan had filled her lungs, her lips parted slightly, and she whispered, "I love you. Please be careful."

Terry threw down his crutch. "Haa. There you are. Giving orders again. I told you she'd come back."

Esther hugged Joan, who, exhausted by her effort, drooped forward.

"Great day for the good guys," said Terry, rubbing the top

of one of Joan's hands. "You and me got a lot o' catching up to do, old girl."

All slept well that night. All except Esther, who lay awake, looking at the ceiling. *What a lovely day*, she thought. *P'raps things are beginning to go our way for a change. What did Mom mean when she said, "Be careful"?*

Audeus didn't want her brooding on that. He needed her to be positive.

Ricky turned over and put an arm round her. She picked up his hand and placed it on her breast. This wasn't sexual. It wasn't even for comfort. Suddenly, in their half-sleep, the commitment they had experienced when they married was reinforced. That bonding the pressure of a child suckling brings, which even the threat of death itself cannot break, soothed her fears away.

As Ricky cuddled her, the room, the whole house and all in it seemed to Esther to join in this communion and become an entity. She fell asleep. The feeling widened as Audeus took her soaring away to embrace the Earth.

In her dream Esther wasn't aware of anything below as Audeus' awesome mental power transported them on their journey: just the magnificence of the universe.

In Royal Oak, the reincarnation of evil turned away from the trunk of a tree and faced the horizon to the east. A blaze of colour, erupting on the skyline, seemed to reach out. The cowl tilted back as Audeus' and Esther's combined energy swept nearer in an immense sensation of light. The shadowy figure became as one with the tree.

The light paused, then swept away to the west and disappeared with the evening sunset. Audeus had seen what he needed to.

Chapter 49

Gathering Storm

After seeing Mary and the children off to school Esther sat in the lounge, thinking about Margaret and the events of the previous day.

Presently Elizabeth came in. "Joan's still out. Must've taken a lot out of her," she said.

"Yes. I'll go up in a minute. I phoned the doctor. She'll be OK. I was thinking, is it just me, or was yesterday a really nice day?"

Elizabeth shoved a stool against the bookcase and stood on it. Stretching up, she put the owl on top. She surprised Esther with her answer. "It *was* a lovely day. I'm so glad I came to live here, even though Thomas wouldn't. The rolling hills remind me so much of Margate. It's all built-up now, but Alan and I used to walk the country lanes for hours. It was beautiful in summer. We were young, and really in love."

"How did you meet him?"

"The family came for a holiday. I met Alan, and never went home."

"God, how romantic."

"It was like a roller-coaster. But after we got married that was it. He'd no ambition. Never wanted to go into business, or climb Mount Everest, or anything. My only disappointment was not being able to have kids. But I got used to that. And the extra money to spend on booze, and stuff. By the way, I was really embarrassed that night in the pub—you know, when I said that—about a threesome."

Esther laughed. "Must admit, it shocked me. But I understand what grief feels like now. Don't worry. You were saying?"

"Well, nothing ever happened, really. You know what it's

like. After the honeymoon's over, and you've known each other for a while, you sort of—well, you get into a routine, and forget what it was that brought you together. The years roll by and you do get close. But I tell you, Alan and I were never as close as we were during the last year of his life."

"I never thought you were so deep," said Esther.

"I'm not, really. He was, though. Rubbed off I suppose. Can I ask you a question?"

"Go on."

"What d'you think when someone tells you how beautiful you are?"

"What d'you mean?"

"Well, if somebody were to tell you, let's say, 'you've got a great bum', would you agree?"

Esther thought for a second. "Well—I've always been pretty happy with myself, but my bum sticks out too much. My nose is too pointed. And my teeth are a bit too straight. I hate the beauty spot above my mouth. God. There are loads of things I don't like about myself, aren't there?"

"What I'm trying to say is, none of us are what other people think we are. I want to show you something. Wait there." Elizabeth left the room. Esther, looking through the window, saw the jackdaw fly in across the top paddock and perch in a tree.

Elizabeth came back and handed Esther a piece of paper. "You're the first person I've shown this to. I'd like you to read it. It's a bit of a dirge, I know. But I got so low at one point that writing my feelings down was the only way I could think of to get rid of some of the stress."

Esther opened the piece of paper and found a poem entitled 'Legacy of A Small Lump':

Summer days, alone in the sun,
Walking down lanes, our footsteps as one.
Stretched out in cornfields as clouds passed us by
We held hands so tightly as we gazed at the sky.
Our love—fresh and passionate—was breathtakingly pure,
Our lives were united, of that we were sure.
The years we'd together were precious, but few,

Still, they were the best years, and I spent them with you.
I'm alone now—the dust gathers round,
No reason to hurry, and silence abounds.
I wonder why it happened, not believing you're gone,
Replaced by only pictures and the memories they bring on.
I look out the window, watch a bus passing by,
It's as empty as my heart, no tears left to cry.
Night won't be different, 'cos each night's the same,
A starlit morgue. I whisper your name.
If I could be bothered I'd fire up the stove,
Or light me a stogie and just hit the road.
But that's only geography now you live in my head,
So I sigh me a long sigh and drift off to bed.
I pull on the covers and lay my head down,
My "Goodnight, God bless" an echoing sound.
I'm aware of the space next to me, all empty and cold,
And realise suddenly what it is to feel old.
Tired and worn, with no positive thoughts there to lift me,
I lie still and wonder if I'll ever be free.
Maybe tomorrow will be different, haven't got a clue why,
Can't be bothered to think of it, can't be bothered to try.
So I close my eyes slowly and start to recall
The love that once lifted me and made me feel tall;
When my love lay down beside me, and it was alright,
Then I give myself gladly to what's left of the night.

Esther lowered the paper to her lap. The two women sat without a word being spoken, with Esther looking out through the window. The jackdaw had gone. Just for a moment, she thought she saw a figure dressed in a monk's habit, standing amongst the trees. Then it disappeared in a shuffling of leaves and branches.

"I don't know what to say," she said. "That poem's blown my mind. Where did it come from?"

"Dunno. Grief, I suppose. It was hard. The hardest thing I've ever had to do."

"Write that poem?"

"No. Watch him die. You can suffer your own physical pain. Go to the dentist, or have stitches put in or whatever; but when someone you love is suffering, and you can't do anything about it, and you suddenly realise you might not have time to say all the things you want to say; that situation brings the most amazing emotions. I just don't show them as much as some people."

Esther was astonished. *I've misjudged you*, she thought. *I thought you were such a shallow person, but now you've come up with this.*

Elizabeth carried on. "You asked me earlier if I thought yesterday was a nice day. Well, there was such an atmosphere in the place. It was electric. I thought I was going to faint. When the children started laughing after Terry came in, I started to laugh. D'you remember when you last laughed?"

The nature of Esther's challenge would take immense concentration, and faith. Her thoughts were not entirely her own from then on, as Audeus prepared her—repeating Elizabeth's words in her mind. *"Electric atmosphere," she said. That's empathy. A shared feeling. The unspoken bond she formed with Alan. I've got that with Ricky. It's a powerful emotion. It's energy.*

Esther smiled. "When I last laughed? Erm—not really."

"Nor me. Well, I tell you—for me it was like a release of all those built-up emotions. But I actually did think I was going to faint."

"What was your biggest disappointment? When you were young. The thing that made you think your heart would break?"

Elizabeth's eyes lit up. "Dad tried to win me a doll once. When we were on holiday. You know—you put a penny in, and get one go at grabbing the doll before the claw shuts and the wire takes it back up."

"And every time he caught hold of one and dropped it, your heart sank?"

"Yes."

"Did he get one?"

"He must've put a pound in, but he got one. Then I screamed my head off."

"Did you ever think he wouldn't get one?"

"That's the amazing thing. I can remember being frantic,

but somehow I always knew he'd get one in the end."

"So you had faith?"

"I had faith in my Dad. As far as religious faith is concerned, I don't know. Alan was a deep thinker. That reminds me. The nearest I ever came to thinking there might be a hereafter was just before he died."

"What happened?"

"Well, he'd been in a terrible state. He'd not long come back from surgery, and the stent they put in his windpipe was bothering him. He was struggling to breathe. It was desperate, having to watch him sit there, banging the bed in frustration. Then all of a sudden he went quiet. He looked into my eyes for an age. I've never seen his eyes so blue, or sharp. He looked over my shoulder, as if he'd seen something. Then he smiled, closed his eyes, and died."

Esther had the feeling she was only saying what both women already knew when she then said, "He'd seen memories. You know, I think the greater the disappointment, or sacrifice, or the deeper hurt goes, so long as we've faith, the better prepared we are for what's to come."

Esther gave Elizabeth the poem, and hugged her. "Thanks for letting me read that. I'll go and look at Mom. Then I've got a letter to write."

"That's OK. I'm glad I've shown it to you. I'll bring you up a cuppa."

Later that day Esther looked at the blank page lying on the desk in front of her. After half an hour she hadn't written a word. She looked out the window, hoping for inspiration. Then the soft purr of the phone by her side interrupted her train of thought. "Miss Clayton?" a man's voice said.

"Yes."

"My name's Branston. James Branston, calling from America."

"Oh. I was about to write to you."

"I missed you at the memorial service. I've a couple of photographs of you and your brother and sister, I believe."

For a second Esther felt an impulse to put the receiver down. Audeus coaxed her.

"Can you put them in the post?" she said.

"I'd like to meet you, if I may. I didn't know about you, but I knew Margaret."

"Did you. How?"

"She was my wife."

Esther closed her eyes as her heart threatened to leap through her mouth. She opened them to see Ricky coming into the room. She stretched out a hand to greet him. "Oh," she said.

"I'd like to meet you, if that's alright."

Esther, her mind in a whirl, struggled to take it in, until Audeus boosted the endorphin level in her brain a little. She answered automatically thereafter each time Branston put a question to her.

"If I make the arrangements, would you fly to Detroit? I'll have my car waiting for you at the airport. It's only a short drive from there."

"OK."

"When would be convenient? I'd like it to be as soon as possible. Would this weekend be alright?"

"Yes."

"D'you have a fax? If you have, I'll send the details later on today."

"Yes."

"Good. I look forward to meeting you. Oh, and your husband, of course. I'll see you at the weekend, then."

"Yes. It's the same as the phone number."

The endorphin level eased while Esther replaced the receiver.

"You OK?" said Ricky. "You're shivering. Who was that?"

"I have to go to America."

"I thought you were never going there again."

Esther looked out the window again. "I have to go. Margaret's there. He has a photograph."

"You're not making sense."

"Margaret married an American."

"Good grief. Who?"

"I don't know, but he wants to meet us."

"When?"

"This weekend."

"Esther. Look at me. What's going on? What about the baby?"

She pulled him down and kissed him on the cheek. "Where's your sense of adventure? The morning sickness has gone, now. We could do with a break, and it's only for a weekend. Besides, I have to go."

"OK. But I hope you know what you're doing."

Esther slept well that night. But Ricky didn't. He was tired; mentally exhausted from the emotional highs and lows of the past eight years. Unable to settle, he slipped out of bed and went to the children's room in the early hours.

Paul lay flat on his back on his bed, head to one side. One ear on the headpiece of a Batman outfit, lying at an oblique angle to his nose, fluttered each time he breathed. Ricky decided to leave him.

Sheila sat hunched up, supported by the angles of the walls her bed was adjacent to. Eyes tight shut, she sucked her left thumb while holding her right ear with her other hand. Ricky watched them for a moment; then, distracted by the hoot of an owl, perched in one of the trees in the lower paddock, he turned to the window.

He opened the curtains a little and sat sideways in the deep bay window. A full moon lit up the scene like a floodlight. The cold, pristine beauty of it took his breath away. Yet he was happy to be where he was. Halfway between the world he could see—only just outside, but in a way unreachable—and his world, which lived and breathed gently behind him and in the bedroom he shared with the woman he loved. Any doubts he had about going to America with Esther disappeared as he closed the curtains and went to settle his children down for the night.

Sheila twitched as he eased one hand behind the back of her head and the other under her bottom. "Daad," she groaned.

"It's OK, darling. Daddy's here. I love you."

He slid Sheila under the duvet and tucked her in, then untangled Paul from the Batman outfit. Paul yawned and turned over. As if in a trance he opened his eyes, then, sensing someone was there, half-turned towards Ricky. "Can I? Where are you...?"

Paul went back to sleep as Ricky pulled the duvet up to his chin, and everything was fine.

On his way back to his own bedroom, Ricky thought about Margaret and the unknown American.

And when the thousand years are expired,
Satan shall be loosed out of his prison;
to gather them to battle: the number of
whom is as the sand of the sea
Rev: 20:7—8.

Chapter 50

The Final Battle

In his office Branston put down the phone and pressed the button on the wall. Henry, dishevelled, having come straight from his room, appeared five minutes later. "Yas'm," he said.

Branston's head jerked up. "Why are you talking like that?"

Henry composed himself (outwardly). "I'm sorry, sir. A momentary lapse. Can I help you?"

"Have you seen Carrie?"

"Miss Carrie left yesterday afternoon, sir, after a note arrived saying that her mother was ill."

"Did she say when she'd be back?"

"Only that she'd be away a few days, sir."

"Well, I'm expecting guests at the weekend. If she's back by then, tell her we'll be dining at eight on Saturday evening. It's formal."

"Yes, sir. Shall I tell cook how many?"

"There'll be four for dinner, but you'll need to prepare a guest room."

"Very well, sir."

Branston wondered about Carrie. He hadn't actually told her that he'd married Margaret. Carrie was, after all, a servant at the time, even if they'd had occasional liaisons before. But she must've noticed their rings. "Course she knows," he said, getting up. "And I didn't seduce her. *She* came to *me*."

A thought crossed his mind as he left the office. *Trouble is, we've been at it like rabbits since July 5th. She might expect more now. If she comes back before Saturday I'll just say I've invited them out of respect.* He stretched. "Think I'll go back to bed for an hour."

A minute bleed began to exert pressure on the surrounding tissue in Branston's brain. *Wish I'd got Henry to fetch me an aspirin while he was here,* he thought.

Esther slept throughout the entire flight from Heathrow to New York. The jet, which Branston had provided, transferred Ricky and herself to Wayne County airport, where his limousine and driver waited to transport them to Royal Oak.

Esther was sure she could feel Margaret as she sat in the limo's soft, leather seat. She recalled the moment she opened Margaret's bag and smelled inside. *Is this going to happen every time I sit in a seat she might've sat in, or use a towel?* she wondered. She sighed, and closed her eyes.

Ricky squeezed her hand. "You OK?" he said.

"Fine. You?"

Ricky glanced to his right as the limo swept round a bend on its way out of the airport. The clock on the terminal building showed 17.00. "I'll be glad when we get this over and done with."

Esther squeezed back. "Me too." Then she dozed, as Margaret had when accompanied by Colin Cattell.

Tyres crunching in the gravel in front of the house brought Carrie to her bedroom window. As she leaned forward to get a better view of the limousine, Henry appeared from under the gable and opened the car door. Carrie raised her eyebrows when Esther took Henry's hand and got out. "Big sister, huh. It's a good job he didn't meet her first."

She turned away and drew out the shoebox from under her bed. Opening it, she laid a fresh airline ticket on top of the one she'd used when depositing Margaret's cheque the week before.

Don't see why I've got to stay in my room till dinner, she thought. *Anyway, I don't care. I'll be gone for good tomorrow, now the cheque's cleared. They'll do anything for a few bucks in L.A.*

Don't like him, thought Ricky as Branston introduced himself. *Talking like an old man.* Branston shook Esther's hand warmly, but with an appropriate amount of decorum considering the circumstances. Like Margaret before her, Esther was impressed.

"My dear. This is such a pleasure," he said.

Ricky didn't much like the hunched posture of the man genuflecting in front of Esther either, but for her sake remained cordial when Branston turned his attentions to him. But he squeezed the outstretched hand with enough force to send the brain on the other end a message. "How d'you do," he said.

"My husband, Ricky," said Esther.

Ricky liked Branston even less after he said, "Ah. The famous Richmond Bates. Poker player extraordinaire. Come in, please, do come in."

Haslemere

"Time for kip, sweetheart. I'll get Elizabeth to help you into bed," said Terry, hopping off his bed. He pushed Joan's wheelchair to one side and got himself out onto the landing, using a line of chairs he'd positioned, pointing to the bedroom door, for support.

"Aye, aye," he shouted from the top of the stairs.

"Coming," said Elizabeth.

Terry hopped to the bathroom to do what he had to. He'd shove the beds together when he got back—just in case. Even though Joan hadn't completed a sentence since Paul's birthday, she looked at him when he spoke to her, and squeezed his hand. And she was definitely trying to communicate.

Terry flexed his biceps in front of the bathroom mirror. "Half a flippin' male Venus de Milo, that's me," he said. "A marvel of ancient Greece. You never know, kid. Never do know."

Elizabeth finished brushing Joan's hair and let the ends spread. "There you are. If I'm not mistaken, your old man will come back smelling like a fleet of battleships, never mind 'Old Spice', in a minute. Better batten down the hatches if you want any peace tonight."

Joan mumbled something unintelligible as Elizabeth helped her into bed.

Elizabeth tucked her in and kissed her forehead. "Yes, dear. Everything's going to be fine. Night night. See you in the morning."

Terry patted Elizabeth on the bottom as he hopped past her on the landing. "You should be so lucky, mister," she said, switching off the landing light.

Royal Oak

Carrie danced down the stairs and walked into the lounge to be introduced to Esther and Ricky. Meanwhile, Henry was switching on the downstairs lights. Branston also noticed the dimming outside, and went to the window. "Must be burning stubble," he said as Carrie waltzed in. "Ah, Carrie. Esther, meet Carrie, the mai... erm..." Recovering quickly Branston turned to Ricky. "The man I'm about to introduce you to, Carrie, won two million dollars in a World Poker Tour competition. Ricky, Esther—meet Carrie."

Carrie offered her right hand (deliberately smothered in scented moisturising cream). "How d'you do?" she said, noticing how well the long white evening dress with a slit in its side suited Esther.

The silence was palpable, and the delay in Esther taking Carrie's hand worrying for Ricky. In an effort to lighten the situation, he pushed his hand in front of Esther, who was staring at the red novelty ring glinting on Carrie's finger. "Pleased to meet you. Just in time for dinner. Don't know about you, but my stomach thinks my throat's been cut. What d'you say, James? Shall we tackle those cuttlefish, or whatever they are?"

"The red abalone. A delicacy. I have them flown up from California. Cook does a very nice *Mariniére* with them. Please come this way. Henry, tell Cook we're ready."

"Yes, sir."

Branston led the way, seating his party in the dining room. Presently, Henry brought in a silver tureen and served a cold watercress soup, laced with fresh cream. He then placed the bowl on a sideboard. Noticing the open curtains, he prepared to pull them to. A dark cloud rising in the east, just about where Belle Isle Park would be, seemed to lift and move towards him. He quickly shut the curtains, then got out as fast as he could.

Haslemere

Joan threw the sheets off the bed, and screamed.

Terry jumped awake. "What's happened?"

Joan was staring at the window. Sounds of swaying trees filtered through, and shadows danced across the glass. Joan slowly got out of bed. Then the house seemed to fill with Esther's presence. Joan suddenly felt that Esther wanted her to be there, keeping the house, this lifeline, open. The house under whose roof the family came together, and faced both good and bad times with the same stoic resilience. "He's coming for her," she said.

"Who's coming for who, sweetheart?" said Terry, struggling with his false leg.

Joan, heading for the door, walked past Elizabeth as she burst into the room.

"Help me get this flipping leg on, will you?" said Terry.

"You'll have to manage yourself. I've got to look after Joan. Phone for the doctor."

Royal Oak

Esther put down her soup spoon. *She's wearing Margaret's ring. Something evil is happening here*, she thought. *Well, they won't win. This is my task. What's that vibration underneath me?*

"Aren't you enjoying the soup, my dear?" said Branston.

Esther wasn't listening. She was getting up. *The tomb. She's in the tomb.*

"Esther. What's the matter? Where are you going?" said Ricky. He put a hand on her arm. A force he instantly knew he couldn't combat rejected it. He could only follow.

While Ricky watched Esther move up the hill, Carrie pulled out the shoebox and ran downstairs. She fell at the

341

bottom and dropped the box, spilling its contents across the reception hall. Looking up, she saw Branston leaning against the lift door, trying frantically to stop blood seeping from the stitch-marks round his skull.

Carrie screamed and ran out, leaving everything behind her.

Esther was unaware of the trees or the wind rushing through their branches. She was the reservoir from which Pythagoras and Audeus would launch their telepathic power at the dark hordes, and her gaze never wavered. With her brain once more in a soporific state, she stopped at the top of the hill and turned to face the east.

In her mind Esther sought Michael and stretched out her arms, as she had the day Audeus and Pythagoras had transmigrated to her. Once again she was swirled away into the blue of the universe.

Ricky fell against a tree as the ground began to move. First one insect burst through and whirred away. Then another, and another, till they poured out to make a hate-filled swarm facing Esther. Ricky reached out to her. His shout of "Esther" became merely a whisper in the wind.

A new resident in Royal Oak ran outside his house. "What's happening?" he shouted to his neighbour.

"Cicadas. They feed on the roots of trees. After seventeen years they all come out together. Billions of them."

Haslemere

Joan, looking out across the Devil's Punchbowl, raised her arm and pointed to the horizon.

"I'm here," she whispered.

Royal Oak

A blue light emanating from Esther surrounded her. Ricky watched as her diminutive figure, covered by insects bouncing off the aura, stood firm. He looked past her and saw a creeping darkness begin to dominate the sky. The sound of a billion wings, all beating in unison, rose in a nerve-shattering crescendo.

Ricky pulled his jacket over his head as the vibration threatened to burst his eardrums. Still he couldn't take his eyes off Esther. Ricky saw Esther's chin lift. When her head stopped rising, her stare fixed on the evil mass confronting her. She raised her arms and pointed to it. Instantly, her fingers, like an acetylene torch being lit, produced searing energy. Ricky, blinded for a second, shielded his eyes.

When Ricky looked back he saw the spectre of Audeus appear from her left hand and disappear into the dark cloud hovering over Esther. It began to swell and contract as Audeus cut a swathe through its ranks. It soared higher into the sky, then crashed to the ground, only to rise again even higher.

Esther's chin lowered a little in the face of myriad arrow-like, stinging darts. So many that their numbers seemed bound to break through and smother her. She was struggling to maintain control.

Detroit

In Belle Island Park, dry leaves rustled as the same young girl who had used the seclusion of Elisha's tomb to make love to her boyfriend, pulled her knickers up and over her white Bobby Sox. She sat up. "What's that?" she said, then jumped up screaming. The ground beneath her was moving.

She stared at the heaving earth, then looked up as a shadow fell across her long coat of many colours. She and the boy stood petrified, as the shadow became the figure of the shroud-covered man. Their eyes were drawn to his face, revealed as the cowl lifted. Even in their terror they looked for his eyes, seeking an explanation for what was happening.

But there were no eyes. The voids in their place drew the couple in...

The figure turned its attention to the coat. From underneath, a red-eyed, yellow-legged bug wriggled free from the earth and took to the air. He slowly raised an arm. The bug responded by settling on his long, gnarled fingers.

Dozens more burst from their warm, underground nests as he spoke quietly to his angels of death. Within minutes a trillion fat, sap-filled insects would emerge from the earth in Washington DC, Pennsylvania and Michigan States. Their long gestation at an end, each was as evil as the memory it hosted.

Royal Oak

Ricky realised that Esther was becoming noticeably weaker.. Even though her gaze was still focused, her head was appreciably lower now, and the energy pouring from her fingers, though still intense, was definitely receding. "Esther," he shouted. Immediately he was surrounded by buzzing insects. Esther blinked for the first time in response to his call, but didn't turn her head. Instead, a burst of energy peeled off from the mainstream and blasted through the melée with enough force to slam him against the tree. The bugs broke off their attack as a thin, protective blue film shimmered around Ricky's stunned body.

Gradually Ricky regained his senses, except that his hearing seemed to be dulled. Only muffled sound filtered through for a moment. Then he realised that the noise *had* abated. The reason for this became apparent when he opened his eyes.

The swarm was flying off down the hill to the edge of the woods, where the cowled figure of Walt Jackson stood, his arms raised in greeting.

* * *

The relative quiet that pervades a battlefield just before the final conflict descended on the scene, as if the protagonists had been given the order to break off hostilities.

The spectre of Audeus reappeared from the swarm, and dissolved back into Esther, who lowered her arms and face.

The army of bugs rose high into the sky before streaming down in a torrent of red, yellow and black colour, to be sucked into the voids where Walt Jackson's eyes had been. He moved slowly up the field, shedding every vestige of human life as he went.

Ricky was mesmerised. He couldn't take his eyes off this *thing*, which was changing into a nightmarish apparition in front of him. It became difficult for him to breathe as the air thickened. A dreadful, suffocating feeling of helplessness threatened to draw him into the void as a chilling wail, like a wolf howling to its pack, emanated from the thing and echoed throughout.

"Oh, God," said Ricky.

Movement from Esther's direction helped break the spell. She was lifting her face again. No fear showed in her eyes, which fixed on the swollen apparition.

Dark, wispy creatures appeared behind Esther, attempting to burrow through her protective shield. Still she held firm.

Esther raised her arms for the last time and pointed at the head of the object, which had again parted to reveal the voids. This time, as the blue fire spread outwards, the flowing, fair-haired spectre of Pythagoras and Audeus combined called upon the power of the universe as it soared into the heavens.

Instantly, in the place where the Great Oak had once stood, and in all parts of the world where people hosted memories of the dead, telepathic energy left, assembled, and rose into the sky.

St Mary's Vicarage

Michael *had* to get to the church. Slowly he hauled himself out of bed and made for the door. *It's happening,* he thought. *She's calling. I must get to the church.*

Wearing only pyjamas, Michael staggered the short distance to the church. He looked at the open bell-tower as the wind, rushing through, caused the rope to hit the bell, producing a muted clang.

Once inside he felt comfortable. He switched the lights on and turned to look at the altar. What he saw made his heart miss a beat. The cross of Christ crucified, hanging from the roof in the centre of the church, was surrounded by a faint blue glow.

Michael rushed forward and fell to his knees. Unable to

speak for a moment, he bowed his head and gathered his thoughts. *I can feel her calling. The time has come. She needs my support.* He put his hands together, looked at the cross, and prayed: "I believe in one God, the Father Almighty, Maker of Heaven and Earth and of all things visible and invisible."

Michael licked his lips and swallowed, desperately trying to get moisture to dry vocal cords. Then he spoke quickly: "And in one Lord Jesus Christ, the only begotten Son of God, who for us men and for our salvation came from Heaven, and was incarnate by the Holy Ghost of the Virgin Mary. If it be thy will, help this woman in her hour of need. Give us the strength to overcome this evil pervading the world, and in thy name restore—through faith—thy holy work."

Sweat poured from Michael. He could do no more. Propping himself against the altar, he closed his eyes and let his mind go to Esther.

Royal Oak

Telepathic energy illuminated the horizon. It was as if lightning, carrying the limitless power of the forces for good, reversed its strike and answered Pythagoras' call.

Ricky felt, rather than saw, the person approaching from behind, and didn't recognise the figure as that of the same man who had returned the nightstick to him at the Stratosphere Hotel, and given Terry the magazine and copy of *Snow White* either.

Ricky tried to grab hold of the dusty, ankle-length coat to warn him, as it brushed his outstretched foot. Ricky's words, "Mister, you can't go up there," tapered off to a whisper as the man's purposeful stride took him past Ricky and up to where Esther stood. The man, his long search over, positioned himself behind her.

This was the defining moment of the battle. As host to the positive energies that were fighting this battle, Esther was not in charge. But they couldn't manage without her. At the point of the transmigration of Pythagoras and Audeus from Michael to her, she hadn't fought it, but had chosen to give herself to it.

In her soporific state, she now heard Audeus' thoughts, and

the echo of Michael's prayer of support—and gave herself once again.

The aura behind Esther parted slightly. Immediately, the bugs tried to attack, but only the spectre of the man was let in, fusing into her.

In response, the thing reared and blasted out manifestations of evil. Screaming dervishes, cursing the Harmony of the Spheres, hurled themselves at the barrier protecting Esther. Apparitions showing the naked vices of mankind, and offering temptations of every kind, swooned and fawned in front of them. And still the bugs came in their millions.

Exhausted by the prolonged strain of emotional pressure, and no longer able to define the earth from the sky behind the black cloud, Ricky lay back against the tree and let his eyes droop.

Esther, her presence enhanced to invincibility now, never wavered, however; and when Ricky reopened his eyes he realised that the attack on her was less frenzied. The sun was beginning to rise, unseen behind the darkness.

Suddenly, like a dimmer-switch acting in reverse, light, with Pythagoras and Audeus at its head, broke through from the horizon again, strengthening the barrier around Esther. The blue fire pouring from her fingers intensified, then slowly spread out, to envelop the main body of her assailant. Then it squeezed...

In the face of the fresh, icy cold of a new day dawning, and being deprived of the life-giving sap which they needed to sustain flight, the cicadas began to slow. Hate alone was insufficient.

The mass inside attempted to force itself free. Time and time again it contracted, then threw itself at the blue wall surrounding it, in a titanic effort to break out. To no avail. Slowly, the unrelenting pressure overpowered the mass, which became liquid and, like a bubble imploding, collapsed into a swirling, black constellation.

The spectres of Pythagoras and Audeus returned to Esther as she slowly lowered her outstretched arms towards the ground. Controlling the bubble, she moved it around, swallowing up the rest of the swarm. Then, in one last explosion of power, she hurled it through the air vents.

Esther, her ordeal at an end, closed her eyes and slumped to the ground.

* * *

Branston lurched out of the lift deep underground, and ran down the corridor. Rounding a corner, he collided with staff, running the opposite way and shouting: "The tubes. They're all breaking out..."

Branston fell to the floor.

No-one made it. The roaring mass inside the ducts gathered speed and gushed into the corridor. Every part of the complex was filled, then sealed inside an impenetrable blue film.

Outside, Ricky sat beside Esther, now sleeping peacefully. He heard a bird flutter past, and watched it perch in the tree. When it ruffled up its wings, as if indignant at the disturbance, he realised that his heart, still pounding madly, was the loudest sound. Putting his arms underneath Esther, he gently lifted her up and carried her down the hill, towards the house.

Henry, holding the shoebox, opened the door as Ricky approached. "Good morning, sir," he said.

"Did you see that, Henry?"

"See what, sir?"

"Did you say morning?"

"Yes, sir. It's six o'clock, just turned."

I don't understand. We were eating soup ten minutes ago. Why didn't he see it?

"Is the lady in difficulty, sir? Is there anything I can do?"

Ricky laid Esther down on the settee in the lounge and looked at her. *Lady? Yes, she is a lady. A special lady. I don't understand what I've just seen, but I know if it hadn't been for her...*

Henry, perfectly dressed, even down to his white gloves, stood waiting.

"Are you sure you didn't see anything?" said Ricky.

"If you'll pardon me saying so, sir, I saw the lady in my dream. She made things OK again, didn't she?"

Ricky smoothed his fingers through his hair. *Dream? Did I dream it all?* he wondered, looking at Henry and trying to unscramble his thoughts. *Branston. Where's Branston?*

"Yes. But I'd like to take the lady home, now. Where's the master?"

"The master's nowhere to be found, sir. Nor Miss Carrie."

Ricky looked at Esther. *I couldn't care less*, he thought. *I need to get her away from here.*

"Well, when the master returns, tell him we had to go home, please. Can you organise the car for us?"

"Yes, sir," said Henry, holding out the shoebox.

"What's this?"

"I believe the contents belonged to Miss Margaret, sir."

St Mary's Church

Rays of sunshine, bursting through the windows high on the walls, flickered on Michael's face. He opened his eyes, got up, and looked at the Cross. All seemed to be normal again. "Thanks be to God," he said, crossing himself.

Haslemere

Dawn broke. "It's over, she's OK," said Joan.

"D'you know, that's the first time you've said more than two words to me in ages," said Terry, putting his arm round her waist. Joan put a hand on his bottom and said, "Time to put the kettle on, then."

Chapter 51

Epilogue—Haslemere

Esther remained unconscious for two days, and remembered nothing when she did wake. "What happened?" she asked.

* * *

She gave birth to a boy, whom she named Christopher, at home. After he'd been weighed and was lying in her arms, she turned to Ricky. Her hair was matted, and perspiration glistened on her forehead. But her cheeks were pink and healthy, and her eyes sparkled at the sight of him. She put a hand on the side of his face, and said, "Bet you don't think I'm beautiful now."

Ricky looked at her solemnly for a moment, then leaned over and kissed her. "I think no early morning, dew-covered rose could look as beautiful as you do now. I love you very much."

"Flatterer," she said. Then, more seriously, "And I love you too. Now we can begin to live."

The following summer, Ricky, Esther and the children attended a service at St Mary's Church, and were pleased to find Michael, much improved, taking the service. Afterwards they introduced Christopher to him. Michael took him in his arms and looked into his eyes. "He's a lovely boy," he said. "It was quite a year, last year. Especially July and August. Did you take a holiday? Go anywhere? Was the weather fine where you were?"

Ricky, standing slightly behind Esther, felt the nightstick in his pocket grow warm. A warmth which seemed to reach out to Michael as they exchanged looks.

An overwhelming sense of relief coursed through Ricky's

body. Words almost gushed from him; but knowing he couldn't say anything now, he mouthed "She doesn't remember" instead.

Michael nodded, handed Christopher back, and said, "Well, that's good. Everything's alright, then."

"Yes, fine, thanks. You must come and visit us in Haslemere some time," said Esther.

New generations of children came to run up and down the moat. To swing on ropes, tied to other trees now, and daydream in the den where the Great Oak tree had once stood. As they played, they fell about and knocked themselves. Sometimes they scratched their knees... and picked up splinters...